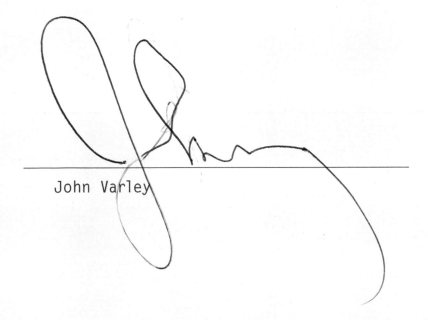

John Varley

GOOD-BYE,
ROBINSON CRUSOE
and Other Stories

GOOD-BYE,
ROBINSON CRUSOE
and Other Stories

John Varley

Subterranean Press 2013

Good-bye, Robinson Crusoe and Other Stories
Copyright © 2013 by John Varley. All rights reserved.

First Edition

ISBN
978-1-59606-528-4

Subterranean Press
PO Box 190106
Burton, MI 48519

www.subterraneanpress.com

TABLE OF CONTENTS

INTRODUCTION

When Bill Schafer first proposed this book, he sent me a list of my stories that were not currently available in book form. There were eleven of them, and he wanted to know what order I'd prefer to have them appear. I wrote them all down and thought about them (for the first time in years, in some cases), pondered what they were about and other ways of ordering them. Many of them go back to the 1970s, and like most of us, I was a very different person that long ago.

I wasn't getting anywhere with it, and then it occurred to me to consider the settings of these stories. Many of them were written during a time when we were making new discoveries about our solar system, some of which pulled the rug out from under our old pictures of the planets. Jupiter had rings and a lot more moons than we thought (66 at current count). Saturn's rings were almost infinitely more complex than we thought. Mars had the largest mountain in the system, and a gigantic canyon. Deimos looked like a potato.

The moneyed British classes used to do something called the "Grand Tour" of Europe. By train and steamship they would visit all the cultural landmarks of the continent, from Paris to Venice, from Moscow to Madrid. The theory ran something like "If you go to these places, some of the culture will rub off on you."

And I realized that I could order some of the stories as a sort of Grand Tour of the Solar System.

Not all of them fit—the last two stories here are more essays than stories, and another is a one-off that has nothing to do with anything else I have written.

And I won't be able to take you to all the planets.

There's no Mars story here. If you want one, try "In the Hall of the Martian Kings," in my collection *The John Varley Reader*, or my novels *Red Thunder*, *Red Lightning*, and *Rolling Thunder*. (Or there are the excellent Mars series by Kim Stanley Robinson and Joe Haldeman.)

There is no Jupiter story. If you want to read one, try *Rolling Thunder*.

There is no Uranus story. If you want to read one that visits the Uranian moons, try my novel *The Golden Globe*.

There is no Neptune story. If you want to read one…well, the cruise ship *SS Varley* never got around to docking there. Sorry about that. And offhand, I can't recall any memorable stories by other authors set around Neptune.

But I do have a Pluto story—"Good-bye, Robinson Crusoe"—written back when the poor little icy world was still a planet. Now it's a "dwarf planet," along with Ceres, Haumea (which even has two moons of its own!), Makemake, Eris, and maybe Orcus, Quaoar, Sedna, and one so new it's not even named yet: 2007 OR. You can't blame me for not including *them* on the itinerary since, except for Ceres, they hadn't even been discovered when I wrote these stories.

I do wish I'd written a story about Neptune, though…

THE FUNHOUSE EFFECT

You've probably heard the old joke about the (insert presumed-to-be-stupid-minority-group here) plan to send astronauts to land on the sun. When asked if they weren't worried about being burned up, they replied that it was no problem, they planned to land at night.

Calling our tiny section of the galaxy "the solar system" seems to me to be imparting entirely too much importance to a scattering of rocks and balls of gas. The sun accounts for 99.86 percent of the mass of the system. It is a G2 star, which means it's too small to ever go supernova. Before you sigh in relief, you should know that it's only about a billion years before it will heat up enough to boil off all Earth's air and water, and only ten billion years until it will enter a brief red giant phase, during which it will expand to beyond Earth's orbit. So make your plans accordingly, and don't say I didn't warn you.

Every second, the sun fuses 620,000,000 tons of hydrogen into helium. In the process it turns four million tons of matter into energy, in the form of neutrinos and radiation. It's been doing that for four and a half billion years. Everything in the solar system derives from and depends on the sun. So it seems like the logical place to start our Grand Tour.

But what sort of ship should we take for our voyage? Well, first we shouldn't plan to land on the sun. We couldn't even if we wanted to, because it doesn't really have a surface as we understand it. Like Jupiter, it has denser and denser regions, getting hotter and hotter. The temperatures range from about ten thousand degrees F in the part we can see, right up to three million degrees at the core. So I figure that's right out.

So how about visiting the corona? That's the part you can see during a total eclipse (which I was privileged to see near Goldendale, Washington, on February 26, 1979). Oddly enough, the corona is much hotter than the surface…but since it is very, very tenuous, it might be possible to pass through it without too much harm, if we could design a spaceship that could withstand the great heat. In fact, there are plans on the drawing board for a flyby of around four million miles with something called Solar Probe Plus, scheduled to launch in 2018 unless Congress or NASA cuts the funding.

But wait a minute. There are bodies that visit the corona regularly. I'm talking about comets. Some of them have regular orbits that we have measured, and some malinger out in the most distant reaches of the system until some gravitational whim gives them a nudge, and they start falling toward the sun. How about if we hitched a ride on one of them? We'd lose a little of the ship every time it passed through the corona, but we could choose a big one, and use it multiple times. As an added bonus, every time we approached the sun the people back on Earth would get a great show as the cometary tail stretched out for millions of miles.

And we wouldn't even have to go at night.

"Did you see what's playing at the theater tonight, Mr. Quester?" The stewardess was holding a printed program in her hand.

"No, and I haven't the time now. Where's the captain? There are some things he should—"

"Two old flat movies," she went on, oblivious to his protests. "Have you ever seen one? They're very interesting and entertaining. *A Night to Remember* and *The Poseidon Adventure*. I'll make a reservation for you."

Quester called out to her as she was leaving.

"I'm trying to tell you, there's something badly wrong on this ship. Won't anybody listen?"

But she was gone, vanished into the crowd of merrymakers. She was busy enough without taking time to listen to the wild tales of a nervous passenger.

Quester was not quite right in thinking of *Hell's Snowball* as a ship. The official welcoming pamphlet referred to it as an asterite, but that was advertising jargon. Anyone else would have called it a comet.

Icarus Lines, Inc., the owners, had found it drifting along at a distance of 500 AU. It had been sixty kilometers in diameter, weighing in at about one hundred trillion tons.

Fortunately, it was made up of frozen liquids rich in hydrogen. Moving it was only a matter of installing a very large fusion motor, then sitting back for five years until it was time to slow it down for orbit in the umbra of Mercury.

The company knew they would not get many passengers on a bare snowball. They tunneled into the comet, digging out staterooms and pantries and crew's quarters as they went. The shipfitters went in and paneled the bare ice walls in metal and plastic, then filled the rooms with furniture. There was room to spare, power to spare. They worked on a grand scale, and they had a grand vision. They intended to use the captive comet for sightseeing excursions to the sun.

Things went well for fifty years. The engine would shove the *Snowball* out of the protective shadow and, with the expenditure of ten million tons of ice and ammonia for reaction mass, inject it into a hyperbolic orbit that would actually brush the fringes of the solar corona. Business was good. *Hell's Snowball* became the vacation bonanza of the system, more popular than Saturn's Rings.

But it had to end. This was to be the last trip. Huge as it is, there comes a time when a comet has boiled off too much of its mass to remain stable in a close approach to the sun. *Hell's Snowball* was robbed of a hundred million tons with each trip. The engineers had calculated it was good for only one more pass before it cracked apart from internal heating.

But Quester was beginning to wonder.

There was the matter of the engines. Early on the fourth day of the excursion, Quester had gone on a guided tour of the farside of the comet to see the fusion engines. The guide had quoted statistics all the way through the tunnel, priming the tourists for the mind-wrenching sight of them. They were the largest rocket engines ever constructed. Quester and everyone else had been prepared to be impressed.

He *had* been impressed; first at the size of the pits that showed where the engines had been, then at the look of utter amazement on the face of the tour guide. Also impressive had been the speed with which the expression had been masked. The guide sputtered for only a moment, then quickly filled in with a story that almost sounded logical.

"I wish they'd tell me these things," he laughed. Did the laugh sound hollow? Quester couldn't tell for sure. "The engines weren't due for removal until tomorrow. It's part of our accelerated salvage program, you see, whereby we remove everything that can be of use in fitting-out the *Icarus*, which you all saw near Mercury when you boarded. It's been decided not to slow *Hell's Snowball* when we complete this pass, but to let it coast on out where it came from. Naturally, we need to strip it as fast as possible. So equipment not actually needed for this trip has been removed already. The rest of it will be taken off on the other side of the sun, along with the passengers. I'm not a physicist, but evidently there is a saving in fuel. No need to worry about it; our course is set and we'll have no further need of the engines." He quickly shepherded the buzzing group of passengers back into the tunnel.

Quester was no physicist, either, but he could work simple equations. He was unable to find a way whereby Icarus Lines would save anything by removing the engines. The fuel was free; by their own admission whatever was left on the comet was to be discarded anyway. So why did it matter if they burned some more? Further, ships removing passengers and furnishings from the *Snowball* on the other side would have to match with its considerable velocity, then expend even more to slow down to solar system speeds. It sounded wasteful.

He managed to put this out of his mind. He was along for the ride, to have fun, and he wasn't a worrier. He had probably dropped a decimal point somewhere in his calculations, or was forgetting a little-known fact of ballistics. Certainly no one else seemed worried.

When he discovered that the lifeboats were missing, he was more angry than frightened.

"What are they doing to us?" he asked the steward who had come when he pressed the service bell. "Just because this is the last trip, does that mean we're not entitled to full protection? I'd like to know what's going on."

The steward, who was an affable man, scratched his head in bewilderment as he once more examined the empty lifeboat cradle.

"Beats me," he said, with a friendly grin. "Part of the salvage operation, I guess. But we've never had a spot of trouble in over fifty years. I hear the *Icarus* won't even carry lifeboats."

Quester fumed. If, sometime in the past, an engineer had decided *Hell's Snowball* needed lifeboats, he'd have felt a damn sight better if the ship still *had* lifeboats.

"I'd like to talk to someone who knows something about it."

"You might try the purser," the steward ventured, then quickly shook his head. "No, I forgot. The purser didn't make this trip. The first mate...no, she's...I guess that leaves the captain. You might talk to him."

Quester grumbled as he swam down the corridor toward the bridge. The company had no right to strip the ship before its final cruise. On the way there, he heard an announcement over the public address system.

"Attention. All passengers are to report to A Deck at 1300 hours for lifeboat drill. The purser...correction, the second officer will call the roll. Attendance is required of all passengers. That is all."

The announcement failed to mollify him, though he was puzzled.

The door to the bridge was ajar. There was a string spanning the open doorway with a hand-lettered sign hanging from it.

"The captain can be found at the temporary bridge," it read, "located on F Deck aft of the dispensary." Inside the room, a work crew was removing the last of the electronic equipment. There was the smell of ozone and oil, and the purple crackle of sparks. The room was little more than an ice-walled shell.

"What...?" Quester began.

"See the captain," the boss said tiredly, pulling out one of the last memory banks in a shower of shorting wires. "I just work here. Salvage crew."

Quester was reminded more of a wrecking crew. He started back toward F Deck.

"Correction on that last announcement," the PA said. "Lifeboat drill has been cancelled. The social director wishes to announce that he is no longer taking reservations for tours of the engine room. The second officer...correction, the third officer has requested all personnel to stay clear of the reactor room. There has been a slight spillage during the salvage program. Passengers are not to worry; this incident presents no danger to them. The power requirements of the ship are being taken over by the auxiliary reactor. The social director wishes to announce that tours of the auxiliary reactor are suspended. That is all."

"Is it just me?" Quester asked himself as he drifted by the groups of other passengers, none of whom seemed upset by any of this.

He located the temporary bridge, at the end of a little-used corridor that was stacked high with plastic crates marked "Immediate Removal—Rush, Urgent, Highest Priority." He insinuated his way past them with difficulty and was about to knock on the door when he was stopped by the sound of voices on the other side. The voices were angry.

"I tell you, we should abort this trip at once. I've lost the capability to maneuver the ship in the event of an emergency. I told you I wanted the attitude thrusters to remain in place until after perihelenion."

"Captain, there is no use protesting now," said another voice. "Maybe I agree with you; maybe I don't. In any case, the engines are gone now, and there's no chance of installing them again. There is to be no argument with these orders. The company's in bad shape, what with outfitting the new asterite. Can you picture what it would cost to abort this trip and refund the fares to seven thousand passengers?"

"Hang the company!" the captain exploded. "This ship is *unsafe*! What about those new calculations I gave you—the ones from Lewiston? Have you looked them over?"

The other voice was conciliatory. "Captain, Captain, you're wasting energy worrying about that crackpot. He's been laughed out of the Lunar Academy; his equations simply do not work."

"They look sound enough to me."

"Take it from me, Captain, the best minds in the system have assured us that the *Snowball* will hold together. Why, this old hunk of junk is good for a dozen more trips, and you know it. We've erred, if at all, on the conservative side."

"Well, maybe," the captain grumbled. "I still don't like that lifeboat situation, though. How many did you say we had left?"

"Twenty-eight," the other soothed.

Quester felt the hair stand up on the back of his neck.

He peeked into the room, not knowing what he would say. But there was no one there. The voices were coming from a speaker on the wall. Evidently the captain was in another part of the ship.

He considered going to his cabin and getting drunk, then decided it was a bad idea. He would go to the casino and get drunk.

On the way he passed a lifeboat cradle that was not empty. It was the site of bustling activity, with crews hurrying up and down ramps into the ship. He stuck his head in, saw that the seats had been stripped and the interior was piled high with plastic crates. More were being added every minute.

He stopped one of the workers and asked her what was going on.

"Ask the captain," she shrugged. "They told me to stack these boxes in here, that's all I know."

He stood back and watched until the loading was complete, then was told to stand clear as the nullfield was turned off to allow the boat to drift clear of the *Snowball*. At a distance of two kilometers, the engines fired and the boat was away, blasting back toward the inner planets.

"Twenty-seven," Quester mumbled to himself and headed for the casino.

"Twenty-seven?" the woman asked.

"Probably less by now," Quester said with a broad shrug. "And they only hold fifty people."

They were sitting together at the roulette table, pressed into close company by the random currents of humanity that ebbed and flowed through the room. Quester was not gambling; his legs had just happened to give out, and the nearest place to collapse had been the chair he was sitting in. The woman had materialized out of his alcoholic mist.

It was nice to get back to gravity after the weightless levels of the *Snowball*. But, he discovered, getting drunk in a weightless state was less hazardous. One needn't worry about one's balance. Here in the casino there was the problem of standing. It was too much of a problem for Quester.

The casino was located at one end of a slowly rotating arm, which was mounted horizontally on a pivoted mast that extended straight up from *Hell's Snowball*. On the other end of the arm were the restaurants that served the passengers. Both modules were spherical; the structure resembled an anemometer with silver balls instead of cups on the ends. The view was tremendous. Overhead was the silver sphere that contained the restaurants. To one side was the slowly moving surface of the comet, a dirty gray even in the searing sunlight. To the other side were the stars and the main attraction: Sol itself, blemished with a choice collection of spots. The viewing was going to be good this trip. If anyone was alive to view it, Quester added to himself.

"Twenty-seven, you say?" the woman asked again.

"That's right, twenty-seven."

"One hundred Marks on number twenty-seven," she said and placed her bet. Quester looked up, wondering how many times he would have to repeat himself before she understood him.

The ball clattered to a stop, on number twenty-seven, and the croupier shoveled a tottering stack of chips to the woman. Quester looked around him again at the huge edifice he was sitting in, the incalculable tonnage of the spinning structure, and laughed.

"I wondered why they built this place," he said. "Who needs gravity?"

"Why did they build it?" she asked him, picking up the chips.

"For him," he said, pointing to the croupier. "That little ball would just hang there on the rim without gravity." He felt himself being lifted to his feet, and stood in precarious balance. He threw his arms wide.

"For that matter, that's what all the gravity in the system's for. To bring those little balls down to the number, the old wheel of fortune; and when they've got your number, there's nothing you can do because your number's up, that's all there is, twenty-seven, that's all…"

He was sobbing and mumbling philosophical truths as she led him from the room.

The ride in the elevator to the hub of the rotating structure sobered Quester considerably. The gradually decreasing weight combined with the Coriolis effect that tended to push him against one wall was more than an abused stomach could take. The management knew that and had provided facilities for it. Quester vomited until his legs were shaky. Luckily, by then he was weightless and didn't need them.

The woman towed him down the passageway like a toy balloon. They ended up in the grand ballroom.

The ballroom was a hemisphere of nullfield sitting on the surface of the *Snowball*. From inside it was invisible. The dance area was crowded with couples trying out free-fall dances. Most of them had the easy grace of a somersaulting giraffe.

Quester sobered a bit in the near-zero gee. Part of it was the effect of the antinausea drugs he had taken for free-fall; they also tended to reduce the effects of alcohol.

"What's your name?" he asked the woman.

"Solace. You?"

"I'm Quester. From Tharsis, Mars. I'm…I'm confused about a lot of things."

She floated over to a table, still towing Quester, and fastened him to one of the chairs. He turned his attention from the twisting bodies in the dance area to his companion.

Solace was tall, much taller than a man or a woman would naturally grow. He estimated she was two and a half meters from head to toe, though she had no toes. Her feet had been replaced with peds, oversized hands popular with spacers. They were useful in free-fall, and for other things, as he discovered when she reached across the table with one slender leg and cupped his cheek with her ped. Her legs were as limber and flexible as her arms.

"Thanks," she said, with a smile. "For the luck, I mean."

"Hmmm? Oh, you mean the bet." Quester had to drag his attention back from the delightful sensation on his cheek. She was beautiful. "But I wasn't advising you on a bet. I was trying to tell you…"

"I know. You were saying something about the lifeboats."

"Yes. It's astounding, I…" He stopped, realizing that he couldn't remember what was astounding. He was having trouble focusing on her. She was wearing a kaleidoholo suit, which meant she was naked but for a constantly shifting pattern of projections. There seemed to be fifty or sixty different suits contained in it, none persisting for longer than a few seconds. It would melt smoothly from a silver sheath dress to an almost military uniform with gold braid and buttons to a garland of flowers to Lady Godiva. He rubbed his eyes and went on.

"They're salvaging the ship," he said. "The last I heard there were only twenty-seven lifeboats left. And more are leaving every hour. They're taking the electronic equipment with them. And the furnishings and the machinery and who knows what else. I overheard the captain talking to a company representative. *He's* worried, the *captain*! But no one else seems to be. Am I worrying over nothing, or what?"

Solace looked down at her folded hands for a moment, then brought her eyes back up to his.

"I've been uneasy, too," she said in a low voice. She leaned closer to him. "I've shared my apprehensions with a group of friends. We…get together and share what we have learned. Our friends laugh at us when we tell them of our suspicions, but…" She paused and looked suspiciously around her. Even in his befuddled state Quester had to smile.

"Go on," he said.

She seemed to make up her mind about him and leaned even closer.

"We'll be meeting again soon. Several of us have been scouting around—I was covering the casino when we met—and we'll share our findings and try to come to a consensus on what to do. Are you with us?"

Quester fought off the feeling, quite strong since his suspicions began to haunt him, that he was somehow trapped in an adventure movie. But if he was, he was just getting to the good part.

"You can count me in."

With no further ado, she grabbed his arm in one of her peds and began towing him along, using her hands to grab onto whatever was handy. He thought of objecting, but she was much better than he at weightless maneuvering.

"May I have your attention, please?"

Quester looked around and spotted the captain standing in the center of the stage, in front of the band. He was not alone. On each side of him were women dressed in black jumpsuits, their eyes alertly scanning the audience. They were armed.

"Please, please." The captain held up his arms for quiet and eventually got it. He wiped his brow with a handkerchief.

"There is no cause for alarm. No matter what you may have been hearing, the ship is in no danger. The stories about the main engines having been removed are lies, pure and simple. We are looking for the people who planted these rumors and will soon have all of them in custody. The chief engineer wishes to announce that tours of the engine room will be resumed—"

One of the women shot the captain a glance. He mopped his brow again and consulted a slip of paper in his hand. The hand was shaking.

"Ah, a correction. The engineer announces that tours will *not* be resumed. There is, ah…that is, they are being overhauled, or…or something." The woman relaxed slightly.

"The rumor that the main reactor has been shut down is unfounded. The surgeon has told me that there has been no spillage of radioactive material, and even if there had been, the amount was insignificant and would only have been a danger to those passengers with high cumulative exposures. The surgeon will be collecting dosimeters at 1400 hours tomorrow.

"Let me repeat: there is no cause for alarm. As captain of this ship, I take a very dim view of rumormongering. Anyone caught disseminating stories about the unspaceworthiness of this vessel in the future will be dealt with sternly."

"Lifeboat drill will be held tomorrow on A Deck, as scheduled. Anyone who has not as yet been checked out on his life jacket will do so by noon tomorrow, ship's time. That is…is that all?" This last was addressed to the woman to his left, in a whisper. She nodded curtly, and the three of them walked off the stage, their magnetized shoes sticking to the deck like flypaper.

Solace nudged Quester in the ribs.

"Are those women bodyguards?" she whispered. "Do you think his life is in danger?"

Quester looked at the way the women gripped the captain's elbows. Not bodyguards, but guards, certainly…

"Say, I just remembered I still have some unpacking to do," he said. "Maybe I can join you and your friends later on. I'll just nose around, see what I can pick up, you know, and—"

But he couldn't squirm free of her grip. Those peds were *strong*.

"May I have your attention, please? Lifeboat drill for tomorrow has been canceled. Repeat, canceled. Passengers showing up at the cradles for lifeboat drill will be interrogated, by order of the captain. That is all."

On the way to Solace's room, the two were shoved out of the way by a group of people in uniform. Their faces were determined, and some of them carried clubs.

"Where does that corridor lead?" he asked.

"To the bridge. But they won't find anything there, it's been—"

"I know."

"I think we're being followed."

"Wha'?" He looked behind him as he bounced along in her wake. There was someone back there, all right. They turned a corner and Solace hauled Quester into a dimly lit alcove, bumping his head roughly against the wall. He was getting fed up with this business of being dragged. If this was an adventure, he was Winnie-the-Pooh following Christopher Robin up the stairs. He started to object, but she clapped a hand around his mouth, holding him close.

"Shhh," she hissed.

A fine thing, Quester grumbled to himself. Can't even speak my mind. He thought he was better off before, alone and puzzled, then he was with this mysterious giantess towing him around.

Of course, things could have been worse, he reflected. She was warm and naked to the touch no matter what his eyes told him. And *tall*. Floating there in the hall, she extended above and below him by a third of a meter.

"How can I think of something like that at a time like this?" he began, but she hushed him again and her arms tightened around him. He realized she was really scared, and he began to be so himself. The liquor and the sheer unlikelihood of recent events had detached him; he was drifting along, rudderless. Nothing in his life had prepared him to cope with things like the black-suited man who now eased slowly around the corner in shadowy pursuit of them.

They watched him from the concealment of the alcove. Many of the lights in the corridor were not working or were mere empty sockets. Earlier, Quester had been alarmed at this, adding it to his list of ways not to run a spaceship. Now, he was grateful.

"He doesn't look much like a man at all," Solace whispered. And sure enough, he didn't. Nor a woman. He didn't look too human.

"Humanoid, I'd say," Quester whispered back. "Pity no one told us. Obviously the system's been invaded by the first intelligent race of humanoids."

"Don't talk nonsense. And be quiet." The man, or whatever it was, was very close now. They could see the ill-fitting pink mask, the lumps and nodules in odd places under his sweater and pants. He passed them by, leaving a pungent odor of hydrogen sulfide.

Quester found himself laughing. To his surprise, Solace laughed along with him. The situation was so grotesque that he had to either laugh or scream.

"Listen," he said, "I don't *believe* in sinister humanoid invaders."

"No? But you believe in superhuman heavy-planet Invaders like the ones that have occupied the Earth, don't you? And you haven't even *seen* them."

"Are you telling me you do believe that thing was an...an alien?"

"I'm not saying anything. But I'm wondering what those people were doing, earlier, armed with clubs. Do you believe in mutiny?"

"Solace, I'd *welcome* a mutiny, I'd throw a party, give away all my worldly wealth to charity if only such a normal, everyday thing would happen. But I don't think it will. I think we've fallen through the looking glass."

"You think you're crazy?" She looked at him skeptically.

"Yep. I'm going to turn myself in right now. You're obviously not even here. Maybe this ship isn't even here."

She twisted slightly in the air, bringing her legs up close to his chest.

"I'll prove to you I'm here," she said, working with all four hands and peds at unbuttoning him.

"Hold it. What are you…how can you think of that at a time like…" It sounded familiar. She laughed, holding his wrists with her hands as her peds quickly stripped him.

"You've never been in danger before," she said. "I have. It's a common reaction to get aroused in a tight spot, especially when the danger's not immediate. And you are, and so am I."

It was true. He was, but didn't like doing it in the hallway.

"There's not room here," he protested. "Another of those critters could come along."

"Yes, isn't it exciting?" Her eyes were alight by now, and her breath was fast and shallow. "And if you think there isn't room, you haven't done it in free-fall yet. Ever tried the Hermesian Hyperbola?"

Quester sighed, and submitted. Soon he was doing more than submitting. He decided she was as crazy as everyone else, or, alternatively, he was crazy and she was as sane as everybody else. But she was right about the free-fall. There was plenty of room.

They were interrupted by a crackle of static from the public address. They paused to listen to it.

"Attention, your attention please. This is the provisional captain speaking. The traitor running-dog lackey ex-captain is now in chains. Long Live the Revolutionary Committee, who will now lead us on the true path of Procreative Anti-Abortionism."

"Free-Birthers!" Quester yelped. "We've been hijacked by Free-Birthers!"

The new captain, who sounded like a woman, started to go on, but her voice was cut short in a hideous gurgle.

"Long Live the Loyalist Faction of the Glorious Siblings of the—" a new voice began, but it, too, was cut short. Voices shouted in rapid succession.

"The counterrevolution has been suppressed," shouted yet another captain. "Liberate our wombs! Our gonads—our Freedom! Attention, attention! All female persons aboard this ship are ordered to report at once to the infirmary for artificial insemination. Shirkers will be obliterated. That is all."

Neither of them said anything for a long time. At last Solace eased herself away a bit and let him slip out of her. She let out a deep breath.

"I wonder if I could plead double jeopardy?"

"Insanity four, reality nothing," Quester giggled. He was in high spirits as they skulked their way down the dim corridors.

"Are you still on that?" Solace shot back. She sounded a bit tired of him. She kept having to hang back as he struggled to keep up with her supple quadridexterous pace. "Listen, if you want to get fitted for a straitjacket, the tailor's in the other direction. Me, I don't care how ridiculous the situation gets. I'll keep coping."

"I can't help it," he admitted. "I keep feeling that I *wrote* this story several years ago. Maybe in another life. I dunno."

She peered around another corner. They were on their way to the temporary bridge. They had stopped three times already to watch black-suited figures drift by. Everyone else they had seen—those dressed in holiday clothes—had ducked into doorways as quickly as they themselves. At least it seemed that the passengers were no longer in the holiday mood, were aware that there was something wrong.

"You a writer?" she asked.

"Yes. I write scientifiction. Maybe you've heard of it. There's a cult following, but we don't reach the general public."

"What's it about?"

"Scientifiction deals with life on Earth. It's set in the future—each of us creates our own hypothetical future with our own ground rules and set of assumptions. The basic assumption is that we figure out a way to fight the Invaders and reclaim the Earth, or at least a beachhead. In my stories we've managed to rout the Invaders, but the dolphins and whales are still around, and they want their allies back, so humans fight them. It's adventure stuff, purely for thrills. I have a hero called the Panama Kid."

She glanced back at him, and he couldn't read the expression. He was used to taking the defensive about his vocation.

"Is there a living in that?"

"I managed to get aboard the *Snowball* for the final trip, didn't I? That wasn't cheap, but then you know that. Say, what do you do for a living?"

"Nothing. My mother was a holehunter. She made a strike in '45 and got rich. She went out again and left the money to me. She's due back in about fifty years, unless she gets swallowed by a hole."

"So you were born on Pluto?"

"No. I was born in free-fall, about one hundred AU from the sun. I think that's a record so far." She grinned back at him, looking pleased with herself. "You made up your mind yet?"

"Huh?"

"Have you decided if you're the author or a character? If you really think you're crazy, you can shove off. What can you do but accept the reality of your senses?"

He paused and really thought about it for the first time since he met her.

"I do," he said firmly. "It's all happening. Holy Cetacean, *it really is happening.*"

"Glad to have you with us. I *told* you you couldn't experience the Hermesian Hyperbola and still doubt your senses.

It hadn't been the love-making, Quester knew. That could be as illusory as anything else; he had the stained sheets to prove it. But he believed in *her*, even if there was something decidedly illogical about the goings-on around her.

"Attention, attention."

"Oh, shit. What now?" They slowed near a speaker so they could listen without distortion.

"Glad tidings! This is the provisional captain, speaking for the ad hoc steering committee. We have decided to steer this comet into a new, closer approach to the sun, thus gaining speed for faster departure from solar space. It has been decided to convert this vessel hereafter to be referred to as the *Spermatozoa*, into an interstellar colony ship to spread the seed of humanity to the stars. All passengers are hereby inducted into the Proletarian Echelon of the Church of Unlimited Population. Conversion of all resources into a closed-ecology system will begin at once. Save your feces! Breathe shallowly until this crisis is past. Correction, correction, there is no crisis. Do not panic. Anyone found panicking will be shot. The steering committee has determined that there is no crisis. All surviving officers with knowledge of how to work these little gadgets on the bridge are ordered to report immediately."

Quester looked narrowly at Solace.

"Do you know anything about them?"

"I can pilot a ship, if that's what you mean. I've never flown any-thing quite this…*enormous*…but the principles are the same. You aren't suggesting that we help them, are you?"

"I don't know," he admitted. "I didn't really think in terms of plans until a few minutes ago. What was *your* plan? Why are we headed for the bridge?"

She shrugged. "Just to see what the hell's going on, I guess. But maybe we ought to make some preparations. Let's get some life jackets."

They found a locker in the hall containing emergency equipment. Inside were twenty of the nullfield devices called life jackets. More accu-rately, they were emergency spacesuit generators, with attached water recyclers and oxygen supply. Each of them was a red cylinder about thirty centimeters long and fifteen in diameter with shoulder straps and a single flexible tube with a metal connector on the end. They were worn strapped to the back with the tube reaching over the shoulder.

In operation, the life jackets generated a nullfield that conformed closely to the contours of the wearer's body. The field oscillated between one and one and a half millimeters from the skin, and the resulting bellows action forced waste air through the exhaust nozzle. The device attached itself to a tiny metal valve that was surgically implanted in all the passengers. The valve's external connection was located under Quester's left collarbone. He had almost forgotten it was there. It was just a brass-colored flower that might be mistaken for jewelry but was actually part of a plumbing system that could route venous blood from his pulmonary artery to the oxygenator on his back. It then returned through a parallel pipe to his left auricle and on to his body.

Solace helped him get into it and showed him the few manual con-trols. Most of it was automatic. It would switch on the field around him if the temperature or pressure changed suddenly.

Then they were off again through the silent corridors to confront the hijackers.

At the last turn in the corridor before reaching the temporary bridge, they stopped to manually switch on their suit fields. Solace instantly became a mirror in the shape of a woman. The field reflected all elec-tromagnetic radiation except through pupil-sized discontinuities over her eyes which let in controlled quanta of visible light. It was disquieting. The funhouse effect, it was called, and it looked as if her body had been twisted through another spatial dimension. She almost disappeared, except for a pattern of distortions that hurt Quester's eyes when he looked at it.

They reached the door leading to the bridge and stopped for a moment. It was a perfectly ordinary door. Quester wondered why he was here with this impulsive woman.

"Do we knock first, or what?" she mused. "What do you think, Quester? What would the Panama Kid do?"

"He'd knock it down," Quester said without hesitation. "But he wouldn't have gotten here without his trusty laser. Say, do you think we ought to go back and..."

"No. We'd better do it now before we think about it too hard. These suits are protections against any weapon I know of. The most they can do is capture us."

"Then what?"

"Then you can talk us out of it. You're the one who's fast with words, aren't you?"

Quester remained silent as she backed up and planted herself against the opposite wall, coiled and ready to hit the door with her shoulder. He didn't want to point out that skill with a typer and skill at oratory are not necessarily related. Besides, if she wanted to risk forcible insemination, it was her business.

Just on the off chance, he touched the door plate with his palm. It clicked, and the door opened. It was too late. Solace howled and barreled end-over-end into the room, reaching out with all four limbs like a huge silver starfish to grab onto something. Quester rushed after her, then stopped short as soon as he was into the room. There was no one in it.

"Talk about your anticlimax," Solace breathed, getting herself sorted out from a pile of crates at the far end of the room. "I...never mind. It was my fault. Who'd have thought it'd be unlocked?"

"*I* did," Quester pointed out. "Hold it a minute. We're sort of, well, we're being pretty hasty, aren't we? I haven't really had time to stop and think since we got going, but I think we're going at this the wrong way, I really do. Damn it, this isn't an adventure where everything goes according to a set pattern. I've written enough of them, I ought to know. This is life, and that means there's got to be a rational explanation."

"So what is it?"

"I don't know. But I don't think we'll find it this way. Things have been happening...well, think about the announcements over the PA, for instance. They are *crazy*! No one's that crazy, not even Free-Birthers."

Quester's chain of thought was interrupted by the noisy entrance of four people in life jackets. He and Solace jumped up, banged their heads on the ceiling, and were quickly captured.

"All right, which one of you is the provisional captain?"

There was a short silence, then Solace broke it with a laugh.

"Lincoln?" she asked.

"Solace?"

The four were part of Solace's short-lived cabal. It seemed the ship was crawling with people who were concerned enough about the situation to try and do something about it. Before Quester caught all the names, they were surprised by another group of four, with three more close on their heels. The situation threatened to degenerate into a pitched battle of confused identities until someone had a suggestion.

"Why don't we hang a sign on the door? Anybody who comes in here thinks we're the hijackers." They did, and the sign said the provisional captain was dead. While new arrivals were pondering that and wondering what to do next, someone had time to explain the situation.

Someone arrived with a tray of drinks, and soon the would-be liberators were releasing their tensions in liquor and argument. There were fifteen pet theories expounded in as many minutes.

Now that he felt he had his feet under him, Quester adopted a wait-and-see attitude. The data was still insufficient.

"'When you have eliminated the impossible,'" he quoted, "'whatever is left, however improbable, must be the truth.'"

"So what does that gain us?" Solace asked.

"Only a viewpoint. Me, I think we'll have to wait until we get back to Mercury to find out what's been happening. Unless you bring me a live alien, or Free-Birther, or...some physical evidence."

"Then let's go look for it," Solace said.

"Attention, attention. This is the ship's computer speaking. I have grave news for all passengers. The entire crew has been assassinated. Until now, I have been blocked by a rogue program inserted by the revolutionaries which has prevented me from regaining control of operations. Luckily, this situation has been remedied. Unluckily, the bridge is still in the hands of the pirates! They have access to all my manual controls from their position, and I'm afraid there is but one course open to those of you who wish to avoid a catastrophe. We are on a trajectory that will soon intersect with the solar chromosphere, and I am powerless to correct it until the bridge is regained. Rally to me! Rise in righteous fury and repulse the evil usurpers! Storm the bridge! Long live the counterrevolution!"

There was a short silence as the implications sank in, then a babble of near panic. Several people headed for the door, only to come back and bolt it. There was an ominous roar from outside.

"…chromosphere? Where the hell *are* we? Has anyone been out on the surface lately?"

"…some pleasure cruise. I haven't even *seen* the sun and now they say we're about to…"

"…pirates, revolutions, counterrevolutions, Free-Birthers, *aliens*, for heaven's sake…"

Solace looked helplessly around her, listened to the pounding on the door. She located Quester hunkered down beside an instrument console and crouched beside him.

"Talk your way out of *this* one, Panama Kid," she yelled in his ear.

"My dear, I'm much too busy to talk. If I can get the back off this thing…" He worked at it and finally pulled off a metal cover. "There was a click from here when the computer came on the line."

There was a recorder inside, with a long reel of tape strung between playback heads. He punched a button that said rewind, watched the tape cycle briefly through, and hit the play button.

"Attention, attention. This is the ship's computer speaking. I have grave news for all passengers."

"We've *heard* that one already," someone shouted. Quester held his head in his hands for a moment, then looked up at Solace. She opened her mouth to say something, then bit her lip, her eyebrows almost touched in a look of puzzlement so funny that Quester would have laughed out loud. But the roof of the bridge evaporated.

It took only a few seconds. There was a blinding white light and a terrible roaring sound; then he was whisked into the air and pulled toward the outside. In an instant, everyone was covered in a nullfield and milling around the hole in the roof like a school of silverfish. In twos and threes they were sucked through. Then the room was empty and Quester was still in it. He looked down and saw Solace's hand around his ankle. She was grasping the firmly anchored computer console with one ped. She hauled him down to her and held him close as he found handholds. His teeth were chattering.

The door burst open, and there was another flurry of astonished passengers sucked through the roof. It didn't take as long this time; the hole in the roof was much larger. Beyond the hole was blackness.

Quester was surprised to see how calm he was once his initial shock had dissipated. He thanked Solace for saving him, then went on with what he had been about to say before the blowout.

"Did you talk to anyone who actually saw a mutineer, or a Free-Birther, or whatever?"

"Huh? Is this the time to…? No, I guess I didn't. But we saw those aliens, or whatever they—"

"Exactly. Whatever they were. They could have been anything. Someone is playing an awfully complicated trick on us. Something's happening, but it isn't what we've been led to believe."

"We've been led to believe something?"

"We've been given clues. Sometimes contradictory, sometimes absolutely insane, and encouraged to think a mutiny is going on; and this recorder proves it isn't happening. Listen." And he played back the recordings of various announcements they had heard earlier. It sounded tinny in their middle-ear receivers.

"But what does that prove?" Solace wanted to know. "Maybe this thing just taped them as they happened."

Quester was dumfounded for a moment. The theory of a vast conspiracy had appealed to him, even if he didn't know the reason for it.

He played past the point of the computer's announcement and sighed with relief when he heard that there was more. They let it natter on to no one about crises in the engine room, spillage in the second auxiliary reactor, and so on. It was obvious that it was playing a scenario that could no longer happen. Because the ship had already broken down completely and they were headed directly for…

They seemed to reach that thought simultaneously and scrambled up toward a hole in the ceiling to see what was going on. Quester forgot, as usual, to hang onto something and would have drifted straight up at near-escape velocity but for Solace's grasping hands.

The sun had eaten up the sky. It was huge, *huge.*

"That's what we paid to see," Solace said, weakly.

"Yeah. But I thought we'd see it from the ballroom. It's sort of…*big,* isn't it?"

"Do you think we're…?"

"I don't know. I never thought we'd get this close. Something the captain said—no, wait, it wasn't the captain, was it? But one of the recordings said something about…"

The ground heaved under them.

Quester saw the revolving casino complex off to his right. It swayed, danced, and came apart. The twin balls broke open, still rotating, and spilled tables and roulette wheels and playing cards and dishes and walls and carpets to the waiting stars. The debris formed a glittering double spiral of ejecta, like droplets of water spraying from the tips of a lawn sprinkler. Bits of it twisted in the sunlight, cartwheeling, caroming, semaphoring, kicking.

"Those are people."

"Are they…?" Quester couldn't ask it.

"No," Solace answered. "Those suits will protect them. Maybe they can be picked up later. You see, when you hit something wearing one of these suits, you—"

She didn't have time to finish, but Quester soon had a demonstration of what she was talking about. The ground opened a few meters from them. They were swept off their feet and tumbled helplessly across the dirty white surface until they hung suspended over the pit.

Quester hit the far side of the rift and bounced. He felt little of the impact, though he hit quite hard, because the suit field automatically stiffened when struck by a fast-moving object. He had cause to be thankful for that fact, because the rift began to close. He clawed his way along the surface toward the sunlight, but the walls of ice closed on him like a book snapped shut.

For a brief moment he was frozen while the ice and rock around him shook and vaporized under the incredible pressures of shearing force. He saw nothing but white heat as frozen methane and water became gas in an instant without an intermediate liquid stage. Then he was shot free as the masses came apart again.

He was still frozen into a climbing position, but now he could see. He was surrounded by chunks of debris, ranging from fistsized rocks glowing bright red to giant icebergs that sublimated and disappeared before his eyes. Each time the suit began to lose its rigidity he was hit by another object and frozen into a new position as the suit soaked up the kinetic energy.

In a surprisingly short time, everything had vanished. Every particle of the explosion was impelled away from every other particle by the pressures of expanding superheated steam.

But Solace was still clinging to his ankle. She was the only thing left in his universe apart from a few tiny flashing stars of debris far in the distance, tumbling, tumbling.

And the sun.

He could look directly at it as it swung past his field of vision once every ten seconds. It could barely be seen as a sphere; each second it looked more like a flat, boiling plane. The majestic, crushing presence of it flattened his ego with a weight he could barely tolerate. He found Solace in his arms. He looked at her face, which was endless mirrors showing a vanishing series of suns rebounding from his face to hers and back to infinity. The funhouse effect, so disconcerting only an hour ago, seemed familiar and reassuring now in comparison to the chaos below him. He hugged her and closed his eyes.

"Are we going to hit it?" he asked.

"I can't tell. If we do, it'll be the hardest test these suits have ever had. I don't know if they have limits."

He was astounded. "You mean we might actually...?"

"I tell you, I don't know. Theoretically, yes, we could graze the chromosphere and not feel a thing, not from the heat, anyway. But it would be bound to slow us down pretty quickly. The deceleration could kill us. The suits protect us from outside forces almost completely, but internal accelerations can break bones and rupture organs. This suit doesn't stop gravity or inertia from working."

There was no use thinking too long on that possibility.

They were hurtling through the corona now, building up a wake of ionized particles that trailed after them like the tail of a tiny comet. They looked around them for other survivors but could find nothing. Soon, they could see little but a flickering haze as the electrical potential they had built up began discharging in furry feathers of hot plasma. It couldn't have lasted longer than a few minutes; then it began to fade slowly away.

There came a time when the sun could be seen to have shrunk slightly. They didn't speak of it, just held onto each other.

"What are our chances of pickup?" Quester wanted to know. The sun was now much smaller, receding almost visibly behind them. They were concerned only for the next twenty hours, which was the length of their oxygen reserves.

"How should I know? Someone must know by now that something's happened, but I don't know if any ships can get to us in time. It would depend on where they were at the time of the disaster."

Quester scanned the stars as they swept past his field of vision. They had no way to slow their rotation; so the stars still went around them every ten seconds.

He didn't expect to see anything but was not surprised when he did. It was the next-to-last in a long series of incongruities. There was a ship closing in on them. A voice over the radio told them to stand by to come aboard and asked them how they enjoyed the trip.

Quester was winding up for a reply, but the speaker said one word, slowly and clearly:

"Frightfulness."

And everything changed.

I woke up and found out it had all been a dream.

The very first story I wrote, back when I was five years old, ended with words very much like that last sentence. I'm not ashamed of it. The thought was not new, but it was original with me. It was only later that I learned it's not a fair way to end a story, that the reader deserves more than that.

So here's more.

I woke up and found out it had *almost* all been a dream. The word, "frightfulness," was a posthypnotic trigger that caused me to remember all the things which had been blocked from me by earlier suggestion.

I don't know why I'm bothering to explain all this. I guess old writing habits die hard. No matter that this is being written for a board of psychists, mediartists, and flacks; I have to preserve the narrative thread. I've broken the rules by changing to first person at the end, but I found I could not write the account Icarus Lines requested of me unless I did it in the third person.

"I" am Quester, though that's not my real name. I am a scientifiction writer, but I have no character named the Panama Kid. Solace's name is something else. It was suggested that I change the names.

I signed aboard *Hell's Snowball* knowing that it was going to break apart along the way. That's why so much of it had been stripped. They retained only enough to preserve a tenuous illusion that the trip was a normal one, then threw in everything they could think of to scare the daylights out of us.

We knew they would. We agreed to and submitted to a hypnotic treatment that would fool us into thinking we were on a normal trip and were released into the crazy world they cooked up for us. It's the first time they had ever tried it, and so they threw in everything in the book: aliens, accidents, mutiny, confusion, crackpots, and I didn't even see it all. The experience is different for each passenger, but the basic theme is to put us into a scary situation with evident peril of life and limb; shake well, and then let us come through the experience safe and sound.

There was no danger, not from the first to the last. We were on a stable, carefully calculated orbit. The life jackets were enough to keep us absolutely safe against anything we would encounter, and we were conditioned to have them on at the right time. As proof of this, not a single passenger was injured.

We were *all* nearly scared to death.

It says here you want to know the motive. I remember it clearly now, though I remembered an entirely different one at the time. I went on the Disaster Express because I had just sold a novel and wanted to do something wild, out of character. That was the wildest thing I could think of, and I could wish I had gone to a museum instead. Because the next question you want me to answer is how I feel about it now that it's over, and you won't like it. I hope I'm in the majority and you people at Icarus will give this thing up and never run another like it.

There used to be something called a "haunted house." One was led blindfolded through it and encountered various horrors, the effect being heightened by the unknown nature of the things one touched and was touched by. People have done things like that for as long as we have history. We go to movies to be scared, ride on roller coasters, read books, go to funhouses. Thrills are never cheap, no matter what they say. It takes skill to produce them, and art, and a knowledge of what will be genuinely thrilling and what will be only amusing.

You people had mixed success. Part of it was the kitchen-sink approach you took on this first trip. If you unified your theme the next time, stuck to a mutiny or an invasion, for instance, instead of mucking it up with all the other insanity you put in…but what am I saying? I don't want you to improve it. It's true that I was a little bemused by the unreality of the opener, but it was stark terror all the way when we approached the sun. My stomach still tightens just to think about it.

But—and I must cry it from the rooftops—you have gone too far. I'm basically conservative, as are all scientifiction writers, being concerned as we are with the past on Earth rather than the future in the stars. But I can't avoid thinking how frivolous it all was. Have we come to this? While our precious home planet remains under the three-hundred-year Occupation, do we devote ourselves to more and more elaborate ways of finding thrills?

I hope not.

There is a second consideration, one that I find it difficult to put into words. You hear of the "shipboard romance," when passengers become involved with each other only to part forever at their destination. Something of the sort happened to me and to Solace. We grew close on that loop through the corona. I didn't write about it. It's still painful. We clung to each other for two days. We made love with the stars at our feet.

We might even have remained involved, if our minds had been our own. But upon the utterance of that magic word we suddenly found that we were not the people we had been presenting ourselves as being. It's difficult enough to find out that one you care for is not the person she seemed to be; how much harder when it is *you* who are not what you thought you were?

It is a tremendous identity crisis, one that I am only now getting over. I, Quester, would not have behaved as I did aboard the *Snowball* if I had been in possession of all my faculties. We were tested, destructively tested in a way, to see if the injunction against discovering the underlying facts was strong enough to hold. It was, though I was beginning to see through the veils at the end. With a more consistent emergency I'm sure I would have had no inkling that it was anything but real. And that would be *much* worse. As it was, I was able to retain a degree of detachment, to entertain the notion that I might be insane. I was *right*.

The trip to the sun is thrill enough. Leave it at that, please, so that we may be sure of our loves and fears and not come to think that all might be illusion. I'll always have the memory of the way Solace looked when she woke from the dream she shared with me. The dream was gone; Solace was not the person I thought she might be. I'll have to look for solace elsewhere.

RETROGRADE SUMMER

I wonder how many science fiction stories were rendered obsolete by the discovery, in 1965, that Mercury did *not* turn one face eternally to the sun? I'll bet it is dozens, if not hundreds. The idea that the closest planet to the sun was incredibly hot on one side, and on the other side possibly the coldest planet of them all—colder than Pluto because the dark side *never* got any sunlight—was just too good for an SF writer to pass up. Hot enough to melt lead on one side, and just a few miles away temperatures down around absolute zero.

But I don't think anyone *laughs* at those stories these days. I certainly don't. We SF writers always proceed with the best information available at the time. It's all we can do. Many, many other stories have been undercut by things we've learned later. It's happened to me, both from new scientific discoveries and new history. In my novel *Millennium*, for instance, I mentioned that no one had ever found the *Titanic* because it had been taken into the future, where the remaining passengers were saved from drowning, taken off, and used to repopulate a dying human race. Today, you can go down to the wreck and explore it yourself…if you have the $68,000 for a ticket, or are James Cameron with your own submersible.

What are you gonna do? We just keep *discovering* things.

But with the old picture busted, an even more interesting fact emerged. Mercury is indeed tide-locked, but instead of having a rotation, a "day," taking eighty-eight Earth days, the same time of the Mercury "year," it turns out that it rotates once in fifty-nine days, which is a ratio of 3:2. And, since Mercury's orbit is highly eccentric, its orbital speed varies tremendously. The result is that, at certain times, the sun will appear to set…and then pop up again, before finally setting. The same thing can be seen in the morning, with a brief sunrise, a sunset, and sunrise again. Or, if the sun is overhead, it will stop, and then move backwards for a while, a "retrograde" motion, before resuming its path across the sky. Isn't that neat? So I had my title, and all I needed were people, and a story. I had no trouble finding them, and this story is the result.

I was at the spaceport an hour early on the day my clone-sister was to arrive from Luna. Part of it was eagerness to see her. She was three E-years older than me, and we had never met. But I admit that I grab every chance I can get to go to the port and just watch the ships arrive and depart. I've never been off-planet. Someday I'll go, but not as a paying passenger. I was about to enroll in pilot-training school.

Keeping my mind on the arrival time of the shuttle from Luna was hard, because my real interest was in the liners departing for all the far-off places in the system. On that very day the *Elizabeth Browning* was lifting off on a direct, high-gee run for Pluto, with connections for the cometary zone. She was sitting on the field a few kilometers from me, boarding passengers and freight. Very little of the latter. The *Browning* was a luxury-class ship where you paid a premium fare to be sealed into a liquid-filled room, doped to the gills, and fed through a tube for the five-gee express run. Nine days later, at wintertime Pluto, they decanted you and put you through ten hours of physical rehabilitation. You could have made it in fourteen days at two gees and only have been mildly uncomfortable, but maybe it's worth it to some people. I had noticed that the *Browning* was never crowded.

I might not have noticed the arrival of the Lunar shuttle, but the tug was lowering it between me and the *Browning*. They were berthing it in Bay 9, a recessed area a few hundred meters from where I was standing. So I ducked into the tunnel that would take me there.

I arrived in time to see the tug cut the line and shoot into space to meet the next incoming ship. The Lunar shuttle was a perfectly reflective sphere sitting in the middle of the landing bay. As I walked up to it, the force-field roof sprang into being over the bay, cutting off the summertime sunlight. The air started rushing in, and in a few minutes my suit turned off. I was suddenly sweating, cooking in the heat that hadn't been dissipated as yet. My suit had cut off too soon again. I would have to have that checked. Meantime, I did a little dance to keep my bare feet away from the too-hot concrete.

When the air temperature reached the standard 24 degrees, the field around the shuttle cut off. What was left behind was an insubstantial latticework of decks and bulkheads, with people gawking out of the missing outer walls of their rooms.

I joined the crowd of people clustered around the ramp. I had seen a picture of my sister, but it was an old one. I wondered if I'd recognize her.

There was no trouble. I spotted her at the head of the ramp, dressed in a silly-looking loonie frock coat and carrying a pressurized suitcase. I was sure it was her because she looked just like me, more or less, except that she was a female and she was frowning. She might have been a few centimeters taller than me, but that was from growing up in a lower gravity field.

I pushed my way over to her and took her case.

"Welcome to Mercury," I said in my friendliest manner. She looked me over. I don't know why, but she took an instant dislike to me, or so it seemed. Actually, she had disliked me before we ever met.

"You must be Timmy," she said. I couldn't let her get away with that. There are limits.

"Timothy. And you're my sister, Jew."

"Jubilant."

We were off to a great start.

She looked around her at the bustle of people in the landing bay. Then she looked overhead at the flat black underside of the force-roof and seemed to shrink away from it.

"Where can I rent a suit?" she asked. "I'd like to get one installed before you have a blowout here."

"It isn't that bad," I said. "We do have them more often here than you do in Luna, but it can't be helped." I started off in the direction of General Environments, and she fell in beside me. She was having difficulty walking. I'd hate to be a loonie; just about anywhere they go, they're too heavy.

"I was reading on the trip that you had a blowout here at the port only four lunations ago."

I don't know why, but I felt defensive. I mean, sure we have blowouts here, but you can hardly *blame* us for them. Mercury has a lot of tidal stresses; that means a lot of quakes. Any system will break down if you shake it around enough.

"All right," I said, trying to sound reasonable. "It happens I was here during that one. It was in the middle of the last dark year. We lost pressure in about ten percent of the passages, but it was restored in a few minutes. No lives were lost."

"A few minutes is more than enough to kill someone without a suit, isn't it?" How could I answer that? She seemed to think she had won a point. "So I'll feel a lot better when I get into one of your suits."

"Okay, let's get a suit into you." I was trying to think of something to restart the conversation and drawing a blank. Somehow she seemed to have a low opinion of our environmental engineers on Mercury and was willing to take her contempt out on me.

"What are you training for?" I ventured. "You must be out of school. What are you going to do?"

"I'm going to be an environmental engineer."

"Oh."

I was relieved when they finally had her lie on the table, made the connection from the computer into the socket at the back of her head, and turned off her motor control and sensorium. The remainder of the trip to GE had been a steady lecture about the shortcomings of the municipal pressure service in Mercury Port. My head was swimming with facts about quintuple-redundant failless pressure sensors, self-sealing locks, and blowout drills. I'm *sure* we have all those things, and just as good as the ones in Luna. But the best anyone can do with the quakes shaking everything up a hundred times a day is achieve a 99 percent safety factor. Jubilant had sneered when I trotted out that figure. She quoted one to me with fifteen decimal places, all of them nines. That was the safety factor in Luna.

I was looking at the main reason why we didn't need that kind of safety, right in the surgeon's hands. He had her chest opened up and the left lung removed, and he was placing the suit generator into the cavity. It looked pretty much like the lung he had removed except it was made of metal and had a mirror finish. He hooked it up to her trachea and the stump ends of the pulmonary arteries and did some adjustments. Then he closed her and applied somatic sealant to the incisions. In thirty minutes she would be ready to wake up, fully healed. The only sign of the operation would be the gold button of the intake valve under her left collarbone. And if the pressure were to drop by two millibars in the next instant, she would be surrounded by the force field that is a Mercury suit. She would be safer than she had ever been in her life, even in the oh-so-safe warrens in Luna.

The surgeon made the adjustment in my suit's brain while Jubilant was still out. Then he installed the secondary items in her; the peasized voder in her throat so she could talk without inhaling and exhaling, and the binaural radio receptors in her middle ears. Then he pulled the plug out of her brain, and she sat up. She seemed a little more friendly. An hour of sensory deprivation tends to make you more open and relaxed when you come out of it. She started to get back into her loonie coat.

"That'll just burn off when you go outside," I pointed out.

"Oh, of course. I guess I expected to go by tunnel. But you don't have many tunnels here, do you?"

You can't keep them pressurized, can you?

I really *was* beginning to feel defensive about our engineering.

"The main trouble you'll have is adjusting to not breathing."

We were at the west portal, looking through the force-curtain that separated us from the outside. There was a warm breeze drifting away from the curtain, as there always is in summertime. It was caused by the heating of the air next to the curtain by the wavelengths of light that are allowed to pass through so we can see what's outside. It was the beginning of retrograde summer, when the sun backtracks at the zenith and gives us a triple helping of very intense light and radiation. Mercury Port is at one of the hotspots, where retrograde sun motion coincides with solar noon. So even though the force-curtain filtered out all but a tiny window of visible light, what got through was high-powered stuff.

"Is there any special trick I should know?"

I'll give her credit; she wasn't any kind of fool, she was just overcritical. When it came to the operation of her suit, she was completely willing to concede that I was the expert.

"Not really. You'll feel an overpowering urge to take a breath after a few minutes, but it's all psychological. Your blood will be oxygenated. It's just that your brain won't feel right about it. But you'll get over it. And don't try to breathe when you talk. Just subvocalize, and the radio in your throat will pick it up."

I thought about it and decided to throw in something else, free of charge.

"If you're in the habit of talking to yourself, you'd better try to break yourself of it. Your voder will pick it up if you mutter, or sometimes if you just think too loud. Your throat moves sometimes when you do that, you know. It can get embarrassing."

She grinned at me, the first time she had done it. I found myself liking her. I had always *wanted* to, but this was the first chance she had given me.

"Thanks. I'll bear it in mind. Shall we go?"

I stepped out first. You feel nothing at all when you step through a force-curtain. You can't step through it at all unless you have a suit generator installed, but with it turned on, the field just forms around your body as you step through. I turned around and could see nothing but a perfectly flat, perfectly reflective mirror. It bulged out as I watched in the shape of a nude woman, and the bulge separated from the curtain. What was left was a silver-plated Jubilant.

The suit generator causes the field to follow the outlines of your body, but from one to one-and-a-half millimeters from the skin. It oscillates between those limits, and the changing volume means a bellows action forces the carbon dioxide out through your intake valve. You expel waste gas and cool yourself in one operation. The field is perfectly reflective except for two pupil-sized discontinuities that follow your eye movements and let in enough light to see by, but not enough to blind you.

"What happens if I open my mouth?" she mumbled. It takes a while to get the knack of subvocalizing clearly.

"Nothing. The field extends over your mouth, like it does over your nostrils. It won't go down your throat."

A few minutes later: "I sure would like to take a breath." She would get over it. "Why is it so hot?"

"Because at the most efficient setting your suit doesn't release enough carbon dioxide to cool you down below about thirty degrees. So you'll sweat a bit."

"It feels like thirty-five or forty."

"It must be your imagination. You can change the setting by turning the nozzle of your air valve, but that means your tank will be releasing some oxygen with the CO_2, and you never know when you'll need it."

"How much of a reserve is there?"

"You're carrying forty-eight hours' worth. Since the suit releases oxygen directly into your blood, we can use about ninety-five percent of it, instead of throwing most of it away to cool you off, like your loonie suits do." I couldn't resist that one.

"The term is Lunarian," she said, icily. Oh, well. I hadn't even known the term was derogatory.

"I think I'll sacrifice some margin for comfort now. I feel bad enough as it is in this gravity without stewing in my own sweat."

"Suit yourself. You're the environment expert."

She looked at me, but I don't think she was used to reading expressions on a reflective face. She turned the nozzle that stuck out above her left breast, and the flow of steam from it increased.

"That should bring you down to about twenty degrees, and leave you with about thirty hours of oxygen. That's under ideal conditions, of course, sitting down and keeping still. The more you exert yourself, the more oxygen the suit wastes keeping you cool."

She put her hands on her hips. "Timothy, are you telling me that I shouldn't cool off? I'll do whatever you say."

"No, I think you'll be all right. It's a thirty-minute trip to my house. And what you say about the gravity has merit; you probably need the relief. But I'd turn it up to twenty-five as a reasonable compromise."

She silently readjusted the valve.

Jubilant thought it was silly to have a traffic conveyor that operated in two-kilometer sections. She complained to me the first three or four times we got off the end of one and stepped onto another. She shut up about it when we came to a section knocked out by a quake. We had a short walk between sections of the temporary slideway, and she saw the crews working to bridge the twenty-meter gap that had opened beneath the old one.

We only had one quake on the way home. It didn't amount to anything, just enough motion that we had to do a little dance to keep our feet under us. Jubilant didn't seem to like it much. I wouldn't have noticed it at all, except Jubilant yelped when it hit.

Our house at that time was situated at the top of a hill. We had carried it up there after the big quake seven darkyears before that had shaken down the cliffside where we used to live. I had been buried for ten hours in that one—the first time I ever needed digging out. Mercurians don't like living in valleys. They have a tendency to fill up with debris during the big quakes. If you live at the top of a rise, you have a better chance of being near the top of the rubble when it slides down. Besides, my mother and I both liked the view.

Jubilant liked it, too. She made her first comment on the scenery as we stood outside the house and looked out over the valley we had just crossed. Mercury Port was sitting atop the ridge, thirty kilometers away. At that distance you could just make out the hemispherical shape of the largest buildings.

But Jubilant was more interested in the mountains behind us. She pointed to a glowing violet cloud that rose from behind one of the foothills and asked me what it was.

"That's quicksilver grotto. It always looks like that at the start of retrograde summer. I'll take you over there later. I think you'll like it."

Dorothy greeted us as we stepped through the wall.

I couldn't put my finger on what was bothering Mom. She seemed happy enough to see Jubilant after seventeen years. She kept saying inane things about how she had grown and how pretty she looked. She had us stand side by side and pointed out how much we looked like each other. It was true, of course, since we were genetically identical. She was five centimeters taller than me, but she could lose that in a few months in Mercury's gravity.

"She looks just like you did two years ago, before your last Change," she told me. That was a slight misstatement; I hadn't been quite as sexually mature the last time I was a female. But she was right in essence. Both Jubilant and I were genotypically male, but Mom had had my sex changed when I first came to Mercury, when I was a few months old. I had spent the first fifteen years of my life female. I was thinking of Changing back, but wasn't in a hurry.

"You're looking well yourself, Glitter," Jubilant said.

Mom frowned for an instant. "It's Dorothy now, honey. I changed my name when we moved here. We use Old Earth names on Mercury."

"I'm sorry, I forgot. My mother always used to call you Glitter when she spoke of you. Before she, I mean before I—"

There was an awkward silence. I felt like something was being concealed from me, and my ears perked up. I had high hopes of learning some things from Jubilant, things that Dorothy had never told me no matter how hard I prodded her. At least I knew where to start in drawing Jubilant out.

It was a frustrating fact at that time that I knew little of the mystery surrounding how I came to grow up on Mercury instead of in Luna, and why I had a clone-sister. Having a clone-twin is a rare enough thing that it was inevitable I'd try to find out how it came to pass. It wasn't socially debilitating, like having a fraternal sibling or something scandalous like that. But I learned early not to mention it to my friends. They wanted to know how it happened, how my mom managed to get around the laws that forbid that kind of unfair preference. One Person, One Child: that's the first moral lesson any child learns, even before Thou Shalt Not Take a Life. Mom wasn't in jail, so it must have been legal. But how? And why? She wouldn't talk, but maybe Jubilant would.

Dinner was eaten in a strained silence, interrupted by awkward attempts at conversation. Jubilant was suffering from culture shock and an attack of nerves. I could understand it, looking around me with her eyes. Loonies—pardon me, Lunarians—live all their lives in burrows down in the rock and come to need the presence of solid, substantial walls around them. They don't go outside much. When they do, they are wrapped in a steel-and-plastic cocoon that they can feel around them, and they look out of it through a window. Jubilant was feeling terribly exposed and trying to be brave about it. When inside a force-bubble house, you might as well be sitting on a flat platform under the blazing sun. The bubble is invisible from the inside.

When I realized what was bothering her, I turned up the polarization. Now the bubble looked like tinted glass.

"Oh, you needn't," she said, gamely. "I have to get used to it. I just wish you had *walls* somewhere I could look at."

It was more apparent than ever that something was upsetting Dorothy. She hadn't noticed Jubilant's unease, and that's not like her. She should have had some curtains rigged to give our guest a sense of enclosure.

I did learn some things from the intermittent conversation at the table. Jubilant had divorced her mother when she was ten E-years old, an absolutely extraordinary age. The only grounds for divorce at that age are really incredible things like insanity or religious evangelism. I didn't know much about Jubilant's foster mother—not even her name—but I did know that she and Dorothy had been good friends back in Luna. Somehow, the question of how and why Dorothy had abandoned her child and taken me, a chip off the block, to Mercury, was tied up in that relationship.

"We could never get close, as far back as I can remember," Jubilant was saying. "She told me crazy things, she didn't seem to fit in. I can't really explain it, but the court agreed with me. It helped that I had a good lawyer."

"Maybe part of it was the unusual relationship," I said, helpfully. "You know what I mean. It isn't all that common to grow up with a foster mother instead of your real mother." That was greeted with such a dead silence that I wondered if I should just shut up for the rest of dinner. There were meaningful glances exchanged.

"Yes, that might have been part of it. Anyway, within three years of your leaving for Mercury, I knew I couldn't take it. I should have gone with you. I was only a child, but even then I wanted to come with you." She looked appealingly at Dorothy, who was studying the table. Jubilant had stopped eating.

"Maybe I'd better not talk about it."

To my surprise, Dorothy agreed. That cinched it for me. They wouldn't talk about it because they were keeping something from me.

Jubilant took a nap after dinner. She said she wanted to go to the grotto with me but had to rest from the gravity. While she slept I tried once more to get Dorothy to tell me the whole story of her life on the moon.

"But *why* am I alive at all? You say you left Jubilant, your own child, three years old, with a friend who would take care of her in Luna. Didn't you *want* to take her with you?"

She looked at me tiredly. We'd been over this ground before.

"Timmy, you're an adult now, and have been for three years. I've told you that you're free to leave me if you want. You will soon, anyway. But I'm not going into it any further."

"Mom, you know I can't insist. But don't you have enough respect for me not to keep feeding me that story? There's more behind it."

"Yes! Yes, there is more behind it. But I prefer to let it lie in the past. It's a matter of personal privacy. Don't you have enough respect for *me* to stop grilling me about it?" I had never seen her this upset. She got up and walked through the wall and down the hill. Halfway down, she started to run.

I started after her, but came back after a few steps. I didn't know what I'd say to her that hadn't already been said.

We made it to the grotto in easy stages. Jubilant was feeling much better after her rest, but still had trouble on some of the steep slopes.

I hadn't been to the grotto for four lightyears and hadn't played in it for longer than that. But it was still a popular place with the kids. There were scores of them.

We stood on a narrow ledge overlooking the quicksilver pool, and this time Jubilant was really impressed. The quicksilver pool is at the bottom of a narrow gorge that was blocked off a long time ago by a quake. One side of the gorge is permanently in shade, because it faces north and the sun never gets that high in our latitude. At the bottom of the gorge is the pool, twenty meters across, a hundred meters long, and about five meters deep. We *think* it's that deep, but just try sounding a pool of mercury. A lead weight sinks through it like thick molasses, and just about everything else floats. The kids had a fairsized boulder out in the middle and were using it for a boat.

That's all pretty enough, but this was retrograde summer, and the temperature was climbing toward the maximum. So the mercury was near the boiling point, and the whole area was thick with the vapor. When the streams of electrons from the sun passed through the vapor, it lit up, flickering and swirling in a ghostly indigo storm. The level was down, but it would never all boil away because it kept condensing on the dark cliffside and running back into the pool.

"Where does it all come from?" Jubilant asked when she got her breath.

"Some of it's natural, but the majority comes from the factories in the port. It's a by-product of some of the fusion processes that they can't find any use for, and so they release it into the environment. It's too heavy to drift away, and so during darkyear, it condenses in the valleys. This one is especially good for collecting it. I used to play here when I was younger."

She was impressed. There's nothing like it on Luna. From what I hear, Luna is plain dull on the outside. Nothing moves for billions of years.

"I never saw anything so pretty. What do you do in it, though? Surely it's too dense to swim in?"

"Truer words were never spoken. It's all you can do to force your hand half a meter into the stuff. If you could balance, you could stand on it and sink in just about fifteen centimeters. But that doesn't mean you can't swim, you swim *on* it. Come on down, I'll show you."

She was still gawking at the ionized cloud, but she followed me. That cloud can hypnotize you. At first you think it's all purple; then you start seeing other colors out of the corners of your eyes. You can never see them plainly, they're too faint. But they're there. It's caused by local impurities of other gases.

I understand people used to make lamps using ionized gases: neon, argon, mercury, and so forth. Walking down into quicksilver gully is exactly like walking into the glow of one of those old lamps.

Halfway down the slope, Jubilant's knees gave way. Her suit field stiffened with the first impact when she landed on her behind and started to slide. She was a rigid statue by the time she plopped into the pool, frozen into an awkward posture trying to break her fall. She slid across the pool and came to rest on her back.

I dived onto the surface of the pool and was easily carried all the way across to her. She was trying to stand up and finding it impossible. Presently she began to laugh, realizing that she must look pretty silly.

"There's no way you're going to stand up out here. Look, here's how you move." I flipped over on my belly and started moving my arms in a swimming motion. You start with them in front of you, and bring them back to your sides in a long circular motion. The harder you dig into the mercury, the faster you go. And you keep going until you dig your toes in. The pool is frictionless.

Soon she was swimming along beside me, having a great time. Well, so was I. Why is it that we stop doing so many fun things when we grow up? There's nothing in the solar system like swimming on mercury. It was coming back to me now, the sheer pleasure of gliding along on the mirror-bright surface with your chin plowing up a wake before you. With your eyes just above the surface, the sensation of speed is tremendous.

Some of the kids were playing hockey. I wanted to join them, but I could see from the way they eyed us that we were too big and they thought we shouldn't be out here in the first place. Well, that was just tough. I was having too much fun swimming.

After several hours, Jubilant said she wanted to rest. I showed her how it could be done without going to the side, forming a tripod by sitting with your feet spread wide apart. That's about the only thing you can do except lie flat. Any other position causes your support to slip out from under you. Jubilant was content to lie flat.

"I still can't get over being able to look right at the sun," she said. "I'm beginning to think you might have the better system here. With the internal suits, I mean."

"I thought about that," I said. "You loo...Lunarians don't spend enough time on the surface to make a forcesuit necessary. It'd be too much trouble and expense, especially for children. You wouldn't believe what it costs to keep a child in suits. Dorothy won't have her debts paid off for twenty years."

"Yes, but it might be worth it. Oh, I can see you're right that it would cost a lot, but I won't be outgrowing them. How long do they last?"

"They should be replaced every two or three years." I scooped up a handful of mercury and let it dribble through my hands and onto her chest. I was trying to think of an indirect way to get the talk onto the subject of Dorothy and what Jubilant knew about her. After several false starts, I came right out and asked her what they had been trying not to say.

She wouldn't be drawn out.

"What's in that cave over there?" she asked, rolling over on her belly.

"That's the grotto."

"What's in it?"

"I'll show you if you'll talk."

She gave me a look. "Don't be childish, Timothy. If your mother wants you to know about her life in Luna, she'll tell you. It's not my business."

"I won't be childish if you'll stop treating me like a child. We're both adults. You can tell me whatever you want without asking my mother."

"Let's drop the subject."

"That's what everyone tells me. All right, go on up to the grotto by yourself." And she did just that. I sat on the lake and glowered at everything. I don't enjoy being kept in the dark, and I especially don't like having my relatives talk around me.

I was just a little bemused to find out how important it had become to find out the real story of Dorothy's trip to Mercury. I had lived seventeen years without knowing, and it hadn't harmed me. But now that I had thought about the things she told me as a child, I saw that they didn't make sense. Jubilant arriving here had made me reexamine them. Why *did* she leave Jubilant in Luna? Why take a cloned infant instead?

The grotto is a cave at the head of the gully, with a stream of quicksilver flowing from its mouth. That happens all lightyear, but the stream gets more substantial during the height of summer. It's caused by the mercury vapor concentrating in the cave, where it condenses and drips off the walls. I found Jubilant sitting in the center of a pool, entranced. The ionization glow in the cave seems much brighter than outside, where it has to compete with sunlight. Add to that the thousands of trickling streams of mercury throwing back reflections, and you have a place that has to be entered to be believed.

"Listen, I'm sorry I was pestering you. I—"

"Shhh." She waved her hands at me. She was watching the drops fall from the roof to splash without a ripple into the isolated pools on the floor of the cave. So I sat beside her and watched it, too.

"I don't think I'd mind living here," she said, after what might have been an hour.

"I guess I never really considered living anywhere else."

She faced me, but turned away again. She wanted to read my face, but all she could see was the distorted reflection of her own.

"I thought you wanted to be a ship's captain."

"Oh, sure. But I'd always come back here." I was silent for another few minutes, thinking about something that had bothered me more and more lately.

"Actually, I might get into another line of work."

"Why?"

"Oh, I guess commanding a spaceship isn't what it used to be. You know what I mean?"

She looked at me again, this time tried even harder to see my face.

"Maybe I do."

"I know what you're thinking. Lots of kids want to be ship's captains. They grow out of it. Maybe I have. I think I was born a century too late for what I want. You can hardly find a ship anymore where the captain is much more than a figurehead. The real master of the ship is a committee of computers. They handle *all* the work. The captain can't even overrule them anymore."

"I wasn't aware it had gotten that bad."

"Worse. All of the passenger lines are shifting over to totally automated ships. The high-gee runs are already like that, on the theory that after a dozen trips at five gees, the crew is pretty much used up."

I pondered a sad fact of our modern civilization: the age of romance was gone. The solar system was tamed. There was no place for adventure.

"You could go to the cometary zone," she suggested.

"That's the only thing that's kept me going toward pilot training. You don't need a computer out there hunting for black holes. I thought about getting a job and buying passage last darkyear, when I was feeling really low about it. But I'm going to try to get some pilot training before I go."

"That might be wise."

"I don't know. They're talking about ending the courses in astrogation. I may have to teach myself."

"You think we should get going? I'm getting hungry."

"No. Let's stay here a while longer. I love this place."

I'm sure we had been there for five hours, saying very little. I had asked her about her interest in environmental engineering and gotten a surprisingly frank answer. This was what she had to say about her chosen profession: "I found after I divorced my mother that I was interested in making safe places to live. I didn't feel very safe at that time." She found other reasons later, but she admitted that it was a need for security that still drove her. I meditated on her strange childhood. She was the only person I ever knew who didn't grow up with her natural mother.

"I was thinking about heading outsystem myself," she said after another long silence. "Pluto, for instance. Maybe we'll meet out there someday."

"It's possible."

There was a little quake; not much, but enough to start the pools of mercury quivering and make Jubilant ready to go. We were threading our way through the pools when there was a long, rolling shock, and the violet glow died away. We were knocked apart and fell in total darkness.

"What was that?" There was the beginning of panic in her voice.

"It looks like we're blocked in. There must have been a slide over the entrance. Just sit tight and I'll find you."

"Where are you? I can't find you. Timothy!"

"Just hold still and I'll run into you in a minute. Stay calm, just stay calm, there's nothing to worry about. They'll have us out in a few hours."

"Timothy, I can't find you, I can't—" She smacked me across the face with one of her hands, then was swarming all over me. I held her close and soothed her. Earlier in the day I might have been contemptuous of her behavior, but I had come to understand her better. Besides, no one likes to be buried alive. Not even me. I held her until I felt her relax.

"Sorry."

"Don't apologize, I felt the same way the first time. I'm glad you're here. Being buried alone is much worse than just being buried alive. Now sit down and do what I tell you. Turn your intake valve all the way to the left. Got it? Now we're using oxygen at the slowest possible rate. We have to keep as still as possible so we don't heat up too much."

"All right. What next?"

"Well, for starters, do you play chess?"

"What? Is that all? Don't we have to turn on a signal or something?"

"I already did."

"What if you're buried solid and your suit freezes to keep you from being crushed? How do you turn it on then?"

"It turns on automatically if the suit stays rigid for more than one minute."

"Oh. All right. Pawn to king four."

We gave up on the game after the fifteenth move. I'm not that good at visualizing the board, and while she was excellent at it, she was too nervous to plan her game. And I was getting nervous. If the entrance was blocked with rubble, as I had thought, they should have had us out in under an hour. I had practiced estimating time in the dark and made it to be two hours since the quake. It must have been bigger than I thought. It could be a full day before they got around to us.

"I was surprised when you hugged me that I could touch you. I mean your skin, not your suit."

"I thought I felt you jump. The suits merge. When you touch me, we're wearing one suit instead of two. That comes in handy sometimes."

We were lying side by side in a pool of mercury, arms around each other. We found it soothing.

"You mean…I see. You can make love with your suit on. Is that what you're saying?"

"You should try it in a pool of mercury. That's the best way."

"We're in a pool of mercury."

"And we don't dare make love. It would overheat us. We might need our reserve."

She was quiet, but I felt her hands tighten behind my back.

"Are we in trouble, Timothy?"

"No, but we might be in for a long stay. You'll get thirsty by and by. Can you hold out?"

"It's too bad we can't make love. It would have kept my mind off it."

"Can you hold out?"

"I can hold out."

"Timothy, I didn't fill my tank before we left the house. Will that make a difference?"

I don't think I tensed, but she scared me badly. I thought about it, and didn't see how it mattered. She had used an hour's oxygen at most getting to the house, even at her stepped-up cooling rate. I suddenly remembered how cool her skin had been when she came into my arms.

"Jubilant, was your suit set at maximum cooling when you left the house?"

"No, but I set it up on the way. It was so *hot*. I was about to pass out from the exertion."

"And you didn't turn it down until the quake?"

"That's right."

I did some rough estimates and didn't like the results. By the most pessimistic assumptions, she might not have more than about five hours of air left. At the outside, she might have twelve hours. And she could do simple arithmetic as well as I; there was no point in trying to hide it from her.

"Come closer to me," I said. She was puzzled, because we were already about as close as we could get. But I wanted to get our intake valves together. I hooked them up and waited three seconds.

"Now our tank pressures are equalized."

"Why did you do that? Oh, no, Timothy, you shouldn't have. It was my own fault for not being careful."

"I did it for me, too. How could I live with myself if you died in here and I could have saved you? Think about that."

"Timothy, I'll answer any question you want to ask about your mother."

That was the first time she got me mad. I hadn't been angry with her for not refilling the tank. Not even about the cooling. That was more my fault than hers. I had made it a game about the cooling rate, not really telling her how important it was to maintain a viable reserve. She hadn't taken me seriously, and now we were paying for my little joke. I had made the mistake of assuming that because she was an expert at Lunar safety, she could take care of herself. How could she do that if she didn't have a realistic estimate of the dangers?

But this offer sounded like repayment for the oxygen, and you don't do that on Mercury. In a tight spot, air is always shared freely. Thanks are rude.

"*Don't* think you owe me anything. It isn't right."

"That's not why I offered. If we're going to die down here, it seems silly for me to be keeping secrets. Does that make sense?"

"No. If we're going to die, what's the use in telling me? What good will it do me? And that doesn't make sense, either. We're not even *near* dying."

"It would at least be something to pass the time."

I sighed. At that time, it really wasn't important to know what I had been trying to learn from her.

"All right. Question one: Why did Dorothy leave you behind when she came here?" Once I had asked it, the question suddenly became important again.

"Because she's not our mother. I divorced our mother when I was ten."

I sat up, shocked silly.

"Dorothy's not…then she's…she's my foster mother? All this time she said she was—"

"No, she's not your foster mother, not technically. She's your father."

"*What?*"

"She's your father."

"Who the hell—*father?* What kind of crazy game is this? Who the hell ever knows who their *father* is?"

"I do," she said simply. "And now you do."

"I think you had better tell it from the top."

She did, and it all stood up, bizarre as it was.

Dorothy and Jubilant's mother (*my* mother!) had been members of a religious sect called the First Principles. I gathered they had a lot of screwy ideas, but the screwiest one of all had to do with something called the "nuclear family." I don't know why they called it that, maybe because it was invented in the era when nuclear power was first harnessed. What it consisted of was a mother and a father, *both living in the same household*, and dozens of kids.

The First Principles didn't go that far; they still adhered to the One Person-One Child convention—and a damn good thing, too, or they might have been lynched instead of queasily tolerated—but they liked the idea of both biological parents living together to raise the two children.

So Dorothy and Gleam (that was her name; they were Glitter and Gleam back in Luna) "married," and Gleam took on the female role for the first child. She conceived it, birthed it, and named it Jubilant.

Then things started to fall apart, as any sane person could have told them it would. I don't know much history, but I know a little about the way things were back on Old Earth. Husbands killing wives, wives killing husbands, parents beating children, wars, starvation—all those things. I don't know how much of that was the result of the nuclear family, but it must have been tough to "marry" someone and find out too late that it was the wrong someone. So you took it out on the children. I'm no sociologist, but I can see that much.

Their relationship, while it may have glittered and gleamed at first, went steadily downhill for three years. It got to the point where Glitter couldn't even share the same planet with his spouse. But he loved the child and had even come to think of her as his own. Try telling that to a court of law. Modern jurisprudence doesn't even recognize the *concept* of fatherhood, any more than it would recognize the divine right of kings. Glitter didn't have a legal leg to stand on. The child belonged to Gleam.

But my mother (*foster* mother, I couldn't yet bring myself to say father) found a compromise. There was no use mourning the fact that he couldn't take Jubilant with him. He had to accept that. But he could take a piece of her. That was me. So he moved to Mercury with the cloned child, changed his sex, and brought me up to adulthood, never saying a word about First Principles.

I was calming down as I heard all this, but it was certainly a revelation. I was full of questions, and for a time survival was forgotten.

"No, Dorothy isn't a member of the church any longer. That was one of the causes of the split. As far as I know, Gleam is the *only* member today. It didn't last very long. The couples who formed the church pretty much tore each other apart in marital strife. That was why the court granted my divorce; Gleam kept trying to force her religion on me, and when I told my friends about it, they laughed at me. I didn't want that, even at age ten, and told the court I thought my mother was crazy. The court agreed."

"So…so Dorothy hasn't had her one child yet. Do you think she can still have one? What are the legalities of that?"

"Pretty cut-and-dried, according to Dorothy. The judges don't like it, but it's her birthright, and they can't deny it. She managed to get permission to have you grown because of a loophole in the law, since she was going to Mercury and would be out of the jurisdiction of the Lunar courts. The loophole was closed shortly after you left. So you and I are pretty unique. What do you think about that?"

"I don't know. I think I'd rather have a normal family. What do I say to Dorothy now?"

She hugged me, and I loved her for that. I was feeling young and alone. Her story was still settling in, and I was afraid of what my reaction might be when I had digested it.

"I wouldn't tell her anything. Why should you? She'll probably get around to telling you before you leave for the cometary zone, but if she doesn't, what of it? What does it matter? Hasn't she been a mother to you? Do you have any complaints? Is the biological fact of motherhood all that important? I think not. I think love is more important, and I can see that it was there."

"But she's my father! How do I relate to that?"

"Don't even try. I suspect that fathers loved their children in pretty much the same way mothers did, back when fatherhood was more than just insemination."

"Maybe you're right. I think you're right." She held me close in the dark.

"Of course I'm right."

Three hours later there was a rumble and the violet glow surrounded us again.

We walked into the sunlight hand in hand. The rescue crew was there to meet us, grinning and patting us on the back. They filled our tanks, and we enjoyed the luxury of wasting oxygen to drive away the sweat.

"How bad was it?" I asked the rescue boss.

"Medium-sized. You two are some of the last to be dug out. Did you have a hard time in there?"

I looked at Jubilant, who acted as though she had just been resurrected from the dead, grinning like a maniac. I thought about it.

"No. No trouble."

We climbed the rocky slope and I looked back. The quake had dumped several tons of rock into quicksilver gully. Worse still, the natural dam at the lower end had been destroyed. Most of the mercury had drained out into the broader valley below. It was clear that quicksilver grotto would never be the magic place it had been in my youth. That was a sad thing. I had loved it, and it seemed that I was leaving a lot behind me down there.

I turned my back on it and walked toward the house and Dorothy.

IN THE BOWL

Oh, for the long-lost swamps of Venus! Some of my favorite stories of all time were set there. I recall fondly Robert A. Heinlein's *Between Planets*, with its intelligent Venerian dragons, and *Space Cadet*, with its aquatic humanoid beings. Both took place on the traditional, eternal, planet-wide swamp.

Why a swamp? The only reason I can think of is that Venus is eternally cloudy. We took the clouds to be water vapor, and eternal rain would likely mean an eternal swamp, right?

Well, not if the surface of the planet was a toasty 860 degrees F, with an atmosphere that is 96 percent carbon dioxide, only .002 percent water, and a surface pressure of 1350 psi.

Farewell, swamps of Venus.

But just as with Mercury, though our new knowledge wiped out the scientific background for hundreds of stories, the new data also opened up new possibilities. The one that appealed to me was the pressure. Gas at that pressure will bend light significantly. I read an article that said it would bend light so much that you would appear to be standing at the bottom of a bowl as light from over the horizon was bent downward toward your eye. So I had my title.

I have since asked myself a couple of questions. In fact, I considered them even before I wrote the story. One, would there be enough light down there to see *anything*? Well, they could see with some sort of infrared scope, okay? And two, would the air be clear enough? I suspect it wouldn't, but what the hell? It *might* be clear enough, and that's good enough for me.

Never buy anything at a secondhand organbank. And while I'm handing out good advice, don't outfit yourself for a trip to Venus until you *get* to Venus.

I wish I had waited. But while shopping around at Coprates a few weeks before my vacation, I happened on this little shop and was talked into an infraeye at a very good price. What I should have asked myself was, what was an infraeye doing on Mars in the first place?

Think about it. No one wears them on Mars. If you want to see at night, it's much cheaper to buy a snooperscope. That way you can take the damn thing off when the sun comes up. So this eye must have come back with a tourist from Venus. And there's no telling how long it sat there in the vat until this sweet-talking old guy gave me his line about how it belonged to a nice little old schoolteacher who never…ah, well. You've probably heard it before.

If only the damn thing had gone on the blink before I left Venusburg. You know Venusburg: town of steamy swamps and sleazy hotels where you can get mugged as you walk down the public streets, lose a fortune at the gaming tables, buy any pleasure in the known universe, hunt the prehistoric monsters that wallow in the fetid marshes that are just a swamp-buggy ride out of town. You do? Then you should know that after hours—when they turn all the holos off and the place reverts to an ordinary cluster of silvery domes sitting in darkness and eight-hundred-degree temperature and pressure enough to give you a sinus headache just *thinking* about it, when they shut off all the tourist razzle-dazzle—it's no trouble to find your way to one of the rental agencies around the spaceport and get medicanical work done. They'll accept Martian money. Your Solar Express Card is honored. Just walk right in, no waiting.

However…

I had caught the daily blimp out of Venusburg just hours after I touched down, happy as a clam, my infraeye working beautifully. By the time I landed in Cui-Cui town, I was having my first inklings of trouble. Barely enough to notice; just the faintest hazing in the rightside peripheral vision. I shrugged it off. I had only three hours in CuiCui before the blimp left for Last Chance. I wanted to look around. I had no intention of wasting my few hours in a bodyshop getting my eye fixed. If it was still acting up at Last Chance, then I'd see about it.

IN THE BOWL

Cui-Cui was more to my liking than Venusburg. There was not such a cast-of-thousands feeling there. On the streets of Venusburg the chances are about ten to one against meeting a real human being; everyone else is a holo put there to spice up the image and help the streets look not quite so *empty*. I quickly tired of zoot-suited pimps that I could see right through trying to sell me boys and girls of all ages. What's the *point*? Just try to touch one of those beautiful people.

In Cui-Cui the ratio was closer to fifty-fifty. And the theme was not decadent corruption but struggling frontier. The streets were very convincing mud, and the wooden storefronts were tastefully done. I didn't care for the eight-legged dragons with eyestalks that constantly lumbered through the place, but I understand they are a memorial to the fellow who named the town. That's all right, but I doubt if he would have liked to have one of the damn things walk through him like a twelve-ton tank made of pixie dust.

I barely had time to get my feet "wet" in the "puddles" before the blimp was ready to go again. And the eye trouble had cleared up. So I was off to Last Chance.

I should have taken a cue from the name of the town. And I had every opportunity to do so. While there, I made my last purchase of supplies for the bush. I was going out where there wasn't an air station on every corner, and so I decided I could use a tagalong.

Maybe you've never seen one. They're modern science's answer to the backpack. Or maybe to the mule train, though in operation they remind you of the safari bearers in old movies, trudging stolidly along behind the White Hunter with bales of supplies on their heads. The thing is a pair of metal legs exactly as long as your legs, with equipment on the top and an umbilical cord attaching the contraption to your lower spine. What it does is provide you with the capability of living on the surface for four weeks instead of the five days you get from your Venus-lung.

The medico who sold me mine had me lying right there on his table with my back laid open so he could install the tubes that carry air from the tanks in the tagalong into my Venus-lung. It was a golden opportunity to ask him to check the eye. He probably would have, because while he was hooking me up he inspected and tested my lung and charged me nothing. He wanted to know where I bought it, and I told him Mars. He clucked and said it seemed all right. He warned me to never let the level of oxygen in the lung get too low, to always charge it up before I left a pressure dome, even if I was only going out for a few minutes. I assured him that I knew all that and would be careful. So he connected the nerves into a metal socket in the small of my back and plugged the tagalong into it. He tested it several ways and said the job was done.

And I didn't ask him to look at the eye. I just wasn't thinking about the eye then. I'd not even gone out on the surface yet, so I'd no real occasion to see it in action. Oh, things looked a little different, even in visible light. There were different colors and very few shadows, and the image I got out of the infraeye was fuzzier than the one from the other eye. I could close one eye, then the other, and see a real difference. But I wasn't thinking about it.

So I boarded the blimp the next day for the weekly scheduled flight to Lodestone, a company mining town close to the Fahrenheit Desert. Though how they were able to distinguish a desert from anything else on Venus was still a mystery to me. I was enraged to find that, though the blimp left half-loaded, I had to pay two fares: one for me and one for my tagalong. I thought briefly of carrying the damn thing in my lap but gave it up after a ten-minute experiment in the depot. It was full of sharp edges and poking angles, and the trip was going to be a long one. So I paid. But the extra expense had knocked a large hole in my budget.

From Cui-Cui the steps got closer together and harder to reach. Cui-Cui is two thousand kilometers from Venusburg, and it's another thousand to Lodestone. After that the passenger service is spotty. I did find out how Venusians defined a desert, though. A desert is a place not yet inhabited by human beings. So long as I was able to board a scheduled blimp, I wasn't there yet.

The blimps played out on me in a little place called Prosperity, population seventy-five humans and one otter. I thought the otter was a holo playing in the pool in the town square. The place didn't look prosperous enough to afford a real pool like that with real water. But it was. It was a transient town catering to prospectors. I understand that a town like that can vanish overnight if the prospectors move on. The owners of the shops just pack up and haul the whole thing away. The ratio of the things you see in a frontier town to what really is there is something like a hundred to one.

I learned with considerable relief that the only blimps I could catch out of Prosperity were headed in the direction I had come from. There was nothing at all going the other way. I was happy to hear that and felt it was only a matter of chartering a ride into the desert. Then my eye faded out entirely.

I remember feeling annoyed; no, more than annoyed. I was really angry. But I was still viewing it as a nuisance rather than a disaster. It was going to be a matter of some lost time and some wasted money.

I quickly learned otherwise. I asked the ticket seller (this was in a saloon-drugstore-arcade; there was no depot in Prosperity) where I could find someone who'd sell and install an infraeye. He laughed at me.

"Not out here you won't, brother," he said. "Never have had anything like that out here. Used to be a medico in Ellsworth, three stops back on the local blimp, but she moved back to Venusburg a year ago. Nearest thing now is in Last Chance."

I was stunned. I knew I was heading out for the deadlands, but it had never occurred to me that any place would be lacking in something so basic as a medico. Why, you might as well not sell food or air as not sell medicanical services. People might actually *die* out here. I wondered if the planetary government knew about this disgusting situation.

Whether they did or not, I realized that an incensed letter to them would do me no good. I was in a bind. Adding quickly in my head, I soon discovered that the cost of flying back to Last Chance and buying a new eye would leave me without enough money to return to Prosperity and still make it back to Venusburg. My entire vacation was about to be ruined just because I tried to cut some corners buying a used eye.

"What's the matter with the eye?" the man asked me.

"Huh? Oh, I don't know. I mean, it's just stopped working. I'm blind in it, that's what's wrong." I grasped at a straw, seeing the way he was studying my eye. "Say, you don't know anything about it, do you?"

He shook his head and smiled ruefully at me. "Naw. Just a little here and there. I was thinking if it was the muscles that was giving you trouble, bad tracking or something like that—"

"No. No vision at all."

"Too bad. Sounds like a shot nerve to me. I wouldn't try to fool around with that. I'm just a tinkerer." He clucked his tongue sympathetically. "You want that ticket back to Last Chance?"

I didn't know what I wanted just then. I had planned this trip for two years. I almost bought the ticket, then thought what the hell. I was here, and I should at least look around before deciding what to do. Maybe there was someone here who could help me. I turned back to ask the clerk if he knew anyone, but he answered before I got it out.

"I don't want to raise your hopes too much," he said, rubbing his chin with a broad hand. "Like I say, it's not for sure, but—"

"Yes, what is it?"

"Well, there's a kid lives around here who's pretty crazy about medico stuff. Always tinkering around, doing odd jobs for people, fixing herself up; you know the type. The trouble is she's pretty loose in her ways. You might end up worse when she's through with you than when you started."

"I don't see how," I said. "It's not working at all; what could she do to make it any worse?"

He shrugged. "It's your funeral. You can probably find her hanging around the square. If she's not there, check the bars. Her name's Ember. She's got a pet otter that's always with her. But you'll know her when you see her."

Finding Ember was no problem. I simply backtracked to the square and there she was, sitting on the stone rim of the fountain. She was trailing her toes in the water. Her otter was playing on a small waterslide, looking immensely pleased to have found the only open body of water within a thousand kilometers.

"Are you Ember?" I asked, sitting down beside her.

She looked up at me with that unsettling stare a Venusian can inflict on a foreigner. It comes of having one blue or brown eye and one that is all red, with no white. I looked that way myself, but I didn't have to look at it.

"What if I am?"

Her apparent age was about ten or eleven. Intuitively, I felt that it was probably very close to her actual age. Since she was supposed to be handy at medicanics, I could have been wrong. She had done some work on herself, but of course there was no way of telling how extensive it might have been. Mostly it seemed to be cosmetic. She had no hair on her head. She had replaced it with a peacock fan of feathers that kept falling into her eyes. Her scalp skin had been transplanted to her lower legs and forearms, and the hair there was long, blonde, and flowing. From the contours of her face I was sure that her skull was a mass of file marks and bone putty from where she'd fixed the understructure to reflect the face she wished to wear.

"I was told that you know a little medicanics. You see, this eye has—"

She snorted. "I don't know who would have told you *that*. I know a hell of a lot about medicine. I'm not just a backyard tinkerer. Come on, Malibu."

She started to get up, and the otter looked back and forth between us. I don't think he was ready to leave the pool.

"Wait a minute. I'm sorry if I hurt your feelings. Without knowing anything about you, I'll admit that you must know more about it than anyone else in town."

She sat back down, finally had to grin at me.

"So you're in a spot, right? It's me or no one. Let me guess: you're here on vacation, that's obvious. And either time or money is preventing you from going back to Last Chance for professional work." She looked me up and down. "I'd say it was money."

"You hit it. Will you help me?"

"That depends." She moved closer and squinted into my infraeye. She put her hands on my cheeks to hold my head steady. There was nowhere for me to look but her face. There were no scars visible on her; at least she was that good. Her upper canines were about five millimeters longer than the rest of her teeth.

"Hold still. Where'd you get this?"

"Mars."

"Thought so. It's a Gloom Piercer, made by Northern Bio. Cheap model; they peddle 'em mostly to tourists. Maybe ten, twelve years old."

"Is it the nerve? The guy I talked to—"

"Nope." She leaned back and resumed splashing her feet in the water. "Retina. The right side is detached, and it's flopped down over the fovea. Probably wasn't put on very tight in the first place. They don't make those things to last more than a year."

I sighed and slapped my knees with my palms. I stood up, held out my hand to her.

"Well, I guess that's that. Thanks for your help."

She was surprised. "Where you going?"

"Back to Last Chance, then to Mars to sue a certain organbank. There are laws for this sort of thing on Mars."

"Here, too. But why go back? I'll fix it for you."

We were in her workshop, which doubled as her bedroom and kitchen. It was just a simple dome without a single holo. It was refreshing after the ranch-style houses that seemed to be the rage in Prosperity. I don't wish to sound chauvinistic, and I realize that Venusians need some sort of visual stimulation, living as they do in a cloud-covered desert. Still, the emphasis on illusion there was never to my liking. Ember lived next door to a man who lived in a perfect replica of the palace at Versailles. She told me that when he shut his holo generator off his *real* possessions would have fit in a knapsack. Including the holo generator.

"What brings you to Venus?"

"Tourism."

She looked at me out of the corner of her eye as she swabbed my face with nerve deadener. I was stretched out on the floor, since there was no furniture in the room except a few work tables.

"All right. But we don't get many tourists this far out. If it's none of my business, just say so."

"It's none of your business."

She sat up. "Fine. Fix your own eye." She waited with a half-smile on her face. I eventually had to smile, too. She went back to work, selecting a spoon-shaped tool from a haphazard pile at her knees.

"I'm an amateur geologist. Rock hound, actually. I work in an office, and weekends I get out in the country and hike around. The rocks are an excuse to get me out there, I guess."

She popped the eye out of its socket and reached in with one finger to deftly unhook the metal connection along the optic nerve. She held the eyeball up to the light and peered in to the lens.

"You can get up now. Pour some of this stuff into the socket and squint down on it." I did as she asked and followed her to the workbench.

She sat on a stool and examined the eye more closely. Then she stuck a syringe into it and drained out the aqueous humor, leaving the orb looking like a turtle egg that's dried in the sun. She sliced it open and started probing carefully. The long hairs on her forearms kept getting in the way. So she paused and tied them back with rubber bands.

"Rock hound," she mused. "You must be here to get a look at the blast jewels."

"Right. Like I said, I'm strictly a small-time geologist. But I read about them and saw one once in a jeweler's shop on Phobos. So I saved up and came to Venus to try and find one of my own."

"That should be no problem. Easiest gems to find in the known universe. Too bad. People out here were hoping they could get rich off them." She shrugged. "Not that there's not some money to be made off them. Just not the fortune everybody was hoping for. Funny; they're as rare as diamonds used to be, and to make it even better, they don't duplicate in the lab the way diamonds do. Oh, I guess they could make 'em, but it's way too much trouble." She was using a tiny device to staple the detached retina back onto the rear surface of the eye.

"Go on."

"Huh?"

"Why can't they make them in the lab?"

She laughed. "You *are* an amateur geologist. Like I said, they could, but it'd cost too much. They're a blend of a lot of different elements. A lot of aluminum, I think. That's what makes rubies red, right?"

"Yes."

"It's the other impurities that make them so pretty. And you have to make them in high pressure and heat, and they're so unstable that they usually blow before you've got the right mix. So it's cheaper to go out and pick 'em up."

"And the only place to pick them up is in the middle of the Fahrenheit Desert."

"Right." She seemed to be finished with her stapling. She straightened up to survey her work with a critical eye. She frowned, then sealed up the incision she had made and pumped the liquid back in. She mounted it in a caliper and aimed a laser at it, then shook her head when she read some figures on a readout by the laser.

"It's working," she said. "But you really got a lemon. The iris is out of true. It's an ellipse, about point two four eccentric. It's going to get worse. See that brown discoloration on the left side? That's progressive decay in the muscle tissue, poisons accumulating in it. And you're a dead cinch for cataracts in about four months."

I couldn't see what she was talking about, but I pursed my lips as if I did.

"But will it last that long?"

She smirked at me. "Are you looking for a six-month warranty? Sorry, I'm not a member of the VMA. But if it isn't legally binding, I guess I'd feel safe in saying it ought to last that long. Maybe."

"You sure go out on a limb, don't you?"

"It's good practice. We future medicos must always be on the alert for malpractice suits. Lean over here and I'll put it in."

"What I was wondering," I said, as she hooked it up and eased it back into the socket, "is whether I'd be safe going out in the desert for four weeks with this eye."

"No," she said promptly, and I felt a great weight of disappointment. "Nor with any eye," she quickly added. "Not if you're going alone."

"I see. But you think the eye would hold up?"

"Oh, sure. But you wouldn't. That's why you're going to take me up on my astounding offer and let me be your guide through the desert."

I snorted. "You think so? Sorry, this is going to be a solo expedition. I planned it that way from the first. That's what I go out rock hunting for the first place: to be alone." I dug my credit meter out of my pouch. "Now, how much do I owe you?"

She wasn't listening but was resting her chin on her palm and looking wistful.

"He goes out so he can be alone, did you hear that, Malibu?" The otter looked up at her from his place on the floor. "Now take me, for instance. Me, I know what being alone is all about. It's the crowds and big cities I crave. Right, old buddy?" The otter kept looking at her, obviously ready to agree to anything.

"I suppose so," I said. "Would a hundred be all right?" That was about half what a registered medico would have charged me, but like I said, I was running short.

"You're not going to let me be your guide? Final word?"

"No. Final. Listen, it's not you, it's just—"

"I know. You want to be alone. No charge. Come on, Malibu."

She got up and headed for the door. Then she turned around.

"I'll be seeing you," she said, and winked at me.

IN THE BOWL

It didn't take me too long to understand what the wink had been all about. I can see the obvious on the third or fourth go-around.

The fact was that Prosperity was considerably bemused to have a tourist in its midst. There wasn't a rental agency or hotel in the entire town. I had thought of that but hadn't figured it would be too hard to find someone willing to rent his private skycycle if the price was right. I'd been saving out a large chunk of cash for the purpose of meeting extortionate demands in that department. I felt sure the locals would be only too willing to soak a tourist.

But they weren't taking. Just about everyone had a skycycle, and absolutely everyone who had one was uninterested in renting it. They were a necessity to anyone who worked out of town, which everyone did, and they were hard to get. Freight schedules were as spotty as the passenger service. And every person who turned me down had a helpful suggestion to make. As I say, after the fourth or fifth such suggestion I found myself back in the town square. She was sitting just as she had been the first time, trailing her feet in the water. Malibu never seemed to tire of the waterslide.

"Yes," she said, without looking up. "It so happens that I *do* have a skycycle for rent."

I was exasperated, but I had to cover it up. She had me over the proverbial barrel.

"Do you always hang around here?" I asked. "People tell me to see you about a skycycle and tell me to look here, almost like you and this fountain are a hyphenated word. What else do you do?"

She fixed me with a haughty glare. "I repair eyes for dumb tourists. I also do body work for everyone in town at only twice what it would cost them in Last Chance. And I do it damn well, too, though those rubes'd be the last to admit it. No doubt Mr. Lamara at the ticket station told you scandalous lies about my skills. They resent it because I'm taking advantage of the cost and time it would take them to get to Last Chance and pay merely inflated prices, instead of the outrageous ones I charge them."

I had to smile, though I was sure I was about to become the object of some outrageous prices myself. She was a shrewd operator.

"How old are you?" I found myself asking, then almost bit my tongue. The last thing a proud and independent child likes to discuss is age. But she surprised me.

"In mere chronological time, eleven Earth years. That's just over six of your years. In real, internal time, of course, I'm ageless."

"Of course. Now about that cycle…"

"Of course. But I evaded your earlier question. What I do besides sit here is irrelevant, because while sitting here I am engaged in contemplating eternity. I'm diving into my navel, hoping to learn the true depth of the womb. In short, I'm doing my yoga exercises." She looked thoughtfully out over the water to her pet. "Besides, it's the only pool in a thousand kilometers." She grinned at me and dived flat over the water. She cut it like a knife blade and torpedoed out to her otter, who set up a happy racket of barks.

When she surfaced near the middle of the pool, out by the jets and falls, I called to her.

"What about the cycle?"

She cupped her ear, though she was only about fifteen meters away.

"I said what about the cycle?"

"I can't hear you," she mouthed. "You'll have to come out here."

I stepped into the pool, grumbling to myself. I could see that her price included more than just money.

"I can't swim," I warned.

"Don't worry, it won't get much deeper than that." It was up to my chest. I sloshed out until I was on tiptoe, then grabbed at a jutting curlicue on the fountain. I hauled myself up and sat on the wet Venusian marble with water trickling down my legs.

Ember was sitting at the bottom of the waterslide, thrashing her feet in the water. She was leaning flat against the smooth rock. The water that sheeted over the rock made a bow wave at the crown of her head. Beads of water ran off her head feathers. Once again she made me smile. If charm could be sold, she could have been wealthy. What am I talking about? Nobody ever sells anything *but* charm, in one way or another. I got a grip on myself before she tried to sell me the north and south poles. In no time at all I was able to see her as an avaricious, cunning little guttersnipe again.

"One billion Solar Marks per hour, not a penny less," she said from that sweet little mouth.

There was no point in negotiating from an offer like that. "You brought me out here to hear *that*? I'm really disappointed in you. I didn't take you for a tease, I really didn't. I thought we could do business. I—"

"Well, if that offer isn't satisfactory, try this one. Free of charge, except for oxygen and food and water." She waited, threshing the water with her feet.

Of course there would be some teeth in that. In an intuitive leap of truly cosmic scale, a surmise worthy of an Einstein, I saw the string. She saw me make that leap, knew I didn't like where I had landed, and her teeth flashed at me. So once again, and not for the last time, I had to either strangle her or smile at her. I smiled. I don't know how, but she had this knack of making her opponents like her even as she screwed them.

"Are you a believer in love at first sight?" I asked her, hoping to throw her off guard. Not a chance.

"Maudlin wishful thinking, at best," she said. "You have *not* bowled me over, Mister—"

"Kiku."

"Nice. Martian name?"

"I suppose so. I never really thought of it. I'm not rich, Ember."

"Certainly not. You wouldn't have put yourself in my hands if you were."

"Then why are you so attracted to me? Why are you so determined to go with me, when all I want from you is to rent your cycle? If I was that charming, I would have noticed it by now."

"Oh, I don't know," she said, with one eyebrow climbing up her forehead. "There's *something* about you that I find absolutely fascinating. Irresistible, even." She pretended to swoon.

"Want to tell me what it is?"

She shook her head. "Let that be my little secret for now."

I was beginning to suspect she was attracted to me by the shape of my neck—so she could sink her teeth into it and drain my blood. I decided to let it lie. Maybe she'd tell me more in the days ahead. Because it looked like there would be days together, many of them.

"When can you be ready to leave?"

"I packed right after I fixed your eye. Let's get going."

Venus is spooky. I thought and thought, and that's the best way I can describe it.

It's spooky partly because of the way you see it. Your right eye—the one that sees what's called visible light—shows you only a small circle of light that's illuminated by your hand torch. Occasionally there's a glowing spot of molten metal in the distance, but it's far too dim to see by. Your infraeye pierces those shadows and gives you a blurry picture of what lies outside the torchlight, but I would have almost rather been blind.

There's no good way to describe how this dichotomy affects your mind. One eye tells you that everything beyond a certain point is shadowy, while the other shows you what's in those shadows. Ember says that after a while your brain can blend the two pictures as easily as it does for binocular vision. I never reached that point. The whole time I was there I was trying to reconcile the two pictures.

I don't like standing in the bottom of a bowl a thousand kilometers wide. That's what you see. No matter how high you climb or how far you go, you're still standing in the bottom of that bowl. It has something to do with the bending of the light rays by the thick atmosphere, if I understand Ember correctly.

Then there's the sun. When I was there it was nighttime, which means that the sun was a squashed ellipse hanging just above the horizon in the east, where it had set weeks and weeks ago. Don't ask me to explain it. All I know is that the sun never sets on Venus. Never, no matter where you are. It just gets flatter and flatter and wider and wider until it oozes around to the north or south, depending on where you are, becoming a flat, bright line of light until it begins pulling itself back together in the west, where it's going to rise in a few weeks.

Ember says that at the equator it becomes a complete circle for a split second when it's actually directly underfoot. Like the lights of a terrific stadium. All this happens up at the rim of the bowl you're standing in, about ten degrees above the theoretical horizon. It's another refraction effect.

You don't see it in your left eye. Like I said, the clouds keep out virtually all of the visible light. It's in your right eye. The color is what I got to think of as infrablue.

It's quiet. You begin to miss the sound of your own breathing, and if you think about that too much, you begin to wonder why you *aren't* breathing. You know, of course, except the hindbrain, which never likes it at all. It doesn't matter to the autonomic nervous system that your Venus-lung is dribbling oxygen directly into your bloodstream; those circuits aren't made to understand things; they are primitive and very wary of improvements. So I was plagued by a feeling of suffocation, which was my medulla getting even with me, I guess.

I was also pretty nervous about the temperature and pressure. Silly, I know. Mars would kill me just as dead without a suit, and do it more slowly and painfully into the bargain. If my suit failed here, I doubt if I'd have felt anything. It was just the thought of that incredible pressure being held one millimeter away from my fragile skin by a force field that, physically speaking, isn't even there. Or so Ember told me. She might have been trying to get my goat. I mean, lines of magnetic force aren't tangible, but they're *there*, aren't they?

I kept my mind off it. Ember was there and she knew about such things.

What she couldn't adequately explain to me was why a skycycle didn't have a motor. I thought about that a lot, sitting on the saddle and pedaling my ass off with nothing to look at but Ember's silver-plated buttocks.

She had a tandem cycle, which meant four seats; two for us and two for our tagalongs. I sat behind Ember, and the tagalongs sat in two seats off to our right. Since they aped our leg movements with exactly the same force we applied, what we had was a four-humanpower cycle.

"I can't figure out for the life of me," I said on our first day out, "what would have been so hard about mounting an engine on this thing and using some of the surplus power from our packs."

"Nothing hard about it, lazy," she said, without turning around. "Take my advice as a fledgling medico; this is much better for you. If you *use* the muscles you're wearing, they'll last you a lot longer. It makes you feel healthier and keeps you out of the clutches of money-grubbing medicos. I *know*. Half my work is excising fat from flabby behinds and digging varicose veins out of legs. Even out here, people don't get more than twenty years' use of their legs before they're ready for a trade-in. That's pure waste."

"I think I should have had a trade-in before we left. I'm about done in. Can't we call it a day?"

She tut-tutted, but touched a control and began spilling hot gas from the balloon over our heads. The steering vanes sticking out at our sides tilted, and we started a slow spiral to the ground.

We landed at the bottom of the bowl—my first experience with it, since all my other views of Venus had been from the air where it isn't so noticeable. I stood looking at it and scratching my head while Ember turned on the tent and turned off the balloon.

The Venusians use null fields for just about everything. Rather than try to cope with a technology that must stand up to the temperature and pressure extremes, they coat everything in a null field and let it go at that. The balloon on the cycle was nothing but a standard globular field with a discontinuity at the bottom for the air heater. The cycle body was protected with the same kind of field that Ember and I wore, the kind that follows the surface at a set distance. The tent was a hemispherical field with a flat floor.

It simplified a lot of things. Air locks, for instance. What we did was to simply walk into the tent. Our suit fields vanished as they were absorbed into the tent field. To leave, one need merely walk through the wall again, and the suit would form around you.

I plopped myself down on the floor and tried to turn my hand torch off. To my surprise, I found that it wasn't built to turn off. Ember turned on the campfire and noticed my puzzlement.

"Yes, it is wasteful," she conceded. "There's something in a Venusian that hates to turn out a light. You won't find a light switch on the entire planet. You may not believe this, but I was shocked silly a few years ago when I heard about light switches. The idea had never occurred to me. See what a provincial I am?"

That didn't sound like her. I searched her face for clues to what had brought on such a statement, but I could find nothing. She was sitting in front of the campfire with Malibu on her lap, preening her feathers.

I gestured at the fire, which was a beautifully executed holo of snapping, crackling logs with a heater concealed in the center of it.

"Isn't that an uncharacteristic touch? Why didn't you bring a fancy house, like the ones in town?"

"I like the fire. I don't like phony houses."

"Why not?"

She shrugged. She was thinking of other things. I tried another tack.

"Does your mother mind you going into the desert with strangers?"
She shot me a look I couldn't read.

"How should I know? I don't live with her. I'm emancipated. I think she's
in Venusburg." I had obviously touched a tender area, so I went cautiously.

"Personality conflicts?"

She shrugged again, not wanting to get into it.

"No. Well, yes, in a way. She wouldn't emigrate from Venus. I wanted
to leave and she wanted to stay. Our interests didn't coincide. So we went
our own ways. I'm working my way toward passage off-planet."

"How close are you?"

"Closer than you might think." She seemed to be weighing something in her mind, sizing me up. I could hear the gears grind and the
cash register bells clink as she studied my face. Then I felt the charm
start up again, like the flicking of one of those nonexistent light switches.

"See, I'm as close as I've ever been to getting off Venus. In a few
weeks, I'll be there. As soon as we get back with some blast jewels.
Because you're going to adopt me."

I think I was getting used to her. I wasn't rocked by that, though
it was nothing like what I had expected to hear. I had been thinking
vaguely along the lines of blast jewels. She picks some up along with me,
sells them, and buys a ticket off-planet, right?

That was silly, of course. She didn't need *me* to get blast jewels. She was
the guide, not I, and it was her cycle. She could get as many jewels as she
wanted, and probably already had. This scheme had to have something to
do with me, personally, as I had known back in town and forgotten about.
There was something she wanted from me.

"That's why you had to go with me? That's the fatal attraction? I
don't understand."

"Your passport. I'm in love with your passport. On the blank labeled
'citizenship' it says 'Mars.' Under age it says, oh…about seventy-three."
She was within a year, though I keep my appearance at about thirty.

"So?"

"So, my dear Kiku, you are visiting a planet which is groping its way
into the Stone Age. A medieval planet, Mr. Kiku, that sets the age of
majority at thirteen—a capricious and arbitrary figure, as I'm sure you'll
agree. The laws of this planet state that certain rights of free citizens are
withheld from minor citizens. Among these are liberty, the pursuit of

happiness, and the ability *to get out of the goddam place!*" She startled me with her fury, coming so hard on the heels of her usual amusing glibness. Her fists were clenched. Malibu, sitting in her lap, looked sadly up at his friend, then over to me.

She quickly brightened and bounced up to prepare dinner. She would not respond to my questions. The subject was closed for the day.

I was ready to turn back the next day. Have you ever had stiff legs? Probably not; if you go in for that sort of thing—heavy physical labor— you are probably one of those health nuts and keep yourself in shape. I wasn't in shape, and I thought I'd die. For a panicky moment I thought I *was* dying.

Luckily, Ember had anticipated it. She knew I was a desk jockey, and she knew how pitifully underconditioned Martians tend to be. Added to the sedentary life-styles of most modern people, we Martians come off even worse than the majority because Mars's gravity never gives us much of a challenge no matter how hard we try. My leg muscles were like soft noodles.

She gave me an old-fashioned massage and a newfangled injection that killed off the accumulated poisons. In an hour I began to take a flickering interest in the trip. So she loaded me onto the cycle and we started off on another leg of the journey.

There's no way to measure the passage of time. The sun gets flatter and wider, but it's much too slow to see. Sometime that day we passed a tributary of the Reynolds-wrap River. It showed up as a bright line in my right eye, as a crusted, sluggish semiglacier in my left. Molten aluminum, I was told. Malibu knew what it was, and barked plaintively for us to stop so he could go for a slide. Ember wouldn't let him.

You can't get lost on Venus, not if you can still see. The river had been visible since we left Prosperity, though I hadn't known what it was. We could still see the town behind us and the mountain range in front of us and even the desert. It was a little way up the slope of the bowl. Ember said that meant it was still about three days' journey away from us. It takes practice to judge distance. Ember kept trying to point out Venusburg, which was several thousand kilometers behind us. She said it was easily visible as a tiny point on a clear day. I never spotted it.

We talked a lot as we pedaled. There was nothing else to do and, besides, she was fun to talk to. She told me more of her plan for getting off Venus and filled my head with her naive ideas of what other planets were like.

It was a subtle selling campaign. We started off with her being the advocate for her crazy plan. At some point it evolved into an assumption. She took it as settled that I would adopt her and take her to Mars with me. I half believed it myself.

On the fourth day I began to notice that the bowl was getting higher in front of us. I didn't know what was causing it until Ember called a halt and we hung there in the air. We were facing a solid line of rock that sloped gradually upward to a point about fifty meters higher than we were.

"What's the matter?" I asked, glad of the rest.

"The mountains are higher," she said matter-of-factly. "Let's turn to the right and see if we can find a pass."

"Higher? What are you talking about?"

"Higher. You know, taller, sticking up more than they did the last time I was around, of slightly greater magnitude in elevation, bigger than—"

"I know the definition of higher," I said. "But why? Are you sure?"

"Of course I'm sure. The air heater for the balloon is going flat-out; we're as high as we can go. The last time I came through here, it was plenty to get me across. But not today."

"Why?"

"Condensation. The topography can vary quite a bit here. Certain metals and rocks are molten on Venus. They boil off on a hot day, and they can condense on the mountaintops where it's cooler. Then they melt when it warms up and flow back to the valleys."

"You mean you brought me here in the middle of winter?"

She threw me a withering glance.

"You're the one who booked passage for winter. Besides, it's night, and it's not even midnight yet. I hadn't thought the mountains would be this high for another week."

"Can't we get around?"

She surveyed the slope critically.

"There's a permanent pass about five hundred kilometers to the east. But that would take us another week. Do you want to?"

"What's the alternative?"

"Parking the cycle here and going on foot. The desert is just over this range. With any luck we'll see our first jewels today."

I was realizing that I knew far too little about Venus to make a good decision. I had finally admitted to myself that I was lucky to have Ember along to keep me out of trouble.

"We'll do what you think best."

"All right. Turn hard left and we'll park."

We tethered the cycle by a long tungsten-alloy rope. The reason for that, I learned, was to prevent it from being buried in case there was more condensation while we were gone. It floated at the end of the cable with its heaters going full blast. And we started up the mountain.

Fifty meters doesn't sound like much. And it's not, on level ground. Try it sometime on a seventy-five degree slope. Luckily for us, Ember had come prepared with alpine equipment. She sank pitons here and there and kept us together with ropes and pulleys. I followed her lead, staying slightly behind her tagalong. It was uncanny how that thing followed her up, placing its feet in precisely the spots where she had stepped. Behind me, my tagalong was doing the same thing. Then there was Malibu, almost running along, racing back to see how we were doing, going to the top and chattering about what was on the other side.

I don't suppose it would have been much for a mountain climber. Personally I'd have preferred to slide on down the mountainside and call it quits. I would have, but Ember just kept going up. I don't think I've ever been so tired as the moment when we reached the top and stood looking over the desert.

Ember pointed ahead of us.

"There's one of the jewels going off now," she said.

"Where?" I asked, barely interested. I could see nothing.

"You missed it. It's down lower. They don't form up this high. Don't worry, you'll see more by and by."

And down we went. This wasn't too hard. Ember set the example by sitting down in a smooth place and letting go. Malibu was close behind her, squealing happily as he bounced and rolled down the slippery rock face. I saw Ember hit a bump and go flying in the air to come down on her head. Her suit was already stiffened. She continued to bounce her way down, frozen in a sitting position.

I followed them down in the same way. I didn't much care for the idea of bouncing around like that, but I cared even less for a slow, painful descent. It wasn't too bad. You don't feel much after your suit freezes in impact mode. It expands slightly away from your skin and becomes harder than metal, cushioning you from anything but the most severe blows that could bounce your brain against your skull and give you internal injuries. We never got going nearly fast enough for that.

Ember helped me up at the bottom after my suit unfroze. She looked like she had enjoyed the ride. I hadn't. One bounce seemed to have impacted my back slightly. I didn't tell her about it, but just started off after her, feeling a pain with each step.

"Where on Mars do you live?" she asked brightly.

"Uh? Oh, at Coprates. That's on the northern slope of the Canyon."

"Yes, I know. Tell me more about it. Where will we live? Do you have a surface apartment, or are you stuck down in the underground? I can hardly wait to see the place."

She was getting on my nerves. Maybe it was just the lower-back pain.

"What makes you think you're going with me?"

"But of course you're taking me back. You said, just—"

"I said nothing of the sort. If I had a recorder I could prove it to you. No, our conversations over the last days have been a series of monologues. You tell me what fun you're going to have when we get to Mars, and I just grunt something. That's because I haven't the heart, or haven't *had* the heart, to tell you what a hare-brained scheme you're talking about."

I think I had finally managed to drive a barb into her. At any rate, she didn't say anything for a while. She was realizing that she had overextended herself and had been counting the spoils before the battle was won.

"What's hare-brained about it?" she said at last.

"Just everything."

"No, come on, tell me."

"What makes you think I want a daughter?"

She seemed relieved. "Oh, don't worry about that. I won't be any trouble. As soon as we land, you can file dissolution papers. I won't contest it. In fact, I can sign a binding agreement not to contest anything before you even adopt me. This is strictly a business arrangement, Kiku. You don't have to worry about being a mother to me. I don't need one. I'll—"

"What makes you think it's just a business arrangement to *me*?" I exploded. "Maybe I'm old-fashioned. Maybe I've got funny ideas. But I won't enter into an adoption of convenience. I've already had my one child, and I was a good parent. I won't adopt you just to get you to Mars. That's my final word."

She was studying my face. I think she decided I meant it.

"I can offer you twenty thousand Marks."

I swallowed hard.

"Where did you get that kind of money?"

"I told you I've been soaking the good people of Prosperity. What the hell is there for me to spend it on out here? I've been putting it away for an emergency like this. Up against an unfeeling Neanderthal with funny ideas about right and wrong, who—"

"That's enough of that." I'm ashamed to say that I was tempted. It's unpleasant to find that what you had thought of as moral scruples suddenly seem not quite so important in the face of a stack of money. But I was helped along by my backache and the nasty mood it had given me.

"You think you can buy me. Well, I'm not for sale. I think it's wrong."

"Well *damn* you, Kiku, damn you to hell." She stomped her foot hard on the ground, and her tagalong redoubled the gesture. She was going to go on damning me, but we were blasted by an explosion as her foot hit the ground.

It had been quiet before, as I said. There's no wind, no animals, hardly anything to make a sound on Venus. But when a sound gets going, watch out. That thick atmosphere is murder. I thought my head was going to come off. The sound waves battered against our suits, partially stiffening them. The only thing that saved us from deafness was the millimeter of low-pressure air between the suit field and our eardrums. It cushioned the shock enough that we were left with just a ringing in our ears.

"What was that?" I asked.

Ember sat down on the ground. She hung her head, uninterested in anything but her own disappointment.

"Blast jewel," she said. "Over that way." She pointed, and I could see a dull glowing spot about a kilometer off. There were dozens of smaller points of light—infralight—scattered around the spot.

"You mean you set it off just by stomping the ground?"

She shrugged. "They're unstable. They're full of nitroglycerine, as near as anyone can figure."

"Well, let's go pick up the pieces."

"Go ahead." She was going limp on me. And she stayed that way, no matter how I cajoled her. By the time I finally got her on her feet, the glowing spots were gone, cooled off. We'd never find them now. She wouldn't talk to me as we continued down into the valley. All the rest of the day we were accompanied by distant gunshots.

We didn't talk much the next day. She tried several times to reopen the negotiations, but I made it clear that my mind was made up. I pointed out to her that I had rented her cycle and services according to the terms she had set. Absolutely free, she had said, except for consumables, which I had paid for. There had been no mention of adoption. If there had, I assured her, I would have turned her down just as I was doing now. Maybe I even believed it.

That was during the short time, the morning after our argument, when it seemed like she was having no more to do with the trip. She just sat there in the tent while I made breakfast. When it came time to go, she pouted and said she wasn't going looking for blast jewels, that she'd just as soon stay right there or turn around.

After I pointed out our verbal contract, she reluctantly got up. She didn't like it, but honored her word.

Hunting blast jewels proved to be a big anticlimax. I'd had visions of scouring the countryside for days. Then the exciting moment of finding one. Eureka! I'd have howled. The reality was nothing like that. Here's how you hunt blast jewels: you stomp down hard on the ground, wait a few seconds, then move on and stomp again. When you see and hear an explosion, you simply walk to where it occurred and pick them up. They're scattered all over, lit up in the infrared bands from the heat of the explosion. They might as well have had neon arrows flashing over them. Big adventure.

When we found one, we'd pick it up and pop it into a cooler mounted on our tagalongs. The jewels are formed by the pressure of the explosion, but certain parts of them are volatile at Venus temperatures. These elements will boil out and leave you with a grayish powder in about three hours if you don't cool them down. I don't know why they lasted as long as they did. They were considerably hotter than the air when we picked them up, so I thought they should have melted right away.

Ember said it was the impaction of the crystalline lattice that gave the jewels the temporary strength to outlast the temperature. Things behave differently in the temperature and pressure extremes of Venus. As they cooled off, the lattice was weakened and a progressive decay set in. That's why it was important to get them as soon as possible after the explosion to get unflawed gems.

We spent the whole day at that. Eventually we collected about ten kilos of gems, ranging from pea size up to a few the size of an apple.

I sat beside the campfire and examined them that night. Night by my watch, anyway. Another thing I was beginning to miss was the twenty-five-hour cycle of night and day. And while I was at it, moons. It would have cheered me up considerably to spot Deimos or Phobos that night. But the sun just squatted up there in the horizon, moving slowly to the north in preparation for its transition to the morning sky.

The jewels were beautiful, I'll say that much for them. They were a wine-red color, tinged with brown. But when the light caught them right, there was no predicting what I might see. Most of the raw gems were coated with a dull substance that hid their full glory. I experimented with chipping some of them. What was left behind when I flaked off the patina was a slippery surface that sparkled even in candlelight. Ember showed me how to suspend them from a string and strike them. Then they would ring like tiny bells, and every once in a while one would shed all its imperfections and emerge as a perfect eight-sided equilateral.

I was cooking for myself that day. Ember had cooked from the first, but she no longer seemed interested in buttering me up.

"I hired on as a guide," she pointed out, with considerable venom. "Webster's defines guide as—"

"I know what a guide is."

"—and it says nothing about cooking. Will you marry me?"

"No." I wasn't even surprised.

"Same reasons?"

"Yes. I won't enter into an agreement like that lightly. Besides, you're too young."

"Legal age is twelve. I'll be twelve in one week."

"That's too young. On Mars you must be fourteen."

"What a dogmatist. You're not kidding, are you? Is it really fourteen?"

That's typical of her lack of knowledge of the place she was trying so hard to get to. I don't know where she got her ideas about Mars. I finally concluded that she made them up whole in her daydreams.

We ate the meal I prepared in silence, toying with our collection of jewels. I estimated that I had about a thousand Marks' worth of uncut stones. And I was getting tired of the Venusian bush. I figured on spending another day collecting, then heading back for the cycle. It would probably be a relief for both of us. Ember could start laying traps for the next stupid tourist to reach town, or even head for Venusburg and try in earnest.

When I thought of that, I wondered why she was still out here. If she had the money to pay the tremendous bribe she had offered me, why wasn't she in town where the tourists were as thick as flies? I was going to ask her that, but she came up to me and sat down very close.

"Would you like to make love?" she asked.

I'd had about enough inducements. I snorted, got up, and walked through the wall of the tent.

Once outside, I regretted it. My back was hurting something terrible, and I belatedly realized that my inflatable mattress would not go through the wall of the tent. If I got it through somehow, it would only burn up. But I couldn't back out after walking out like that. I felt committed. Maybe I couldn't think straight because of the backache; I don't know. Anyway, I picked out a soft-looking spot of ground and lay down.

I can't say it was all that soft.

I came awake in the haze of pain. I knew without trying that if I moved I'd get a knife in my back. Naturally I wasn't anxious to try.

My arm was lying on something soft. I moved my head—confirming my suspicions about the knife—and saw that it was Ember. She was asleep, lying on her back. Malibu was curled up in her arm.

She was a silver-plated doll, with her mouth open and a look of relaxed vulnerability on her face. I felt a smile growing on my lips, just like the ones she had coaxed out of me back in Prosperity. I wondered why I'd been treating her so bad. At least it seemed to me that morning that I'd been treating her bad. Sure, she'd used me and tricked me and seemed to want to use me again. But what had she hurt? Who was suffering for it? I couldn't think of anyone at the moment. I resolved to apologize to her when she woke up and try to start over again. Maybe we could even reach some sort of accommodation on this adoption business.

And while I was at it, maybe I could unbend enough to ask her to take a look at my back. I hadn't even mentioned it to her, probably for fear of getting deeper in her debt. I was sure she wouldn't have taken payment for it in cash. She preferred flesh.

I was about to awaken her, but I happened to glance on my other side. There was something there. I almost didn't recognize it for what it was.

It was three meters away, growing from the cleft of two rocks. It was globular, half a meter across, and glowing a dull reddish color. It looked like a soft gelatin.

It was a blast jewel, before the blast.

I was afraid to talk, then remembered that talking would not affect the atmosphere around me and could not set off the explosion. I had a radio transmitter in my throat and a receiver in my ear. That's how you talk on Venus; you subvocalize and people can hear you.

Moving very carefully, I reached over and gently touched Ember on the shoulder.

She came awake quietly, stretched, and started to get up.

"Don't move," I said, in what I hoped was a whisper. It's hard to do when you're subvocalizing, but I wanted to impress on her that something was wrong.

She became alert, but didn't move.

"Look over to your right. Move very slowly. Don't scrape against the ground or anything. I don't know what to do."

She looked, said nothing.

"You're not alone, Kiku," she finally whispered. "This is one I never heard of."

"How did it happen?"

"It must have formed during the night. No one knows much about how they form or how long it takes. No one's ever been closer to one than about five hundred meters. They always explode before you can get that close. Even the vibrations from the prop of a cycle will set them off before you can get close enough to see them."

"So what do we do?"

She looked at me. It's hard to read expressions on a reflective face, but I think she was scared. I know I was.

"I'd say sit tight."

"How dangerous is this?"

"Brother. I don't know. There's going to be quite a bang when that monster goes off. Our suits will protect us from most of it. But it's going to lift us and accelerate us *very* fast. That kind of sharp acceleration can mess up your insides. I'd say a concussion at the very least."

I gulped. "Then—"

"Just sit tight. I'm thinking."

So was I. I was frozen there with a hot knife somewhere in my back. I knew I'd have to squirm sometime.

The damn thing was moving.

I blinked, afraid to rub my eyes, and looked again. No, it wasn't. Not on the outside anyway. It was more like the movement you can see inside a living cell beneath a microscope. Internal flows, exchanges of fluids from here to there. I watched it and was hypnotized.

There were worlds in the jewel. There was ancient Barsoom of my childhood fairy tales; there was Middle Earth with brooding castles and sentient forests. The jewel was a window into something unimaginable, a place where there were no questions and no emotions but a vast awareness. It was dark and wet without menace. It was growing, and yet complete as it came into being. It was bigger than this ball of hot mud called Venus and had its roots down in the core of the planet. There was no corner of the universe that it did not reach.

It was aware of me. I felt it touch me and felt no surprise. It examined me in passing but was totally uninterested. I posed no questions for it, whatever it was. It already knew me and had always known me.

I felt an overpowering attraction. The thing was exerting no influence on me; the attraction was a yearning within me. I was reaching for a completion that the jewel possessed and I knew I could never have.

Life would always be a series of mysteries for me. For the jewel, there was nothing but awareness. Awareness of everything.

I wrenched my eyes away at the last possible instant. I was covered in sweat, and I knew I'd look back in a moment. It was the most beautiful thing I will ever see.

"Kiku, listen to me."

"What?" I remembered Ember as from a huge distance.

"Listen. Wake up. Don't look at that thing."

"Ember, do you see anything? Do you feel something?"

"I see something. I…I don't want to talk about it. I can't talk about it. Wake up, Kiku, and don't look back."

I felt like I was already a pillar of salt; so why not look back? I knew that my life would never be quite like it had been. It was like some sort of involuntary religious conversion, like I knew what the universe was for all of a sudden. The universe was a beautiful silklined box for the display of the jewel I had just beheld.

"Kiku, that thing should already have gone off. We shouldn't be here. I moved when I woke up. I tried to sneak up on one before and got five hundred meters away from it. I set my foot down soft enough to walk on water and it blew. So this thing can't be here."

"That's nice," I said. "How do we cope with the fact that it *is* here?"

"All right, all right, it is here. But it must not be finished. It must not have enough nitro in it yet to blow up. Maybe we can get away."

I looked back at it, then away again. It was like my eyes were welded to it with elastic bands; they'd stretch enough to let me turn away, but they kept pulling me back.

"I'm not sure I want to."

"I know," she whispered. "I…hold on, don't look back. We have to get away."

"Listen," I said, looking at her with an act of will. "Maybe one of us can get away. Maybe both. But it's more important that you not be injured. If I'm hurt, you can maybe fix me up. If you're hurt, you'll probably die; and if we're both hurt, we're dead."

"Yeah. So?"

"So, I'm the closest to the jewel. You can start backing away from it first, and I'll follow you. I'll shield you from the worst of the blast, if it goes off. How does that sound?"

"Not too good." But she thought it over and could see no flaws in my reasoning. I think she didn't relish being the protected instead of the heroine. Childish, but natural. She proved her maturity by bowing to the inevitable.

"All right. I'll try to get ten meters from it. I'll let you know when I'm there, and you can move back. I think we can survive it at ten meters."

"Twenty."

"But…oh, all right. Twenty. Good luck, Kiku. I think I love you." She paused. "Uh, Kiku?"

"What is it? You should get moving. We don't know how long it'll stay stable."

"All right. But I have to say this. My offer last night, the one that got you so angry?"

"Yeah?"

"Well, it wasn't meant as a bribe. I mean, like the twenty thousand Marks. I just…well, I don't know much about that yet. I guess it was the wrong time?"

"Yeah, but don't worry about it. Just get moving."

She did, a centimeter at a time. It was lucky that neither of us had to worry about holding our breath. I think the tension would have been unbearable.

And I looked back. I couldn't help it. I was in the sanctuary of a cosmic church when I heard her calling me. I don't know what sort of power she used to reach me where I was. She was crying.

"Kiku, please listen to me."

"Huh? Oh, what is it?"

She sobbed in relief. "Oh, Christ, I've been calling you for an hour. *Please* come on. Over here, I'm back far enough."

My head was foggy. "Oh, Ember, there's no hurry. I want to look at it just another minute. Hang on."

"*No!* If you don't start moving right this minute I'm coming back and I'll drag you out."

"You can't do… Oh. All right, I'm coming." I looked over at her sitting on her knees. Malibu was beside her. The little otter was staring in my direction. I looked at her and took a sliding step, scuttling on my back. My back was not something to think about.

I got two meters back, then three. I had to stop to rest. I looked at the jewel, then back at Ember. It was hard to tell which drew me more strongly. I must have reached a balance point. I could have gone either way.

Then a small silver streak came at me, running as fast as it could go. It reached me and dived across.

"*Malibu!*" Ember screamed. I turned. The otter seemed happier than I had ever seen him, even in the waterslide in town. He leaped right at the jewel.

Regaining consciousness was a very gradual business. There was no dividing line between different states of awareness for two reasons: I was deaf, and I was blind. So I cannot say when I went from dreams to reality; the blend was too uniform, there wasn't enough change to notice.

I don't remember learning that I was deaf and blind. I don't remember learning the hand-spelling language that Ember talked to me with. The first rational moment that I can recall as such was when Ember was telling me her plans to get back to Prosperity.

I told her to do whatever she felt best, that she was in complete control. I was desolated to realize that I was not where I had thought I was. My dreams had been of Barsoom. I thought I had become a blast jewel and had been waiting in a sort of detached ecstacy for the moment of explosion.

She operated on my left eye and managed to restore some vision. I could see things that were a meter from my face, hazily. Everything else was shadows. At least she was able to write things on sheets of paper and hold them up to me to see. It made things quicker. I learned that she was deaf too. And Malibu was dead. Or might be. She had put him in the cooler and thought she might be able to patch him up when she got back. If not, she could always make another otter.

I told her about my back. She was shocked to hear that I had hurt it on the slide down the mountain, but she had sense enough not to scold me about it. It was short work to fix it up. Nothing but a bruised disc, she told me.

It would be tedious to describe all of our trip back. It was difficult, because neither of us knew much about blindness. But I was able to adjust pretty quickly. Being led by the hand was easy enough, and I stumbled only rarely after the first day. On the second day we scaled the mountains, and my tagalong malfunctioned. Ember discarded it and we traded off with hers. We could only do it when I was sitting still, as hers was made for a much shorter person. If I tried to walk with it, it quickly fell behind and jerked me off balance.

Then it was a matter of being set on the cycle and pedaling. There was nothing to do but pedal. I missed the talking we had done on the way out. I missed the blast jewel. I wondered if I'd ever adjust to life without it.

But the memory had faded when we arrived back at Prosperity. I don't think the human mind can really contain something of that magnitude. It was slipping away from me by the hour, like a dream fades away in the morning. I found it hard to remember what it was that was so great about the experience. To this day, I can't really tell about it except in riddles. I'm left with shadows. I feel like an earthworm who has been shown a sunset and has no place to store the memory.

Back in town it was a simple matter for Ember to restore our hearing. She just hadn't been carrying any spare eardrums in her first-aid kit.

"It was an oversight," she told me. "Looking back, it seems obvious that the most likely injury from a blast jewel would be burst eardrums. I just didn't think."

"Don't worry about it. You did beautifully."

She grinned at me. "Yes, I did, didn't I?"

The vision was a larger problem. She didn't have any spare eyes and no one in town was willing to sell one of theirs at any price. She gave me one of hers as a temporary measure. She kept her infraeye and took to wearing an eye patch over the other. It made her look bloodthirsty. She told me to buy another at Venusburg, as our blood types weren't much of a match. My body would reject it in about three weeks.

The day came for the weekly departure of the blimp to Last Chance. We were sitting in Ember's workshop, facing each other with our legs crossed and the pile of blast jewels between us.

They looked awful. Oh, they hadn't changed. We had even polished them up until they sparkled three times as much as they had back in the firelight of our tent. But now we could see them for the rotten, yellowed, broken fragments of bone that they were. We had told no one what we had seen out in the Fahrenheit Desert. There was no way to check on it, and all our experience had been purely subjective. Nothing that would stand up in a laboratory. We were the only ones who knew their true nature. Probably we would always remain the only ones. What could we tell anyone?

"What do you think will happen?" I asked.

She looked at me keenly. "I think you already know that."

"Yeah." Whatever they were, however they survived and reproduced, the one fact we knew for sure was that they couldn't survive within a hundred kilometers of a city. Once there had been blast jewels in the very spot where we were sitting. And humans do expand. Once again, we would not know what we were destroying.

I couldn't keep the jewels. I felt like a ghoul. I tried to give them to Ember, but she wouldn't have them either.

"Shouldn't we tell someone?" Ember asked.

"Sure. Tell anyone you want. Don't expect people to start tiptoeing until you can prove something to them. Maybe not even then."

"Well, it looks like I'm going to spend a few more years tiptoeing. I find I just can't bring myself to stomp on the ground."

I was puzzled. "Why? You'll be on Mars. I don't think the vibrations will travel that far."

She stared at me. "What's this?"

There was a brief confusion; then I found myself apologizing profusely to her, and she was laughing and telling me what a dirty rat I was, then taking it back and saying I could play that kind of trick on her anytime I wanted.

It was a misunderstanding. I honestly thought I had told her about my change of heart while I was deaf and blind. It must have been a dream, because she hadn't gotten it and had assumed the answer was a permanent no. She had said nothing about adoption since the explosion.

"I couldn't bring myself to pester you about it anymore, after what you did for me," she said, breathless with excitement. "I owe you a lot, maybe my life. And I used you badly when you first got here."

I denied it, and told her I had thought she was not talking about it because she thought it was in the bag.

"When did you change your mind?" she asked.

I thought back. "At first I thought it was while you were caring for me when I was so helpless. Now I can recall when it was. It was shortly after I walked out of the tent for that last night on the ground."

She couldn't find anything to say about that. She just beamed at me. I began to wonder what sort of papers I'd be signing when we got to Venusburg: adoption, or marriage contract.

I didn't worry about it. It's uncertainties like that that make life interesting. We got up together, leaving the pile of jewels on the floor. Walking softly, we hurried out to catch the blimp.

BLUE CHAMPAGNE

This story doesn't take place on the third planet from the sun, it takes place in a large resort in orbit *around* the Earth. Seeing the movies astronauts made aboard Skylab, seeing the way water behaved in zero gee, had always fascinated me. So I began to envision a really *big* bubble of water, a space pool, and it seemed to open a lot of possibilities. How would one make and stabilize such a monster bubble of water, with a bubble of air inside? I have no idea. Like many if not most SF writers, I leave that to the engineers. I merely postulate that it could be done.

The other factor in the story is another technological wonder—at the time, at least. That is Megan's powered exoskeleton. My first wife had polio as a child, wore a leg brace and sometimes used a crutch, later moving to a powered wheelchair as she weakened from post-polio syndrome. She was very politically involved in the disability rights movement. (Without her and her friends there wouldn't be those reserved parking spaces and wide bathroom stalls and ramps, among many other excellent changes.) So I came up with this device. I always knew it was possible, and just a few days ago I saw a YouTube of a big, clunky thing that enabled a paralyzed man to walk. These machines are sure to get better, but it is my hope that advances in medicine will make them pointless, as we learn to regenerate spinal tissue so that paraplegics and quadriplegics can walk (and run!) again.

Megan Galloway arrived in the Bubble with a camera crew of three. With her breather and her sidekick she was the least naked nude woman any of the lifeguards had ever seen.

"I bet she's carrying more hardware than any of her crew," Glen said.

"Yeah, but it hardly shows, you know?"

Q.M. Cooper was thinking back as he watched her accept the traditional bulb of champagne. "Isn't that some kind of record? Three people in her crew?"

"The President of Brazil brought twenty-nine people in with her," Anna-Louise observed. "The King of England had twenty-five."

"Yeah, but only one network pool camera."

"So that's the Golden Gypsy," Leah said.

Anna-Louise snorted. "More like the Brass Transistor."

They had all heard that one before, but laughed anyway. None of the lifeguards had much respect for Trans-sisters. Yet Cooper had to admit that in a profession which sought to standardize emotion, Galloway was the only one who was uniquely herself. The others were interchangeable as News Anchors.

A voice started whispering in their ears, over the channel reserved for emergency announcements and warnings.

"Entering the Bubble is Megan Galloway, representing the Feelie Corporation, a wholly-owned subsidiary of GWA Conglom. Feeliecorp: bringing you the best in experiential tapes and erotix. Blue Champagne Enterprises trusts you will not impede the taping, and regrets any disturbance."

"Commercials, yet," Glen said in disgust. To those who loved the Bubble—as all the lifeguards did—this was something like using the walls of the Taj Mahal for the Interconglomerate Graffiti Championship finals.

"Stick around for the yacht races," Cooper said. "They should have at least told us she was coming. What about that sidekick? Should we know anything about it if she gets into trouble?"

"Maybe she knows what she's doing," Leah said, earning sour looks from the other four. It was an article of faith that *nobody* on a first visit to the Bubble knew what they were doing.

"You think she'll take the sidekick into the water?"

"Well, since she can't move without it I sort of doubt she'll take it off," Cooper said. "Stu, you call operations and ask why we weren't notified. Find out about special precautions. The rest of you get back to work. A.L., you take charge here."

"What will *you* be doing, Q.M.?" Anna-Louise asked, arching one eyebrow.

"I'm going to get a closer look." He pushed off, and flew toward the curved inner surface of the Bubble.

The Bubble was the only thing Q.M. Cooper ever encountered which caught his imagination, held it for years, and did not prove a disappointment when he finally saw it. It was love at first sight.

It floated in lunar orbit with nothing to give it perspective. Under those conditions the eye can see the Earth or Luna as hunks of rock no bigger than golf balls, or a fleck of ice millimeters from the ship's window can seem to be a distant, tumbling asteroid. When Cooper first saw it the illusion was perfect: someone had left a champagne glass floating a few meters from the ship.

The constricted conic-shape was dictated by the mathematics of the field generators that held the Bubble. It was made of an intricate network of fine wires. No other configuration was possible; it was mere chance that the generator resembled the bowl and stem of a wine glass.

The Bubble itself had to be weightless, but staff and visitors needed a spin-gravity section. A disc was better than a wheel for that purpose, since it provided regions of varying gravity, from one gee at the rim to free-fall at the hub. The most logical place for the disc was at the base of the generator stem, which also made it the base of the glass. It was rumored that the architect of the Bubble had gone mad while designing it and that, since he favored martinis, he had included in the blueprints a mammoth toothpick spearing a giant green olive.

But that was only the station. It was beautiful enough in itself, but was nothing compared to the Bubble.

It floated in the shallow bowl of the generators, never touching them. It was two hundred million liters of water held between two concentric spherical fields of force, one of them one hundred meters in diameter, the other one hundred and forty. The fields contained a shell of water massing almost a million tonnes, with a five-hundred-thousand-cubic-meter bubble of air in the middle.

Cooper knew the relevant numbers by heart. Blue Champagne Enterprises made sure no one entered the Bubble without hearing them at least once. But numbers could not begin to tell what the Bubble was really like. To know that, one had to ride the elevator up through the glass swizzle stick that ended in the center of the air bubble, step out of the car, grab one of the monkeybar struts near the lifeguard station, and hold on tight until one's emotions settled down enough to be able to *believe* in the damn thing.

The lifeguards had established six classes of visitor. It was all unofficial; to BCE, everyone was an honored guest. The rankings were made by a guest's behavior and personal habits, but mostly by swimming ability.

Crustaceans clung to the monkeybars. Most never got their feet wet. They came to the Bubble to be seen, not to swim. Plankton thought they could swim, but it was no more than a fond hope. Turtles and frogs really could swim, but it was a comical business.

Sharks were excellent swimmers. If they had added brains to their other abilities the lifeguards would have loved them. Dolphins were the best. Cooper was a dolpin-class swimmer, which was why he had the job of chief lifeguard for the third shift.

To his surprise, Megan Galloway ranked somewhere between a frog and a shark. Most of her awkward moves were the result of being unaccustomed to the free-fall environment. She had obviously spent a lot of time in flat water.

He pulled ahead and broke through the outer surface of the Bubble with enough speed to carry him to the third field, which kept air in and harmful radiation out. On his way he twisted in the air to observe how she handled the breakthrough. He could see gold reflections from the metal bands of her sidekick while she was just an amorphous shape beneath the surface. The water around her was bright aquamarine from the camera lights. She had outdistanced her crew.

He had an immediate and very strong reaction: what a ghastly way to live. Working in the Bubble was very special to him. He griped about the clients, just like everyone did, complained when he had to ferry some damn crustacean who couldn't even get up enough speed to return to the monkeybars, or when he had to clean up one of the excretory nuisances that got loose in surprising numbers when somebody got disoriented and scared. But the basic truth was that, for him, it never got old. There was always some new way of looking at the place, some fresh magic to be found. He wondered if he could feel that way about it if he lived in the middle of a traveling television studio with the whole world watching.

He was starting to drift back toward the water when she burst free of it. She broke the surface like a golden mermaid, rising, trailing a plume of water that turned into a million quivering crystals as it followed her into the air. She tumbled in the middle of a cloud of water globes, a flesh and metal Aphrodite emerging from the foam.

Her mouthpiece fell from her lips to dangle from its airhose, and he heard her laugh. He did not think she had noticed him. He was fairly sure she thought she was alone, for once, if only for a few seconds. She sounded as delighted as a child, and her laughter went on until the camera crew came grumbling out of the water.

They made her go back and do it over.

"She's not worth the effort, Q.M."

"Who? Oh, you mean the Golden Gypsy."

"You want your bedroom technique studied by ninety million slobs?"

Cooper turned to look at Anna-Louise, who sat behind him on the narrow locker room bench, tying her shoelaces. She glanced over her shoulder and grinned. He knew he had a reputation as a starfucker. When he first came to work at the Bubble he had perceived one of the fringe benefits to be the opportunity to meet, hob-nob with, and bed famous women, and had done so with more than a few. But he was long over that.

"Galloway doesn't make heavy-breathers."

"Not yet. Neither did Lyshia Trumbull until about a year ago. Or that guy who works for ABS...Chin. Randall Chin."

"Neither did Salome Hassan," someone chimed in from across the room. Cooper looked around and saw the whole shift was listening.

"I thought you were all above that," he said. "Turns out we're a bunch of feelie-groupies."

"You can't help hearing the names," Stu said, defensively.

Anna-Louise pulled her shirt over her head and stood up. "There's no sense denying I've tried tapes," she said. "The trans-sisters have to make a living. She'll do them. Wetdreams are the coming thing."

"They're coming, all right," Stu said, with an obscene gesture.

"Why don't you idiots knock it off and get out of here?" Cooper said.

They did, gradually, and the tiny locker room at the gee/10 level was soon empty but for Cooper and Anna-Louise. She stood at the mirror, rubbing a lotion over her scalp to make it shine.

"I'd like to move to the number two shift," she said.

"You're a crazy Loonie, you know that?" he shot back, annoyed.

She turned at the waist and glared at him.

"That's redundant and racist," she said. "If I wasn't such a sweet person I'd resent it."

"But it's true."

"That's the other reason I'm not going to resent it."

He got up and embraced her from behind, nuzzling her ear. "Hey, you're all wet," she laughed, but did not try to stop him, even when his hands lifted her shirt and went down under the waistband of her pants. She turned and he kissed her.

Cooper had never really understood Anna-Louise, even though he had bunked with her for six months. She was almost as big as he was, and he was not small. Her home was New Dresden, Luna. Though German was her native tongue, she spoke fluent, unaccented English. Her face would inspire adjectives like strong, healthy, glowing, and fresh, but never a word like glamorous. In short, she was physically just like all the other female lifeguards. She even shaved her head, but where the others did it in an attempt to recapture past glory, to keep that Olympic look, she had never done any competitive swimming. That alone made her unique in the group, and was probably what made her so refreshing. All the other women in the lifeguard force were uncomplicated jocks who liked two things: swimming, and sex, in that order.

Cooper did not object to that. It was a pretty fair description of himself. But he was creeping up on thirty, getting closer every day. That is never a good time for an athlete. He was surprised to find that it hurt when she told him she wanted to change shifts.

"Does this have anything to do with Yuri Feldman?" he asked, between kisses.

"Is that his shift?"

"Are we still going to be bunkmates?"

She drew back. "Are we going to talk? Is that why you're undressing me?"

"I just wanted to know."

She turned away, buckling her pants.

"Unless you want to move out, we're still bunkmates. I didn't think it really meant a hell of a lot. Was I wrong?"

"I'm sorry."

"It's just that it might be simpler to sleep alone, that's all." She turned back and patted his cheek. "Hell, Q.M. It's just sex. You're very good at it, and so long as you stay interested we'll do just fine. Okay?" Her hand was still on his cheek. Her expression changed as she peered intently into his eyes. "It *is* just sex, isn't it? I mean—"

"Sure, it's—"

"—if it *isn't*...but you've never said anything that would—"

"God, no," he said. "I don't want to get tied down."

"Me, either." She looked as if she might wish to say more, but instead touched his cheek again, and left him alone.

Cooper was so preoccupied that he walked past the table where Megan Galloway sat with her camera crew.

"Cooper! Your name is Cooper, right?"

When he turned he had his camera smile in place. Though being recognized had by that time become a rare thing, the reflexes were still working. But the smile was quickly replaced by a more genuine expression of delight. He was surprised and flattered that she had known who he was.

Galloway had her hand to her forehead, looking up at him with comical intensity. She snapped her fingers, hit her forehead again.

"I've been trying to think of the name since I saw you in the water," she said. "Don't tell me...I'll get it...it was a nickname..." She trailed off helplessly, then plunked both elbows on the table and put her chin in her hands, glowering at him.

"I can't think of it."

"It's—"

"Don't *tell me*."

He had been about to say it was not something he revealed, but instead he shrugged and said nothing.

"I'll get it, if you'll just give me time."

"She will, too," said the other woman, who then gestured to an empty seat and extended a hand to him. "I'm Consuela Lopez. Let me buy you a drink."

"I'm…Cooper."

Consuela leaned closer and murmured, "If she doesn't have the goddam name in ten minutes, tell her, huh? Otherwise she won't be worth a damn until she gets it. You're a lifeguard."

He nodded, and his drink arrived. He tried to conceal his amazement. It was *impossible* to impress the waiters at the promenade cafes. Yet Galloway's party did not even have to order.

"Fascinating profession. You must tell me all about it. I'm a producer, studying to be a pimp." She swayed slightly, and Cooper realized she was drunk. It didn't show in her speech. "That devilish fellow with the beard is Markham Montgomery, director and talent prostitute." Montgomery glanced at Cooper, made a gesture that could have been the step-outline for a nod. "And the person of debatable sex is Coco-89 (Praisegod), recordist, enigma, and devotee of a religiosexual cult so obscure even Coco isn't sure what it's about." Cooper had seen Coco in the water. He or she had the genitals of a man and the breasts of a woman, but androgynes were not uncommon in the Bubble.

"Cheers," Coco said, solemnly raising a glass. "Accly your am tance to deep make honored."

Everyone laughed but Cooper. He could not see the joke. Lopez had not bothered him—he had heard cute speeches from more rich/sophisticated people than he could count—but Coco sounded crazy.

Lopez lifted a small, silver tube over the edge of the table, squeezed a trigger, and a stream of glittering silver powder sprayed toward Coco. It burst in a thousand pinpoint scintillations. The androgyne inhaled with a foolish grin.

"Wacky Dust," Lopez said, and pointed the tube at Cooper. "Want some?" Without waiting for an answer she fired again. The stuff twinkled around his head. It smelled like one of the popular aphrodisiacs.

"What is it?" he asked.

"A mind-altering drug," she said, theatrically. When she saw his alarm she relented a little. "The trip is very short. In fact, I gave you such a little squirt you'll hardly notice it. Five minutes, tops."

"What does it do?"

She was eyeing him suspiciously. "Well, it should have done it already. Are you left-handed?"

"Yes."

"That explains it. Most of it's going to the wrong side of your head. What it does is scramble your speech center."

Montgomery roused himself enough to turn his head. He looked at Cooper with something less than total boredom. "It's like inhaling helium," he said. "You talk funny for a while."

"I didn't think that was possible," Cooper said, and everyone laughed. He found himself grinning reflexively, not knowing what was funny until he played his words back in his head and realized he had said something like "Pos that ib think unt I bull..."

He gritted his teeth and concentrated.

"I," he said, and thought some more. "Don't. Like. This." They seemed delighted. Coco babbled gibberish, and Lopez patted him on the back.

"Not many people figure it out that fast," she said. "Stick to one-word sentences and you're okay."

"The Wacky Dust scrambles the sentence-making capability of the brain," Montgomery said. He was sounding almost enthusiastic. Cooper knew from experience that the man was speaking of one of the few things that could excite him, that being his current ten-minute's wonder, the thing that everyone of any importance was doing today and would forget about tomorrow. "Complex thoughts are no longer—"

Cooper slammed his fist on the table and got the expected silence. Montgomery's eyes glazed and he looked away, bored by poor sportsmanship. Cooper stood.

"You," he said, pointing at all of them. "Stink."

"Quarter-meter!" Galloway shouted, pointing at Cooper. "Quarter-meter Cooper! Silver medal in Rio, bronze at Shanghai, 1500-meter freestyle, competed for United N.A., then for Ryancorp." She was grinning proudly, but when she looked around her face fell. "What's wrong?"

Cooper walked away from them. She caught him when he was almost out of sight around the curved promenade floor.

"Quarter-meter, please don't—"

"Don't me call that!" he shouted, jerking his arm away from her touch, not caring how the words came out. Her hand sprang back poised awkwardly, each joint of her fingers twinkling with its own golden band.

"Mr. Cooper, then." She let her hand fall, and her gaze with it, looked at her booted feet. "I want to apologize for her. She had no right to do that. She's drunk, if you hadn't—"

"I no…ticed."

"You'll be all right now," she said, touching his arm lightly, remembering, and pulling it away with a sheepish smile.

"There are no lasting effects?"

"We hope not. There haven't been so far. It's experimental."

"And illegal."

She shrugged. "Naturally. Isn't everything fun?"

He wanted to tell her how irresponsible that was, but he sensed she would be bored with him if he belabored it and while he did not care if Montgomery was bored with him, he did not want to be tiresome with her. So when she offered another tentative smile, he smiled back, and she grinned, showing him that gap between her front teeth which had made a fortune for the world's dentists when one hundred million girls copied it.

She had one of the most famous faces in the world, but she did not closely resemble herself as depicted on television. The screen missed most of her depth, which centered on her wide eyes and small nose, was framed by her short blonde curls. A faint series of lines around her mouth betrayed the fact that she was not twenty, as she looked at first glance, but well into her thirties. Her skin was pale, and she was taller than she seemed in pictures, and her arms and legs were even thinner.

"They compensate for that with camera angles," she said, and he realized she was not reading his mind but merely noticing where he was looking. He had given her a stock reaction, one she got every day, and he hated that. He resolved not to ask any questions about her sidekick. She had heard them all and was surely as sick of them as he was of his nickname.

"Will you join us?" she asked. "I promise we won't misbehave again."

He looked back at the three, just visible at their table before the curved roof cut off his view of the corridor promenade, gee/1 level.

"I'd rather not. Maybe I shouldn't say this, but those are pretty stock types. I always want to either sneer at them or run away from them."

She leaned closer.

"Me too. Will you rescue me?"

"What do you mean?"

"Those three could teach limpets a thing or two about clinging. That's their job, but the hell with them."

"What do you want to do?"

"How should I know? Whatever people do around here for a good time. Bob for apples, ride on the merry-go-round, screw, play cards, see a show."

"I'm interested in at least one of those."

"So you like cards, too?" She glanced back at her crew. "I think they're getting suspicious."

"Then let's go." He took her arm and started to walk away with her. Suddenly she was running down a corridor. He hesitated only a second, then was off after her.

He was not surprised to see her stumble. She recovered quickly, but it slowed her enough for him to catch her.

"What happened?" she said. "I thought I was falling—" She pulled back her sleeve and stared at the world's most complicated wristwatch. He realized it was some sort of monitor for her sidekick.

"It isn't your hardware," he said, leading her at a fast walk. "You were running with the spin. You got heavier. You should bear in mind that what you're feeling isn't gravity."

"But how will we get away if we can't run?"

"By going just a little faster than they do." He looked back, and as he had expected, Lopez was already down. Coco was wavering between turning back to help and following Montgomery, who was still coming, wearing a determined expression. Cooper grinned. He had finally succeeded in getting the man's attention. He was making off with the star.

Just beyond stairwell C Cooper pulled Galloway into an elevator whose door was closing. He had a glimpse of Montgomery's outraged face.

"What good will this do us?" Galloway wanted to know. "He'll just follow us up the stairs. These things are slow as the mid-town express."

"They're slow for a very good reason, known as coriolis force," Cooper said, reaching into his pocket for his keys. He inserted one in the control board of the elevator. "Since we're on the bottom level, Montgomery will go up. It's the only direction the stairs go." He twisted the key, and the elevator began to descend.

The two "basement" levels were the parts of the Champagne Hotel complex nearest hard vacuum. The car stopped on B level and he held the door for her. They walked among exposed pipes, structural cables, and beams not masked by the frothy decorations of the public levels. The only light came from bare bulbs spaced every five meters. The girders and the curved floor made the space resemble the innards of a zeppelin.

"How hard will they look for you?"

She shrugged. "They won't be fooling around. They'll keep it up until they find me. It's only a question of time."

"Can they get me in trouble?"

"They'd love to. But I won't let them."

"Thanks."

"It's the least I could do."

"So my room is out. First place they'd look."

"No, they'd check my room first. It's better equipped for playing cards."

He was mentally kicking himself. She was playing games with him, he knew that, but what was the game? If it was just sex, that was okay. He'd never made love with a woman in a sidekick.

"About your nickname…" she said, leaving the sentence unfinished to see how he would react. When he said nothing, she started over. "Is it your favorite swimming distance? I seem to recall you were accused of never exerting yourself more than the situation required."

"Wouldn't it be foolish if I did?" But the label still rankled. It was true he had never turned in a decent time just swimming laps, and that he seldom won a race by more than a meter. The sports media had never warmed to him because of that, even before he failed to win the gold. For some reason, they thought of him as lazy, and most people assumed his nickname meant he would prefer to swim races of no more than a quarter of a meter.

"No, that's not it," was all he would say, and she dropped the subject.

The silence gave him time to reflect, and the more he did, the less happy he was. She had said she could keep him out of trouble, but could she? When it came to a showdown, who had more clout with BCE? The Golden Gypsy, or her producers? He might be risking a lot, and she was risking nothing at all. He knew he should ditch her but, if he spurned her now, she might withdraw what protection she could offer.

"I sense you don't care for your nickname," she said, at last. "What should I call you? What's your real name?"

"I don't like that, either. Call me Q.M."

"Must I?" she sighed.

"Everybody else does."

He took her to Eliot's room because Eliot was in the infirmary and because Montgomery and company would not look for them there. They drank some of Eliot's wine, talked for a while, and made love.

The sex was pleasant, but nothing to shout about. He was surprised at how little the sidekick got in his way. Though it was all over her body, it was warm and most of it was flexible, and he soon forgot about it.

Finally she kissed him and got dressed. She promised to see him again soon. He thought she said something about love. It struck him as a grotesque thing to say, but by then he was not listening very hard. There was an invisible wall between them and most of it belonged to her. He had tried to penetrate it—not very hard, he admitted to himself—but a good ninety-nine percent of her was in a fiercely-guarded place he was sure he'd never see. He shrugged mentally. It was certainly her right.

He was left with a bad post-coital depression. It had not been one of his finer moments. The best thing to do about it was to put it behind him and try not to do it again. It was not long before he realized he was doing uncommonly well at that already. Reclining naked on the bed, gazing at the ceiling, he could not recall a single thing she had said.

What with one thing and another, he did not get back to his room until late. He did not turn on the light because he did not want to wake Anna-Louise. And he walked with extra care because he was not balancing as well as he might. There had been a few drinks.

Still, she woke up, as she always did. She pressed close to him under the covers, her body warm and humid and musky, her breath a little sour as she kissed him. He was half-drunk and she was half-awake, but when her hands began to pull and her hips to thrust forward insistently he found to his surprise that he was ready and so was she. She guided him, then eased over onto her side and let him nestle in behind her. She drew her knees up and hugged them. Her head was pillowed on his arm. He kissed the back of her smooth scalp and nibbled her ear, then let his head fall into the pillow and moved against her slowly for a peaceful few minutes. At last she stretched, squeezing him, making small fists, digging her toes into his thighs.

"How did you like her?" she mumbled.

"Who?"

"You know who."

He was pretty sure he could pull off a lie, because Anna-Louise couldn't be *that* sure, and then he frowned in the darkness, because he had never wanted to lie to her before.

So he said, "Do you know me that well?"

She stretched again, this time more sensually, to more of a purpose than simply getting the sleepiness out of her system.

"How should I know? My nose didn't give me a chance to find out. I smelled the liquor on your breath when you came in, but I smelled her on my fingers after I touched you."

"Come *on.*"

"Don't get mad." She reached around to pat his buttocks while at the same time pressing herself back against him. "Okay, so I guessed at the identity. It didn't take much intuition."

"It was lousy," he admitted.

"I'm so sorry." He knew she really was, and did not know if that made him happy or sad. It was a hell of a thing, he thought, not to know something as basic as that.

"It's a damn shame," she went on. "Fucking should never be lousy."

"I agree."

"If you can't have fun doing it, you shouldn't do it."

"You're one hundred per cent right."

He could just see her teeth in the darkness; he had to imagine the rest of her grin, but he knew it well.

"Do you have anything left for me?"

"There's a very good chance that I do."

"Then what do you say we just skip the next part and *wake up*?"

She shifted gears so fast he had a hard time keeping up at first; she was all over him and she was one of the strongest women he knew. She liked to wrestle. Luckily, there were no losers in her matches. It was everything the encounter with Galloway had not been. That was no surprise; it *always* was. Sex with Anna-Louise was very good indeed. For that matter, so was everything else.

He lay there in the dark long after she had gone to sleep, their bodies spooned together just as they had begun, and he thought long and hard and as clearly as he could. Why not? Why not Anna-Louise? She could care if he gave her the chance. And maybe he could, too.

He sighed, and hugged her tighter. She murmured like a big, happy cat, and began to snore.

He would talk to her in the morning, tell her what he had been thinking. They would begin the uncertain process of coming to know each other.

Except that he woke with a hangover, Anna-Louise had already showered, dressed, and gone, and someone was knocking on his door.

He stumbled out of bed and it was her, Galloway. He had a bad moment of disorientation, wishing that famous face would get back on the television screen where it belonged. But somehow she was in his room, though he did not recall standing aside to admit her. She was smiling, smiling, and talking so fast he could barely understand her. It was an inane rattle about how good it was to see him and how nice the room was, as her eyes swept him and the room from head to toe and corner to corner until he was sure she knew Anna-Louise better than he did himself, just from the faint traces she had left on the bare impersonal cubicle.

This was going to be difficult. He closed the door and padded to the bed, where he sank gratefully and put his face in his hands.

When she finally ran down he looked up. She was perched on the edge of the room's only chair, hands laced together on her knees. She looked so bright and chipper he wanted to puke.

"I quit my job," she said. It took a while for that to register. In time, he was able to offer a comment.

"Huh?" he said.

"I quit. Just said screw this and walked out. All over, ka-put, down the toilet. Fuck it." Her smile looked unhealthy.

"Oh." He thought about that, listening to the dripping of the bathroom faucet. "Ah...what will you do?"

"Oh, no problem, no problem." She was bouncing a little now. One knee bobbed in four-four time while the other waltzed. Perhaps that should have told him something. Her head jerked to the left, and there was a whine as it slowly straightened.

"I've had offers from all over," she went on. "CBS would sacrifice seven virgin vice-presidents on a stone altar to sign me up. NAAR and Telecommunion are fighting a pitched battle across Sixth Avenue at this very moment, complete with tanks and nerve gas. Shit, I'm already pulling down half the GNP of Costa Rica, and they all want to triple that."

"Sounds like you'll do all right," he ventured. He was alarmed. The head movement was repeating now, and her heels were hammering the floor. He had finally figured out that the whining noise was coming from her sidekick.

"Oh, bugger them, too," she said easily. "Independent production, that's for me. Doing my own thing. I'll show you some tapes. No more LCD, no more Trendex. Just me and a friend or two."

"LCD?"

"Lowest common denominator. My audience. Eight-year-old minds in thirty-one-point-three-six-year-old bodies. Demographics. Brain-cancer victims."

"Television made them that way," he said.

"Of course. And they loved it. Nobody could ever underestimate them, and nobody could ever give them enough crap. I'm not even going to try anymore."

She stood up, turned at the waist, and knocked the door off its hinges. It clattered into the hallway, teetering around the deep dimple her fist had made in the metal.

All that would have been bizarre enough, but when the noise had finally stopped she still stood there, arm extended, fist clenched, half turned at the waist. The whining sound was louder now, accompanied by something resembling the wail of a siren. She looked over her shoulder.

"Oh, darn it," she said, in a voice that rose in pitch with every word. "I think I'm stuck." And she burst into tears.

Cooper was no stranger to the ways of the super-rich and super-famous. He had thought he understood clout. He soon learned he knew nothing about it.

He got her calmed in a few minutes. She eventually noticed the small crowd that had gathered beyond the space where his door had been, whispering and pointing at the woman sitting on Cooper's bed with her arm stuck in an odd position. Her eyes grew cold, and she asked for his telephone.

Thirty seconds after her first call, eight employees of BCE arrived in the hallway outside. Guards herded the audience away and engineers erected a new door, having to remove two twisted hinges to do so. It was all done in less than four minutes, and by then Galloway had completed her second call.

She made three calls, none of them over two minutes long.

In one, she merely chatted with someone at the Telecommunion Network and mentioned, in passing, that she had a problem with her sidekick. She listened, thanked the person on the other end, and hung up. The call to GM&L, the conglom that owned Sidekick, Incorporated, was businesslike and short.

Two hours later a repairman from Sidekick knocked at the door. It was not until the next day that Cooper realized the man had been on the Earth's surface when he got the call, that his trip had involved a special ship boosting at one gee all the way and carrying no cargo but himself and his tool kit, which he opened and plugged into the wall computerminal before starting to work on the sidekick.

But in those two hours...

"If you'd like me to leave, I'll leave," she said, sipping her third glass of Cooper's wine.

"No, please."

She was still frozen like a frame from a violent film. Her legs worked and so did her right arm, but from her hips all the way up her back and down her left arm the sidekick had shorted out. It looked awfully uncomfortable. He asked if there was anything he could do.

"It's okay, really," she said, resting her chin on the arm that crossed in front of her.

"Will they be able to fix it?"

"Oh, sure." She tossed down the rest of the wine. "And if they can't, I'll just stay here and you'll have a real conversation piece. A human hatrack." She picked her shirt off the couch beside her and draped it over her frozen arm, then smiled at him. It was not a pretty smile.

He had helped her get the shirt off. It had been like undressing a statue. The idea had been to check the sidekick core for hot spots and visible cracks, which would necessitate the quick removal of the apparatus. It was clearly a project she did not relish. But as far as he had been able to see the thing was physically intact. The damage was on the electronic level.

It was the closest look he had yet taken at the technological marvel of the age, closer even than the night before, when he had made love to her. Then, manners had prevented him from staring. Now he had a perfect excuse, and he used it.

When he thought about it, it was frightening that they could pack so much power into a mechanism that, practically speaking, was hardly even there. The most massive part of the sidekick was the core, which was segmented, padded in flesh-toned soft plastic, and hugged her spine from the small of the back to the nape of her neck. Nowhere was it more than three centimeters thick.

Radiating from the core was an intricate network of gold chains, bands, and bracelets, making such a cunningly contrived system that one could almost believe it was all decoration rather than the conductors for energized fields that allowed her to move. Woven belts of fine gold wire criss-crossed like bandoliers between her breasts and just happened to connect, via a fragile gold chain, with the sinuous gooseneck that was concealed by her hair before it attached to the back of the golden tiara that made her look like Wonder Woman. Helical bands fashioned to look like snakes coiled down her arms, biting each other's tails until the last ones attached to thick, jewel-encrusted bracelets around her wrists, which in turn sprouted hair-fine wires that transformed themselves into finger rings, one for each joint, each inset with a single diamond. Elsewhere the effect was much the same. Each piece, taken by itself, was a beautiful piece of jewelry. The worst that could be said about Megan Galloway in the "nude" was that she was ostentatiously bejeweled. If one didn't mind that, she was absolutely stunning: a gilded Venus, or a fantasy artist's Amazon in full, impractical armor. Dressed, she was just like anyone else except for the tiara and the rings. There were no edges on her sidekick to savage clothes or poke out at unnatural angles. Cooper guessed this was as important to Galloway as the fact that the sidekick was a beautiful object, emphatically not an orthopedic appliance.

"It's unique," she said. "One of a kind."

"I didn't mean to stare."

"Heavens," she said. "You weren't staring. You are so pointedly *not* staring that your fascination must be intense. And no...don't say anything." She held up her free hand and waited for him to settle back in his chair. "Please, no more apologies. I've got a pretty good idea of the problem I present to somebody with both manners and curiosity, and it was shitty of me to say that about not staring. That puts you in the wrong whatever you do, huh?" She leaned back against the wall, getting comfortable as she could while waiting for the repairman to arrive.

"I'm proud of the damned thing, Cooper. That's probably obvious. And of course I've answered the same questions so many times that it bores me, but for you, since you're providing me a refuge in an embarrassing moment, I'll tell you anything you want to know."

"Is it really gold?"

"Twenty-four carat, solid."

"That's where your nickname comes from, I presume."

She looked puzzled for a moment, then her face cleared.

"Touché. I don't like that nickname any more than you like yours. And no, it's no more correct than yours is. At first, *I* wasn't the Golden Gypsy. The sidekick was. That was the name of this model sidekick. But they've still only made one of them, and before long, the name rubbed off on me. I discourage it."

Cooper understood that too well.

He asked more questions. Before long the explanations got too technical for him. He was surprised that she knew as much about it as she did. Her knowledge stopped short of the mathematics of Tunable Deformation Fields, but that was her only limit. TDF's were what had made the Bubble possible, since they could be made to resonate with particular molecular or atomic structures. The Bubble's fields were turned to attract or repel H_2O, while the fields generated by Galloway's sidekick influenced gold, Au^{197}, and left everything else alone. She went on to tell him far more than he could absorb about the ways in which the fields were generated in the sidekick core, shaped by wave guides buried in the jewelry, and deformated ("Physics terms are usually inelegant," she apologized), to the dictates of nanocomputers scattered throughout the hardware, operating by a process she called "augmented neuro-feedback holistitopology."

"The English of which is…" he pleaded.

"…that I think of pressing the middle valve down, the music goes round and round and it comes out here." She held out her hand and depressed the middle finger. "You would weep to know how many decisions the core made to accomplish that simple movement."

"On the other hand," he said, and rushed on when he remembered what had happened to her other hand, "what goes on in my brain to do the same thing is complex, but I don't have to program it. It's done for me. Isn't it much the same with you?"

"Much. Not exactly. If they made one of these for you and plugged you in right now, you'd twitch a lot. In a few weeks you'd patty-cake pretty well. But in a year you'd not even think about it. The brain re-trains itself. Which is a simple way of saying you struggle day and night for six or seven months with something that feels totally unnatural and eventually you learn to do it. Having done it, you know that learning to tap-dance on the edge of a razor blade would be a snap."

"You say you've heard all the questions. What's your least favorite?"

"God, you're merciless, aren't you? There's no contest. 'How did you hurt yourself?' To answer the question you so cleverly didn't ask, I broke my fool neck when me and my hang-glider got into an argument with a tree. The tree won. Many years later I went back and chopped that tree down, which just *may* be the stupidest thing I ever did, not counting today." She looked at him and raised one eyebrow. "Aren't you going to ask me about that?"

He shrugged.

"The funny thing is, that's the question I *want* you to ask. Because it's tied up with what we did yesterday, and that's really what I came here to talk to you about."

"So talk," he said, wondering what she could have to say about it beyond the fact that it had been hideous, and demeaning to both of them.

"It was the worst sexual experience I ever had," she said. "And you bear zero percent responsibility for that. Please don't interrupt. There are things you don't know about.

"I know you don't think much of my profession—I really don't want you to interrupt, or I'll never get all this out; if you disagree you can tell me when I'm through.

"You'd be a pretty strange lifeguard if you were a fan of the transtapes, or if you didn't feel superior to the kind of people who buy them. You're young, fairly well-educated and fairly articulate, you've got a good body and an attractive face and the opposite sex neither terrifies nor intimidates you. You are out on the end of *all* the bell-curves, demographically. You are *not* my audience, and people who *aren't* my audience tend to *look down* on my audience, and usually on me and my kind, too. And I don't blame them. Me and my kind have taken what might have been a great art-form and turned it into something so exploitative that even Hollywood and Sixth Avenue gag at it.

"You know as well as I do that there are many, many people growing up now who wouldn't know an honest, genuine, self-originated emotion if it kicked them in the behind. If you take their Transers away from them they're practically zombies.

"For a long time I've flattered myself that I'm a little better than the industry in general. There are some tapes I've made that will back me up on that. Things I've taken a chance on, things that try to be more complex than the LCD would dictate. *Not* my bread-and-butter tapes. Those are as simple-headed as the worst hack travelogue. But I've tried to be like the laborers in other artistic sweatshops of the past. Those few who managed to turn out something with some merit, like some directors of Hollywood westerns which were never meant to be anything but crowd pleasers and who still produced some works of art, or a handful of television producers who…none of this is familiar to you, is it? Sorry, I didn't mean to get academic. I've made a study of it, of art in the mass culture.

"All those old art-forms had undergrounds, independents who struggled along with no financing and produced things of varying quality but with some *vision*, no matter how weird. Trans-tapes are more expensive than films or television but there is an underground. It's just so far under it practically never comes to light. Believe it or not, it's possible to produce great art in emotional recording. I could name names, but you will not have heard of any of them. And I'm not talking about the people who make tapes about how it feels to kill somebody; that's another underground entirely.

"But things are getting tight. It used to be that we could make a good living and still stay away from the sex tapes. Let me add that I don't feel contempt for the people who make sex tapes. Given the state of our audience, it has become necessary that many of them have their well-worn jerk-off cassette, so when they get horny they know what to do with it. Most of them wouldn't have the vaguest notion otherwise. I just didn't want to make them myself. It's axiomatic in the trade that love is the one emotion that cannot be recorded, and if I can't have—"

"I'm sorry," Cooper said, "but I have to interrupt there. I've never heard that. In fact, I've heard just the opposite."

"You've been listening to our commercials," she reproved. "Get that shit out of your head, Cooper. It's pure hype." She rubbed her forehead, and sighed. "Oh, all right. I wasn't precise enough. I can make a tape of how I love my mother or my father or anybody I'm already in love with. It's not easy to do—it's the less subtle emotions that are more readily transed. But nobody has ever recorded the process of falling in love. It's sort of a Heisenberg Principle of transing, and nobody's sure if the limitation is in the equipment or in the person being recorded, but it exists, and there are some very good reasons to think nobody will ever succeed in recording that kind of love."

"I don't see why not," Cooper confessed. "It's supposed to be very intense, isn't it? And you said the strong emotions are the easiest to tape."

"That's true. But…well, try to visualize it. I've got my job because I'm better at ignoring all the hardware involved in transing. It's because of my sidekick; I mean, if I can learn to forget I'm operating *that* I can ignore anything. That's why the nets scour the trauma wards of hospitals looking for potential stars. It's like...well, in the early days of sex research they had people fuck in laboratories, with wires taped to them. A lot of people just couldn't do it. They were too self-conscious. Hook most people up to a transcorder and what you get is 'Oh, how interesting it is to be making a tape, look at all those people watching me, look at all those cameras, how interesting, now I have to forget about them, I must forget about them I just *must* forget—"

Cooper held up his hand, nodding. He was recalling seeing her burst from the water that first day in the Bubble, and his feelings as he watched her.

"So the essence of making a tape," she went on, "is the ability to ignore the fact that you're making one. To react just as you would have reacted if you *weren't* doing it. It calls for some of the qualities of an actor, but most actors can't do it. They think too much about the process. They can't be natural about it. That's my talent: to feel natural in unnatural circumstances.

"But there are limits. You can fuck up a storm while transing, and the tape will record how good everything feels and how goddam happy you are to be fucking. But it all falls apart when the machine is confronted with that moment of first falling in love. Either that, or the person being recorded just can't get into the *frame of mind* to fall in love while transing. The distraction of the transer itself makes that emotional state impossible.

"But I really got off on a tangent there. I'd appreciate it if you'd just hear me out until I've said what I have to say." She rubbed her forehead again, and looked away from him.

"We were talking economics. You have to make what sells. My sales have been dropping off. I've specialized in what we call 'elbow-rubbers.' 'You, too, can go to fancy places with fancy people. You, too, can be important, recognized, appreciated.'" She made a face. "I also do the sort of thing we've been making in the Bubble. Sensuals, short of sex. Those, frankly, are not selling so well anymore. The snob-tapes still do well, but everybody makes those. What you're marketing there is your celebrity, and mine is falling off. The competition has been intense.

"That's why I...well, it was Markham who talked me into it. I've been on the verge of going into heavy-breathers." She lifted her eyes. "I assume you know what those are."

Cooper nodded, remembering what Anna-Louise had said. So even Galloway could not stay out of it.

She sighed deeply, but no longer looked away from him.

"Anyway, I wanted to make something just a *little bit* better than the old tired in-and-outers. You know: 'Door-to-door salesman enters living room; "I'd like to show you my samples, ma'am." Woman rips open nightgown; "Take a look at these samples, buster." Fade to bed.' I thought that for my first sex-tape I'd try for something more erotic than salacious. I wanted a romantic situation, and if I couldn't get some love in it at least I'd try for affection. It would be with a handsome guy I met unexpectedly. He'd have some aura of romance about him. Maybe there'd be an argument at first, but the irresistible attraction would bring us together in spite of it, and we'd make love and part on a slightly tragic note since we'd be from different worlds and it could never…"

Tears were running down her cheeks. Cooper realized his mouth was open. He was leaning toward her, too astonished at first to say anything.

"You and me…" he finally managed to say.

"Shit, Cooper, *obviously* you and me."

"And you thought that…that what we did last night…did you really think that was worth a tape? I knew it was bad, but I had no inkling *how* bad it could be. I knew you were using me—hell, I was using you, too, and I didn't like that any better—but I never thought it was so cynical—"

"No, no, *no, no, no!*" She was sobbing now. "It wasn't that. It was *worse* than that! It was supposed to be *spontaneous,* damn it! *I* didn't pick you out. *Markham* was going to do that. He would find someone, coach him, arrange a meeting, conceal cameras to tape the meeting and in the bedroom later. I'd never really *know.* We've been studying an old show called *Candid Camera* and using some of their techniques. They're *always* throwing something unexpected at me, trying to help me stay fresh. That's Markham's job. But how surprised can I be when you show up at my table? Just look at it: in the romantic Bubble, the handsome lifeguard—*lifeguard,* for pete's sake!—an Olympic athlete familiar to millions from their television sets, gets pissed at my rich, decadent friends…I couldn't have gotten a more clichéd script from the most drug-brained writer in Television City!"

For a time there was no sound in the room but her quiet sobs. Cooper looked at it from all angles, and it didn't look pretty from any of them. But he had been just as eager to go along with the script as she had.

"I wouldn't have your job for anything," he said.

"Neither would I," she finally managed to say. "And I *don't*, damn it. You want to know what happened this morning? Markham showed me just how original he really is. I was eating breakfast and this guy—he was a lifeguard, are you ready?—he tripped over his feet and dropped his plate in my lap. Well, while he was cleaning me up he started dropping cute lines at a rate that would have made Neil Simon green. Sorry, getting historical again. Let's just say he sounded like he was reading from a script...he made that shitty little scene we played out together yesterday seem just wonderful. His smile was phony as a brass transistor. I realized what had happened, what I'd done to you, so I pushed the son of a bitch down into his French toast, went to find Markham, broke his fucking jaw for him, quit my job, and came here to apologize. And went a little crazy and broke your door. So I'm sorry, I really am, and I'd leave but I've busted my sidekick and I can't *stand* to have people staring at me like that, so I'd like to stay here a little longer, until the repairman gets here, and I don't have any notion of what I'm going to *do*."

What composure she had managed to gather fell apart once again, and she wept bitterly.

By the time the repairman arrived Galloway was back in control.

The repairman's name was Snyder. He was a medical doctor as well as a cybertechnician, and Cooper supposed that combination allowed him to set any price he fancied for his services.

Galloway went into the bedroom and got all the clean towels. She spread them on the bed, then removed her clothes. She reclined, face down, with the towels making a thick pad from her knees to her waist. She made herself as comfortable as she could with her arm locked in the way, and waited.

Snyder fiddled with the controls in his tool kit, touched needle-sharp probes to various points on the sidekick core, and Galloway's arm relaxed. He made more connections, there was a high whine from the core, and the sidekick opened like an iron maiden. Each bracelet, chain, amulet and ring separated along invisible join lines. Snyder then went to the bed, grasped the sidekick with one hand around the center of the core, and lifted it away from her. He set it on its "feet," where it promptly assumed a parade-rest stance.

There was an Escher print Cooper had seen, called "Rind," that showed the bust of a woman as if her skin had been peeled off and arranged in space to suggest the larger thing she had once been. Both the inner and outer surfaces of the rind could be seen, like one barber-pole stripe painted over an irregular, invisible surface. Galloway's sidekick, minus Galloway, looked much like that. It was one continuous, though convoluted, entity, a thing of springs and wires, too fragile to stand on its own but doing it somehow. He saw it shift slightly to maintain its balance. It seemed all too alive.

Galloway, on the other hand, looked like a rag doll. Snyder motioned to Cooper with his eyes, and the two of them turned her on her back. She had some control of her arms, and her head did not roll around as he had expected it to. There was a metal wire running along her scarred spine.

"I was an athlete, too, before the accident," she said.

"Were you?"

"Well, not in your class. I was fifteen when I cracked my neck, and I wasn't setting the world on fire as a runner. For a girl that's already too old."

"Not strictly true," Cooper said. "But it's a lot harder after that." She was reaching for the blanket with hands that did not work very well. Coupled with her inability to raise herself from the bed, it was a painful process to watch. Cooper reached for the edge of the blanket.

"No," she said, matter-of-factly. "Rule number one. Don't help a crip unless she asks for it. No matter how badly she's doing something, just don't. She's got to learn to ask, and you've got to learn to let her do what she *can* do."

"I'm afraid I've never known any crips."

"Rule number two. A nigger can call herself a nigger and a cripple can call herself a cripple, but lord help the able-bodied white who uses either word."

Cooper settled back in his chair.

"Maybe I'd better just shut up until you fill me in on all the rules."

She grinned at him. "It'd take all day. And frankly, maybe some of them are self-contradictory. We can be a pretty prickly lot, but I ain't going to apologize for it. You've got your body and I don't have mine. That's not your fault, but I think I hate you a little because of it."

Cooper thought about that. "I think I probably would too."

"Yeah. It's nothing serious. I came to terms with it a long time ago, and so would you, after a bad couple of years." She still hadn't managed to reach the blanket, and at last she gave it up and asked him to do it for her. He tucked it around her neck.

There were other things he thought he would like to know, but he felt she must have reached the limits of questioning, no matter what she said. And he was no longer quite so eager to know the answers. He had been about to ask what the towels on the bed were for, then suddenly it was obvious what they were for and he couldn't imagine why he hadn't known it at once. He simply knew nothing about her, and nothing about disability. And he was a little ashamed to admit it, but he was not sure he *wanted* to know any more.

There was no way he could keep the day's events from Anna-Louise, even if he had wanted to. The complex was buzzing with the story of how the Golden Gypsy had blown a fuse, though the news about her quitting her job was still not general knowledge. He was told the story three different times during his next shift. Each story was slightly different, but all approximated the truth. Most of the tellers seemed to think it was funny. He supposed he would have, too, yesterday.

Anna-Louise inspected the door hinges when they got back from work. "She must have quite a right hook," she said.

"Actually, she hit it with her left. Do you want to hear about it?"

"I'm all ears."

So he told her the whole story. Cooper had a hard time figuring out how she was taking it. She didn't laugh, but she didn't seem too sympathetic, either. When he was through—mentioning Galloway's incontinence with some difficulty—Anna-Louise nodded, got up, and started toward the bathroom.

"You've led a sheltered life, Q.M."

"What do you mean?"

She turned, and looked angry for the first time.

"I mean you sound as if incontinence was the absolute worst thing you'd ever heard of in your life."

"Well, what is it, then? No big thing?"

"It certainly isn't to *that* woman. For most people with her problem, it means catheters and feces bags. Or diapers. Like my grandfather wore for the last five years of his life. The operations she's had to fix it, and the hardware, implanted and external…well, it's damn expensive, Q.M. You can't afford it on the money grandfather was getting from the State, and Conglomerate health plans won't pay for it, either."

"Oh, so that's it. Just because she's rich and can afford the best treatment, her problems don't amount to anything. Just how would *you* like to—"

"Wait a minute, hold on…" She was looking at him with an expression that would not hold still, changing from sympathy to disgust. "I don't want to fight with you. I know it wouldn't be pleasant to have my neck broken, even if I was a trillionaire." She paused, and seemed to be choosing her words carefully.

"I'm bothered by something here," she said, at last. "I'm not even sure what it is. I'm concerned about you, for one thing. I still think it's a mistake to get involved with her. I like you. I don't want to see you hurt."

Cooper suddenly remembered his resolve of the night before, as she lay sleeping at his side. It confused him terribly. Just what *did* he feel for Anna-Louise? After the things Galloway had told him about love and the lies of the Transer commercials, he didn't know what to think. It was pitiful, when he thought about it, that he was as old as he was and hadn't the vaguest notion what love might be, that he had actually assumed the place to find it, when the time came, was on trans-tapes. It made him angry.

"What are you talking about, hurt?" he retorted. "She's not dangerous. I'll admit she lost control there for a moment, and she's strong, but—"

"Oh, help!" Anna-Louise moaned. "What am I supposed to do with these emotionally stunted smoggies who think nothing is real unless they've been told by somebody on the—"

"Smoggies? You called me a racist when—"

"Okay, I'm sorry." He complained some more but she just shook her head and wouldn't listen and he eventually sputtered to a stop.

"Finished? Okay. I'm getting crazy here. I've only got one more month before I go back home. And I do find most Earthlings—is that a neutral enough term for you?—I find them weird. *You're* not so bad, most of the time, except you don't seem to have much notion about what life is *for*. You like to screw and you like to swim. Even *that* is twice as much purpose as most sm—, Terrans seem to have."

"You...you're going?"

"Surprise!" Her tone dripped sarcasm.

"But why didn't you tell me?"

"You never asked. You never asked about a lot of things. I don't think you ever realized I might like to tell you about my life, or that it might be any different from yours."

"You're wrong. I sensed a difference."

She raised an eyebrow and seemed about to say something, but changed her mind. She rubbed her forehead, then took a deep, decisive breath.

"I'm almost sorry to hear that. But I'm afraid it's too late to start over. I'm moving out." And she began packing.

Cooper tried to argue with her but it did no good. She assured him she wasn't leaving because she was jealous; she even seemed amused that he thought that might be the reason. And she also claimed she was not going to move in with Yuri Feldman. She intended to live her last month in the Bubble alone.

"I'm going back to Luna to do what I planned to do all along," she said, tying the drawstring of her duffel bag. "I'm going to the police academy. I've saved enough now to put me through."

"Police?" Cooper could not have been more astonished if she had said she intended to fly to Mars by flapping her arms.

"You had no inkling, right? Well, why should you? You don't notice other people much unless you're screwing them. I'm not saying that's your fault; you've been trained to be that way. Haven't you ever wondered what I was doing here? It isn't the working conditions that drew me. I despise this place and all the people who come to visit. I don't even like water very much, and I *hate* that monstrous obscenity they call the Bubble."

Cooper was beyond shock. He had never imagined anyone could exist who would not be drawn by the magic of the Bubble.

"Then why? Why work here, and why do you hate it?"

"I hate it because people are starving in Pennsylvania," she said, mystifying him completely. "And I work here, God help me, because the pay is good, which you may not have noticed since you grew up comfortable. I would have said rich, but by now I know what real rich is. I grew up poor, Q.M. Another little detail you never bothered to learn. I've worked hard for everything, including the chance to come here to this disgusting pimp-city to provide a safety service for rich degenerates, because BCE pays in good, hard GWA Dollars. You probably never noticed, but Luna is having serious economic troubles because it's caught between a couple of your corporation-states…ah, forget it. Why worry your cute little head with things like that?"

She went to the door, opened it, then turned to look at him.

"Honestly, Q.M., I don't dislike you. I think I feel sorry for you. Sorry enough that I'm going to say once more you'd better watch out for Galloway. If you mess around with her right now, you're going to get hurt."

"I still don't understand how."

She sighed, and turned away.

"Then there's nothing more I can say. I'll see you around."

Megan Galloway had the Mississippi Suite, the best in the hotel. She didn't come to the door when Cooper knocked, but just buzzed him in.

She was sitting tailor-fashion on the bed, wearing a loose nightgown and a pair of wire-rimmed glasses and looking at a small box in front of her. The bed resembled a sternwheeler, with smoke and sparks shooting from the bedposts, and was larger than his entire room and bath. She put her glasses at the end of her nose and peered over them.

"Something I can do for you?"

He came around until he could see the box, which had a picture flickering dimly on one side of it.

"What's that?"

"Old-timey television," she said. "*Honey West*, circa 1965, American Broadcasting Company. Starring Anne Francis, John Ericson, and Irene

Hervey, Friday nights at 2100. Spin-off from *Burke's Law*, died 1966. What's up?"

"What's wrong with the depth?"

"They didn't have it." She removed her glasses and began to chew absently on one rubber tip. "How are you doing?"

"I'm surprised to see you wear glasses."

"When you've had as many operations as I have, you skip the ones you think you can do without. Why is it I sense you're having a hard time saying whatever it is you came here to say?"

"Would you like to go for a swim?"

"Pool's closed. Weekly filtering, or something like that."

"I know. Best possible time to go for a swim."

She frowned. "But I was told no one is admitted during the filtering."

"Yeah. It's illegal. Isn't everything that's fun?"

The Bubble was closed one hour in every twenty-four for accelerated filtering. At one time the place had been open all day, with filteration constantly operating, but then a client got past the three safety systems, where he was aerated, churned, irradiated, centrifuged, and eventually forced through a series of very fine screens. Most of him was still in the water in one form or another, and his legend had produced the station's first ghost.

But long before the Filtered Phantom first sloshed down the corridors the system had been changed. The filters never shut down completely, but while people were in the pool they were operated at slow speed. Once a day they were turned to full power.

It still wasn't enough. So every ten days BCE closed the pool for a longer period and gave the water an intensive treatment.

"I can't believe no one even watches it," Megan whispered.

"It's a mistake. Security is done by computer. There's twenty cameras in here but somebody forgot to tell the computer to squeal if it sees anybody enter during filteration. I got that from the computer itself, which thinks the whole fuck-up is very funny."

The hordes of swimmers had been gone for over two hours, and the clean-up crew had left thirty minutes before. Megan Galloway had probably thought she knew the Bubble pretty well, on the basis of her two visits. She was finding out now, as Cooper had done long ago, that she knew nothing. The difference between a resort beach on a holiday weekend and on a day in mid-winter was nothing compared to what she saw now.

It was perfectly still, totally clear: a crystal ball as big as the world.

"Oh, Cooper." He felt her hand tighten on his arm.

"Look. Down there. No, to the left." She followed his pointing finger and saw a school of the Bubble goldfish far below the surface, moving like lazy submarines, big and fat as watermelons and tame as park squirrels.

"Can I touch it, daddy?" she whispered, with the hint of a giggle. He pretended to consider it, then nodded. "I almost don't want to, you know?" she said. "Like a huge field covered in new snow, before anybody tracks across it."

"Yeah, I know." He sighed. "But it might as well be us. Hurry, before somebody beats you to it." He grinned at her, and pushed off slowly from his weightless perch on the sundeck tier that circled the rim of the champagne glass.

She pushed off harder and passed him before he was halfway there, as he had expected her to. The waves made by her entry spread out in perfect circles, then he broke the surface right behind her.

It was a different world.

When the Bubble had first been proposed, many years before, it had been suggested that it be a solid sphere of water, and that nothing but weightlessness and surface tension be employed to maintain it. Both forces came free of charge, which was a considerable factor in their favor.

But in the end, the builders had opted for TDF fields. This was because, while any volume of water would assume a spherical shape in free-fall, surface tension was not strong enough to keep it that way if it was disturbed. Such a structure would work fine so long as no swimmers entered to upset the delicate balance.

The TDF's provided the necessary unobtrusive force to keep things from getting messy. Tuned to attract or repel water, they also acted to force foreign matter toward either the inner or outer surfaces; in effect, making things that were *not* water float. A bar of lead floated better than a human body. Air bubbles also were pushed out. The fields were deliberately tuned to a low intensity. As a result, humans did not bob out of the water like corks but drifted toward a surface slowly, where they floated quite high in the water. As a further result, when the pool was open it was always churned by a billion bubbles.

When Cooper and Galloway entered the water the bubbles left behind by the happy throngs had long since merged with one of the larger volumes of air. The Bubble had become a magic lens, a piece of water with infinite curvature. It was nearly transparent with an aquamarine tint. Light was bent by it in enchanting ways, to the point that one could fancy the possibility of seeing all the way around it.

It distorted the world outside itself. The lifeguard station, cabanas, bar, and tanning chairs in the center were twisted almost beyond recognition, as if vanishing down the event horizon of a black hole. The rim of the glass, the deep violet field-dome that arched over it, and the circle of tanning chairs where patrons could brown themselves under genuine sunlight bent and flowed like a surrealist landscape. And everything, inside and outside the Bubble, oozed from one configuration to another as one changed position in the water. Nothing remained constant.

There was one exception to that rule. Objects in the water were not distorted. Galloway's body existed in a different plane, moved against the flowing, twisting background as an almost jarring intrusion of reality: pink flesh and golden metal, curly yellow hair, churning arms and legs. The stream of air ejected from her mouthpiece cascaded down the front of her body. It caressed her intimately, a thousand shimmering droplets of mercury, before it was thrashed to foam by her feet. She moved like a sleek aerial machine, streamlined, leaving a contrail behind her.

He customarily left his mouthpiece and collar-tank behind when he swam alone, but he was wearing it now, mostly so Galloway would not insist on removing hers, too. He felt the only decent way to swim was totally nude. He conceded the breathers were necessary for the crustaceans and plankton who did not understand the physical laws of the Bubble and who would never take the time to learn them. It was possible to get hopelessly lost, to become disoriented, unable to tell which was the shortest distance to air. Though bodies would float to a surface eventually, one could easily drown on the way out. The Bubble had no ends, deep or shallow. Thus the mouthpieces were required for all swimmers. They consisted of two semi-circular tanks that closed around the neck, a tube, a sensor that clipped to the ear, and the mouthpiece itself. Each contained fifteen minutes of oxygen, supplied on demand or when blood color changed enough to indicate it was needed. The devices automatically notified both the user and the lifeguard station when they were nearly empty.

It was a point of honor among the lifeguards to turn them in as full as they had been issued.

There were things one could do in the Bubble that were simply impossible in flat water. Cooper showed her some of the tricks, soon had her doing them herself. They burst from the water together, described long, lazy parabolas through the air, trailing comet tails of water. The TDF fields acted on the water in their bodies at all times, but it was such a lackadaisical force that it was possible to remain in the air for several minutes before surrendering to the inexorable center-directed impulse. They laced the water with their trails of foam, be-spattered the air with fine mist. They raced through the water, cutting across along a radial line, building up speed until they emerged on the inner surface to barrel across the width of the Bubble and re-enter, swam some more, and came up outside in the sunlight. If they went fast enough their momentum would carry them to the dark sun-field, which was solid enough to stand on.

He had had grave misgivings about asking her to come here with him. In fact, it had surprised him when he heard himself asking. For hours he had hesitated, coming to her door, going away, never knocking. Once inside it hadn't seemed possible to talk to her, particularly since he was far from sure he knew what he wanted to say. So he had brought her here, where talking was unnecessary. And the biggest surprise was that he was glad. It was fun to share this with someone. He wondered why he had never done it before. He wondered why he had never brought Anna-Louise, remembered the revelation of her real opinions of the place, and then turned away from thoughts of her.

It was strenuous play. He was in pretty good shape but was getting tired. He wondered if Galloway ever got tired. If she did, she seemed sustained by the heady joy of being there. She summed it up to him in a brief rest period at the outer rim.

"Cooper, you're a genius. We've just hijacked a swimming pool!"

The big clock at the lifeguard station told him it was time to quit, not so much because he needed the rest as because there was something he wanted her to see, something she would not expect. So he swam up to her and took her hand, motioned toward the rim of the glass, and saw her nod. He followed her as she built up speed.

He got her to the rim just in time. He pointed toward the sun, shielding his eyes, just as the light began to change. He squinted, and there it was. The Earth had appeared as a black disc, beginning to swallow the sun.

It ate more and more of it. The atmosphere created a light show that had no equal. Arms of amber encircled the black hole in the sky, changing colors quickly through the entire spectrum: pure, luminous colors against the deepest black imaginable. The sun became a brilliant point, seemed to flare sharply, and was gone. What was left was one side of the corona, the halo of Earth's air, and stars.

Millions of stars. If tourists ever complained about anything at the Bubble, it was usually that. There were no stars. The reason was simple: space was flooded with radiation. There was enough of it to fry an unprotected human. Any protection that could shut out that radiation would have to shut out the faint light of the stars as well. But now, with the sun in eclipse, the sensors in the field turned it clear as glass. It was still opaque to many frequencies, but that did not matter to the human eye. It simply vanished, and they were naked in space.

Cooper could not imagine a better time or place to make love, and that is exactly what they did.

"Enjoyed that a little more, did you?" she said.

"Uh." He was still trying to catch his breath. She rested her head against his chest and sighed in contentment.

"I can still hear your heart going crazy."

"My heart has seldom had such a workout."

"Nor a certain quarter of a meter, from the look of things."

He laughed. "So you figured that out. It's exaggerated."

"But a fifth of a meter would be an understatement, wouldn't you say?"

"I suppose so."

"So what's between? Nine fortieths? Who the hell needs a nickname like 'Nine-fortieths-of-a-meter Cooper'? That is about right, isn't it?"

"Close enough for rock and roll."

She thought about that for a time, then kissed him. "I'll bet you know, *exactly*. To the goddamn tenth of a millimeter. You'd *have* to, with a nickname like that." She laughed again, and moved in his arms. He opened his eyes and she was looking into them.

"This time I rock, and *you* roll," she suggested.

"I guess I'm getting older," he admitted, at last.

"You'd be a pretty odd fellow if you weren't."

He had to smile at that, and he kissed her again. "I only regret that we didn't get to see the sun come out."

"Well, I regret a little more than *that*." She studied his face closely, and seemed puzzled by what she found. "Damn. I never would have expected it, but I don't think you're really upset. For some reason, I don't feel the need to soothe your wounded ego."

He shrugged. "I guess not."

"What's your secret?"

"Just that I'm a realist, I guess. I never claimed to be superman. And I had a fairly busy night." He shut his eyes, not wanting to remember it. But the truth was that something *was* bothering him, and something else was warning him not to ask about it. He did, anyway.

"Not only did I have a rather full night," he said, "but I think I sensed a certain…well, you were less than totally enthusiastic, the second time. I think that put me off slightly."

"Did it, now?"

He looked at her face, but she did not seem angry, only amused.

"Was I right?"

"Certainly."

"What was wrong?"

"Not much. Only that I have absolutely no sensation from my toes to…right about here." She was holding her arm over her chest, just below her shoulders.

It was too much for him to take in all at once. When he began to understand what she was saying, he felt a terror beside which fear of impotence would have been a very minor annoyance.

"You can't mean...nothing I did had...you were faking it? Faking everything, the whole time? You felt—"

"That first night, yes, I was. Totally. Not very well, I presume, from your reaction."

"...but just now..."

"Just now, it was something different. I really don't know if I could explain it to you."

"Please try." It was very important that she try, because he felt despair such as he had never imagined. "Can you...is it all going through the motions? Is that it? You can't have sex, really?"

"I have a full and satisfying sex life," she assured him. "It's different than yours, and it's different from other women's. There are a lot of adaptations, a lot of new techniques my lovers must learn."

"Will you—" Cooper was interrupted by high-pitched, chittering squeals from the water. He glanced behind him, saw Charlie the Dolphin had been allowed to re-enter the Bubble, signaling the end of their privacy. Charlie knew about Cooper, was in on the joke, and always warned him when people were coming.

"We have to go now. Can we go back to your room, and...and will you teach me how?"

"I don't know if it's a good idea, friend. Listen, I enjoyed it, I loved it. Why don't we leave it that way?"

"Because I'm very ashamed. It never occurred to me."

She studied him, all trace of levity gone from her face. At last, she nodded. He wished she looked more pleased about it.

But when they returned to her room she had changed her mind. She did not seem angry. She would not even talk about it. She just kept putting him off each time he tried to start something, not unkindly, but firmly, until he finally stopped pursuing the matter. She asked him then if he wanted to leave. He said no, and he thought her smile grew a little warmer at that.

So they built a fire in her fireplace with logs of real wood brought up from Earth. ("This fireplace must be the least energy-efficient heater humans have ever built," she said.) They curled up on the huge pillows scattered on the rug, and they talked. They talked long into the night, and this time Cooper had no trouble at all remembering what she said. Yet he would have been hard put to relate the conversation to anyone else. They spoke of trivia and of heartbreaks, sometimes in the same sentence, and it was hard to know what it all meant.

They popped popcorn, drank hot buttered rum from her autobar until they were both feeling silly, kissed a few times, and at last fell asleep, chaste as eight-year-olds at a slumber party.

For a week they were separated only when Cooper was on duty. He did not get much sleep, and he got no sex at all. It was his longest period of abstinence since puberty, and he was surprised at how little he felt the lack. There was another surprise, too. Suddenly he found himself watching the clock while he was working. The shift could not be over soon enough to suit him.

She was educating him, he realized that, and he did not mind. There was nothing dry or boring about the things they did together, nor did she demand that he share all her interests. In the process he expanded his tastes more in a week than he had in the previous ten years.

The outer, promenade level of the station was riddled with hole-in-the-wall restaurants, each featuring a different ethnic cuisine. She showed him there was more to food than hamburgers, steaks, potato chips, tacos, and fried chicken. She never ate *anything* that was advertised on television, yet her diet was a thousand times more varied than his.

"Look around you," she told him one night, in a Russian restaurant she assured him was better than any to be found in Moscow. "These are the people who own the companies that make the food you've been eating all your life. They pay the chemists who formulate the glop-of-the-month, they hire the advertising agencies who manufacture a demand for it, and they bank the money the proles pay for it. They do everything with it but *eat* it."

"Is there really something wrong with it?"

She shrugged. "Some of it used to cause problems, like cancer. Most of it's not very nutritious. They watched for carcinogens, but that's because a consumer with cancer eats less. As for nutrition, the more air the better. My rule of thumb is if they have to flog the stuff on television it *has* to be bad."

"Is everything on television bad, then?"

"Yes. Even me."

He was indifferent to clothes but liked to shop for them. She did not patronize the couturiers but put her wardrobe together from unlikely sources.

"Those high-priced designers work according to ancient laws," she told him. "They all work more or less together—though they don't plan it that way. I've decided that trite ideas are born simultaneously in mediocre minds. A fashion designer or a television writer or a studio executive cannot really be said to possess a mind at all. They're hive mentalities; they eat the sewage that floats on the surface of the mass culture, digest it, and then get creative diarrhea—all at once. The turds look and smell exactly alike, and we call them this year's fashions, hit shows, books, and movies. The key to dressing is to look at what everyone else is wearing then avoid it. Find a creative person who had never thought of designing clothes, and ask her to come up with something."

"You don't look like that on television," he pointed out.

"Ah, my *dear*. That's my job. A Celebrity must be homogenized with the culture that believes she *is* a Celebrity. I couldn't even get *on* the television dressed like I am now; the Taste Arbiter would consult its trendex and throw up its hands and have a screaming snit. But take note; the way I'm dressed now is the way everyone will be dressed in about a month."

"Do you like that?"

"Better than I like getting into costume for a guest spot on the *Who's Hot, Who's Shit?* show. This way the designers are watching me instead of the other way around." She laughed, and nudged him with her elbow. "Remember drop-seat pajamas, about a year and a half ago? That was mine. I wanted to see how far they'd go. They ate it up. Didn't you think that was funny?"

Cooper did recall thinking they were funny when they first came around. But then, somehow, they looked sexy. Soon a girl looked frumpy without that rectangle of flannel flapping against the backs of her thighs. Later, another change had happened, the day he realized the outfits were old-fashioned.

"Remember tail-fins on shoes? That was mine too."

One night she took him through part of her library of old tapes.

After her constant attacks on television, he was not prepared for her fondness, her genuine love, for the buried antiques of the medium.

"Television is the mother that eats its young," she said, culling through a case of thumbnail-sized cassettes. "A television show is senile about two seconds after the phosphor dots stop glowing. It's dead after one re-run, and it doesn't go to heaven." She came back to the couch with her selection and dumped them on the table beside the ancient video device.

"My library is hit-and-miss," she said. "But it's one of the best there is. In the real early days they didn't even save the shows. They made some films, lost most of those, then went to tape and erased most of them after a few years in the vault. Shows you how valuable the product was, in their own estimation. Here, take a look at this."

What she now showed him lacked not only depth, but color as well. It took him a few minutes to reliably perceive the picture, it was so foreign to him. It flickered, jumped, it was all shades of gray, and the sound was tinny. But in ten minutes he was hypnotized.

"This is called *Faraway Hill*," she said. "It was the first net soap. It came on Wednesday nights at 2100, on the DuMont Net, and it ran for twelve weeks. This is, so far as I know, the only existing episode, and it didn't surface until 1990."

She took him back, turning the tiny glass screen into a time machine. They sampled *Toast of the Town, One Man's Family, My Friend Irma, December Bride, Pete and Gladys, Petticoat Junction, Ball Four, Hunky & Dora, Black Vet, Kunklowitz, Kojak,* and *Koonz*. She showed him wonderfully inventive game shows, serials that made him deeply involved after only one episode, adventures so civilized and restrained he could barely believe they were on television. Then she went on to the Golden Age of the Sitcom for *Gilligan's Island* and *Family Affair*.

"What I can't get over," he said, "is how good it is. It's so much better than what we see today. And they did it all with no sex and practically no violence."

"No nudity, even," she said. "There was no frontal nudity on network TV until *Koonz*. Next season, *every* show had it, naturally. There was no actual intercourse until much later, in *Kiss My Ass*." She looked away from him, but not before he caught a hint of sadness in her eyes. He asked her what was wrong.

"I don't know, Q.M. I mean...I don't know exactly. Part of it is knowing that most of these shows were panned by the critics when they came out. And I've showed you some flops, but mostly these were hits. And I *can't tell the difference.* They all look good. I mean, none of them have people you'd expect to meet in real life, but they're all recognizably human, they act more or less like humans act. You can care for the characters in the dramas, and the comedies are witty."

"So those critics just had their heads up their asses."

She sighed. "No. What I fear is that it's *us*. If you're brought up eating shit, rotten soyaloid tastes great. I really do think that's what's happened. It's possible to do the moral equivalent of the anatomical impossibility you just mentioned. I know, because I'm one of the contortionists who does it. What frightens me is that I've been kidding myself all along, that I'm *stuck* in that position. That none of us can unbend our spines any longer."

She had other tapes.

It was not until their second week together that she brought them out, rather shyly, he thought. Her mother had been a fanatic home vidmaker; she had documented Megan's life in fine detail.

What he saw was a picture of lower-upper-class life, not too different in its broad outlines from his own upper-middle milieu. Cooper's family had never had any financial troubles. Galloway's were not fabulously wealthy, though they brought in twenty times the income of Cooper's. The house that appeared in the background shots was much larger than the one Cooper had grown up in. Where his family had biked, hers had private automobiles. There was a woman in the early tapes that Megan identified as her nurse; he did not see any other servants. But the only thing he saw that really impressed him was a sequence of her receiving a pony for her tenth birthday. Now, there was class.

Little Megan Galloway, pre-sidekick, emerged as a precocious child, perhaps a trifle spoiled. It was easy to see where at least part of her composure before the Transer came from; her mother had been everywhere, aiming her vidcam. Her life was *cinema verité*, with Megan either totally ignoring the camera or playing to it expertly, as her mood dictated. There were scenes of her reading fluently in three languages at the age of seven, others showing her hamming it up in amateur theatricals staged in the back yard.

"Are you sure you want to see more?" she asked, for the third or fourth time.

"I tell you, I'm fascinated. I forgot to ask you where all this is happening. California, isn't it?"

"No, I grew up in *La Barrio Cercada*, *Veintiuno*, one of the sovereign enclaves the congloms carved out of Mexico for exec families. Dual United States and GWA citizenship. I never saw a real Mexican the whole time I lived there. I just thought I ought to ask you," she went on, diffidently. "Home vids can be deadly boring."

"Only if you don't care about the subject. Show me more."

Somewhere during the next hour of tapes, control of the camera was wrested from Megan's mother and came to reside primarily with Megan herself and with her friends. They were as camera-crazy as her mother had been, but not quite so restrained in subject matter. The children used their vidcams as virtually every owner had used them since the invention of the device: they made dirty tapes. The things they did could usually better be described as horseplay than as sex, and they generally stopped short of actual intercourse, at least while the tape was rolling.

"My god," Megan sighed, rolling her eyes. "I must have a million kilometers of this sort of kiddie-porn. You'd think we invented it."

He observed that she and her crowd were naked a lot more than he and his friends had been. The students at his school had undressed at the beach, to participate in athletics, and to celebrate special days like Vernal Equinox and The Last Day of School. Megan's friends did not seem to dress at all. Most of them were Caucasian, but all were brown as coffee beans.

"It's true," she said. "I never wore *anything* but a pair of track shoes."

"Even to school?"

"They didn't believe in dictating things like that to us."

He watched her develop as a woman in a sequence that lap-dissolved her from the age of ten, like those magic time-lapses of flowers blooming.

"I call this 'The Puberieties of 2073,'" she said, with a self-deprecating laugh. "I put it together years ago, for something to do."

He had already been aware of the skilled hand which had assembled these pieces into a whole which was integrated, yet not artificially slick. The arts learned during her years in the business had enabled her to produce an extended program which entranced him far longer than its component parts, seen raw, could ever have done. He remembered Anna-Louise's accusations, and wondered what she would think if she could see him now, totally involved in someone else's life.

A hand-lettered title card appeared on the screen: "The Broken Blossom: An Act of Love. By Megan Allegra Galloway and Reginald Patrick Thomas." What followed had none of the smooth flow of what had gone before. The cuts were jerky. The camera remained stationary at all times, and there were no fades. He knew this bit of tape had been left untouched from the time a young girl had spliced it together many years ago. The children ran along the beach in slow-motion, huge waves breaking silently behind them. They walked along a dirt road, holding hands, stopping to kiss. The music swelled behind them. They sat in an infinite field of yellow flowers. They laughed, tenderly fondled each other. The boy covered Megan with showers of petals.

They ran through the woods, found a waterfall and a deep pool. They embraced under the waterfall. The kisses became passionate and they climbed out onto a flat rock where—coincidentally—there was an inflatable mattress. ("When we rehearsed it," Megan explained, "that damn rock didn't feel half as romantic as it looked.") The act was consummated. The sequence was spliced from three camera angles; in some of the shots Cooper could see the legs of one of the other tripods. The lovers lay in each other's arms, spent, and more ocean breakers were seen. Fade to black.

Galloway turned off the tape player. She sat for a time examining her folded hands.

"That was my first time," she said.

Cooper frowned. "I was sure I saw—"

"No. Not with me, you didn't. The other girls, yes. And you saw me doing a lot of other things. But I was 'saving' that." She chuckled. "I'd read too many old romances. My first time was going to be with someone I loved. I know it's silly."

"And you loved him?"

"Hopelessly." She brushed her eyes with the back of her hand, then sighed. "He wanted to pull out at the end and ejaculate on my belly, because that's the way they always do it on television. I had to argue with him for hours to talk him out of that. He was an idiot." She considered that for a moment. "We were both idiots. He believed real life should imitate television, and I believed it wasn't real unless it was on television. So I had to record it, or it might all fade away. I guess I'm still doing that."

"But you know it's not true. You do it for a living."

She regarded him bleakly. "This makes it better?"

When he did not answer she fell silent for a long time, studying her hands again. When she spoke, she did not look up.

"There are more tapes."

He knew what she meant, knew it would no longer be fun, and knew just as certainly that he must view them. He told her to go on.

"My mother shot this."

It began with a long shot of a silver hang-glider. Cooper heard Megan's mother shout for her daughter to be careful. In response, the glider banked sharply upward, almost stalled, then came around to pass twenty meters overhead. The camera followed. Megan was waving and smiling. There was a chaotic moment—shots of the ground, of the sky, a blurred glimpse of the glider nearing the tree—then it steadied.

"I don't know what was going through her mind," Megan said, quietly. "But she responded like an old pro. It must have been reflex."

Whatever it was, the camera was aimed unerringly as the glider turned right, grazed the tree, and flipped over. It went through the lower branches, and impaled itself. The image was jerky as Megan's mother ran. There was a momentary image of Megan dangling from her straps. Her head was at a horrifying angle. Then the sky filled one half of the screen and the ground the other as the camera continued to record after being flung aside.

Things were not nearly so comprehensive after that. The family at last had no more inclination to tape things. There were some hasty shots of a bed with a face—Megan, so wrapped and strapped and tucked that nothing else showed—pictures of doctors, of the doors of operating rooms and the bleak corridors of hospitals. And suddenly a girl with ancient eyes was sitting in a wheelchair, feeding herself laboriously with a spoon strapped to her fist.

"Things pick up a little now," Megan said. "I told them to start taping again. I was going to contrast these tapes with the ones they would make a year from now, when I was walking again."

"They told you you would walk?"

"They told me I would *not*. But everyone thinks they're the exception. The doctors tell you you'll regain some function, and hell, if you can regain some you can regain it all, right? You start to believe in mind over matter, and you're sure God will smile on you alone. Oh, by the way, there's trans-tape material with some of these."

The implications of the casual statement did not hit him for a moment. When he understood, he knew she would not mention it again. It was an invitation she would never make more directly than she had just done.

"I'd like to run them, if you wouldn't mind." He had hoped for a tone of voice as casual as hers had been, and was not sure he had pulled it off. When she looked at him her eyes were measuring.

"It would be bad form for me to protest," she said, at last. "Obviously, I want very much for you to try them. But I'm not sure you can handle them. I should warn you, they're—"

"—not much fun? Damn it, Megan, don't insult me."

"All right." She got up and went to a cabinet, removed a very small, very expensive Transer unit and helmet. As she helped him mount it she would not look into his eyes, but babbled nervously about how the Feelie Corporation people had showed up in the hospital one day, armed with computer printouts that had rated her a good possibility for a future contract with the company. She had turned them away the first time, but they were used to that. Transing had still been a fairly small industry at the time. They were on the verge of breakthroughs that would open the mass market, but neither Feelie-Corp nor Megan knew that. When she finally agreed to make some tapes for them it was not in the belief that they would lead to stardom. It was to combat her growing fear that there was very little she could do with her life. They were offering the possibility of a job, something she had never worried about when she was rich and un-injured. Suddenly, any job looked good.

"I'll start you at low intensity," she said. "You don't have a tolerance for transing, I presume, so there's no need for power boosters. This is fragmented stuff. Some of the tapes have trans-tracks, and others don't, so you'll—"

"Will you get on with it, please?"

She turned on the machine.

On the screen, Megan was in a therapy pool. Two nurses stood beside her, supporting her, stretching her thin limbs. There were more scenes of physical therapy. He was wondering when the transing would begin. It should start with a shifting of perspectives, as though he had (*The television expanded; he passed through the glass and into the world beyond.*) actually *entered*—

"Are you all right?"

Cooper was holding his face in his hands. He looked up, and shook his head, realized that she would misinterpret the gesture, and nodded.

"A touch of vertigo. It's been awhile."

"We could wait. Do it another time."

"No. Let's go."

He was sitting in the wheelchair, dressed in a fine lace gown that covered him from his neck to his toes. The toes were already beginning to look different. There was no more muscle tone in them. Most important, he could no longer feel them.

He felt very little sensation. There was a gray area just above his breasts where everything began to fade. He was a floating awareness, suspended above the wheelchair and the body attached to it.

He was aware of all this, but he was not thinking about it. It was already a common thing. The awful novelty was long gone.

Spring had arrived outside his window. (Where was he? This was not Mexico, he was sure, but his precise location eluded him. No matter.) He watched a squirrel climbing a tree just outside his window. It might be nice to be a squirrel.

Someone was coming to visit real soon. It would only be a few more hours. He felt good about that. He was looking forward to it. Nothing much had happened today. There had been therapy (his shoulders still ached from it) and a retraining session (without thinking about it, he made the vast, numb mittens that used to be his hands close together strongly—which meant he had exerted almost enough force to hold a sheet of paper between thumb and bunched fingers). Pretty soon there would be lunch. He wondered what it would be.

Oh, yes. There had been that unpleasantness earlier in the day. He had been screaming hysterically and the doctor had come with the needle. That was all still down there. There was enough sadness to drown in, but he didn't feel it. He felt the sunlight on his arm and was grateful for it. He felt pretty good. Wonder what's for lunch?

"You still okay?"

"I'm fine." He rubbed his eyes, trying to uncross them. It was the transition that always made him dizzy; that feeling as though a taut rubber band had snapped and he had popped out of the set and back into his own head, his own body. He rubbed his arms, which felt as though they had gone to sleep. On the screen, Megan still sat in her wheelchair, looking out the window with a vague expression. The scene changed.

He sat as still as he could so he wouldn't disturb the sutures in the back of his neck, but it was worth a little pain. On the table in front of him, the tiny metal bug shuddered, jerked forward, then stopped. He concentrated, telling it to make a right turn. He thought about how he would have turned right while driving a car. Foot on the accelerator, hands on the wheel. Shoulder muscles holding the arms up, fingers curled, thumbs...what had he done with his thumbs? But then he had them, he felt the muscles of his arms as he began turning the wheel. He tapped the brake with his foot, trying to feel the tops of his toes against the inside of his shoe as his foot lifted, the steady pressure on the sole as he pushed down. He took his right hand off the wheel as his left crossed in front of him...

On the table, the metal bug whirred as it turned to the right. There was applause from the people he only vaguely sensed standing around him. Sweat dripped down his neck as he guided the device through a left turn, then another right. It was too much. The bug reached the edge of the table and try as he might, he could not get it straightened out. One of the doctors caught it and placed it in the center of the table.

"Would you like to rest, Megan?"

"No," he said, not allowing himself to relax. "Let me try again." Behind him, an entire wall flashed and blinked as the computer found itself taxed to

its limits, sorting the confusing neural impulses that gathered on the stump of his spinal cord, translating the information, and broadcasting it to the servos in the remotalog device. He made it start, then stopped it before it reached the edge of the table. Just how he had done it was still mostly mysterious, but he felt he was beginning to get a handle on it. Sometimes it worked best if he tried to trick himself into thinking he could still walk and then just did it. Other times the bug just sat there, not fooled. It knew he could not walk. It knew he was never going to—

A white-sheeted form was being wheeled down the corridor toward the door to the operating room. Inside, from the gallery, he saw them transfer the body onto the table. The lights were very bright. He blinked, confused by them. But they were turning him over now, and that made it much better. Something cool touched the back of his neck—

"A thousand pardons, sir," Megan said, briskly fast-forwarding the tape. "You're not ready for that. *I'm* not ready for that."

He was not sure what she was talking about. He knew he needed the operation. It was going to improve the neural interfaces, which would make it easier for him to operate the new remotes they were developing. It was exciting to be involved in the early stages of…

"Oh. Right. I'm…"

"Q.M. Cooper," she said, and looked dubiously into his eyes. "Are you sure you wouldn't rather wait?"

"No. Show me more."

The nights were the worst. Not all of them, but when it was bad it was very bad. During the day there was acceptance, or some tough armor that contained the real despair. For days at a time he could be happy, he could accept what had happened, know that he must struggle but that the struggle was worth it. For most of his life he knew that what had happened was not the end of the world, that he could lead a full, happy life. There were people who cared about him. His worst fears had not been realized. Pleasure was still possible, happiness could be attained. Even sexual pleasures had not vanished. They were different and sometimes awkward, but he didn't mind.

But alone at night, it could all fall apart. The darkness stripped his defenses and he was helpless, physically and emotionally.

He could not move. His legs were dead meat. He was repulsive, disgusting, rotting away, a hideous object no one could ever love. The tube had slipped out and the sheets were soaked with urine. He was too ashamed to buzz for the nurse.

He wept silently. When he was through, he coldly began plotting the best way to end his life.

She held him until the worst of the shaking passed. He cried like a child who cannot understand the hurt, and like a weary old man. For the longest time he could not seem to make his eyes open. He did not want to see anything.

"Do I...do I have to see the next part?" He heard the whine in his voice.

She covered his face with kisses, hugging him, giving him wordless reassurance that everything would be all right. He accepted it gratefully.

"No. You don't have to see anything. I don't know why I showed you as much as I have, but I can't show you that part even if I wanted to because I destroyed it. It's too dangerous. I'm no more suicidal now than anybody else, but transing that next tape would strip me naked and maybe drive me crazy, or anybody who looked at it. The strongest of us is pretty fragile, you know. There is so much primal despair just under our surfaces that you don't dare fool around with it."

"How close did you come?"

"Gestures," she said, easily. "Two attempts, both discovered in plenty of time." She kissed him again, looked into his eyes and gave him a tentative smile. She seemed satisfied with what she saw, for she patted his cheek and reached for the transer controls again.

"One more little item," she said, "and we'll call it a night. This is a happy tape. I think we could both use it."

There was a girl in a sidekick. This machine was to the Golden Gypsy what a Wright Brothers Flyer was to a supersonic jet. Megan was almost invisible. Chromed struts stuck out all over, hydraulic cylinders hissed. There were welds visible where the thing had been bashed into shape. When she moved, the thing whined like a sick dog. Yet she was moving, and under her own control, placing one foot laboriously in front of the other, biting her tongue in concentration as she pondered her next step. Quick cut to—

—next year's model. It was still ponderous, it poked through her clothes, it was hydraulic and no-nonsense orthopedic. But she was moving well. She was able to walk naturally; the furrows of concentration were gone from her brow. This one had hands. They were heavy metal gauntlets, but she could move each finger separately. The smile she gave the camera had more genuine warmth than Cooper had seen from her since the accident.

"The new Mark Three," said an off-camera voice, and Cooper saw Megan running. She did high kicks, jumped up and down. And yet this new model was actually bulkier than the Mark Two had been. There was a huge bulge on her back, containing computers which had previously been external to the machine. It was the first self-contained sidekick. No one would ever call it pretty, but he could imagine the feeling of freedom it must have given Megan, and wondered why she wasn't playing the trans-track. He started to look away from the screen *but this was no time to worry about things like that. He was free!*

He held his hands before his face, turning them, looking at the trim leather gloves he would always have to wear, and not caring, because they were so much better than the mailed fists, or the fumbling hooks before that. It was the first day in his new sidekick, and it was utterly glorious. He ran, he shouted and jumped and cavorted, and everyone laughed with him and applauded his every move. He was powerful! He was going to change the world. Nothing could stop him. Some day, everyone would know the name of Me(Q.M.)gan Gallo(Cooper)way. There was nothing, nothing in the world he couldn't do. He would—

"Oh!" He clapped his hands to his face to shock. "Oh! You turned it off!"

"Sort of coitus interruptus, huh?" she said, smugly.

"But I want more!"

"That would be a mistake. It's not good to get too deeply into someone else's joy or sadness. Besides, how do you know it stays that good?"

"How could it not? You have everything now, you—" He stopped, and looked into her face. She was smiling. He would come back to the moment many times in days to come, searching for a hint of mockery, but he would never find it. The walls were gone. She had showed him everything there was to know about her, and he knew his life would never be the same.

"I love you," he said.

Her expression changed so slightly he might have missed it had he not been so exquisitely attuned to her emotions. Her lower lip quivered, and sadness outlined her eyes. She drew a ragged breath.

"This is sudden. Maybe you should wait until you've recovered from—"

"No." He touched her face with his hands and made her look at him. "No. I could only put it into words just now, in that crazy moment. It wasn't an easy thing for me to say."

"Oh boy," she said, in a quiet monotone.

"What's the matter?" When she wouldn't talk, he shook her head gently back and forth between his hands. "You don't love me, is that it? I'd rather you came out and said it now."

"That's not it. I do love you. You've never been in love before, have you?"

"No. I wondered if I'd know what it would feel like. Now I know."

"You don't know the half of it. Sometimes, you almost wish it was a more rational thing, that it wouldn't hit you when you feel you can least cope with it."

"I guess we're really helpless, aren't we?"

"You said it." She sighed again, then rose and took his hand. She pulled him toward the bed.

"Come on. You're going to have to learn to make love."

He had feared it would be bizarre. It was not. He had thought about it a great deal in the last weeks and had come up with no answers. What would she do? If she could feel nothing below the collarbone, how could any sexual activity have any meaning for her?

One answer should have been obvious. She still felt with her shoulders, her neck, her face, lips, and ears. A second answer had been there for him to see, but he had not made the connection. She was still capable of erection. Sensation from her genitals never reached her brain, but the nerves from her clitoris to her spinal cord were undamaged. Complex things happened, things she never explained completely, involving secondary and tertiary somatic effects, hormones, transfer arousal, the autonomic and vascular systems of the body.

"Some of it is natural adaptation," she said, "and some of it has been augmented by surgery and microprocessors. Quadraplegics could do this before the kind of nerve surgery we can do today, but not as easily as I can. It's like a blind person, whose sense of hearing and touch sharpen in compensation. The areas of my body I can still feel are now more sensitive, more responsive. I know a woman who can have an orgasm from having her elbow stimulated. With me, elbows are not so great."

"With all they can do, why can't they bridge the gap where your spinal cord was cut? If they can make a machine to read the signals your brain sends out, why can't they make one to put new signals into the rest of your body, and take the signals that come from your lower body and put them into—"

"It's a different problem. They're working on it. Maybe in fifteen or twenty years."

"Here?"

"More around here. All around my neck, from ear to ear...that's it. Keep doing that. And why don't you find something for your hands to do?"

"But you can't feel this. Can you?"

"Not directly. But nice things are happening. Just look."

"Yeah."

"Then don't worry about it. Just keep doing it."

"What about this?"

"Not particularly."

"This?"

"You're getting warmer."

"But I thought you—"

"Why don't you do a little less thinking? Come on, put it in. I want this to be good for you, too. And don't think it won't do something for me."

"Whatever you say. Oh, lord, that feels...hey, how did you do that?"

"You ask a lot of questions."

"Yeah, but you can't move any muscles down there."

"A simple variation on the implants that keep me from making a mess of myself. Now, honestly, Q.M. Don't you think the time for questions is over?"

"I think you're right."

"You want to see something funny?" she asked.

They were sprawled in each other's arms, looking at the smoke belching from her ridiculous bedposts. She had flipped on the holo generators, and her bedroom had vanished in a Mark Twain illusion. They floated down the Mississippi River. The bed rocked gently. Cooper felt indecently relaxed.

"Sure."

"Promise you won't laugh?"

"Not unless it's funny."

She rolled over and spread her arms and legs, face down on the bed. The sidekick released her, stood up, found the holo control, and turned off the river. It put one knee on the bed, carefully turned Megan onto her back, crossed her legs for her, then sat beside her on the edge of the bed and crossed its own legs, swinging them idly. By then he was laughing, as she had intended. It sat beside her and encased her left forearm and hand, lit a cigarette and placed it in her mouth, then released her hand again. It went to a chair across the room and sat down.

He jumped when she touched him. He turned and saw a thin hand on his elbow, not able to grasp him, not strong enough to do more than nudge.

"Will you put this out?" She inclined her head toward him. He carefully removed the cigarette from her lips, cupping his hand under the ash. When he turned back to her, her eyes were guarded.

"This is me, too," she said.

"I know that." He frowned, and tried to get closer to the truth, for his own sake as well as hers. "I hadn't thought about it much. You look very helpless like this."

"I *am* very helpless."

"Why are you doing it?"

"Because *nobody* sees me like this, except doctors. I wanted to know if it made any difference."

"No. No difference at all. I've seen you this way before. I'm surprised you asked."

"You shouldn't be. I hate myself like this. I disgust myself. I expect everyone else to react the way I do."

"You expect wrong." He hugged her, then drew back and studied her face. "Do you...would you like to make love again? Not this second, I mean, but a little later. Like this."

"God, no. But thanks for offering." When she was inside the side-kick again she touched his face with her be-ringed hand. Her expression was an odd mixture of satisfaction and uncertainty.

"You keep passing the tests, Cooper. As fast as I can throw them at you. I wonder what I'm going to do with you?"

"Are there more tests?"

She shook her head. "No. Not for you."

"You're going to be late for work," Anna-Louise said, as Cooper lifted one of her suitcases and followed her out of the shuttleport waiting room.

"I don't care." Anna-Louise gave him an odd look. He knew why. When they had been together he had always been eager for his shift to begin. By now he was starting to hate it. When he worked he could not be with Megan.

"You've really got it bad, don't you?" she said.

He smiled at her. "I sure do. This is the first time I've been away from her in weeks. I hope you aren't angry."

"Me? No. I'm flattered that you came to see me off. You...well, you wouldn't have thought of something like that a month ago. Sorry."

"You're right." He put the suitcase down beside the things she had been carrying. A porter took them through the lock and into the shuttle. Cooper leaned against the sign that announced "New Dresden, Clavius, Tycho Under." "I didn't know if you'd be angry, but I thought I ought to be here."

Anna-Louise smiled wryly. "Well, she's certainly changed you. I'm happy for you. Even though I still think she's going to hurt you, you'll gain something from it. You've come alive since the last time I saw you."

"I wanted to ask you about that," he said, slowly. "Why do you think she'll hurt me?"

She hesitated, hitching at her pants and awkwardly scuffing her shoes on the deck.

"You don't like your work as much as you did. Right?"

"Well...yeah. I guess not. Mostly because I'd like to spend more time with her."

She looked at him, cocking her head.

"Why don't you quit?"

"What...you mean—"

"Just quit. She wouldn't even notice the money she spent to support you."

He grinned at her. "You've got the wrong guy, A.L.. I don't have any objections to being supported by a woman. Did you really think I was that old-fashioned?"

She shook her head.

"But you think money will be a problem."

She nodded. "Not the fact that she has it. The fact that you don't."

"Come on. She doesn't care that I'm not rich."

Anna-Louise looked at him a long time, then smiled.

"Good," she said, and kissed him. She hurried into the shuttle, waving over her shoulder.

Megan received a full sack of mail every day. It was the tip of the iceberg; she employed a staff on Earth to screen it, answer fan mail with form letters, turn down speaking engagements, and repel parasites. The remainder was sent on, and fell into three categories. The first, and by far the largest, was the one out of a thousand matters that came in unsolicited and, after sifting, seemed to have a chance of meriting her attention. She read some, threw most away, unopened.

The last two categories she always read. One was job offers, and the other was material from facilities on Earth doing research into the nervous system. Often the latter was accompanied by requests for money. She usually sent a check.

At first she tried to keep him up on the new developments but she soon realized he would never have her abiding and personal interest in matters neurological. She was deeply involved with what is known as the cutting edge of the research. Nothing new was discovered, momentous or trivial, that did not end up on her desk the next day. There were odd side effects: The Wacky Dust which had figured in their first meeting had been sent by a lab which had stumbled across it and didn't know what to do with it.

Her computer was jammed with information on neurosurgery. She could call up projections of when certain milestones might be reached, from minor enhancements all the way up to complete regeneration of the neuron net. Most of the ones Cooper saw looked dismal. The work was not well funded. Most money for medical research went to the study of radiation disease.

Reading the mail in the morning was far from the high point of the day. The news was seldom good. But he was not prepared for her black depression one morning two weeks after Anna-Louise's departure.

"Did someone die?" he asked, sitting down and reaching for the coffee.

"Me. Or I'm in the process."

When she looked up and saw his face she shook her head.

"No, it's not medical news. Nothing so straightforward." She tossed a sheet of paper across the table at him. "It's from *Allgemein Fernsehen Gesellschaft*. They will pay any price…if I'll do essentially what I've been doing all along for Feelie-corp. They regret that the board of directors will not permit the company to enter any agreement wherein AFG has less than total creative control of the product."

"How many does that make now?"

"That you've seen? Seventeen. There have been many more that never got past the preliminary stage."

"So independent production isn't going to be as easy as you thought."

"I never said it would be easy."

"Why not use your own money? Start your own company."

"We've looked into it, but the answers are all bad. The war between GWA and Royal Dutch Shell makes the tax situation…" She looked at him, quickly shifted gears. "It's hard to explain."

That was a euphemism for "you wouldn't understand." He did not mind it. She had tried to explain her business affairs to him and all it did was frustrate them both. He had no head for it.

"Okay. So what do you do now?"

"Oh, there's no crisis yet. My investments are doing all right. Some war losses, but I'm getting out of GWA. The bank balance is in fair shape." That was another euphemism. She had begun using it when she realized he was baffled by the baroque mechanism that was *Gitano de Oro*, her corporate self. He had seen some astounding bills from Sidekick Inc., but if she said she was not hurting he would believe her.

She had been toying with the salt shaker while her eggs benedict grew cold. Now she gave a derisive snort, and glanced at him.

"The funny thing is, I've just proved all the theoreticians wrong. I've made a breakthrough no one believed was possible. I could set the whole industry on its ear, and I can't get a job."

It was the first he heard of it. He raised one eyebrow in polite inquiry.

"Damn it, Cooper. I've been wondering how to tell you this. The problem is I didn't realize until something you said a few days ago that you didn't know my transcorder is built in to my sidekick."

"I thought your camera crew—"

"I know you did, now. I swear I didn't realize that. No, the crew makes nothing but visual tapes. It's edited into the trans-tape which is made by my sidekick. I leave it on all the time."

He chewed on that one for a while, and frowned at her.

"You're saying you got love on tape."

"The moment of falling in love. I got it all."

"Why didn't you tell me?"

She sighed. "Trans-tapes have to be developed. They aren't like viddies. They just came back from the lab yesterday. I transed them last night, while you slept."

"I'd like to see them."

"Maybe someday," she hedged. "For right now, it's too personal. I want to keep this just for myself. Can you understand that? God knows I've never sought privacy very hard in my life, but this…" She looked helpless.

"I guess so." He considered it a little longer. "But if you sell them, it'll hardly be personal then, will it?"

"I don't want to sell them, Q.M."

He said nothing, but he had been hoping for something a little stronger than that. For the first time, he began to feel alarmed.

He did not think about money, or about trans-tapes, in the next two weeks. There was too much else to do. He took his accumulated vacation and sick leave and the two of them traveled to Earth. It might as well have been a new planet.

It was not only that he went to places he had never seen. They went there in a style to which he was not accustomed. It was several steps above what most people thought of as first class. Problems did not exist on this planet. Luggage took care of itself. He never saw any money. There was no schedule that had to be met. Cars and planes and hypersonic shuttles were always ready to whisk them anywhere they wanted to go. When he mentioned that all this might be costing too much she explained that she was paying for none of it. Everything was provided by eager corporate suitors. Cooper thought they behaved worse than any love-smitten adolescent. They were as demonstrative as puppies, and as easily forgiving when she snubbed them while accepting their gifts.

She did not seem afraid of kidnapping, either, though he saw little in the way of security. When he asked, she told him that security one kept tripping over was just amateur guntoting. She advised him never to think of it again, that it was all taken care of.

"You wouldn't market that tape, would you?" There, he finally had it out in the open.

"Well, let me put it this way. When I first came to you, I was near a nervous breakdown from just thinking about going into the sex tape business. This is much more personal, much dearer to me than plain old intercourse."

"Ah. I feel better."

She reached across the bed and squeezed his hand, looked at him fondly.

"You really don't want me to market it, do you?"

"No. I really don't. The first day I saw you, a good friend warned me that if I got into bed with you my technique would be seen by ninety million slobs."

She laughed. "Well, Anna-Louise was wrong. You can put that possibility right out of your mind. For one thing, there were no vidicams around, so no one will ever see you making love to me. For another, they wouldn't use my sensations while I'm making love if I ever get into the sex-tape business. Those are a little esoteric for my audience. That would all be put together in the editing room. There would be visuals and emotionals from me—showing me making love in the regular way—and there'd be a stand-in for the physical sensations."

"Pardon my asking," he said, "but wasn't your reaction that first day a little overblown, then?"

She laughed. "Much ado about nothing?"

"Yeah. I mean, it'd be your body on the screen—"

"—but I've already shown you I don't care about that."

"And if you were making love in the conventional way, you'd hardly be emotionally transported—"

"It would register as sheer boredom."

"—so I presume you'd splice in the emotional track from some other source, too." He frowned, no longer sure of what he was trying to say.

"You're catching on. I told you this business was all fake. And I can't really explain why it bothers me so much, except to say I don't want to surrender that part of myself, even a little bit. I *taped* my first intercourse, but I didn't show it to anybody until you saw it. And what about you? You're worried that I might sell a tape of falling in love with you. You wouldn't be on it at all."

"Well, it was something we shared."

"Exactly. I don't want to share it with anyone else."

"I'm glad you don't plan to sell it."

"My darling, I would hate that as much as you would."

It was not until later that he realized she had never ruled out the possibility.

151

They went back to the Bubble when Cooper's vacation time was over. She never suggested he quit his job. They checked into a different suite. She said the cost had little to do with it, but this time he was not so sure. He had begun to see a haunted expression around her eyes as she read letter after letter rejecting increasingly modest proposals.

"They really know the game," she told him bitterly, one night. "Every one of those companies will give me any salary I want to name, but I have to sign their contract. You begin to think it's a conspiracy."

"Is it?"

"I really don't know. It may be just shrewdness. I talk about how stupid they are, and artistically they live up to that description. Morally, there's not one of them who wouldn't pay to have his daughter gang-raped if it meant a tenth-point ratings jump. But financially, you can't fault them. These are the folks who have suppressed the cures for a dozen diseases because they didn't cost enough to use. I'm speaking of the parent congloms, of course, the real governments. If they ever find a way to profit off nuclear war we'll be having them every other week. And they have obviously decided that television outside their control is dangerous."

"So what does it mean to you and me?"

"I got into the business by accident. I won't go crazy if I'm not working."

"And the money?"

"We'll get along."

"Your expenses must be pretty high."

"They are. No sense lying about that. I can cut out a lot, but the sidekick is never going to be cheap."

As if to underscore her words of the night before, the Golden Gypsy chose the next morning to get temperamental. The middle finger of Megan's right hand was frozen in the extended position. She joked about it.

"As they say, 'The perversity of the universe tends toward the maximum.' Why the *middle* finger? Can you answer me that?"

"I guess you'll have the repairman up here before I get back."

"Not this time," she decided. "It'll be hard, but I'll struggle through. I'll wait until we return to Earth, and drop by the factory."

She called Sidekick while he dressed for work. He could hear her without being able to make out the words. She was still on the phone when he came out of the bathroom and started for the door. She punched the hold button and caught him, turned him around, and kissed him hard.

"I love you very much," she said.

"I love you, too."

She was not there when he returned. She had left a tape playing. When he went to turn it off he found the switch had been sealed. On the screen, a younger Megan moved through the therapy room in her Mark One sidekick. It was a loop, repeating the same scene.

He waited for almost an hour, then went to look for her. Ten minutes later he learned she had taken the 0800 shuttle for Earth.

A day later he realized he was not going to be able to get her on the telephone. That same day he heard the news that she had signed a contract with Telecommunion, and as he turned off the set he saw the trans-tape which had been sitting on top of it, unnoticed.

He got out the Transer she had left behind, donned the headset, inserted the cassette, turned on the machine. Half an hour later it turned itself off, and he came back to reality with a beatific smile on his face.

Then he began to scream.

They released him from the hospital in three days. Still numb from sedation, he went to the bank and closed his account. He bought a ticket for New Dresden.

He located Anna-Louise in the barracks of the police academy. She was surprised to see him, but not as much as he had expected. She took him to a lunar park—an area of trees with a steel roof and corridors radiating in all directions—sat him down, and let him talk.

"…and you were the only one who seemed to have understood her. You warned me the first day. I want to know how you did that, and I want to know if you can explain it to me."

She did not seem happy, but he could see it was not directed at him.

"You say the tape really did what she claimed? It captured love?"

"I don't think anyone could doubt it."

She shivered. "That frightens me more than anything I've heard in a long time." He waited, not knowing exactly what she meant by that. When she spoke again, it was not about her fears. "Then it proved to your satisfaction that she really *was* in love with you."

"Absolutely."

She studied his face. "I'll take your word for it. You look like someone who would recognize it." She got up and began to walk, and he followed her. "Then I've done her an injustice. I thought at first that you were just a plaything to her. From what you said, I changed my mind, even before I left the station."

"But you were still sure she'd hurt me. Why?"

"Cooper, have you studied much history? Don't answer that. Whatever you learned, you got from corporate-run schools. Have you heard of the great ideological struggles of the last century?"

"What the hell does that have to do with me?"

"Do you want my opinions or not? You came a long way to hear them." When she was sure he'd listen, she went on.

"This is very simplified. I don't have time to give you a history lesson, and I'm pretty sure you aren't in the mood for one. But there was capitalism, and there was communism. Both systems were run, in the end, by money. The capitalists said money was really a good thing. The communists kept trying to pretend that money didn't actually exist. They were both wrong, and money won in the end. It left us where we are now. The institutions wholly devoted to money swallowed up *all* political philosophies."

"Listen, I know you're a crazy Loonie and you think Earth is—"

"Shut up!" He was caught off guard when she spun him around. For a moment he thought she would hit him. "Damn you, that might have been funny in the Bubble, but now you're on *my* territory and *you're* the crazy one. I don't have to listen to your smoggie shit!"

"I'm sorry."

"Forget it!" she shouted, then ran her hand through her short hair. "Forget the history lesson, too. Megan Galloway is trying to make it as best she can in a world that rewards nothing so well as it rewards total self-interest. So am I, and so are you. Today or yesterday, Earth or Luna, it doesn't really matter. It's probably always been like that. It'll be that way tomorrow. I am *very sorry*, Q.M., I was right about her, but *she had no choice*, and I could see that from the start."

"That's what I want you to explain to me."

"If she was anybody but the Golden Gypsy, she might have gone with you to the ends of the world, endured any poverty. She might not have cared that you were never going to be rich. I'm not saying you wouldn't have had your problems, but you'd have had the same chance anyone else has to overcome them. But there is only one Golden Gypsy, and there's a reason for that."

"You're talking about the machine now. The sidekick."

"Yes. She called me yesterday. She was crying. I didn't know what to say to her, so I just listened. I felt sorry for her, and I don't even *like* her. I guess she knew you'd seek me out. She wanted you to hear some things she was ashamed to tell you. I *really* don't like her for that, but what can I do?

"There is only one Golden Gypsy. It is not owned by Megan Galloway. Rich as she is, she couldn't afford that. She leases it, at a monthly fee that is more than you or I will ever see in our lives, and she pays for a service contract that is almost that much money again. She had not been on television for over a month. Babe, it's not like there aren't other people who would like to use a machine like that. There must be a million of them or more. If you ran a conglom that owned that machine, who would you rent it to? Some nobody, or someone who will wear it in ten billion homes every night, along with a promo for your company?"

"That's what they told her on the phone? That they were going to take the machine away."

"The way she put it was they threatened to take her *body* away."

"But that's not enough!" He was weeping again, and he had thought he was past that stage. "I would have understood that. I told her I didn't care if she was in a sidekick, in a wheelchair, in bed, or whatever."

"Your opinion is hardly the one that matters, there," Anna-Louise pointed out.

"No, what I'm saying is, I don't *care* if she had to sign a contract she didn't like to do things she hates. Not if it means that much to her. If having the Golden Gypsy is that important. That wasn't enough reason to walk out on me."

"Well, I think she gave you credit for that much. She was less certain you'd forgive her for the other thing she had to do, which was sell the tape she made of her falling in love with you. But maybe she'd have tried to make you understand why she had to do that, too…except that wasn't her real problem. The thing is, *she* couldn't live with it, not with her betrayal of herself, if you were around to remind her of the magnitude of the thing she had sold."

He looked at it from all angles, taking his time. He thought it would be too painful to put into words, but he gave it a try.

"She could keep me, or she could keep her body. She couldn't keep both."

"I'm afraid that's the equation. There's a rather complex question of self-respect in there, too. I don't think she figured she could save much of that either way."

"And she chose the machine."

"You might have, too."

"But she *loved* me. Love is supposed to be the strongest thing there is."

"Get your brain out of the television set, Q.M."

"I think I hate her."

"That would be a big mistake."

But he was no longer listening.

He tried to kill her, once, shortly after the tape came out, more because it seemed like the right thing to do than because he really wanted to. He never got within a mile of her. Her security had his number, all right.

The tape was a smash, the biggest thing ever to hit the industry. Within a year, all the other companies had imitations, mostly bootlegged from the original. Copyright skirmishes were fought in Hollywood and Tokyo.

He spent his time beachcombing, doing a lot of swimming. He found that he now preferred flat water. He roamed, with no permanent address, but the checks found him, no matter where he was. The first was accompanied with a detailed royalty statement showing that he was getting fifty percent of the profits from sales of the tape. He tore it up and mailed it back. The second one was for the original amount plus interest plus the new royalties. He smeared it with his blood and paid to have it hand-delivered to her.

The tape she had left behind continued to haunt him. He had kept it, and viewed it when he felt strong enough. Again and again the girl in the wheezing sidekick walked across the room, her face set in determination. He remembered her feeling of triumph to be walking, even so awkwardly.

Gradually, he came to focus on the last few meters of the tape. The camera panned away from Megan and came to rest on the face of one of the nurses. There was an odd expression there, as subtle and elusive as the face of the Mona Lisa. He knew this was what Megan had wanted him to see, this was her last statement to him, her final plea for understanding. He willed himself to supply a trans-track for the nurse, to see with her eyes and feel with her skin. He could let no nuance escape him as he watched Megan's triumphant walk, the thing the girl had worked so long and hard to achieve. And at last he was sure that what the woman was feeling was an uglier thing than mere pity. That was the image Megan had chosen to leave him with: the world looking at Megan Galloway. It was an image to which she would never return, no matter what the price.

In a year he allowed himself to view the visual part of the love tape. They had used an actor to stand in for him, re-playing the scene in the Bubble and in the steam-boat bed. He had to admit it: she had never lied to him. The man did not even resemble Cooper. No one would be studying his lovemaking.

It was some time later before he actually transed the tape again. It was both calming and sobering. He wondered what they could sell using this new commodity, and the thought frightened him as much as it had Anna-Louise. But he was probably the only spurned lover in history who knew, beyond a doubt, that she actually *had* loved him.

Surely that counted for something.

✦

His hate died quickly. His hurt lasted much longer, but a day came when he could forgive her.

Much later, he knew she had done nothing that needed his forgiveness.

BAGATELLE

I've written a lot of stories set on the moon. Many of them are in what I call my "Eight Worlds" future history. The central postulate of those stories is that the Earth has been invaded by creatures from a gas giant planet. Humanity on our home planet has been wiped out, all our works destroyed, because we were seen as an infection that threatened the only true intelligent beings on Earth, namely dolphins and whales. These stories originated when the ecology movement was really gathering steam, and I had been reading the books of John Lilly concerning his work with dolphins. It seemed possible to me—still does—that we might not recognize a completely different form of intelligence, one that does not use tools, but could in some ways we will never fathom be even more intelligent than we are. And it stood to reason that beings from, say, Jupiter, would float in that incredible stew of atmosphere much like whales do in water.

Then there was another set of stories, not really organized as such (I'm no Heinlein or Niven when it comes to constructing future histories), starring Anna-Louise Bach, a cop on Luna. Some readers have assumed these stories were part of the Eight Worlds, but they're not, really. Officer Bach's universe is harsher, with crime problems that I never addressed in the Eight Worlds. I have written of her as a rookie beat cop, and all the way up to chief of police in the underground city of New Dresden. This story concerns the worst threat she ever faced.

There was a bomb on the Leystrasse, level forty-five, right outside the Bagatelle Flower and Gift Shoppe, about a hundred meters down the promenade from Prosperity Plaza.

159

"I am a bomb," the bomb said to passersby. "I will explode in four hours, five minutes, and seventeen seconds. I have a force equal to fifty thousand English tons of trinitrololuene."

A small knot of people gathered to look at it.

"I will go off in four hours, four minutes, and thirty-seven seconds."

A few people became worried as the bomb talked on. They remembered business elsewhere and hurried away, often toward the tube trains to King City. Eventually, the trains became overcrowded and there was some pushing and shoving.

The bomb was a metal cylinder, a meter high, two meters long, mounted on four steerable wheels. There was an array of four television cameras mounted on top of the cylinder, slowly scanning through ninety degrees. No one could recall how it came to be there. It looked a little like the municipal street-cleaning machines; perhaps no one had noticed it because of that.

"I am rated at fifty kilotons," the bomb said, with a trace of pride.

The police were called.

A *nuclear* bomb, you say?" Municipal Police Chief Anna-Louise Bach felt sourness in the pit of her stomach and reached for a box of medicated candy. She was overdue for a new stomach, but the rate she went through them on her job coupled with the size of her paycheck had caused her to rely more and more on these stopgap measures. And the cost of cloned transplants was going up.

"It says fifty kilotons," said the man on the screen. "I don't see what else it could be. Unless it's just faking, of course. We're moving in radiation detectors."

"You said 'it says.' Are you speaking of a note, or phone call, or what?"

"No. It's talking to us. Seems friendly enough, too, but we haven't gotten around to asking it to disarm itself. It could be that its friendliness won't extend that far."

"No doubt." She ate another candy. "Call in the bomb squad, of course. Then tell them to do nothing until I arrive, other than look the situation over. I'm going to make a few calls, then I'll be there. No more than thirty minutes."

"All right. Will do."

There was nothing for it but to look for help. No nuclear bomb had ever been used on Luna. Bach had no experience with them, nor did her bomb crew. She brought her computer on line.

Roger Birkson liked his job. It wasn't so much the working conditions—which were appalling—but the fringe benefits. He was on call for thirty days, twenty-four hours a day, at a salary that was nearly astronomical. Then he got eleven months paid vacation. He was paid for the entire year whether or not he ever had to exercise his special talents during his thirty days duty. In that way, he was like a firefighter. In a way, he *was* a firefighter.

He spent his long vacations in Luna. No one had ever asked Birkson why he did so; had they asked, he would not have known. But the reason was a subconscious conviction that one day the entire planet Earth would blow up in one glorious fireball. He didn't want to be there when it happened.

Birkson's job was bomb disarming for the geopolitical administrative unit called CommEcon Europe. On a busy shift he might save the lives of twenty million CE Europeans.

Of the thirty-five Terran bomb experts vacationing on Luna at the time of the Leystrasse bomb scare, Birkson happened to be closest to the projected epicenter of the blast. The Central Computer found him twenty-five seconds after Chief Bach rang off from her initial report. He was lining up a putt on the seventeenth green of the Burning Tree underground golf course, a half kilometer from Prosperity Plaza, when his bag of clubs began to ring.

Birkson was wealthy. He employed a human caddy instead of the mechanical sort. The caddy dropped the flag he had been holding and went to answer it. Birkson took a few practice swings, but found that his concentration had been broken. He relaxed, and took the call.

"I need your advice," Bach said, without preamble. "I'm the Chief of Municipal Police for New Dresden, Anna-Louise Bach. I've had a report on a nuclear bomb on the Leystrasse, and I don't have anyone with your experience in these matters. Could you meet me at the tube station in ten minutes?"

"Are you crazy? I'm shooting for a seventy-five with two holes to go, an easy three-footer on seventeen and facing a par five on the last hole, and you expect me to go chasing after a hoax?"

"Do you know it to be a hoax?" Bach asked, wishing he would say yes.

"Well, no, I just now heard about it, myself. But ninety percent of them are, you know."

"Fine. I suggest you continue your game. And since you're so sure, I'm going to have Burning Tree sealed off for the duration of the emergency. I want you right there."

Birkson considered this.

"About how far away is this 'Leystrasse'?"

"About six hundred meters. Five levels up from you, and one sector over. Don't worry. There must be dozens of steel plates between you and the hoax. You just sit tight, all right?"

Birkson said nothing.

"I'll be at the tube station in ten minutes," Bach said. "I'll be in a special capsule. It'll be the last one for five hours." She hung up.

Birkson contemplated the wall of the underground enclosure. Then he knelt on the green and lined up his putt. He addressed the ball, tapped it, and heard the satisfying rattle as it sank into the cup.

He looked longingly at the eighteenth tee, then jogged off to the clubhouse.

"I'll be right back," he called over his shoulder.

Bach's capsule was two minutes late, but she had to wait another minute for Birkson to show up. She fumed, trying not to glance at the timepiece embedded in her wrist.

He got in, still carrying his putter, and their heads were jerked back as the capsule was launched. They moved for only a short distance, then came to a halt. The door didn't open.

"The system's probably tied up," Bach said, squirming. She didn't like to see the municipal services fail in the company of this Terran.

"Ah," Birkson said, flashing a grin with an impossible number of square teeth. "A panic evacuation, no doubt. You didn't have the tube system closed down, I suppose?"

"No," she said. "I…well, I thought there might be a chance to get a large number of people away from the area in case this thing does go off."

He shook his head, and grinned again. He put this grin after every sentence he spoke, like punctuation.

"You'd better seal off the city. If it's a hoax, you're going to have hundreds of dead and injured from the panic. It's a lost cause trying to evacuate. At most, you might save a few thousand."

"But…"

"Keep them stationary. If it goes off, it's no use anyway. You'll lose the whole city. And no one's going to question your judgment because you'll be dead. If it doesn't go off, you'll be sitting pretty for having prevented a panic. Do it. I *know*."

Bach began to really dislike this man right then, but decided to follow his advice. And his thinking did have a certain cold logic. She phoned the station and had the lid clamped on the city. Now the cars in the cross-tube ahead would be cleared, leaving only her priority capsule moving.

They used the few minutes delay while the order was implemented to size each other up. Bach saw a blonde, square-jawed young man in a checkered sweater and gold knickers. He had a friendly face, and that was what puzzled her. There was no trace of worry on his smooth features. His hands were steady, clasped calmly around the steel shaft of his putter. She wouldn't have called his manner cocky or assured, but he did manage to look cheerful.

She had just realized that he was looking her over, and was wondering what he saw, when he put his hand on her knee. He might as well have slapped her. She was stunned.

"What are you…get your hand off me you…you groundhog."

Birkson's hand had been moving upward. He was apparently unfazed by the insult. He turned in his seat and reached for her hand. His smile was dazzling.

"I just thought that since we're stalled here with nothing else to do, we might start getting to know each other. No harm in that, is there? I just hate to waste any time, that's all."

She wrenched free of his grasp and assumed a defensive posture, feeling trapped in a nightmare. But he relented, having no interest in pursuing the matter when he had been rebuffed.

"All right. We'll wait. But I'd like to have a drink with you, or maybe dinner. After this thing's wrapped up, of course."

"'This thing…' How can you think of something like that…?"

"At a time like this. I know. I've heard it. Bombs get me horny, is all. So okay, so I'll leave you alone." He grinned again. "But maybe you'll feel different when this is over."

For a moment she thought she was going to throw up from a combination of revulsion and fear. Fear of the bomb, not this awful man. Her stomach was twisted into a pretzel, and here he sat, thinking of sex. What was he, anyway?

The capsule lurched again, and they were on their way.

The deserted Leystrasse made a gleaming frame of stainless steel storefronts and fluorescent ceiling for the improbable pair hurrying from the tube station in the Plaza: Birkson in his anachronistic golf togs, cleats rasping on the polished rock floor, and Bach half a meter taller than him, thin like a Lunarian. She wore the regulation uniform of the Municipal Police, which was a blue armband and cap with her rank of chief emblazoned on them, a shoulder holster, an equipment belt around her waist from which dangled the shining and lethal-looking tools of her trade, cloth slippers, and a few scraps of clothing in arbitrary places. In the benign environment of Lunar corridors, modesty had died out ages ago.

They reached the cordon which had been established around the bomb, and Bach conferred with the officer in charge. The hall was echoing with off-key music.

"What's that?" Birkson asked.

Officer Walters, the man to whom Bach had been speaking, looked Birkson over, weighing just how far he had to go in deference to this grinning weirdo. He was obviously the bomb expert Bach had referred to in an earlier call, but he was a Terran, and not a member of the force. Should he be addressed as 'sir'? He couldn't decide.

"It's the bomb. It's been singing to us for the last five minutes. Ran out of things to say, I guess."

"Interesting." Swinging the putter lazily from side to side, he walked to the barrier of painted steel crowd-control sections. He started sliding one of them to the side.

"Hold it…ah, sir," Walters said.

"Wait a minute, Birkson," Bach confirmed, running to the man and almost grabbing his sleeve. She backed away at the last moment.

"It said no one's to cross that barrier," Walters supplied to Bach's questioning glance. "Says it'll blow us all to the Farside."

"What is that damn thing, anyway?" Bach asked, plaintively.

Birkson withdrew from the barrier and took Bach aside with a tactful touch on the arm. He spoke to her with his voice just low enough for Walters to hear.

"It's a cyborged human connected to a bomb, probably a uranium device," he said. "I've seen the design. It's just like one that went off in Johannesburg three years ago. I didn't know they were still making them."

"I heard about it," Bach said, feeling cold and alone. "Then you think it's really a bomb? How do you know it's a cyborg? Couldn't it be tape recordings, or a computer?"

Birkson rolled his eyes slightly, and Bach reddened. Damn it, they were reasonable questions. And to her surprise, he could not defend his opinion logically. She wondered what she was stuck with. Was this man really the expert she took him to be, or a plaid-sweatered imposter?

"You can call it a hunch. I'm going to talk to this fellow, and I want you to roll up an industrial X-ray unit on the level below this while I'm doing it. On the level above, photographic film. You get the idea?"

"You want to take a picture of the inside of this thing. Won't that be dangerous?"

"Yeah. Are your insurance premiums paid up?"

Bach said nothing, but gave the orders. A million questions were spinning through her head, but she didn't want to make a fool of herself by asking a stupid one. Such as: how much radiation did a big industrial X-ray machine produce when beamed through a rock and steel floor? She had a feeling she wouldn't like the answer. She sighed, and decided to let Birkson have his head until she felt he couldn't handle it. He was about the only hope she had.

And he was strolling casually around the perimeter, swinging his goddamn putter behind him, whistling bad harmony with the tune coming from the bomb. What was a career police officer to do? Back him up on the harmonica?

The scanning cameras atop the bomb stopped their back and forth motion. One of them began to track Birkson. He grinned his flashiest, and waved to it. The music stopped.

"I am a fifty kiloton nuclear bomb of the uranium-235 type," it said. "You must stay behind the perimeter I have caused to be erected here. You must not disobey this order."

Birkson held up his hands, still grinning, and splayed out his fingers.

"You got me, bud. I won't bother you. I was just admiring your casing. Pretty nice job, there. It seems a shame to blow it up."

"Thank you," the bomb said, cordially. "But that is my purpose. You cannot divert me from it."

"Never entered my mind. Promise."

"Very well. You may continue to admire me, if you wish, but from a safe distance. Do not attempt to rush me. All my vital wiring is safely protected, and I have a response time of three milliseconds. I can ignite long before you can reach me, but I do not wish to do so until the alloted time has come."

Birkson whistled. "That's pretty fast, brother. Much faster than me, I'm sure. It must be nice, being able to move like that after blundering along all your life with neural speeds."

"Yes, I find it very gratifying. It was a quite unexpected benefit of becoming a bomb."

This was more like it, Bach thought. Her dislike of Birkson had not blinded her to the fact that he had been checking out his hunch. And her questions had been answered: no tape array could answer questions like that, and the machine had as much as admitted that it had been a human being at one time.

Birkson completed a circuit, back to where Bach and Walters were standing. He paused, and said in a low voice, "Check out that time."

"What time?"

"What time did you say you were going to explode?" he yelled.

"In three hours, twenty-one minutes, and eighteen seconds," the bomb supplied.

"That time," he whispered. "Get your computers to work on it. See if it's the anniversary of any political group, or the time something happened that someone might have a grudge about." He started to turn away, then thought of something. "But most important, check the birth records."

"May I ask why?"

He seemed to be dreaming, but came back to them. "I'm just feeling this character out. I've got a feeling this might be his birthday. Find out who was born at that time—it can't be too many, down to the second—and try to locate them all. The one you can't find will be our guy. I'm betting on it."

"What are you betting? And how do you know for sure it's a man?"

That look again, and again she blushed. But, damn it, she had to ask questions. Why should he make her feel defensive about it?

"Because he's chosen a male voice to put over his speakers. I know that's not conclusive, but you get hunches after a while. As to what I'm betting...no, it's not my life. I'm sure I can get this one. How about dinner tonight if I'm right?" The smile was ingenuous, without the trace of lechery she thought she had seen before. But her stomach was still crawling. She turned away without answering.

For the next twenty minutes, nothing much happened. Birkson continued his slow stroll around the machine, stopping from time to time to shake his head in admiration. The thirty men and women of Chief Bach's police detail stood around nervously with nothing to do, as far away from the machine as pride would allow. There was no sense in taking cover.

Bach herself was kept busy coordinating the behind-the-scenes maneuvering from a command post that had been set up around the corner, in the Elysian Travel Agency. It had phones and a computer output printer. She sensed the dropping morale among her officers, who could see nothing going on. Had they known that surveying lasers were poking their noses around trees in the Plaza, taking bearings to within a thousandth of a millimeter, they might have felt a little better. And on the floor below, the X-ray had arrived.

Ten minutes later, the output began to chatter. Bach could hear it in the silent, echoing corridor from her position halfway between the travel agency and the bomb. She turned, and met a young officer with the green armband of a rookie. The woman's hand was ice-cold as she handed Bach the sheet of yellow printout paper. There were three names printed on it, and below that, some dates and events listed.

"This bottom information was from the fourth expansion of the problem," the officer explained. "Very low probability stuff. The three people were all born either on the second or within a three-second margin of error, in three different years. Everyone else has been contacted."

"Keep looking for these three, too," Bach said. As she turned away, she noticed that the young officer was pregnant, about in her fifth month. She thought briefly of sending her away from the scene, but what was the use?

Birkson saw her coming, and broke off his slow circuits of the bomb. He took the paper from her and scanned it. He tore off the bottom part without being told if was low probability, crumpled it, and let it drop to the floor. Scratching his head, he walked slowly back to the bomb.

"Hans?" he called out.

"How did you know my name?" the bomb asked.

"Ah, Hans, my boy, credit us with some sense. You can't have got into this without knowing that the MuniPol can do very fast investigations. Unless I've been underestimating you. Have I?"

"No," the bomb conceded. "I knew you would find out who I was. But it doesn't alter the situation."

"Of course not. But it makes for easier conversation. How has life been treating you, my friend?"

"Terrible," mourned the man who had become a fifty kiloton nuclear weapon.

Every morning Hans Leiter rolled out of bed and padded into his cozy water closet. It was not the standard model for residential apartment modules, but a special one he had installed after he moved in. Hans lived alone, and it was the one luxury he allowed himself. In his little palace, he sat in a chair that massaged him into wakefulness, washed him, shaved him, powdered him, cleaned his nails, splashed him with scent, them made love to him with a rubber imitation that was a good facsimile of the real thing. Hans was awkward with women.

He would dress, walk down three hundred meters of corridor, and surrender himself to a pedestrian slideway which took him as far as the Cross-Crisium Tube. There, he allowed himself to be fired like a projectile through a tunnel below the Lunar surface.

Hans worked in the Crisium Heavy Machinery Foundry. His job there was repairing almost anything that broke down. He was good at it; he was much more comfortable with machines than with people.

One day he made a slip and got his leg caught in a massive roller. It was not a serious accident, because the failsafe systems turned off the machine before his body or head could be damaged, but it hurt terribly and completely ruined the leg. It had to be taken off. While he was waiting for the cloned replacement limb to be grown, Hans had been fitted with a prosthetic.

It had been a revelation to him. It worked like a dream, as good as his old leg and perhaps better. It was connected to his severed leg nerve, but was equipped with a threshold cut-off circuit, and one day when he barked his artificial shin he saw that it had caused him no pain. He recalled the way that same injury had felt with his flesh and blood leg, and again he was impressed. He thought, too, of the agony when his leg had been caught in the machine.

When the new leg was ready for transplanting, Hans had elected to retain the prosthetic. It was unusual, but not unprecedented.

From that time on, Hans, who had never been known to his co-workers as talkative or social, withdrew even more from his fellow humans. He would speak only when spoken to. But people had observed him talking to the stamping press, and the water cooler, and the robot sweeper.

At night, it was Hans' habit to sit on his vibrating bed and watch the holovision until one o'clock. At that time, his kitchen would prepare him a late snack, roll it to him in his bed, and he would retire for the night.

For the last three years Hans had been neglecting to turn the set on before getting into bed. Nevertheless, he continued to sit quietly on the bed staring at the empty screen.

When she finished reading the personal data printout, Bach was struck once more at the efficiency of the machines in her control. This man was almost a cipher, yet there were nine thousand words in storage concerning his uneventful life, ready to be called up and printed into an excruciatingly boring biography.

"...so you came to feel that you were being controlled at every step in your life by machines," Birkson was saying. He was sitting on one of the barriers, swinging his legs back and forth. Bach joined him and offered the long sheet of printout. He waved it away. She could hardly blame him.

"But it's true!" the bomb said. "We all are, you know. We're part of this huge machine that's called New Dresden. It moves us around like parts on an assembly line, washes us, feeds us, puts us to bed and sings us to sleep."

"Ah," Birkson said, agreeably. "Are you a Luddite, Hans?"

"No!" the bomb said in a shocked voice. "Roger, you've missed the whole point. I don't want to destroy the machines. I want to serve them better. I wanted to become a machine, like my new leg. Don't you see? We're part of the machine, but we're the most inefficient part."

The two talked on, and Bach wiped the sweat from her palms. She couldn't see where all this was going, unless Birkson seriously hoped to talk Hans Leiter out of what he was going to do in—she glanced at the clock—two hours and forty-three minutes. It was maddening. On the one hand, she recognized the skill he was using in establishing a rapport with the cyborg. They were on a first-name basis, and at least the damn machine cared enough to argue its position. On the other hand, so what? What good was it doing?

Walters approached and whispered into her ear. She nodded, and tapped Birkson on the shoulder.

"They're ready to take the picture whenever you are," she said.

He waved her off.

"Don't bother me," he said, loudly. "This is getting interesting. So if what you say is true," he went on to Hans, getting up and pacing intently back and forth, this time inside the line of barriers, "maybe I ought to look into this myself. You really like being cyborged better than being human?"

"Infinitely so," the bomb said. He sounded enthusiastic. "I need no sleep now, and I no longer have to bother with elimination or eating. I have a tank for nutrients, which are fed into the housing where my brain and central nervous system are located." He paused. "I tried to eliminate the ups and downs of hormone flow and the emotional reactions that followed," he confided.

"No dice, huh?"

"No. Something always distracted me. So when I heard of this place where they would cyborg me and get rid of all that, I jumped at the chance."

Inactivity was making Bach impulsive. She *had* to say or do something.

"Where did you get the work done, Hans?" she ventured.

The bomb started to say something, but Birkson laughed loudly and slapped Bach hard on the back. "Oh, no, Chief. That's pretty tricky, right Hans? She's trying to get you to rat. That's not done, Chief. There's a point of honor involved."

"Who is that?" the bomb asked, suspiciously.

"Let me introduce Chief Anna-Louise Bach, of the New Dresden Police. Ann, meet Hans."

"Police?" Hans asked, and Bach felt goose-pimples when she detected a note of fright in the voice. What was this maniac trying to do, frightening the guy like that? She was close to pulling Birkson off the case. She held off because she thought she could see a familiar pattern in it, something she could use as a way to participate, even if ignominiously. It was the good guy-bad guy routine, one of the oldest police maneuvers in the book.

"Aw, don't be like that," Birkson said to Hans. "Not all cops are brutes. Ann here, she's a nice person. Give her a chance. She's only doing her job."

"Oh, I have no objection to police," the bomb said. "They are necessary to keep the social machine functioning. Law and order is a basic precept of the coming new Mechanical Society. I'm pleased to meet you, Chief Bach. I wish the circumstances didn't make us enemies."

"Pleased to meet you, Hans." She thought carefully before she phrased her next question. She wouldn't have to take the hardline approach to contrast herself with affable, buddy-buddy Birkson. She needn't be an antagonist, but it wouldn't hurt if she asked questions that probed at his motives.

"Tell me, Hans. You say you're not a Luddite. You say you like machines. Do you know how many machines you'll destroy if you set yourself off? And even more important, what you'll do to this social machine you've been talking about? You'll wipe out the whole city."

The bomb seemed to be groping for words. He hesitated, and Bach felt the first glimmer of hope since this insanity began.

"You don't understand. You're speaking from an organic viewpoint. Life is important to you. A machine is not concerned with life. Damage to a machine, even the social machine, is simply something to be repaired. In a way, I hope to set an example. I wanted to become a machine—"

"And the best, the very ultimate machine," Birkson put in, "is the atomic bomb. It's the end point of all mechanical thinking."

"Exactly," said the bomb, sounding very pleased. It was nice to be understood. "I wanted to be the very best machine I could possibly be, and it had to be this."

"Beautiful, Hans," Birkson breathed. "I see what you're talking about. So if we go on with that line of thought we logically come to the conclusion…" and he was off into an exploration of the fine points of the new Mechanistic world view.

Bach was trying to decide which was the crazier of the two, when she was handed another message. She read it, then tried to find a place to break into the conversation. But there was no convenient place. Birkson was more and more animated, almost frothing at the mouth as he discovered points of agreement between the two of them. Bach noticed her officers standing around nervously, following the conversation. It was clear from their expressions that they feared they were being sold out, that when zero hour arrived they would still be here watching intellectual pingpong. But long before that, she could have a mutiny on her hands. Several of them were fingering their weapons, probably without even knowing it.

She touched Birkson on the sleeve, but he waved her away. Damn it, this was too much. She grabbed him and nearly pulled him from his feet, swung him around until her mouth was close to his ear and growled.

"Listen to me, you idiot. They're going to take the picture. You'll have to stand back some. It's better if we're all shielded."

"Leave me *alone*," he shot back, and pulled from her grasp. But he was still smiling. "This is just getting interesting," he said, in a normal tone of voice.

Birkson came near to dying in that moment. Three guns were trained on him from the circle of officers, awaiting only the order to fire. They didn't like seeing their Chief treated that way.

Bach herself was damn near to giving the order. The only thing that stayed her hand was the knowledge that with Birkson dead, the machine might go off ahead of schedule. The only thing to do now was to get him out of the way and go on as best she could, knowing that she was doomed to failure. No one could say she hadn't given the expert a chance.

"But what I was wondering about," Birkson was saying, "was why today? What happened today? Is this the day Cyrus McCormick invented the combine harvester, or something?"

"It's my birthday," Hans said, somewhat shyly.

"Your *birthday*?" Birkson managed to look totally amazed to learn what he already knew. "Your birthday, That's *great*, Hans. Many happy returns of the day, my friend." He turned and took in all of the officers with an expansive sweep of his hands. "Let's sing, people. Come on, it's his birthday, for heaven's sake. *Happy birthday to you, happy birthday to you, happy birthday dear Hans…*"

He bellowed, he was off-key, he swept his hands in grand circles with no sense of rhythm. But so infectious was his mania that several of the officers found themselves joining in. He ran around the circle, pulling the words out of them with great scooping motions of his hands.

Bach bit down hard on the inside of her cheek to keep herself steady. *She had been singing, too.* The scene was so ridiculous, so blackly improbable…

She was not the only one who was struck the same way. One of her officers, a brave man who she knew personally to have shown courage under fire, fell on his face in a dead faint. A woman officer covered her face with her hands and fled down the corridor, making helpless coughing sounds. She found an alcove and vomited.

And still Birkson capered. Bach had her gun halfway out of the shoulder holster, when he shouted.

"What's a birthday without a party?" he asked. "Let's have a big party." He looked around, fixed on the flower shop. He started for it, and as he passed Bach he whispered, "Take the picture *now.*"

It galvanized her. She desperately wanted to believe he knew what he was doing, and just at the moment when his madness seemed total he had shown her the method. *A distraction.* Please, let it be a distraction. She turned and gave the prearranged signal to the officer standing at the edge of Prosperity Plaza.

She turned back in time to see Birkson smash in the window of the flower shop with his putter. It made a deafening crash.

"Goodness," said Hans, who sounded truly shocked. "Did you have to do that? That's private property."

"What does it matter?" Birkson yelled. "Hell, man, you're going to do much worse real soon. I'm just getting things started." He reached in and pulled out an armload of flowers, signaling to others to give him a hand. The police didn't like it, but soon were looting the shop and building a huge wreath just outside the line of barriers.

"I guess you're right," said Hans, a little breathlessly. A taste of violence had excited him, whetted his appetite for more to come. "But you startled me. I felt a real thrill, like I haven't felt since I was human."

"Then let's do it some more." And Birkson ran up and down one side of the street, breaking out every window he could reach. He picked up small articles he found inside the shops and threw them. Some of them shattered when they hit.

He finally stopped. Leystrasse had been transformed. No longer the scrubbed and air-conditioned Lunar environment, it had become as shattered, as chaotic and uncertain as the tension-filled emotional atmosphere it contained. Bach shuddered and swallowed the rising taste of bile. It was a precursor of things to come, she was sure. It hit her deeply to see the staid and respectable Leystrasse ravaged.

"A cake," Birkson said. "We have to have a cake. Hold on a minute, I'll be right back." He strode quickly toward Bach, took her elbow and turned her, pulled her insistently away with him.

"You have to get those officers away from here," he said, conversationally. "They're tense. They could explode at any minute. In fact," and he favored her with his imbecile grin, "they're probably more dangerous right now than the bomb."

"You mean you think it's a fake?"

"No. It's for real. I know the psychological pattern. After this much trouble, he won't want to be a dud. Other types, they're in it for the attention and they'd just as soon fake it. Not Hans. But what I mean is, I have him. I can get him. But I can't count on your officers. Pull them back and leave only two or three of your most trusted people."

"All right." She had decided again, more from a sense of helpless futility than anything else, to trust him. He *had* pulled a neat diversion with the flower shop and the X-ray.

"We may have him already," he went on, as they reached the end of the street and turned the corner. "Often, the X-ray is enough. It cooks some of the circuitry and makes it unreliable. I'd hope to kill him outright, but he's shielded. Oh, he's probably got a lethal dosage, but it'd take him days to die. That doesn't do us any good. And if his circuitry

174

is knocked out, the only way to find out is to wait. We have to do better than that. Here's what I want you to do."

He stopped abruptly and relaxed, leaning against the wall and gazing out over the trees and artificial sunlight of the Plaza. Bach could hear songbirds. They had always made her feel good before. Now all she could think of was incinerated corpses. Birkson ticked off points on his fingers.

She listened to him carefully. Some of it was strange, but no worse than she had already witnessed. And he really did have a plan. He really did. The sense of relief was so tremendous that it threatened to create a mood of euphoria in her, one not yet justified by the circumstances. She nodded curtly to each of his suggestions, then again to the officer who stood beside her, confirming what Birkson had said and turning it into orders. The young man rushed off to carry them out and Birkson started to return to the bomb. Bach grabbed him.

"Why wouldn't you let Hans answer my question about who did the surgical work on him? Was that part of your plan?" The question was half belligerant.

"Oh. Yeah, it was, in a way. I just grabbed the opportunity to make him feel closer to me. But it wouldn't have done you any good. He'll have a block against telling that, for sure. It could even be set to explode the bomb if he tries to answer that question. Hans is a maniac, but don't underestimate the people who helped him get where he is now. They'll be protected."

"Who are they?"

Birkson shrugged. It was such a casual, uncaring gesture that Bach was annoyed again.

"I have no idea. I'm not political, Ann. I don't know the Antiabortion Movement from the Freedom for Mauretania League. They build 'em, I take 'em apart. It's as simple as that. *Your* job is to find out how it happened. I guess you ought to get started on that."

"We already have," she conceded. "I just thought that…well, coming from Earth, where this sort of thing happens all the time, that you might know…damn it, Birkson. *Why?* Why is this happening?"

He laughed, while Bach turned red and went into a slow boil. Any of her officers, seeing her expression, would have headed for the nearest blast shelter. But Birkson laughed on. Didn't he give a damn about anything?

"Sorry," he forced out. "I've heard that question before, from other police chiefs. It's a good question." He waited, a half-smile on his face. When she didn't say anything, he went on.

"You don't have the right perspective on this, Ann."

"That's Chief Bach to you, damn you."

"Okay," he said, easily. "What you don't see is that this thing is no different from a hand grenade tossed into a crowd, or a bomb sent through the mail. It's a form of communication. It's just that today, with so many people, you have to shout a little louder to get any attention."

"But...who? They haven't even identified themselves. You're saying that Hans is a tool of these people. He's been wired into the bomb, with his own motives for exploding. Obviously he didn't have the resources to do this himself, I can see that."

"Oh, you'll hear from them. I don't think they expect him to be successful. He's a warning. If they were *really* serious they could find the sort of person they want, one who's politically committed and will die for the cause. Of course, they don't *care* if the bomb goes off; they'll be pleasantly surprised if it does. Then they can stand up and pound their chests for a while. They'll be famous."

"But where did they get the uranium? The security is..."

For the first time, Birkson showed a trace of annoyance.

"Don't be silly. The path leading to today was irrevocably set in 1945. There was never any way to avoid it. The presence of a tool implies that it will be used. You can try your best to keep it in the hands of what you think of as responsible people, but it'll never work. And it's *no different*, that's what I'm saying. This bomb is just another weapon. It's a cherry bomb in an anthill. It's gonna cause one hill of ants a hell of a lot of trouble, but it's no threat to the race of ants."

Bach could not see it that way. She tried, but it was still a nightmare of entirely new proportions to her. How could he equate the killing of millions of people with a random act of violence where three or four might be hurt? She was familiar with that. Bombs went off every day in her city, as in every human city. People were always dissatisfied.

"I could walk down...no, it's up here, isn't it?" Birkson mused for a moment on cultural differences. "Anyway, give me enough money and I'll bet I could go up to your slum neighborhoods right this minute and buy you as many kilos of uranium or plutonium as you want. Which is something you ought to be doing, by the way. Anything can be bought. *Anything.* For the right price, you could have bought weapons-grade material on the black market as early as 1960 or so. It would have been very expensive; there wasn't much of it. You'd have had to buy a *lot* of people. But now…well, you think it out." He stopped, and seemed embarrassed by his outburst.

"I've read a little about this," he apologized.

She did think it out as she followed him back to the cordon. What he said was true. When controlled fusion proved too costly for wide-scale use, humanity had opted for fast breeder reactors. There had been no other choice. And from that moment, nuclear bombs in the hands of terrorists had been the price humanity accepted. And the price they would continue to pay.

"I wanted to ask you one more question," she said. He stopped and turned to face her. His smile was dazzling.

"Ask away. But are you going to take me up on that bet?"

She was momentarily unsure of what he meant.

"Oh. Are you saying you'd help us locate the underground uranium ring? I'd be grateful…"

"No, no. Oh, I'll help you. I'm sure I can make a contact. I used to do that before I got into this game. What I meant was, are you going to bet I can't find some? We could bet…say, a dinner together as soon as I've found it. Time limit of seven days. How about it?"

She thought she had only two alternatives: walk away from him, or kill him. But she found a third.

"You're a betting man. I guess I can see why. But that's what I wanted to ask you. How can you stay so calm? Why doesn't this get to you like it does to me and my people? You can't tell me it's simply that you're used to it."

He thought about it. "And why not? You can get used to anything, you know. Now what about that bet?"

"If you don't stop talking about that," she said, quietly, "I'm going to break your arm."

"All right." He said nothing further, and she asked no further questions.

The fireball grew in milliseconds into an inferno that could scarcely be described in terms comprehensible to humans. Everything in a half-kilometer radius simply vanished into super-heated gases and plasma: buttresses, plate-glass windows, floors and ceilings, pipes, wires, tanks, machines, gewgaws and trinkets by the million, books, tapes, apartments, furniture, household pets, men, women, and children. They were the lucky ones. The force of the expanding blast compressed two hundred levels below it like a giant sitting on a Dagwood sandwich, making holes through plate steel turned to putty by the heat as easily as a punch press through tinfoil. Upwards, the surface bulged into the soundless Lunar night and split to reveal a white hell beneath. Chunks flew away, chunks as large as city sectors, before the center collapsed back on itself to leave a crater whose walls were a maze of compartments and ant-tunnels that dripped and flowed like warm gelatin. No trace was left of human bodies within two kilometers of the explosion. They had died after only the shortest period of suffering, their bodies consumed or spread into an invisible layer of organic film by the combination of heat and pressure that passed through walls, entered rooms where the doors were firmly shut. Further away, the sound was enough to congeal the bodies of a million people before the heat roasted them, the blast stripped flesh from bones to leave shrunken stick figures. Still the effects attenuated as the blast was channeled into corridors that were structurally strong enough to remain intact, and that very strength was the downfall of the inhabitants of the maze. Twenty kilometers from the epicenter, pressure doors popped through steel flanges like squeezed watermelon seeds.

What was left was five million burnt, blasted corpses, and ten million injured so hideously that they would die in hours or days. But Bach had been miraculously thrown clear by some freak of the explosion. She hurtled through the void with fifteen million ghosts following her, and each carried a birthday cake. They were singing. She joined in.

"Happy birthday to you, happy birthday..."

"Chief Bach."

"Huh?" She felt a cold chill pass over her body. For a moment she could only stare down into the face of Roger Birkson.

"You all right now?" he asked. He looked concerned.

"I'm...what happened?"

He patted her on both arms, then shook her heartily.

"Nothing. You drifted off for a moment." He narrowed his eyes. "I think you were daydreaming. I want to be diplomatic about this…ah, what I mean…I've seen it happen before. I think you were trying to get away from us."

She rubbed her hands over her face.

"I think I was. But I sure went in the wrong direction. I'm all right now." She could remember it now, and knew she had not passed out or become totally detached from what was going on. She had watched it all. Her memories of the explosion, so raw and real a moment before, were already the stuff of nightmares.

Too bad she hadn't come awake into a better world. It was so damn unfair. That was the reward at the end of a nightmare, wasn't it? You woke up to find everything was all right.

Instead, here was a long line of uniformed officers, bearing birthday cakes to a fifty kiloton atomic bomb.

Birkson had ordered the lights turned off in the Leystrasse. When his order had not been carried out, he broke out the lights with his putter. Soon, he had some of the officers helping him.

Now the beautiful Leystrasse, the pride of New Dresden, was a flickering tunnel through hell. The light of a thousand tiny birthday candles on five hundred cakes turned everything red-orange and made people into shadowed demons. Officers kept arriving with hastily wrapped presents, flowers, balloons. Hans, the little man who was now nothing but a brain and nerve network floating in a lead container; Hans, the cause of all this, the birthday boy himself, watched it all in unconcealed delight from his battery of roving television cameras. He sang loudly.

"I am a bomb! I am a bomb!" he yelled. He had never had so much fun.

Bach and Birkson retreated from the scene into the darkened recess of the Bagatelle Flower Shoppe. There, a stereo viewing tank had been set up.

The X-ray picture had been taken with a moving plate technique that allowed a computer to generate a three dimensional model. They leaned over the tank now and studied it. They had been joined by Sergeant

McCoy, Bach's resident bomb expert, and another man from the Lunar Radiation Laboratory.

"This is Hans," said Birkson, moving a red dot in the tank by means of a dial on the side. It flicked over and around a vague gray shape that trailed dozens of wires. Bach wondered again at the pressures that would allow a man to like having his body stripped from him. There was nothing in that lead flask but the core of the man, the brain and central nervous system.

"Here's the body of the bomb. The two sub-critical masses. The H.E. charge, the timer, the arming barrier, which is now withdrawn. It's an old design, ladies and gentlemen. Old, but reliable. As basic as the bow and arrow. It's very much like the first one dropped on the Nippon Empire at Hiroshima."

"You're sure it'll go off, then?" Bach put in.

"Sure as taxes. Hell, a kid could build one of these in the bathroom, given only the uranium and some shielding equipment. Now let me see." He pored over the phantom in the tank, tracing out wiring paths with the experts. They debated possibilities, lines of attack, drawbacks. At last they seemed to reach a consensus.

"As I see it, we have only one option," Birkson said. "We have to go for his volitional control over the bomb. I'm pretty sure we've isolated the main cable that goes from him to the detonator. Knock that out, and he can't do a thing. We can pry that tin can open by conventional means and disarm that way. McCoy?"

"I agree," said McCoy. "We'd have a full hour, and I'm sure we can get in there with no trouble. When they cyborged this one, they put all their cards on the human operator. They didn't bother with entry blocks, since Hans could presumably blow it up before we could get close enough to do anything. With his control out, we only have to open it up with a torch and drop the damper into place."

The LRL man nodded his agreement. "Though I'm not quite as convinced as Mr. Birkson that he's got the right cable in mind for what he wants to do. If we had more time…"

"We've wasted enough time already," Bach said, decisively. She had swung rapidly from near terror of Roger Birkson to total trust. It was her only defense. She knew she could do nothing at all about the bomb, and had to trust someone.

"Then we go for it. Is your crew in place? Do they know what to do? And above all, are they *good*? Really good? There won't be a second chance."

"Yes, yes, and yes," Bach said. "They'll do it. We know how to cut rock on Luna."

"Then give them the coordinates, and go." Birkson seemed to relax a bit. Bach saw that he had been under some form of tension, even if it was only excitement at the challenge. He had just given his last order. It was no longer in his hands. His fatalistic gambler's instinct came into play and the restless, churning energy he had brought to the enterprise vanished. There was nothing to do about it but wait. Birkson was good at waiting. He had lived through twenty-one of these final countdowns.

He faced Bach and started to say something to her, then thought better of it. She saw doubt in his face for the first time, and it made her skin crawl. Damn it, she had thought he was *sure*.

"Chief," he said, quietly, "I want to apologize for the way I treated you these last few hours. It's not something I can control when I'm on the job. I…"

This time it was Bach's turn to laugh, and the release of tension it brought with it was almost orgasmic. She felt like she hadn't laughed for a million years.

"Forgive me," she said. "I saw you were worried, and thought it was about the bomb. It was just such a relief."

"Oh, yeah," he said, dismissing it. "No point in worrying now. Either your people hit it or they don't. We won't know if they don't. What I was saying, it just sort of comes over me. Honestly. I get horny, I get manic, I totally forget about other people except as objects to be manipulated. So I just wanted to say I like you. I'm glad you put up with me. And I won't pester you anymore."

She came over and put her hand on his shoulder.

"Can I call you Roger? Thanks. Listen, if this thing works, I'll have dinner with you. I'll give you the key to the city, a ticker tape parade, and a huge bonus for a consultant fee…and my eternal friendship. We've been tense, okay? Let's forget about these last few hours."

"All right." His smile was quite different this time.

Outside, it happened very quickly. The crew on the laser drill were positioned beneath the bomb, working from ranging reports and calculations to aim their brute at precisely the right spot.

The beam took less than a tenth of a second to eat through the layer of rock in the ceiling and emerge in the air above the Leystrasse. It ate through the metal sheath of the bomb's underside, the critical wire, the other side of the bomb, and part of the ceiling like they weren't even there. It had penetrated into the level above before it could be shut off.

There was a shower of sparks, a quick sliding sound, then a muffled thud. The whole structure of the bomb trembled, and smoke screeched from the two drilled holes in the top and bottom. Bach didn't understand it, but could see that she was alive and assumed it was over. She turned to Birkson, and the shock of seeing him nearly stopped her heart.

His face was a gray mask, drained of blood. His mouth hung open. He swayed, and almost fell over. Bach caught him and eased him to the floor.

"Roger…what is it? Is it still…will it go off? Answer me, *answer me.* What should I do?"

He waved weakly, pawed at her hands. She realized he was trying to give her a reassuring pat. It was feeble indeed.

"No danger," he wheezed, trying to get his breath back. "No danger. The wrong wire. We hit the wrong wire. Just luck, is all, nothing but luck."

She remembered. They had been trying to remove Hans' control over the bomb. Was he still in control? Birkson answered before she could speak.

"He's dead. That explosion. That was the detonator going off. He reacted just too late. We hit the disarming switch. The shield dropped into place so the masses couldn't come together even if the bomb was set off. Which he did. He set it off. That sound, that *mmmmmmwoooooph!*" He was not with her. His eyes stared back into a time and place that held horror for him.

"I heard that sound—the detonator—once before, over the telephone. I was coaching this woman, no more than twenty-five, because I couldn't get there in time. She had only three more minutes. I heard that sound, then nothing, nothing."

She sat near him on the floor as her crew began to sort out the mess, haul the bomb away for disposal, laugh and joke in hysterical relief. At last Birkson regained control of himself. There was no trace of the bomb except a distant hollowness in his eyes.

"Come on," he said, getting to his feet with a little help from her. "You're going on twenty-four-hour leave. You've earned it. We're going back to Burning Tree and you're going to watch me make a par five on the eighteenth. Then we've got a date for dinner. What place is nice?"

EQUINOCTIAL

So now we hop right over Mars and Jupiter—they must be on the wrong side of the sun to get to easily right now—and the asteroid belt (if you want to read stories about them, try Larry Niven), and arrive at the gaudiest planet for at least four light-years in any direction.

I can recall vividly the first time I saw Saturn in a small telescope. It is one thing to see a photograph, and something else entirely to put your eye to the eyepiece of a decent home telescope and see it for real. *Amazing!* There it is, a tiny bauble a billion miles away. And it really has rings! I have since had the pleasure of showing Saturn to dozens of people who had never seen it except as a bright star in the sky, and the reaction is always the same. They are blown away.

I have taken two shots at imagining a perfect pressure suit. In stories like "Retrograde Summer" and "In the Bowl" and others I described a technological solution to the problem of visiting and living in extremely hostile environments. The result was silver force fields that protected the fragile animal inside from temperature, vacuum, and poisonous gases.

The second was what I hoped was the ultimate suit: a living being genetically designed and tailored to be the perfect symbiotic partner for humans. It would enclose you and enable you to float freely through the rings. And it would be intelligent, a perfect companion in the loneliness.

At the time of writing, the theories concerning the size and shape of the particles that make up Saturn's rings was in flux. Some said grains of sand, others said they could be considerably larger. Then came those pictures from Voyager 1, and better data. Once again the astronomers caught up with me and showed me the real situation was different (and they have never apologized for it!). But it is all worth it for those incredible first shots of the rings as

185

they *really* are, like God's own LP record, with hundreds of thread-like rings looking like grooves waiting for a cosmic tone arm to lower from the sky and play celestial music.

(And it's a little depressing to realize that there are those of you among my readers who have never put a vinyl platter on a spindle and listened to that faint scratchiness as the disc rotated to the first cut. Yes, we called them "cuts" back then, because the sound came from actual cuts in the vinyl, vibrating the needle. Ah, those were the days…days of hiss and pop and disastrous scratches that would make the needle skip. I'll keep my CDs.)

Parameter knew she was being followed. They had been behind her for days, always far enough behind that they couldn't get a permanent fix on her, but never so far that she could lose them. She was in danger, but now was not the time to worry about it.

Now was one of the big moments in her life. She proposed to savor it to the full and refused to be distracted by the hunters. She was giving birth to quintuplets.

Uni, Duo, Tri, Quad… Hopelessly trite. *Doc, Happy, Sneezy, Grumpy*—no, there were seven of those. *Army, Navy, Marine, Airforce, Coastguard?* That was a pentagon, for an interesting pun. But who wanted to be called Coastguard? What was a Coastguard, anyway?

She put the naming ordeal out of her mind. It wasn't important; they would pick their own names when the time came. She just thought it might be nice with *five* to have something to tag them with, if only for bookkeeping purposes.

"They just got another sighting," she thought, but it wasn't her own thought. It was the voice of Equinox. Equinox was Parameter's companion, her environment, her space suit, her alter ego; her Symb. She looked in the direction she had come from.

She looked back on the most spectacular scene in the solar system. She was 230,000 kilometers from the center of Saturn, according to the figures floating in the upper left corner of her field of vision. To one side of her was the yellow bulk of the giant planet, and all around her was a golden line that bisected the universe. She was inside the second and brightest of the Rings.

But Saturn and the Rings was not all she saw. About ten degrees away from Saturn and in the plane of the Rings was a hazy thing like the bell of a trumpet. It was transparent. The wide end of the bell was facing her. Within this shape were four lines of red that were sharp and well-defined far away but became fuzzy as they neared her. These were the hunters. All around her, but concentrated in the plane of the Rings, were slowly moving lines of all colors, each with an arrow at one end, each shifting perspective in a dazzling 3-D ballet.

None of it—the lines, the bells, the "hunters," even Saturn itself—none of it was any more real than the image in a picture tube. Some of it was even less real than that. The shifting lines, for instance, were vector representations of the large chunks of rock and ice within radar range of Equinox.

The bell was closer than it had been for days. That was bad news, because the space-time event it represented was the approach of the hunters and their possible locations projected from the time of the last fix. The fuzzy part was almost touching her. That meant they could be very close indeed, though it wasn't too likely. They were probably back in the stem where the projection looked almost solid, and almost certainly within the four lines that were their most probable location. But it was still too close.

"Since they know where we are, let's get a fix on *them*," Parameter decided, and as she thought it the bell disappeared, to be replaced by four red points that grew tails even as she watched.

"Too close. Way too close." Now they had two fixes on her: one of their own, and the one she had given them by bouncing a signal off them. From this, their Symbs could plot a course; therefore, it was time to alter it.

She couldn't afford to change course in the usual way, by bouncing off a rock. The hunters were close enough that they would detect the change in the rock's velocity and get a better idea of where she was. It was time for thrusters, though she could ill afford the wasted mass.

"Which way?" she asked.

"I suggest you move out of the plane. They won't expect that yet. They don't know you're in labor."

"That's pretty dangerous. There's nothing to hide in out there."

Equinox considered it. "If they get any closer, you'll have to do something at least that drastic, with less chance of success. But I only advise."

"Sure. All right, do it, my green pasture."

The world around her jerked, and all the colored lines started moving down around her, bending as their relative velocity changed. There was a gentle pressure at the small of her back.

"Keep an eye on them. I'm going back to the business of giving birth. How are they doing, by the way?"

"No sweat. One of the girls is in the tube right now—you can feel her—"

"You can tell me *that* three times..."

"—and she's a little puzzled by the pressure. But she's taking it well. She tells you not to worry, she'll be all right."

"Can I talk to her yet?"

"Not for another few hours. Be patient."

"Right. It shouldn't be long now."

And that was very true. She felt the wave of sensation as her uterus contracted again. She looked down at herself, absently expecting to see the first head coming out. But she could no longer see that far; her belly stuck out.

Nothing that Parameter saw was real; all was illusion. Her head was completely enclosed in the thick, opaque substance of Equinox, and all the sensory data she received was through the direct connection from Equinox's senses into her own brain. Much of this information was edited and embellished in ways that made it easier for Parameter to interpret.

So it was that when she looked down at herself she saw not the dark-green surface of Equinox, but her own brown skin. She had asked for that illusion long ago, when it had become a matter of some importance to her to believe she still had her own body. The illusion was flawless. She could see the fingerprints on her hand, the mole on her knee, the color of her nipples, the sentimental scar on her forearm, all illuminated by the soft diffusion of light from the Rings. But if she tried to touch herself, her hand would be stopped while still a good distance from what she saw as the surface of her body. Equinox was invisible to her, but she was certainly there.

She watched as the contraction caused her stomach to writhe and flow like putty. This was more like it. She remembered her other deliveries, before she married Equinox. One had been "natural" and it hadn't worked all that well. She didn't regret it, but it had been painful, not something she would want to repeat. The other had been under anesthetic, and no fun at all. She might as well not have bothered; there had been no pain, no pleasure, no *sensation*. It was like reading about it in the newspaper. But this one, her third birth, was different. It was intense, so intense she had difficulty concentrating on eluding the hunters. But there was no pain. All she felt was a series of waves of pleasure-pain that didn't hurt, and could be related to no other sensation humans had ever experienced.

One of the lines ahead seemed to point almost directly at her. It was a thick red line, meaning it was seventy percent ice and about a million kilograms in mass. The vector was short. It was moving slowly enough that rendezvous would be easy.

She took the opportunity and altered course slightly with the sure instinct she had developed. The line swung, foreshortened even more, then flashed brighter and began to pulse. This was the collision warning from Equinox's plotting sector.

When the rock was close enough to see as an object rather than a simulated projection, she rotated until her legs pointed at it. She soaked up the shock of the landing, then began to scuttle over the surface in a manner quite astonishing, and with a speed not to be believed. She moved with the coordinated complexity of a spider, all four limbs grasping at the rock and ice.

To an observer, she was a comical sight. She looked like a barbell with arms and legs and a bulge at the top that just might be a head. There were no creases or sharp lines anywhere on the outer surface of Equinox; all was gentle curves, absolutely featureless except for short claws on the hands and feet. At the ends of her legs were grasping appendages more like oversized hands than feet. And her legs bent the wrong way. Her knees were hinged to bend away from each other.

But she swarmed over the rock with effortless ease, not even hampered by her pregnancy, though the labor "pains" were getting intense.

When she was where she wanted to be, she pushed off with both hands and peds, rising rapidly. She was now on a course about ninety degrees away from her pursuers. She hoped they would not be expecting this. Now she had to rely on the screening effect of the billions of tiny rocks and ice crystals around her. For the next few hours she would be vulnerable if they beamed in her direction, but she didn't think it likely they would. Their Symbs would be plotting a course for her almost opposite to the one she was actually taking. If she had continued that way they would certainly have caught her later when she was burdened with five infants. Now was the time for audacity.

Having done that, she put the matter out of her mind again, and none too soon. The first baby had arrived.

The head was just emerging as she pushed off the rock. She savored the delicious agony as the head forced its way through her body, struggling to reach the air. It would never reach it. There was no air out here, just another womb that Equinox had prepared, a womb the baby would live in for the rest of its life. No first breath for Parameter's children; no breath at all.

The babies were not full-term. Each had been growing only seven months and would not be able to survive without extensive care. But Equinox was the world's best incubator. She had counseled, and Parameter had agreed, that it would be best to birth them while they were still small and get them out where Equinox could keep a closer eye on them.

Parameter moved her strangely articulated legs, bringing the hand-like peds up to the baby. She pressed slowly and felt the peds sink in as Equinox absorbed the outer covering. Then she felt the head with her own nerve endings. She ran her long fingers over the wet ball. There was another contraction and the baby was out. She was holding it in her peds. She couldn't see much of it, and suddenly she wanted to.

"This is one of the girls, right?"

"Yes. And so are two, three, and five. Navy, Marine, and Coastguard, if you want to get more personal."

"Those were just tags," she laughed. "I didn't even like them."

"Until you think of something else, they'll do."

"*They* won't want them."

"Perhaps not. Anyway, I'm thinking of shifting the boy around to fifth position. There's a little tangling of the cords."

"Whatever you want. I'd like to see her. 'Army,' I mean."

"Do you want a picture, or should I move her?"

"Move her." She knew it was only a semantic quibble as to whether she would actually "see" her child. The projection Equinox could provide would look just as real, hanging in space. But she wanted the picture to coincide with the feel she was getting of the baby against her skin.

By undulating the inner surface of her body, Equinox was able to move the infant around the curve of Parameter's belly until she was visible. She was wet, but there was no blood; Equinox had already absorbed it all.

"I want to touch her with my hands," Parameter thought.

"Go ahead. But don't forget there's another coming in a few minutes."

"Hold it up. I want to enjoy this one first."

She put her hands on the invisible surface of Equinox and they sank in until she was holding the child. It stirred and opened its mouth, but no sound came. There seemed to be no trauma involved for the brand-new human being; she moved her arms and legs slowly but seemed content to lie still for the most part. Compared to most human children, she hadn't really been born at all. Parameter tried to interest her in a nipple, but she didn't want it. She was the prettiest thing Parameter had ever seen.

"Let's get the next one out," she said. "This is so extravagant I still can't believe it. Five!"

She drifted into a wonderful haze as the others arrived, each as pretty as the last. Soon she was covered with tiny bodies, each still tied to an umbilicus. The cords would be left in place until Equinox had finished her childbirth and had five semiautonomous baby Symbs to receive the children. Until then, the children were still a part of her. It was a feeling Parameter loved; she would never be closer to her children.

"Can you hear them yet?" Equinox asked.

"No, not yet."

"You'll have to wait a while longer for mind contact. I'm tuning out. Are you all right? I shouldn't be longer than about two hours."

"Don't worry about me. I'll be fine. In fact, I've never been happier." She stopped verbalizing and let a wave of intense love flood over her; love for her invisible mate. It was answered by such an outpouring of affection that Parameter was in tears. "I love you, earthmother," she said.

"And you, sunshine."

"I hope it'll be as good for you as it was for me."

"I wish I could share it with you. But back to business. I really think we've shaken the hunters. There's been no signal from them for an hour, and their projected path is well away from us. I think we'll be safe, at least for a few hours."

"I hope so. But don't worry about me. I'll get along while you're away. I'm not scared of the dark."

"I know. It won't be for long. See you later."

Parameter felt her mate slipping away. For a moment she *was* afraid, but not of the dark. She was afraid of the loneliness. Equinox would be unavailable to her for the time it took to give birth to her children, and that meant she would be cut off from the outside. That didn't matter, but the absence of Equinox from Parameter's mind was a little frightening. It recalled an unpleasant incident in her past.

But as the lights faded she realized she was not alone. Cut off from sight, sound, smell, and taste by the shutdown of Equinox's interpretative faculties, she still had touch, and that was enough.

She floated in total darkness and felt the sharp tingle as a mouth found a nipple and began to suck. Imperceptibly, she drifted into sleep.

She awoke to a vague feeling of discomfort. It was small and nagging, and impossible to ignore. She felt in her mind for Equinox, and couldn't find her. So she was still in the process of giving birth.

But the feeling persisted. She felt helpless in the dark, then she realized it wasn't totally dark. There was a faint pinkness, like looking into closed eyelids. She could not account for it. Then she knew what was wrong, and it was worse than she could have imagined. The babies were gone.

She felt over her body with increasing panic, but they were nowhere to be found. Before her panic overwhelmed her, she tried to think of what could have happened that would have separated them, and all she could come up with was the hunters. But why would they take the babies? Then she lost control; there was nothing she could do in the darkness without Equinox to create the universe for her.

She was drawn back to rationality by a thought so black she could hardly credit it. In torment, she opened her eyes.

She could see.

She was floating in the center of a room hollowed out of bare rock. There was another person in the room, or rather another symbiote; all she could see was the dark-green, curved form of the Symb.

"Equinox!" she yelled, and heard herself. In a dream, she looked down at her body and felt the bare reality of it. She touched herself; there was no resistance. She was alone. Half of her was gone.

Her mind was dissolving; she watched it go, and knew it to be preferable to facing life without Equinox. She said good-bye to the last shreds of reality, rolled her eyes up into her head, and swallowed her tongue.

The figure looked like a cartoon of a human drawn by a three-year-old, one who was confused about sex. The broad shoulders and bullish neck were ludicrously like the build of a weightlifter, and the narrowing waist and bulbous ass were a moron's idea of a well-built woman. He was green, and featureless except for an oval opening where his mouth should have been.

"Just why do you want to become a Ringer?" The sound issued from the hole in his "face."

Parameter sighed and leaned back in her chair. The operation at Titan was anything but efficient. She had spent three days talking to people who had been no help at all and finally found this man, who seemed to have the authority to give her a Symb. Her patience—never very long—was at an end.

"I should make a tape," she said. "You're the fourth bastard who's asked me that today."

"Nevertheless, I must have your answer. And why don't you keep the smart remarks to yourself? I don't need them. For two cents I'd walk out of here and forget about you."

"Why don't you? I don't think you can even get out of that chair, much less walk out of here. I never expected anything like this. I thought you Consers wanted new people, so why are you giving me such a runaround? I might get up and walk out myself. You people aren't the only Ringers."

He proved her wrong by rising from the chair. He was awkward but steady, and, even more interesting, there was something in his hand that could only be a gun. She was amazed. He was sitting in a bare room, and had been empty-handed. Suddenly there was this gun, out of nowhere.

"If you mean that you're thinking of going over to the Engineers, it's my duty to blow your brains out. You have ten seconds to explain yourself." There was no trace of anger. The gun never wavered.

She swallowed hard, keeping very still.

"Uh, no, that's not what I meant."

The gun dropped slightly.

"It was a foolish remark," she said, her ears burning with shame and anger. "I'm committed to the Conservationists."

The gun vanished into the Symb he was wearing. It could still be in his hand for all she could tell.

"Now you can answer my question."

Keeping her anger rigidly in check, she started her story. She was quite good at it by now, and had it condensed nicely. She recited it in a singsong tone that the interrogator didn't seem to notice.

"I am seventy-seven Earth years old, I was born on Mercury, the Helios Enclave, the child of an extremely wealthy energy magnate. I grew up in the rigid, confining atmosphere that has always existed in Mercury, and I hated it. When I turned twelve, my mother gave me twenty percent of her fortune and said she hoped I'd use it wisely. Luckily for me, I was an adult and beyond her reach, because I disappointed her badly.

"I bought passage on the first ship leaving the planet, which happened to be going to Mars. For the next sixty years I devoted myself to experiencing everything the human organism can experience and still survive.

"It would be tedious and overlong to tell you everything I did, but so you won't think I'm hiding something, I can give you a random sample.

"Drugs: I tried them all. Some only once. Others for years at a time. I had to have my personality rebuilt three times and lost a lot of memory in the process.

"Sex: with two, three, four partners; seven partners; thirty partners; three hundred partners. All-week orgies. Men, women, girls, boys. Infants. Elephants. Pythons. Corpses. I changed sex so many times I'm not sure if I grew up as a male or a female.

"I killed a man. I got away with it. I killed a woman and got away again. I got caught the third time and spent seven years in rehabilitation.

"I traveled. I went to the Belt, to Luna, to the moons of Saturn, Uranus, Neptune. I went to Pluto, and beyond with a holehunter.

"I tried surgery. I joined up with a pair-cult and was connected for a year to another woman as a Siamese twin. I tried out weird new organs and sex systems. I tried on extra limbs.

"A few years ago I joined a passivity cult. They believed all action was meaningless, and demonstrated it by having their arms and legs amputated and relying on the mercy of random strangers to feed them and keep them alive. I lay for months in the public square beneath Coprates. Sometimes I went hungry and thirsty. Sometimes I stewed in my own filth; then someone would clean me up, usually with a stern lecture to quit this way of life and go straight. I didn't care.

"But the second time a dog used me for a urinal, I gave it up. I asked someone to carry me to a doctor, and walked out a changed woman. I decided I had *done* everything and had better start looking for an elaborate and original suicide. I was so bored, so jaded, that *breathing* seemed like too much of a bother.

"Then I thought of two places I'd never been: the sun and the Rings. The sun is the fancy suicide I told you about. The only way to get to the Rings is in a Symb. I tend to sympathize with you people over the Engineers. So here I am."

She settled back in her chair. She was not optimistic about being allowed to join the Conservationist Church, and was already planning ways to get over to the Engineers. If there was ever an unprepossessing story, it was hers, and she knew it. These Consers were supposed to be dedicated people, and she knew she couldn't present a very convincing line. In point of fact, she didn't give any thought at all to the Grand Design of the Engineers. Why should she care if a band of religious fanatics were trying to paint one of Saturn's Rings?

"The next to the last statement was a lie," the man informed her.

"Right," she spat. "You self-righteous bastards. It's the custom in polite society to inform someone when they're undergoing a lie-detector test. Even ask their consent." She got up to go.

"Please sit down, Parameter." She hesitated, then did so.

"It's time some false impressions were cleared up. First, this is not 'polite society,' this is war. Religious war, which is the dirtiest kind. We do what we have to in the interest of security. The sole purpose of this interview was to determine if your story was true. We don't care what you have done, as long as you haven't been consorting with our enemy. Have you?"

"No."

"That is a true statement. Now for the other mistake. We are not self-righteous bastards. We're pragmatists. And we're not religious fanatics, not really, though we all come to believe deeply in what we're doing out here. And that brings us to the third mistake. The primary reasons we're out here have little to do with defeating the Engineers. We're all out here for our own personal reasons, too."

"And what are they?"

"They're personal. Each of us had a different reason for coming. You are out here to satisfy the last dregs of a jaded appetite; that's a common reason. You have some surprises coming up, but you'll stay. You'll have to. You won't be able to bear leaving. And you'll like it. You might even help us fight the Engineers."

She looked at him with suspicion.

"We don't care why you're out here. Your story doesn't impress me one way or the other. You probably expected condemnation or contempt. Don't flatter yourself. As long as you're not here to help paint Ring Beta red, we don't care."

"Then when do I get a Symb?"

"As soon as you can undergo a bit of surgery." For the first time he unbent a little. The corners of the slit that covered his mouth bent up in a silly attempt at a smile. "I must confess that I *was* interested by one thing you said. *How* do you have sex with an elephant?"

Parameter kept a perfectly straight face.

"You don't have sex *with* an elephant. The best you can do is have sex *at* an elephant."

The Symb was a soft-looking greenish lump in the center of the room. With the best will in the world, Parameter could not see that it resembled anything so much as a pile of green cow manure. It was smaller than she had expected, but that was because it had no occupant. She was about to remedy that.

She stumped over to it and looked down dubiously. She had no choice but to walk awkwardly; her legs were no longer built for walking. They had been surgically altered so that the best she could do was a grotesque bowlegged prancing, stepping high so her long fingers would clear the floor. She was now ideally suited for a weightless existence. In a gravitational field, she was clumsy beyond belief.

The man who had interviewed her, whom she now knew by the name of Bushwacker, was the only other occupant of the room. He handled himself better than she did, but only slightly. He was itching to get back to the Rings; this base duty galled him. Gravity was for poor flatfoots.

"Just touch it, that's all?" she said. Now that it had come to it, she was having second thoughts.

"That's right. The Symb will do the rest. It won't be easy. You'll have between six weeks and three months of sensory deprivation while the personality develops. You'd go crazy in two days, but you won't be alone. All you'll have to hang on to will be the mind of the Symb. And it'll be a baby, hard to get along with. You'll grow up together."

She took a deep breath, wondering why she was so reluctant. She had done things easily that were much more repulsive than this. Perhaps it was the dawning realization that this would be much more than a simple lark. It could last a long time.

"Here goes." She lifted her leg and touched one of her ped-fingers to the blob. It stuck. The Symb slowly began stirring.

The Symb was…warm? No, at first she thought so, but it would be more accurate to say it was no temperature at all. It was thirty-seven degrees: blood temperature. It oozed up her leg, spreading itself thinner as it came. In a short time it was inching up her neck.

"Inhale," Bushwacker advised. "It'll help a little."

She did so, just as the Symb moved over her chin. It moved over her mouth and nose, then her eyes.

There was a moment of near-panic when part of her brain told her she *must* take a breath, and she dutifully tried to. Nothing happened, and she wanted to scream. But it was all right. She didn't need to breathe. When she opened her mouth the Symb flowed down her throat and trachea. Soon her lungs were filled with the interface tissue whose function it was to put oxygen in her blood and remove carbon dioxide. It filled her nasal passages, slithered up the eustachian tube to her inner ear. At that point she lost her balance and fell to the floor. Or she thought she did; she could no longer be sure. She had felt no impact. A wave of dizziness swept over her; she wondered what a Symb would do about vomiting. But it didn't happen, and she suspected it never would.

It was a shock, even though she had expected it, when the Symb entered her anus and vagina. Not a *bad* shock. Rather a thrill, actually. It filled the spaces in her uterus, wound into the urethra to fill the bladder, then up the ureter to mingle with the kidneys. Meanwhile another tendril had filled the large and small intestine, consuming the nutrients it found there, and joined with the tendril coming from her mouth. When it was done, she was threaded like the eye of a serpentine needle, and was revealed to any that could see as a topological example of a torus.

The silence closed in. It was absolutely quiet for a period of time she was powerless to measure, but couldn't have been longer than five minutes.

The obvious place where the human brain is accessible without violating any solid membranes is alongside the eyeball and through the supraorbital foramen. But the Symb would not be able to get a very substantial tendril through in the tight confines of the eye. So the genetic engineers, elaborating on the basic design for oxygen breathers received over the Ophiuchi Hotline, had given the Symb the capability of forcing an entry through the top of the skull.

Parameter felt a twinge of pain as a two-centimeter hole was eaten in the top of her head. But it subsided as the Symb began to feel out the proper places to make connections. The Symb was still a mindless thing, but was guided infallibly by the carefully designed instinct built into it.

Suddenly she was surrounded by fear; childish, inconsolable fear that frightened her out of her wits but did not come from her mind. She fought it, but it only became more insistent. In the end, she abandoned herself to it and cried like a baby. She became an infant, sloughing off her seventy-odd years there in the impalpable darkness like they had never happened.

There was nothing; nothing but two very lost voices, crying in the void.

There had been a debate raging for centuries as to whether the Symbiotic Space-Environment Organisms were really a form of artificial intelligence. (Or alien intelligence, depending on your definition.) The people who lived in them were unanimously of the opinion that they were. But the other side—who were mostly psychologists—pointed out that the people who actually *lived* in them were in the worst possible place to judge. Whatever one's opinion on the subject, it was based on personal prejudice, because there could be no objective facts.

The Symbs were genetically tailored organisms that could provide a complete, self-contained environment for a single human being in space. They thrived on human waste products: urine, feces, heat, and carbon dioxide.

They contained several chlorophyll-like enzymes and could accomplish photosynthesis utilizing the human's body heat, though at a low efficiency. For the rest of the energy needs of the pair, the Symb could use sunlight. They were very good at storing energy in chemical compounds that could be broken down later at need. Together with a human, a Symb made a self-contained heat engine. They were a closed ecology, neither host nor parasite: a symbiosis.

To the human being, the Symb was a green pasture, a running brook, a fruit tree, an ocean to swim in. To the Symb, the human was rich soil, sunshine, gentle rain, fertilizer, a pollinating bee. It was an ideal team. Without the other, each was at the mercy of elaborate mechanical aids to survive. Humans were adapted to an environment that no longer existed for their use in a natural state; wherever humans lived since the occupation of the Earth, they had to make their own environment. Now the Symbs were to provide that environment free of charge.

But it hadn't worked that way.

The Symbs were more complicated than they looked. Humans were used to taking from their surroundings, bending or breaking them until they fit human needs. The Symbs required more of humanity; they made it necessary to give.

When inside a Symb, a human was cut off entirely from the external universe. The human component of the symbiosis had to rely on the Symb's faculties. And the sensory data were received in an unusual way.

The Symb extended a connection directly into the human brain and fed data into it. In the process, it had to get tied up in the brain in such a way that it could be difficult to say where human left off and Symb began. The Symb reorganized certain portions of the human brain, freeing its tremendous potential for computation and integration, and using those abilities to translate the sensory data into pictures, sounds, tastes, smells, and touches, going directly through the sensorium. In the process, a mind was generated.

The Symb had no brain of its own, it merely was able to utilize the human brain on a time-sharing basis, and utilize it better than its original owner had been able to. So it would seem impossible that it could have a mind of its own. But every Ringer in the system would swear it had. And that was the crux of the debate: Was it actually an independent mind, parasitically using the human brain as its vehicle for sentient thought, or was it merely schizophrenia, induced by isolation and projection?

It was impossible to decide. Without a human inside it, there is nothing more helpless than a Symb. Without the human brain in combination with the genetic information and enzymatically coded procedures, the Symb can do no more than lie there inert like the green turd it so closely resembles. It has only rudimentary musculature, and doesn't even use that when alone. There is no good analogy for a Symb without a human; nothing else is so dependent on anything else.

Once combined with a human, the pair is transformed, becoming much more than the sum of its parts. The human is protected against the harshest environment imaginable. The livable range with a Symb extends from just outside the orbit of Earth (radiation limit) to the orbit of Neptune (sunlight limit). The pair feed each other, water each other, and respirate each other. The human brain is converted into a supercomputer. The Symb has radio and radar sender and receiver organs, in addition to sensors for radiation and the electromagnetic spectrum from one thousand to sixteen thousand angstroms. The system can gain mass by ingesting rock and ice and the Symb can retain the valuable minerals and water and discard the rest. About all the pair cannot do is change velocity without a chunk of rock to push against. But it is a small matter to carry a rocket thruster instead of the whole apparatus of a space suit. In the Rings, they didn't even do that. The Symb could manufacture enough gas for attitude control. For major velocity changes, the Ringers carried small bottles of compressed gas.

So why weren't all humans in space installed in Symbs?

The reason was that the Symbs needed more than most people were willing to give. It wasn't a simple matter of putting it on when you needed it and taking it off later. When you took off your Symb, the Symb ceased to exist.

It was probably the heaviest obligation a human ever had to face. Once mated with a Symb, you were mated for life. There had never been a closer relationship; the Symb lived *inside your mind*, was with you even when you slept, moving independently through your dreams. Compared with that, Siamese twins were utter strangers who pass in the night.

It was true that all the humans who had ever tried it swore they hadn't even been alive before they joined their Symb. It looked attractive in some ways, but for most people the imagined liabilities outweighed the gains. Few people are able to make a commitment they *know* will be permanent, not when permanent could mean five or six hundred years.

After an initial rush of popularity the Symb craze had died down. Now all the Symbs in the system were in the Rings, where they had made possible a nomadic existence never before known.

Ringers are loners by definition. Humans meet at long intervals, mate if they are of a mind to, and go their separate ways. Ringers seldom see the same person twice in a lifetime.

They are loners who are never alone.

"Are you there?"

?????

"I can sense you. We have to do something. I can't stand this darkness, can you? Listen: *Let there be light!*"

?????

"Oh, you're hopeless. Why don't you get lost?"

Sorrow. Deep and childish sorrow. Parameter was drawn into it, cursing herself and the infantile thing she was caught with. She tried for the thousandth time to thrash her legs, to let someone out there know she wanted *out*. But she had lost her legs. She could no longer tell if she was moving them.

From the depths of the Symb's sorrow, she drew herself up and tried to stand away from it. It was no use. With a mental sob, she was swallowed up again and was no longer able to distinguish herself from the infant alien.

Her chest was rising and falling. There was an unpleasant smell in her nostrils. She opened her eyes.

She was still in the same room, but now there was a respirator clamped to her face, forcing air in and out of her lungs. She rolled her eyes and saw the grotesque shape of the other person in the room with her. It floated, bandy legs drawn up, hands and peds clasped together.

A hole formed in the front of the blank face.

"Feeling any better?"

She screamed and screamed until she thankfully faded back into her dream world.

"You're getting it. Keep trying. No, that's the wrong direction; whatever you were doing just then, do the opposite."

It was tentative; Parameter hadn't the foggiest idea of what opposite was, because she hadn't the foggiest idea of what the little Symb was doing in the first place. But it was progress. There was light. Faint, wavering, tentative; but *light*.

The undefined luminance flickered like a candle, shimmered, blew out. But she felt good. Not half as good as the Symb felt; she was flooded by a proud feeling of accomplishment that was not her own. But, she reflected, what does it matter if it's my own or not? It was getting to where she no longer cared to haggle about whether it was she who felt something or the Symb. If they both had to experience it, what difference did it make?

"That was *good*. We're getting there. You and me, kid. We'll go places. We'll get out of this mess yet."

Go? Fear. Go? Sorrow. Go? Anger?

The emotions were coming labeled with words now, and they were extending in range.

"Anger? Anger, did you say? What's this? Of course, I want to get out of here, why do you think we're going through this? It ain't easy, kid. I don't remember anything so hard to get a grip on since I tried to control my alpha waves, years ago. Now wait a minute…" Fear, fear, fear. "Don't do that, kid, you scare me. Wait. I didn't mean it..." Fear, fear loneliness, fear, FEAR! "Stop! Stop, you're scaring me to death, you're..." Parameter was shivering, becoming a child again.

Black, endless fear. Parameter slipped away from her mind; fused with the other mind; chided herself; consoled herself; comforted herself; loved herself.

"Here, take some water, it'll make you feel better."

"Ggggwwway."

"What?"

"Goway. Gway. Goaway. GO. A. WAY!"

"You'll have to drink some water first. I won't go away until you do."

"Go 'way. Murder. Murder'r."

Parameter was at a loss.

"*Why*, why won't you do it? For me. Do it for Parameter."

Negation.

"You mean 'no.' Where do you get those fancy words?"

Your memory. No. Will not do it.

Parameter sighed, but she had acquired patience, infinite patience. And something else, something that was very like love. At least it was a profound admiration for this spunky kid. But she was still scared, because the Symb was beginning to win her over and it was only with increasing desperation that she hung onto her idea of getting the child to open the outside world so she could tell someone she wanted out.

And the desperation only made matters worse. She couldn't conceal it from the Symb, and the act of experiencing communicated it in all its raw, naked panic.

"Listen to me. We've got to get off this merry-go-round. How can we talk something over intelligently if I keep communicating my fear to you, which makes you scared, which scares me, which makes you panicky, which scares me more, which...now stop that!"

Not my fault. Love, love. You need me. You are incomplete without me. I need commitment before I'll cooperate.

"But I can't. Can't you see I have to be *me*? I can't be you. And it's you who's incomplete without me, not the way you said."

Wrong. Both incomplete without the other. It's too late for you. You are no longer you. You are me, I am you.

"I won't believe that. We've been here for centuries, for eons. If I haven't accepted you yet, I never will. I want to be free, in time to see the sun burn out."

Wrong. Here for two months. The sun is still burning.

"Aha! Tricked you, didn't I? You can see out, you're further along than you told me. Why did you trick me like that? Why didn't you tell me you knew what time it was? I've been aching to know that. Why didn't you tell me?"

You didn't ask.

"What kind of answer is that?"

An honest one.

Parameter simmered. She knew it was honest. She knew she was belaboring the child, who couldn't tell a lie any more than she could. But she clung to her anger with the sinking feeling that it was all she had left of herself.

You hurt me. You are angry. I've done nothing to you. Why do you hate me? Why? ????? I love you. I'm afraid you'll leave me.

"I…I love you. I love you, godhelpme, I really do. But that's not me. No! It's something else. I don't know what yet, but I'll hang on. Hang on to it. Hang on to it."

Where are you?

Parameter?

"I'm here. Go away."

✦

"Go away."

"You have to eat something. Please, try this. It's good for you. Really it is. Try it."

"Eat!" She turned in the air with sudden cramps of hunger and revulsion. She retched up stale air and thin fluid. "Get away from me. Don't touch me. Equinox! Equinox!"

The figure touched her with its hand. The hand was hard and cold.

"Your breasts," he said. "They've been oozing milk. I was wondering…"

"Gone. All gone."

Parameter.

"What is it? Are you ready to try again with that picture?"

No. No need. You can go.

"Huh?"

You can go. I can't keep you. You think you are self-sufficient; maybe you're right. You can go.

Parameter was confused.

"Why? Why so sudden?"

I've been looking into some of the concepts in your memory. Freedom. Self-determination. Independence. You are free to go.

"You know what I think, what I *really* think about those concepts, too. Unproven at best. Fantasies at worst."

You are cynical. I recognize that they may indeed be real, so you should be free. I am detaining you against your will. This is contrary to most ethical codes, including the ones you accept more than any others. You are free to go.

It was an awkward moment. It hurt more than she would have thought possible. And she was unsure of whose hurt she was feeling. Not that it mattered.

What was she saying? Here was what might be her one and only chance, and she was acknowledging what the kid had said all along, that they were already fused. And the kid had heard it, like she heard everything.

Yes, I heard it. It doesn't matter. I can hear your doubts about many things. I can feel your uncertainty. It will be with you always.

"Yes. I guess it will. But you. I can't feel much from you. Not that I can distinguish."

You feel my death.

"No, no. It isn't that bad. They'll give you another human. You'll get along. Sure you will."

Perhaps. Despair. Disbelief.

Parameter kicked herself in the mental butt, told herself that if she didn't get out now, she never would.

"Okay. Let me out."

Fade. A gradual withdrawal that was painful and slow as the tendril began to disengage. And Parameter felt her mind being drawn in two.

It would always be like that. It would never get any better.

"Wait, kid. Wait!"

The withdrawal continued.

"Listen to me. Really! No kidding, I really want to discuss this with you. Don't go."

It's for the best. You'll get along.

"No! No more than you will. I'll die."

No you won't. It's like you said; if you don't get out now, you never will. You'll...all right...bye...

"No! You don't understand. I don't want to go anymore. I'm afraid. Don't leave me like this. You can't leave me."

Hesitation.

"Listen to me. Listen. Feel me. Love. Love. Commitment, pure and honest commitment-forever-and-ever-till-death-us-do-part. Feel me."

"I feel you. We are one."

She had eaten, only to bring it back up. But her jailer was persistent. He was not going to let her die.

"Would it be any better if you got inside with me?"

"No. I can't. I'm half gone. It would be no good. Where is Equinox?"

"I told you I don't know. And I don't know where your children are. But you won't believe me."

"That's right. I don't believe you. Murderer."

She listened groggily as he explained how she came to be in this room with him. She didn't believe him, not for a minute.

He said he had found her by following a radio beacon signaling from a point outside the plane of the Rings. He had found a pseudosymb there; a simplified Symb created by budding a normal one without first going through the conjugation process. A pseudo can only do what any other plant can do: that is, ingest carbon dioxide and give out oxygen from its inner surface. It cannot contract into contact with a human body. It remains in the spherical configuration. A human can stay alive in a pseudosymb, but will soon die of thirst.

Parameter had been inside the pseudo, bruised and bleeding from the top of her head and from her genitals. But she had been alive. Even more remarkable, she had lived the five days it had taken to get her to the Conser emergency station. The Consers didn't maintain many of the stations. The ones they had were widely separated.

"You were robbed by Engineers," he said. "There's no other explanation. How long have you been in the Rings?"

After the third repeat of the question, Parameter muttered, "Five years."

"I thought so. A new one. That's why you don't believe me. You don't know much about Engineers, do you? You can't understand why they would take your Symb and leave you alive, with a beacon to guide help to you. It doesn't make sense, right?"

"I...no, I don't know. I can't understand. They should have killed me. What they did was more cruel."

No emotion could be read on the man's "face," but he was optimistic for the first time that she might pull through. At least she was talking, if fitfully.

"You should have learned more. I've been fighting for a century, and I still don't know all I'd like to know. They robbed you for your children, don't you see? To raise them as Engineers. That's what the real battle is about: population. The side that can produce the most offspring is the one that gains the advantage."

"I don't want to talk."

"I understand. Will you just listen?"

He took her lack of response to mean she would.

"You've just been drifting through your life. It's easy to do out here; we all just drift from time to time. When you think about the Engineers at all, it's just a question of evading them. That isn't too hard. Considering the cubic kilometers out here, the hunted always has the advantage over the hunter. There are so many places to hide; so many ways to dodge."

"But you've drifted into a rough neighborhood. The Engineers have concentrated a lot of people in this sector. Maybe you've noticed the high percentage of red rocks. They hunt in teams, which is not something we Consers have ever done. We're too loose a group to get together much, and we all know our real fight doesn't begin for another thousand years.

"We are the loosest army in the history of humanity. We're volunteers on both sides, and on our side, we don't require that individuals do anything at *all* to combat the Engineers. So you don't know anything about them, beyond the fact that they've vowed to paint Ring Beta red within twenty-five thousand years."

He at last got a rise out of her.

"I know a little more than that. I know they are followers of Ringpainter the Great. I know he lived almost two hundred years ago. I know he founded the Church of Cosmic Engineering."

"You read all that in a book. Do you know that Ringpainter is still alive? Do you know how they plan to paint the Ring? Do you know what they do to Consers they catch?"

He was selective in his interpretations. This time he took her silence to mean she didn't know.

"He is alive. Only he's a she now. Her 'Population Edict' of fifty years ago decreed that each Engineer shall spend ninety percent of her time as a female, and bear three children every year. If they really do that, we haven't got a chance. The Rings would be solid Engineers in a few centuries."

She was slightly interested for the first time in weeks.

"I didn't know it was such a long-term project."

"The longest ever undertaken by humans. At the present rate of coloring, it would take three million years to paint the entire Ring. But the rate is accelerating."

He waited, trying to draw her out again, but she lapsed back into listlessness. He went on.

"The one aspect of their religion you don't seem to know about is their ban on killing. They won't take a human or a Symb life."

That got her attention.

"Equinox! Where..." she started shaking again.

"She's almost certainly alive."

"How could they keep her alive?"

"You're forgetting your children. Five of them."

The last thing anyone said to Parameter for two years was, "Take this, you might want to use it. Just press it to a red rock and forget about it. It lasts forever."

She took the object, a thin tube with a yellow bulb on each end. It was a Bacteriophage Applicator, filled with the tailored DNA that attacked and broke down the deposits of red dust left by the Engineers' Ringvirus. Touching the end of it to a coated rock would begin a chain reaction that would end only when all the surface of the rock was restored to its original color.

Parameter absently touched it to her side, where it sank without a trace in the tough integument of Equinox's outer hide. Then she shoved out the airlock and into fairyland.

"I never saw anything like this, Equinox," she said.

"No, you certainly haven't." The Symb had only Parameter's experiences to draw on.

"Where should we go? What's that line around the sky? Which way is it to the Ring?"

Affectionate laughter. "Silly planteater. We're *in* the Ring. That's why it stretches all around us. All except over in that direction. The sun is behind that part of the Ring, so the particles are illuminated primarily from the other side. You can see it faintly, by reflected light."

"Where did you learn all that?"

"From your head. The facts are there, and the deductive powers. You just never thought about it."

"I'm going to start thinking a lot more. This is almost frightening. I repeat: Where do we go from here?"

"Anywhere at all, as long as it's away from this awful place. I don't think I want to come back to the Ringmarket for about a decade."

"Now, now," Parameter chided her. "Surely we'll have to go back before that. Aren't you feeling the least bit poetic?"

The Ringmarket was the clearinghouse for the wildly variant and irresistibly beautiful art that was the byproduct of living a solitary life in the Rings. Art brokers, musicmongers, poetry sellers, editors, moodmusic vendors...all the people who made a living by standing between the artist and the audience and raking off a profit as works of art passed through their hands; they all gathered at the Ringmarket bazaar and bought exquisite works for the equivalent of pretty-colored beads. The Ringers had no need of money. All exchanges were straight barter: a fresh gas bottle for a symphony that would crash through the mind with unique rhythms and harmonies. A handful of the mineral pellets the Ringers needed every decade to supply trace elements that were rare in the Rings could buy a painting that would bring millions back in civilization. It was a speculative business. No one could know *which* of the thousands of works would catch the public taste at high tide and run away with it. All the buyers knew was that for unknown reasons the art of the Rings had consistently captured the highest prices and the wildest reviews. It was different. It was from a whole new viewpoint.

"I can't feel poetic back there. Besides, didn't you know that when we start to create, it will be music?"

"I didn't know that. How do you know?"

"Because there's a song in my heart. Off-key. Let's get out of here."

They left the metallic sphere of the market and soon it was only a blue vector line, pointed away from them.

They spent two years just getting used to their environment. The wonder never wore off. When they met others, they avoided them. Neither was ready for companionship; they had all they needed.

She was sinking, and glad of it. Every day without Equinox was torture. She had come to hate her jailer, even if his story was true, He was keeping her alive, which was the cruelest thing he could do. But even her hatred was a weak and fitful thing.

She stared into the imaginary distance and seldom noticed his comings and goings.

Then one day there were two of them. She noted it dispassionately, watched as they embraced each other and began to flow. So the other person was a female; they were going to mate. She turned away and didn't see, as the two Symbs merged in their conjugation process and slowly expanded into a featureless green sphere within which the humans would couple silently and then part, probably forever.

But something nagged at her, and she looked back. A bulge was forming on the side of the sphere that was facing her. It grew outward and began to form another, smaller sphere. A pink line formed the boundary between the two globes.

She looked away again, unable to retain an interest as the Symbs gave birth. But something was still nagging.

"Parameter."

The man (or was it the woman?) was floating beside her, holding the baby Symb.

She froze. Her eyes filled with horror.

"You're out of your mind."

"Maybe. I can't force it on you. But it's here. I'm going now, and you'll never see me again. You can live or die, whichever you choose. I've done all I can."

It was a warm day in the Upper Half. But then it was always a warm day, though some were warmer than others.

Ringography is an easy subject to learn. There are the Rings: Alpha, Beta, and the thin Gamma. The divisions are called Cassini and Encke, each having been created by the gravitational tug-of-war between Saturn and the larger moons for possession of the particles that make up the Rings. Beyond that, there is only the Upper Half and the Lower Half, above and below the plane, and Inspace and Outspace. The Ringers never visited Inspace because it included the intense Van Allen-type radiation belts that circle Saturn. Outspace was far from the traveled parts of the Rings, but was a nice place to visit because the Rings were all in one part of the sky from that vantage point. An odd experience for children, accustomed from birth to see the sky cut in half by the Rings.

Parameter was in the Upper Half to feed on the sunlight that was so much more powerful there than in the Rings. Equinox was in her extended configuration. The pair looked like a gauzy parabolic dish, two hundred meters across. The dish was transparent, with veins that made it look like a spider web. The illusion was heightened by the small figure spread-eagled in the center of it, like a fly. The fly was Parameter.

It was delicious to float there. She looked directly at the sun, which was bright even this far away and would have burned her eyes quickly if she had been really looking at it. But she saw only a projection. Equinox's visual senses were not nearly as delicate as human eyes.

The front of her body was bathed in radiance. It was highly sensual, but in a new way. It was the mindless joy of a flower unfolding to the sun that Parameter experienced, not the hotter animal passions she was used to. Energy coursed through her body and out into the light-gathering sheets that Equinox had extended. Her mind was disconnected more completely than she would have believed possible. Her thoughts came hours apart, and were concerned with sluggish, vegetable pleasures. She saw herself as naked, exposed to the light and the wind, floating in the center of a silver circle of life. She could feel the wind on her body in this airless place and wondered vacantly how Equinox could be so utterly convincing in the webs of illusion she spun.

There was a sudden gust.

"Parameter. Wake up, my darling."

"Hmmm?"

"There's a storm coming up. We've got to furl the sails and head into port."

Parameter felt other gusts as she swam through the warm waters back to alertness.

"How far are we from the Ring?"

"We're all right. We can be there in ten minutes if I tack for a bit and then use a few seconds of thrust."

In her extended configuration, Equinox was a moderately efficient solar sail. By controlling the angle she presented to the incoming sunlight she could slowly alter velocity. All Parameter had to do was push off above or below the Rings in a shallow arc. Equinox could bring them back into the Rings in a few days, using solar pressure. But the storm was a danger they had always to keep in mind.

It was the solar wind that Equinox felt, a cloud of particles thrust out from the sun by storms beneath the surface. Her radiation sensors had detected the first speed-of-light gusts of it, and the dangerous stuff would not be far behind.

Radiation was the chief danger of life in the Rings. The outer surface of a Symb was proof against much of the radiation the symbiotic pair would encounter in space. What got through was not enough to worry about, certainly never enough to cause sickness. But stray high-energy particles could cause mutations of the egg and sperm cells of the humans.

The intensity of the wind was increasing as they furled their sails and applied the gas thrusters.

"Did we get moving in time?" Parameter asked.

"There's a good margin. But we can't avoid getting a little hard stuff. Don't worry about it."

"What about children? If I want to have some later, couldn't that be a problem?"

"Naturally. But you'll never give birth to a mutation. I'll be able to see any deviations in the first few weeks and abort it and not even have to tell you."

"But you would tell me, wouldn't you?"

"If you want me to. But it isn't important. No more than the daily control I exert over any of your other bodily processes."

"If you say so."

"I say so. Don't worry, I said. You just handle the motor control and leave the busy work to me. Things don't seem quite real to me unless they're on the molecular level."

Parameter trusted Equinox utterly. So much so that when the really hard wind began buffeting them, she didn't worry for a second. She spread her arms to it, embraced it. It was strange that the "wind" didn't blow her around like a leaf. She would have liked that. All she really missed was her hair streaming around her shoulders. She no longer had any hair at all. It got in the way of the seal between the two of them.

As soon as she thought it, long black hair whipped out behind her, curling into her face and tickling her eyes. She could see it and feel it against her skin, but she couldn't touch it. That didn't surprise her, because it wasn't there.

"Thank you," she laughed. And then she laughed even harder as she looked down at herself. She was covered with hair; long, flowing hair that grew as she watched it.

They reentered the Ring, preceded by a twisting, imaginary train of hair a kilometer long.

Three days later she was still staring at the floating ball.

On the fifth day her hand twitched toward it.

"No. No. Equinox. Where are you?"

The Symb was in its dormant state. Only an infant Symb could exist without a human to feed and water it; once it had become attached to a human, it would die very quickly without one. But in dormancy, they could live for weeks at a low energy level. It only needed the touch of her hand to be triggered into action.

The hunger was eating its way through her body; she ignored it completely. It had become a fact of life, something she clutched to her to forget about the *real* hunger that was in her brain. She would never be forced to accept the Symb from hunger. It didn't even enter the question.

On the ninth day her hand began moving. She watched it, crying for Equinox to stop the movement, to give her strength.

She touched it.

"I think it's time we tried out the new uterus."

"I think you're right."

"If that thing out there is a male, we'll do it."

Equinox had in her complex of capabilities the knack of producing a nodule within her body that could take a cloned cell and nurture it until it grew into a complete organ; any organ she wished. She had done that with one of Parameter's cells. She removed it, cloned it, and let it grow into a new uterus. Parameter's old one had run out of eggs long ago and was useless for procreation, but the new one was brimming with life.

She had operated on her mate, taking out the old one and putting in the new. It had been painless and quick; Parameter had not even felt it.

Now they were ready to have a seed planted in it.

"Male," came the voice of the other figure. Before, Parameter would have answered by saying, "Solitude," and he would have gone on his way.

Now she said, "Female."

"Wilderness," he introduced himself.

"Parameter."

The mating ritual over, they fell silent as they drifted closer. She had computed it well, if a little fast. They hit and clung together with all their limbs. Slowly the Symbs melted into each other.

A sensation of pleasure came over Parameter.

"What is it?"

"What do you think? It's heaven. Did you think that because we're sexless, we wouldn't get any pleasure out of conjugation?"

"I guess I hadn't thought about it. It's…different. Not bad at all. But nothing like an orgasm."

"Stick around. We're just getting started."

There was a moment of insecurity as Equinox withdrew her connections, leaving only the one into her brain. She shuddered as an unfamiliar feeling passed over her, then realized she was holding her breath. She had to start respirating again. Her chest crackled as she brought long-unused muscles into play, but once the reflex was started she was able to forget about it and let her hindbrain handle the chore.

The inner surface started to phosphoresce, and she made out a shadowy figure floating in front of her. The light got brighter until it reached the level of bright moonlight. She could see him now.

"Hello," she said. He seemed surprised she wanted to talk, but grinned at her.

"Hello. You must be new."

"How did you know?"

"It shows. You want to talk. You probably expect me to go through an elaborate ritual." And with that he reached for her and pulled her toward him.

"Hold on there," she said. "I'd like to know you a little better first."

He sighed, but let her go. "I'm sorry. You don't know yet. All right, what would you like to know about me?"

She looked him over. He was small, slightly smaller than her. He was completely hairless, as was she. There didn't seem to be any way to guess his age; all the proper clues were missing. Growing out of the top of his head was a snaky umbilicus.

She discovered there was really little to ask him, but having made a point of it, she threw in a token question.

"How old are you?"

"Old enough. Fourteen."

"All right, let's do it your way." She touched him and shifted in space to accommodate his entry.

To her pleasant surprise, it lasted longer than the thirty seconds she had expected. He was an accomplished lover; he seemed to know all the right moves. She was warming deliciously when she heard him in her head.

"*Now* you know," he said, and her head was filled with his laughter.

Everything before that, good as it was, had been just a warm-up.

Parameter and the baby Symb howled with pain.

"I didn't want you," she cried, hurling waves of rejection at the child and at herself. "All I want is Equinox."

That went on for an endless time. The stars burnt out around them. The galaxy turned like a whirligig. The universe contracted; exploded; contracted again. Exploded. Contracted and gave it up as a waste of time. Time ended as all events came to an end.

The two of them floated, howling at each other.

Wilderness drifted away against the swirling background of stars. He didn't look back, and neither did Parameter. They knew each other too well to need good-byes. They might never meet again, but that didn't matter either, because each carried all they needed of the other.

"In a life full of cheap thrills, I never had anything like that."

Equinox seemed absorbed. She quietly acknowledged that it had, indeed, been superduper, but there was something else. There was a new knowledge.

"I'd like to try something," she said.

"Shoot."

Parameter's body was suddenly caressed by a thousand tiny, wet tongues. They searched out every cranny, all at the same time. They were hot, at least a thousand billion degrees, but they didn't burn; they soothed.

"Where were you keeping *that*?" Parameter quavered when it stopped. "And why did you stop?"

"I just learned it. I was watching while I was experiencing. I picked up a few tricks."

"You've got *more*?"

"Sure. I didn't want to start out with the intense ones until I saw how you liked that one. I thought it was very nice. You shuddered beautifully; the delta waves were fascinating."

Parameter broke up with laughter. "Don't give me that clinical stuff. You liked it so much you scared yourself."

"That comes as close as you can come to describing my reaction. But I was serious about having things I think we'll like even better. I can combine sensations in a novel way. Did you appreciate the subtle way the 'heat' blended into the sensation of feathers with an electric current through them?"

"It sounds hideous when you say it in words. But that was what it was, all right. Electric feathers. But pain had nothing to do with it."

Equinox considered it. "I'm not sure about that. I was deep into the pain-sensation center of you. But I was tickling it in a new way, the same way Wilderness tickled you. There is something I'm discovering. It has to do with the reality of pain. *All* you experience is more a function of your brain than of your nerve endings. Pain is no exception. What I do is connect the two centers—pain and pleasure—and route them through other sensorium pathways, resulting in..."

"Equinox."

?????

"Make love to me."

She was in the center of the sun, every atom of her body fusing in heat so hot it was icy. She swam to the surface, taking her time through the plastic waves of ionized gas, where she grew until she could hold the whole sputtering ball in her hand and rub it around her body. It flicked and fumed and smoked, gigantic prominences responding to her will, wreathing her in fire and smoke that bit and tickled. Flares snaked into her, reaming nerves with needle-sharp pins of gas that were soft as a kiss. She was swallowed whole by something pink that had no name, and slid down the slippery innards to splash in a pool of sweet-smelling sulfur.

It melted her; she melted it. Equinox was there; she picked her up and hurled her and herself in a wave of water, a gigantic wave that was gigatons of pent-up energy, rearing itself into a towering breaker a thousand kilometers high. She crashed on a beach of rubbery skin, which became a forest of snakes that squeezed her until the top of her head blew off and tiny flowers showered around her, all of them Equinox.

She was drawn back together from the far corners of the solar system and put into a form that called itself "Parameter" but would answer to anything at all. Then she was rising on a rocket that thrust deep into her vagina, into recesses that weren't even there but felt like mirrors that showed her own face. She was a fusion warhead of sensation; primed to blow. Sparks whipped around her, and each was a kiss of electric feathers. She was reaching orbital velocity; solar escape velocity; the speed of light. She turned herself inside out and contained the universe. The speed of light was a crawl slower than any snail; she transcended it.

There was an explosion; an implosion. She drew away from herself and fell into herself, and the fragments of her body drifted down to the beach, where she and Equinox gathered them and put them in a pile of quivering parts, each smaller than an atom.

It was a long job. They took their time.

"Next time," Parameter suggested, "try to work in some elephants."

Someone had invented a clock. It ticked.

Parameter woke up.

"Did you do that?"

No answer.

"Shut the damn thing off."

The ticking stopped. She rolled over and went back to sleep. Around her, a trillion years passed.

It was no good; she couldn't sleep.

"Are you there?"

Yes.

"What do you think we ought to do?"

Despair. We've lost Equinox.

"You never knew her."

Part of her will always be with you. Enough to hurt you. We will always hurt.

"I want to live again."

Live with hurt?

"If there's no other way. Come on. Let's start. Try to make a light. Come on, you can do it. I can't tell you how; you have to do that yourself. I love you. Blend with me, wash me clean, wipe out the memory."

Impossible. We cannot alter ourselves. I want Equinox.

"Damn you, you never knew her."

Know her as good as you. Better. In a way, I *am* Equinox. But in another way, I can never be.

"Don't talk in riddles. Merge with me."

Cannot. You do not love me yet.

"You want to sleep on it another few thousand years?"

Yes. You are much nicer when you are asleep.

"Is that an insult?"

No. You have loved me in your sleep. You have talked to me, you have taught me, given me love and guidance, grown me up to an adult. But you still think I'm Equinox. I'm not. I am me.

"Who is that?"

No name. I will have a name when you start really talking to me.

"Go to sleep. You confuse me."

Love. Affection. Rockabye, rockabye, rockabye.

"You have a name yet?"

"Yes. My name is Solstice."

Parameter cried, loud and long, and washed herself clean in her own tears.

It took them four years to work their way around to Ringmarket. They traded a song, one that had taken three years to produce, a sweet-sad dirge that somehow rang with hope, orchestrated for three lutes and synthesizer; traded it and a promise of four more over the next century to a tinpan alleycat for an elephant gun. Then they went out on a trail that was four years cold to stalk the memory of those long-ago pachyderm days.

In the way that an earlier generation of humans had known the shape of a hill, the placement of trees and flowers on it, the smell and feel of it; and another generation could remember at a glance what a street corner looked like; or still another the details of a stretch of corridor beneath the surface of the moon; in that same way, Parameter knew rocks. She would know the rock she had pushed off from on that final day just before Equinox was taken from her, the rock she now knew to have been an Engineer waystation. She knew where it had been going on that day, and how fast, and for how long. She knew where it would be now, and that was where she and Solstice were headed. The neighborhood would be different, but she could find that rock.

They found it, in only three years of search. She knew it instantly, knew every crevice and pit on the side she had landed on. The door was on the other side. They picked a likely rock a few kilometers away and settled down for a long wait.

Seventy-six times Saturn turned below them while they used the telescopic sight of the gun to survey the traffic at the station. By the end of that time, they knew the routine of the place better than the residents did. When the time came for action they had worked over each detail until it was almost a reflex.

A figure came out of the rock and started off in the proper direction. Parameter squinted down the barrel of the gun and drew a bead. The range was extreme, but she had no doubt of a hit. The reason for her confidence was the long red imaginary line that she saw growing from the end of the barrel. It represented the distance the bullet would travel in one-thousandth of a second. The figure she was shooting at also had a line extending in front of it, not nearly so long. All she had to do was bring the ends of the two lines together and squeeze the trigger.

It went as planned. The gun was firing stunbullets, tiny harmonic generators that would knock out the pair for six hours. The outer hide of a Symb was proof against the kinetic energy contained in most projectiles, natural or artificial. She didn't dare use a beam stunner because the Engineers in the station would detect it.

They set out in pursuit of the unconscious pair. There was no hurry; the longer it took to rendezvous, the farther they would be from danger.

It took five hours to reach them. Once in contact, Solstice took over. She had assured Parameter that it would be possible to fuse with an unconscious Symb, and she was right. Soon Parameter was floating in the dark cavity with the Engineer, a female. She put the barrel of the gun under the other's chin and waited.

"I don't know if I can do it, Solstice," she said.

"It won't be something you'll ever be proud of, but you know the reasons as well as I. Just keep thinking of Equinox."

"I wonder if that's a good idea? I'd rather do something for her that I *would* be proud of."

"Want to back out? We can still get away. But if she wakes up and sees us, it could get awkward if we let her live."

"I know. I have to do it. I just don't like it."

The Engineer was stirring. Parameter tightened her grip on the rifle.

She opened her eyes, looked around, and seemed to be listening. Solstice was keeping the other Symb from calling for help.

"I won't give you any trouble," the woman said. "But is it asking too much to allow me a few minutes for my death ritual?"

"You can have that and more if you're a fast talker. I don't want to kill you, but I confess I think I'll have to. I want to tell you some things, and to do it, I'll need your cooperation. If you don't cooperate, I can take what I need from you anyway. What I'm hoping is that there'll be some way you can show me that will make your death unnecessary. Will you open your mind to me?"

A light came into the woman's eyes, then was veiled. Parameter was instantly suspicious.

"Don't be nervous," the Engineer said, "I'll do as you ask. It was just something of a surprise." She relaxed, and Parameter eased herself into the arms of Solstice, who took over as go-between.

They had a lot staked on the outcome of this mutual revelation.

It came in a rush, the impalpable weight of the religious fervor and dedication. And above it all, the Great Cause, the project that would go on long after everyone now alive was dead. The audacity of it! The vision of Humanity the mover, the controller, the artist; the Engineer. The universe would acknowledge the sway of Humanity when it gazed at the wonder that was being wrought in the Rings of Saturn.

Ringpainter the Great was a utopian on a grand scale. He had been bitterly disappointed in the manner in which humanity had invaded the solar system. He thought in terms of terraforming and of shifting planets in their courses. What he saw was burrows in rock.

So he preached, and spoke of Dyson spheres and space arks, of turning stars on and off at will, of remodeling galaxies. To him and his followers, the universe was an immensely complex toy that they could do beautiful things with. They wanted to unscrew a black hole and see what made it tick. They wanted to unshift the red shift. They believed in continuous creation, because the big bang implied an end to all their efforts.

Parameter and Solstice reeled under the force of it; the conviction that this admittedly symbolic act could get humanity moving in the direction Ringpainter wanted. He had an idea that there were beings out there keeping score, and they could be impressed by the Grand Gesture. When they saw what a pretty thing Ring Beta had become, they would step in and give the forces of Ringpainter a hand.

The woman they had captured, whose name they learned was Rosy-Red-Ring 3351, was convinced of the truth of these ideas. She had devoted her life to the furtherance of the Design. But they saw her faith waver as she beheld what they had to show her. She cringed away from the shrunken, hardened, protectively encased memory of the days after the theft of Equinox. They held it up and made her look at it, peeling away the layers of forgetfulness they had protected themselves with and thrusting it at her.

At last they let her go. She crouched, quivering, in the air.

"You've seen what we've been."

"Yes." She was sobbing.

"And you know what we have to do to find Equinox. You saw that in my mind. What I want to know is, can this cup pass from us? Do you know another way? Tell me quick."

"I didn't *know*," she cried. "It's what we do to all the Consers we capture. We can't kill them. It's against the Law. So we separate them, keep the Symb, leave the human to be found. We know most of them are never found, but it's the best we can do. But I didn't know it was so bad. I never thought of it. I almost think—"

"No need to think. You're right. It would be more merciful to kill the human. I don't know about the Symb. I'll have to talk to Equinox about that. At first I wanted to kill all the Engineers in the Rings, with a lot of care put into the project so they didn't die too quick. I can't do that any more. I'm not a Conser. I never was. I'm not anything but a seeker, looking for my friend. I don't care if you paint the Ring; go ahead. But I have to find Equinox, and I have to find my children. You have to answer my question now. Can you think of a way I can let you live and still do what I have to do?"

"No. There's no other way."

Parameter sighed. "All right. Get on with your ritual."

"I'm not sure if I want to any more."

"You'd probably better. Your faith has been shaken, but you might be right about the scorekeepers. If you are, I'd hate to be the cause of you going out the wrong way." She was already putting her distance between herself and this woman she would kill. She was becoming an object, something she was going to do something unpleasant to; not a person with a right to live.

Rosy-Red-Ring 3351 gradually calmed as she went through the motions of her auto-extreme unction. By the time she had finished she was as composed as she had been at the start of her ordeal.

"I've experienced the fullness of it," she said quietly. "The Engineers do not claim to know everything. We were wrong about our policy of separating symbiotic pairs. My only regret is that I can't tell anyone about our mistake." She looked doubtfully at Parameter, but knew it was useless. "I forgive you. I love you, my killer. Do the deed." She presented her white neck and closed her eyes.

"Umm," Parameter said. She had not heard her victim's last words; she had cut herself off and could see only the neck. She let Solstice guide her hands. They found the pressure points as if by instinct, pressed hard, and it was just like Solstice had said it would be. The woman was unconscious in seconds. Now she must be kept alive for a few minutes while Solstice did what she had to do.

"Got it," came Solstice's shaken thought.

"Was it hard?" Parameter had kept away from it.

"Let's don't talk about it. I'll show it to you in about a decade and we can cry for a year. But I have it."

So the other Symb was already dead, and Solstice had been with it as it died. Parameter's job would not be nearly so hard.

She put her thumbs on the woman's neck again, bent her ear to the chest. She pressed, harder this time. Soon the heartbeat fluttered, raced briefly. There was a convulsion, then she was dead.

"Let's get out of here."

What they had acquired was the Symb-Engineer frequency organ. It was the one way the inhabitants of the Rings had of telling friend from foe. The radio organs of the Symbs were tuned from birth to send on a specific frequency, and the Engineers used one band exclusively. The Consers employed another, because they had a stake in identifying friends and foes, too. But Parameter no longer identified with either side, and now had the physical resources to back up her lack of conviction. She could send on either band now, according to the needs of the moment, and so could move freely from one society to the other. If caught, she would be seen as a spy by either side, but she didn't think of herself as one.

It had been necessary to kill the Engineer pair because the organ could not be removed without causing the death of the Symb. The organ could be cloned, and that was the escape Parameter had offered the other two. But it had been refused. So now Solstice had two voices; her own, and the one from the other organ which she had already implanted in herself.

In addition to the double voice, they had picked up information about the life of the Engineers without which it would be impossible to function without immediate exposure. They knew the customs and beliefs of the Engineers and could fit in with them as long as they didn't go into sexual rapport. That could get sticky, but they had a dodge. The most reliable way to avoid intercourse was to be pregnant, and that was what they set out to do.

It didn't seem too important, but his name was Appoggiatura. They had encountered him during the third week after the murder. It was a risk—a small one, but a risk all the same. He had been easy about it. He learned all about Parameter's deeds and plans during their intercourse and remained unperturbed. Fanatic dedication was rare among Consers; the only real fanatic Parameter had met was Bushwhacker, who had offered to shoot her at the hint of treason. Parameter and Solstice were aware that what they were doing was treason to the Conser cause. Appoggiatura didn't seem to care, or if he did, he thought it was justified after what they had been through.

"But have you thought about what you'll do if you find Equinox? I don't know what you think, but it sounds like a thorny problem to me."

"It's thorny, all right," Solstice agreed. "To me, especially. Don't talk to me about problems until you've gone through the insecurity I've felt when I think about that day."

"It's my insecurity, too," Parameter said. "We don't know. But we do know we have to find her. And the children, though that isn't so strong. I only saw them for a few minutes, and they'll be seven years old now. I can't expect much there."

"I wouldn't expect much from Equinox, either," he said. "I know something about what happens to a Symb when it's separated from a human. Something dies; I don't know what. But it has to start over again from the beginning. She'll be a part of one of your children now, which-ever one of them she took over when she was separated from you. You won't know her, and she won't know you."

"Still, we have to do this. I want to leave you now."

For six months they drifted, allowing Parameter's body to swell to the point that it would be obvious she was pregnant and not available for sex. During that time they thought.

Countless times they decided they were being foolish; that to com-plete their search would be to finish their life's mission and be faced with what to do with the next thousand years. But they could not just go through the motions. Perhaps one person could do that, but it wouldn't work with two. There was always that alter ego telling you by her very presence that you were living a lie.

And there was Rosy-Red-Ring 3351. If they quit, her murder would have been for no purpose. That would have been too much to bear. They had her in their memory, always cherishing her, always ashamed of what they had done. And the Symb, whose name Solstice had not yet been able to mention. One day Parameter would have to go through that killing again, but closer. Solstice was, if anything, even more determined than Parameter to verify the necessity of that terrible act.

So they started back to the Engineer-infested sector where so long ago Equinox had been made a prisoner of war.

There was a nervous moment the first time they used the stolen transmitter organ, but it went off smoothly. After that, they were able to move freely in Engineer society. It was a strange world, steeped in ritual that would have instantly confounded a novice. But they had received an instant course in religion and fell back on the memories of Rosy-Red-Ring that were burned into their minds.

They took the name Earth-Revenger 9954f, a common name attached to a random number with the "f" added as a mark of status. Only Engineers who had borne a hundred children were supposed to add the letter to their names. Theoretically, births were supposed to be recorded at Ringpainter Temple, clear across the Ring from them, where what records it was possible to keep in Ring society were stored. But there was no danger once they had verified that their stolen transmitter would fool the Engineers. Even in Engineer society, where social contact was more important than among Consers, the chance of meeting the same person twice was small. The chance of Parameter and Solstice meeting the real Earth-Revenger 9954f was not even worth thinking about.

The place they stayed around was the very rock she had pushed off from on the day of her capture, the rock from which Rosy-Red-Ring had left on her final day. It was a communications center, a social hall, a gossip rendezvous; the means by which the Engineers were able to keep their cohesiveness against the formidable odds of empty space.

She took over the job of station manager, a largely informal, voluntary post that meant you stayed in the station and loosely coordinated the activities there. These consisted of posting in written form information that was too important to entrust to word of mouth, and generally trying to pump each incoming Engineer for that type of information. As such, it was ideally suited for what she wanted to do.

There was the problem of her pregnancy. Pregnant women needed a lot of sunshine and rock and ice, and generally didn't take the job. She faced a lot of questions about it, but got away with her story about just plain liking the job so much she didn't want to give it up.

But the problem of getting enough sunlight was real. The location of the station was deep enough inside the Rings by now that the incident sunlight was low. She should have gone above the plane to where the light wasn't scattered off so many rocks, but she couldn't.

She compromised by spending all her free time outside the station with Solstice in her extended configuration.

The prime topic of conversation was the failure of the Pop Edict, and it was this that led her to information about Equinox.

Under the Edict, each Engineer was to undergo a sex change and spend nine years as a female for every year as a male. Three children were to be borne each of those years. The figures told a different story.

It was the first resistance to an Edict; unorganized, but still disturbing. There was much debate about it, and much solemn rededication. Everyone vowed to bear as many children as she could, but Parameter wondered how sincere it was. Her own sampling of Engineers revealed that females did outnumber males, but only by three to one, not nine to one.

There were several causes discussed for it. One, and the most obvious, was simple preference. Statistically, 90 percent of all people had a preferred sex, and of those, it was evenly divided as to which sex was the preferred one. For the target percentages to be in effect, 35 percent of the Engineers would have to be living as the sex they did not prefer. The actual figures indicated that not many of them were doing so. They were remaining defiantly male.

Then there was the logistical problem. To gain enough useful mass to produce one baby, a Symb-human pair had to ingest almost a thousand kilograms of rock and ice. Only a tiny fraction of it was the chemicals needed to produce a baby. Then, to convert the mass to useful form, energy was required. The pair had to spend long hours in the sunlight. After all that, there was little time for painting the Ring, and that was what most Engineers saw as their prime mission, not becoming baby factories.

It was said that Ringpainter was in meditation, and had been for the past ten years, trying to find a way out of the dilemma. She saw her Grand Gesture being slowed down to the point where it was actually in jeopardy. If, in the far future, the Engineer birthrate didn't outstrip the Conser birthrate, it would mean trouble. The time of the great Conser effort was yet to come. As things now stood, a Conser might not even see a painted rock in three or four days; they were too far apart. But as the number of painted rocks grew, the rate of recoloring would also grow. Then the Engineers would have to depend on the sheer rate of repainting to overpower the negative effect of the Consers. If their populations were nearly equal, it would be a stalemate, and only the Consers could win a stalemate. To accomplish the Grand Design, 90 percent of the rock in Ring Beta must be painted. To reach this figure, the Engineers must outnumber the Consers by ten to one, otherwise the number of painted rocks would stabilize below the target figure. It was a crisis of the first magnitude, though no one alive would see the outcome.

In discussing this with one of the Engineers, a woman named Glorious-Red-Ring 43f, the break came. She was one of the early followers of Ringpainter, had been in the Ring for two hundred years. She had birthed 389 children, and acknowledged it was below her quota. She was living proof that the goals of Ringpainter were unrealistic, but she had unshakable faith that it was the right policy. She blamed herself that she had not had six hundred children, and had dedicated herself to meeting her quota within the next century. To do that, she must bear five hundred children. Parameter thought she was pathetic. She was pregnant with septuplets.

"I see these young ones coming in here with twins in their wombs and wonder how they can call themselves Engineers," she complained. "Only last month I saw one with a single child on the way. One! Can you imagine? How many do you have there?"

"Three. Maybe it should have been more." Parameter tried to sound guilty about it.

"That's all right. Three is the right number. I won't ask if you had three *last* year.

"And the number of males I see makes me weep. I make it 7.43 to 2.57, female to male." She lapsed into a brooding silence.

"If that wasn't bad enough," Parameter prompted, "I understand the Conser birthrate has equalled ours."

"Has it?" She was concerned at this bit of news, and would have been relieved to learn it was totally spurious. Parameter used that line frequently to lead someone into a discussion of Conser women in general and one Conser in particular who had been captured around here several years ago while birthing quints.

"But it shouldn't surprise me," the Engineer said. "So many of the Consers we've taken lately have been pregnant with three, four, even five."

This was more like it. Parameter considered remarks that might draw the woman out.

"I recall, almost ten years ago…or was it five? I get confused. There was this Conser some of our people took. Five children she had just borne."

Parameter was so surprised she almost let the opportunity slip by.

"Five?" she managed to croak. It was enough.

"That's right. How long has it been since you saw one of ours give birth to five? And those anarchists don't even have a Pop Edict to tell them to do it. She was doing it for fun."

"Were you there when it happened? When they captured the woman?"

"I heard about it later. They had the pups around here for a few days. Didn't know what to do with them. No one had heard about the crèche."

"Crèche?"

"You, too. The newsmongering around here has fallen down. It should have been posted and circulated."

"I'll surely see that it's done if you'll tell me about it."

"There's a crèche for POW children about fifty thousand kilometers forward from here. That's where we're supposed to take captured Conser children for indoctrination."

They digested that, didn't like the taste of it.

"The indoctrination's pretty successful, is it?"

"Great Red Ring, I hope so. Haven't been there myself. But we need everything we can get these days."

"Just where is this crèche? I should post the orbital elements around here."

The triplets were a failure. During the tenth month, on the way to the crèche, Solstice notified Parameter that it was hopeless; they hadn't gotten enough energy and raw materials during their stay at the way-station. It was no longer possible to hold their development back, and it was too late to amass the necessary minerals to do the job.

Solstice aborted them and reabsorbed the dead bodies. With the extra energy from the abortion, they were able to make good time to the crèche. It only took two years.

The crèche was deserted; an empty shell. News traveled slowly in the Ring. Inquiring around, Parameter discovered that it had not been operating for fifteen years. So her children had never arrived, though they had set out.

This was the time for despair, but they were beyond despair. Somewhere on the way to the crèche they had stopped believing it was possible to do what they were trying to do. So it wasn't a blow to find the crèche deserted. Still, it was hard to accept that their search ended here; they had been on the trail for nine years.

But the figures were unimpeachable. The volume of Ring Beta was seventy billion cubic kilometers, and any one of them could hide a thousand children.

They hung around the crèche for a few weeks, questioning Engineers, trying to find an angle that would enable them to defeat the statistics. Without a known destination for their children, there was no way out; they could be anywhere, and that was so vast it didn't bear thinking about.

In the end they left, and didn't know where they were bound.

Three days later they encountered another Conser, a male, and mated with him. He was sympathetic to their plight, but agreed with them that there was no chance of finding their children. Solstice carefully saw to it that Parameter was not fertilized. They had had enough of pregnancy for the next century or so.

And after they left the Conser, they found themselves falling asleep. Only they knew it wasn't sleep.

Before she even opened her eyes, Parameter reached frantically for the top of her head.

"Solstice…"

"I'm here. Don't make any sudden moves. We've been captured. I don't know by whom, but he's armed."

She opened her eyes. She was in a conjugation sphere and the tendril from Solstice was still firmly planted in her head. There was another person with her, a small person. He waved his gun at her and she nodded.

"Don't be alarmed," he said. "If you can answer a few questions you'll probably come out of this alive."

"You can set your mind at ease. I won't cause any trouble."

She realized he was a child, about eleven years old. But he seemed to know about stunners.

"We've been watching you for about a week," he said. "You talked to Engineers, so we naturally assumed you were one. But just now you spoke to a Conser, and on the Conser frequency. I want an explanation."

"I was originally a Conser. Recently I killed an Engineer and stole her transmitter organ." She knew she couldn't think of a convincing lie quickly enough to be safe from his stunner. She wasn't sure there *was* a convincing lie to cover her situation.

"Which side do you identify with now?"

"Neither side. I want to be independent if anyone will allow that."

He looked thoughtful. "That may be easier than you know. Why did you kill the Engineer?"

"I had to do it so I could move in Engineer society, so I could hunt for my children and the Symb who was taken from me several years ago. I have been—"

"What's your name?"

"Parameter, and Solstice."

"Right. I've got a message for you, Parameter. It's from your children. They're all right, and looking for you around here. We should be able to find them in a few days' search."

The children recognized the awkwardness of the situation. As they joined the group conjugation, emerging from the walls of the slowly enlarging sphere, they limited themselves to a brief kiss, then withdrew into a tangle of small bodies.

Parameter and Solstice were so jittery they could hardly think. The five children they could get to know, but Equinox? What about her?

They got the distinct feeling that the children recognized Parameter, then realized it was possible. Equinox had been talking to them while still in the womb, urging their minds to develop with pictures and sounds. Some of the pictures would have been of Parameter.

Ring children are not like other human children. They are born already knowing most of what they need to survive in the Rings. Then they are able to join with an infant Symb and help guide its development into an adult in a few weeks. From there, the Symb takes over for three years, teaching them and leading them to the places they need to go to grow up strong and healthy. For all practical purposes they are mature at three years. They must be; they cannot count on being with their mother more than the few weeks it takes them to acquire an adult Symb. From that time, they are on their own. Infant physical shortcomings are made up by the guidance and control of the Symb.

Parameter looked at these strange children, these youngsters whose backyard was billions of cubic kilometers wide and whose toys were stars and comets. What did she know of them? They might as well be another species. But that shouldn't matter; so was Solstice.

Solstice was almost hysterical. She was gripped in fear that in some way she couldn't understand she was going to lose Parameter. She was in danger of losing her mind. One part of her loved Equinox as hopelessly as Parameter did; another part knew there was room for only one Symb for any one human. What if it came to a choice? How would they face it?

"Equinox?"

There was a soundless scream from Solstice. "Equinox?"

?????

"Is that you, Equinox?"

The answer was very faint, very far away. They could not hear it.

"It's me. Parameter."

"And Solstice. You don't know me—"

I know you. You are me. I used to be you. I remember both of you. Interesting.

But the voice didn't sound interested. It was cool.

"I don't understand." No one was sure who said it.

But you do. I am gone. There is a new me. There is a new you. It is over.

"We love you."

Yes. Of course you do. But there is no me left to love.

"We're confused."

You will get over it.

The children floated together: quietly, respectfully; waiting for their mother to come to grips with her new reality. At last she stirred.

"Maybe we'll understand it some day," Parameter said.

One of the girls spoke.

"Equinox is no more, Mother," she said. "And yet she's still with us. She made a choice when she knew we were going to be captured. She reabsorbed her children and fissioned into five parts. None of us got all of her, but we all got enough."

Parameter shook her head and tried to make sense out of it. The child who had brought her here had not been willing to tell her anything, preferring to wait until her children could be with her.

"I don't understand how you came to find me."

"All it took was patience. We never reached the crèche; we were liberated on the way here by Alphans. They killed all the Engineers who were guarding us and adopted us themselves."

"What's an Alphan?"

"Alphans are the Ringers who live in Ring Alpha, who are neither Conser nor Engineer. They are renegades from both sides who have opted out of the conflict. They took care of us, and helped us when we said we wanted to find you. We knew where we had been going, and knew it was only a matter of time until you showed up here, if you were still alive. So we waited. And you got here in only nine years. You're very resourceful."

"Perhaps." She was looking at her children's legs. They were oddly deformed. And what were those blunt instruments at the ends of them? How odd.

"Feet, Mother," the child said. "There are surgeons in Alpha, but we could never afford to go there until we had found you. Now we'll go. We hope you'll go with us."

"Huh? Ah, I guess I should. That's across the Cassini Division, isn't it? And there's no war there? No killing?"

"That's right. We don't care if they paint Ring Beta with stripes and polka dots. They're freaks: Conser and Engineers. We are the true Ringers."

"Solstice?"

"Why not?"

"We'll go with you. Say, what are your names?"

"Army," said one of the girls.

"Navy," said another.

"Marine."

"Airforce."

"And Elephant," said the boy.

GOOD-BYE,
ROBINSON CRUSOE

I've been a little bemused at the uproar over Pluto's demotion to a dwarf planet. I guess part of it is that word: demotion. People just seem to *like* Pluto. It was discovered less than 100 years ago. I've always liked the story of how it was searched for by Percival Lowell and later Clyde Tombaugh, and finally discovered in 1930. Neptune had been discovered in 1846 because something was perturbing the orbit of Uranus. Lowell and Tombaugh thought something was perturbing Neptune in turn, and trained their telescope on the region of the sky where they predicted it would be, and sure enough, there it was. (Turns out that was sheer luck. Pluto is far too small and distant to have much effect on the much larger Neptune.)

We have learned a lot about Pluto since I wrote this story. We have found that it has at least four moons. We know that its axis of rotation is skewed, like that of Uranus, so that it seems to roll around its orbit. We have some grainy "maps" made by computer from Hubble telescope data, about as good as the blurred photos of Mars that were all we had when I was young. And in 2015, if all goes well, we should be getting some really great pictures of the dwarf planet and its moon from the New Horizons spacecraft, which has been on its way there since 2006.

New Horizons will probably tell us a lot more about Pluto's composition, too. The best current thinking is that it is covered with a layer of frozen nitrogen, and under that is a thick mantle of water ice. Beneath that is a rocky core.

But none of that really matters to this story. It takes place in a huge, created environment that could have been on the moon, or Mars, or Mercury, or any planet, dwarf planet, or moon in the solar system. These underground environments reproduce Earthly places, like vast terrariums, and I call them by the generic term "disneyland." To the people forever exiled from the home planet, I thought they'd be a lot more fun than the Matterhorn ride, or even It's a Small World.

It was summer, and Piri was in his second childhood. First, second; who counted? His body was young. He had not felt more alive since his original childhood back in the spring, when the sun drew closer and the air began to melt.

He was spending his time at Rarotonga Reef, in the Pacifica disneyland. Pacifica was still under construction, but Rarotonga had been used by the ecologists as a testing ground for the more ambitious barrier-type reef they were building in the south, just off the "Australian" coast. As a result, it was more firmly established than the other biomes. It was open to visitors, but so far only Piri was there. The "sky" disconcerted everyone else.

Piri didn't mind it. He was equipped with a brand-new toy: a fully operational imagination, a selective sense of wonder that allowed him to blank out those parts of his surroundings that failed to fit with his current fantasy.

He awoke with the tropical sun blinking in his face through the palm fronds. He had built a rude shelter from flotsam and detritus on the beach. It was not to protect him from the elements. The disneyland management had the weather well in hand; he might as well have slept in the open. But castaways *always* build some sort of shelter.

He bounced up with the quick alertness that comes from being young and living close to the center of things, brushed sand from his naked body, and ran for the line of breakers at the bottom of the narrow strip of beach.

His gait was awkward. His feet were twice as long as they should have been, with flexible toes that were webbed into flippers. Dry sand showered around his legs as he ran. He was brown as coffee and cream, and hairless.

Piri dived flat to the water, sliced neatly under a wave, and paddled out to waist-height. He paused there. He held his nose and worked his arms up and down, blowing air through his mouth and swallowing at the same time. What looked like long, hairline scars between his lower ribs came open. Red-orange fringes became visible inside them, and gradually lowered. He was no longer an air-breather.

He dived again, mouth open, and this time he did not come up. His esophagus and trachea closed and a new valve came into operation. It would pass water in only one direction, so his diaphragm now functioned as a pump pulling water through his mouth and forcing it out through the gill-slits. The water flowing through this lower chest area caused his gills to engorge with blood, turning them purplish-red and forcing his lungs to collapse upward into his chest cavity. Bubbles of air trickled out his sides, then stopped. His transition was complete.

The water seemed to grow warmer around him. It had been pleasantly cool; now it seemed no temperature at all. It was the result of his body temperature lowering in response to hormones released by an artificial gland in his cranium. He could not afford to burn energy at the rate he had done in the air; the water was too efficient a coolant for that. All through his body arteries and capillaries were constricting as parts of him stabilized at a lower rate of function.

No naturally evolved mammal had ever made the switch from air to water breathing, and the project had taxed the resources of bio-engineering to its limits. But everything in Piri's body was a living part of him. It had taken two full days to install it all.

He knew nothing of the chemical complexities that kept him alive where he should have died quickly from heat loss or oxygen starvation. He knew only the joy of arrowing along the white sandy bottom. The water was clear, blue-green in the distance.

The bottom kept dropping away from him, until suddenly it reached for the waves. He angled up the wall of the reef until his head broke the surface, climbed up the knobs and ledges until he was standing in the sunlight. He took a deep breath and became an air-breather again.

The change cost him some discomfort. He waited until the dizziness and fit of coughing had passed, shivering a little as his body rapidly underwent a reversal to a warm-blooded economy.

It was time for breakfast.

He spent the morning foraging among the tidepools. There were dozens of plants and animals that he had learned to eat raw. He ate a great deal, storing up energy for the afternoon's expedition on the outer reef.

Piri avoided looking at the sky. He wasn't alarmed by it; it did not disconcert him as it did the others. But he had to preserve the illusion that he was actually on a tropical reef in the Pacific Ocean, a castaway, and not a vacationer in an environment bubble below the surface of Pluto.

Soon he became a fish again, and dived off the sea side of the reef.

The water around the reef was oxygen-rich from the constant wave action. Even here, though, he had to remain in motion to keep enough water flowing past his external gill fringes. But he could move more slowly as he wound his way down into the darker reaches of the sheer reef face. The reds and yellows of his world were swallowed by the blues and greens and purples. It was quiet. There were sounds to hear, but his ears were not adapted to them. He moved slowly through shafts of blue light, keeping up the bare minimum of water flow.

He hesitated at the ten-meter level. He had thought he was going to his Atlantis Grotto to check out his crab farm. Then he wondered if he ought to hunt up Ocho the Octopus instead. For a panicky moment he was afflicted with the bane of childhood: an inability to decide what to do with himself. Or maybe it was worse, he thought. Maybe it was a sign of growing up. The crab farm bored him, or at least it did today.

He waffled back and forth for several minutes, idly chasing the tiny red fish that flirted with the anemones. He never caught one. This was no good at all. Surely there was an adventure in this silent fairyland. He had to find one.

An adventure found him, instead. Piri saw something swimming out in the open water, almost at the limits of his vision. It was long and pale, an attenuated missile of raw death. His heart squeezed in panic, and he scuttled for a hollow in the reef.

Piri called him the Ghost. He had seen him many times in the open sea. He was eight meters of mouth, belly and tail: hunger personified. There were those who said the great white shark was the most ferocious carnivore that ever lived. Piri believed it.

It didn't matter that the Ghost was completely harmless to him. The Pacifica management did not like having its guests eaten alive. An adult could elect to go into the water with no protection, providing the necessary waivers were on file. Children had to be implanted with an equalizer. Piri had one, somewhere just below the skin of his left wrist. It was a sonic generator, set to emit a sound that would mean terror to any predator in the water.

The Ghost, like all the sharks, barracudas, morays, and other predators in Pacifica, was not like his cousins who swam the seas of Earth. He had been cloned from cells stored in the Biological Library on Luna. The library had been created two hundred years before as an insurance policy against the extinction of a species. Originally, only endangered species were filed, but for years before the Invasion the directors had been trying to get a sample of everything. Then the Invaders had come, and Lunarians were too busy surviving without help from Occupied Earth to worry about the library. But when the time came to build the disneylands, the library had been ready.

By then, biological engineering had advanced to the point where many modifications could be made in genetic structure. Mostly, the disneyland biologists had left nature alone. But they had changed the predators. In the Ghost, the change was a mutated organ attached to the brain that responded with a flood of fear when a supersonic note was sounded.

So why was the Ghost still out there? Piri blinked his nictating membranes, trying to clear his vision. It helped a little. The shape looked a bit different.

Instead of moving back and forth, the tail seemed to be going up and down, perhaps in a scissoring motion. Only one animal swims like that. He gulped down his fear and pushed away from the reef.

But he had waited too long. His fear of the Ghost went beyond simple danger, of which there was none. It was something more basic, an unreasoning reflex that prickled his neck when he saw that long white shape. He couldn't fight it, and didn't want to. But the fear had kept him against the reef, hidden, while the person swam out of reach. He thrashed to catch up, but soon lost track of the moving feet in the gloom.

He had seen gills trailing from the sides of the figure, muted down to a deep blue-black by the depths. He had the impression that it was a woman.

Tongatown was the only human habitation on the Island. It housed a crew of maintenance people and their children, about fifty in all, in grass huts patterned after those of South Sea natives. A few of the buildings concealed elevators that went to the underground rooms that would house the tourists when the project was completed. The shacks would then go at a premium rate, and the beaches would be crowded.

Piri walked into the circle of firelight and greeted his friends. Nighttime was party time in Tongatown. With the day's work over, everybody gathered around the fire and roasted a vat-grown goat or lamb. But the real culinary treats were the fresh vegetable dishes. The ecologists were still working out the kinks in the systems, controlling blooms, planting more of failing species. They often produced huge excesses of edibles that would have cost a fortune on the outside. The workers took some of the excess for themselves. It was understood to be a fringe benefit of the job. It was hard enough to find people who could stand to stay under the Pacifica sky.

"Hi, Piri," said a girl. "You meet any pirates today?" It was Harra, who used to be one of Piri's best friends but had seemed increasingly remote over the last year. She was wearing a handmade grass skirt and a lot of flowers, tied into strings that looped around her body. She was fifteen now, and Piri was…but who cared? There were no seasons here, only days. Why keep track of time?

Piri didn't know what to say. The two of them had once played together out on the reef. It might be Lost Atlantis, or Submariner, or Reef Pirates; a new plot line and cast of heroes and villains every day. But her question had held such thinly veiled contempt. Didn't she care about the Pirates anymore? What was the matter with her?

She relented when she saw Piri's helpless bewilderment.

"Here, come on and sit down. I saved you a rib." She held out a large chunk of mutton.

Piri took it and sat beside her. He was famished, having had nothing all day since his large breakfast.

"I thought I saw the Ghost today," he said, casually.

Harra shuddered. She wiped her hands on her thighs and looked at him closely.

"Thought? You thought you saw him?" Harra did not care for the Ghost. She had cowered with Piri more than once as they watched him prowl.

"Yep. But I don't think it was really him."

"Where was this?"

"On the sea-side, down about, oh, ten meters. I think it was a woman."

"I don't see how it could be. There's just you and—and Midge and Darvin with—did this woman have an air tank?"

"Nope. Gills. I saw that."

"But there's only you and four others here with gills. And I know where they all were today."

"You used to have gills," he said, with a hint of accusation.

She sighed. "Are we going through that again? I *told* you, I got tired of the flippers. I wanted to move around the *land* some more."

"I can move around the land," he said, darkly.

"All right, all right. You think I deserted you. Did you ever think that you sort of deserted *me*?"

Piri was puzzled by that, but Harra had stood up and walked quickly away. He could follow her, or he could finish his meal. She was right about the flippers. He was no great shakes at chasing anybody.

Piri never worried about anything for too long. He ate, and ate some more, long past the time when everyone else had joined together for the dancing and singing. He usually hung back, anyway. He could sing, but dancing was out of his league.

Just as he was leaning back in the sand, wondering if there were any more corners he could fill up—perhaps another bowl of that shrimp teriyaki?—Harra was back. She sat beside him.

"I talked to my mother about what you said. She said a tourist showed up today. It looks like you were right. It was a woman, and she was amphibious."

Piri felt a vague unease. One tourist was certainly not an invasion, but she could be a harbinger. And amphibious. So far, no one had gone to that expense except for those who planned to live here for a long time. Was his tropical hideout in danger of being discovered?

"What—what's she doing here?" He absently ate another spoonful of crab cocktail.

"She's looking for *you*," Harra laughed, and elbowed him in the ribs. Then she pounced on him, tickling his ribs until he was howling in help-less glee. He fought back, almost to the point of having the upper hand, but she was bigger and a little more determined. She got him pinned, showering flower petals on him as they struggled. One of the red flowers from her hair was in her eye, and she brushed it away, breathing hard.

"You want to go for a walk on the beach?" she asked.

Harra was fun, but the last few times he'd gone with her she had tried to kiss him. He wasn't ready for that. He was only a kid. He thought she probably had something like that in mind now.

"I'm too full," he said, and it was almost the literal truth. He had stuffed himself disgracefully, and only wanted to curl up in his shack and go to sleep.

Harra said nothing, just sat there getting her breathing under control. At last she nodded, a little jerkily, and got to her feet. Piri wished he could see her face to face. He knew something was wrong. She turned from him and walked away.

Robinson Crusoe was feeling depressed when he got back to his hut. The walk down the beach away from the laughter and singing had been a lonely one. Why had he rejected Harra's offer of companionship? Was it really so bad that she wanted to play new kinds of games?

But no, damn it. She wouldn't play his games, why should he play hers?

After a few minutes of sitting on the beach under the crescent moon, he got into character. Oh, the agony of being a lone castaway, far from the company of fellow creatures, with nothing but faith in God to sustain oneself. Tomorrow he would read from the scriptures, do some more exploring along the rocky north coast, tan some goat hides, maybe get in a little fishing.

With his plans for the morrow laid before him, Piri could go to sleep, wiping away a last tear for distant England.

The ghost woman came to him during the night. She knelt beside him in the sand. She brushed his sandy hair from his eyes and he stirred in his sleep. His feet thrashed.

He was churning through the abyssal deeps, heart hammering, blind to everything but internal terror. Behind him, jaws yawned, almost touching his toes. They closed with a snap.

He sat up woozily. He saw rows of serrated teeth in the line of breakers in front of him. And a tall, white shape in the moonlight dived into a curling breaker and was gone.

"Hello."

Piri sat up with a start. The worst thing about being a child living alone on an island—which, when he thought about it, was the sort of thing every child dreamed of—was not having a warm mother's breast to cry on when you had nightmares. It hadn't affected him much, but when it did, it was pretty bad.

He squinted up into the brightness. She was standing with her head blocking out the sun. He winced, and looked away, down to her feet. They were webbed, with long toes. He looked a little higher. She was nude, and quite beautiful.

"Who...?"

"Are you awake now?" She squatted down beside him. Why had he expected sharp, triangular teeth? His dreams blurred and ran like watercolors in the rain, and he felt much better. She had a nice face. She was smiling at him.

He yawned, and sat up. He was groggy, stiff, and his eyes were coated with sand that didn't come from the beach. It had been an awful night.

"I think so."

"Good. How about some breakfast?" She stood, and went to a basket on the sand.

"I usually—" but his mouth watered when he saw the guavas, melons, kippered herring, and the long brown loaf of bread. She had butter, and some orange marmalade. "Well, maybe just a—" and he had bitten into a succulent slice of melon. But before he could finish it, he was seized by an even stronger urge. He got to his feet and scuttled around the palm tree with the waist-high dark stain and urinated against it.

"Don't tell anybody, huh?" he said, anxiously.

She looked up. "About the tree? Don't worry."

He sat back down and resumed eating the melon. "I could get in a lot of trouble. They gave me a thing and told me to use it."

"It's all right with me," she said, buttering a slice of bread and handing it to him. "Robinson Crusoe never had a portable EcoSan, right?"

"Right," he said, not showing his surprise. How did she know *that*?

Piri didn't know quite what to say. Here she was, sharing his morning, as much a fact of life as the beach or the water.

"What's your name?" It was as good a place to start as any.

"Leandra. You can call me Lee."

"I'm—"

"Piri, I heard about you from the people at the party last night. I hope you don't mind me barging in on you like this."

He shrugged, and tried to indicate all the food with the gesture. "Anytime," he said, and laughed. He felt good. It was nice to have someone friendly around after last night. He looked at her again, from a mellower viewpoint.

She was large; quite a bit taller than he was. Her physical age was around thirty, unusually old for a woman. He thought she might be closer to sixty or seventy, but he had nothing to base it on. Piri himself was in his nineties, and who could have known that? She had the slanting eyes that were caused by the addition of transparent eyelids beneath the natural ones. Her hair grew in a narrow band, cropped short, starting between her eyebrows and going over her head to the nape of her neck. Her ears were pinned efficiently against her head, giving her a lean, streamlined look.

"What brings you to Pacifica?" Piri asked.

She reclined on the sand with her hands behind her head, looking very relaxed.

"Claustrophobia." She winked at him. "Not really. I wouldn't survive long in Pluto with *that*." Piri wasn't even sure what it was, but he smiled as if he knew. "Tired of the crowds. I heard that people couldn't enjoy themselves here, what with the sky, but I didn't have any trouble when I visited. So I bought flippers and gills and decided to spend a few weeks skin-diving by myself."

Piri looked at the sky. It was a staggering sight. He'd grown used to it, but knew that it helped not to look up more than he had to.

It was an incomplete illusion, all the more appalling because the half of the sky that had been painted was so very convincing. It looked like it really was the sheer blue of infinity, so when the eye slid over to the unpainted overhanging canopy of rock, scarred from blasting, painted with gigantic numbers that were barely visible from twenty kilometers below—one could almost imagine God looking down through the blue opening. It loomed, suspended by nothing, gigatons of rock hanging up there.

Visitors to Pacifica often complained of headaches, usually right on the crown of the head. They were cringing, waiting to get conked.

"Sometimes I wonder how *I* live with it," Piri said.

She laughed. "It's nothing for me. I was a space pilot once."

"Really?" This was catnip to Piri. There's nothing more romantic than a space pilot. He had to hear stories.

The morning hours dwindled as she captured his imagination with a series of tall tales he was sure were mostly fabrication. But who cared? Had he come to the South Seas to hear of the mundane? He felt he had met a kindred spirit, and gradually, fearful of being laughed at, he began to tell her stories of the Reef Pirates, first as wishful wouldn't-it-be-fun-if's, then more and more seriously as she listened intently. He forgot her age as he began to spin the best of the yarns he and Harra had concocted.

It was a tacit conspiracy between them to be serious about the stories, but that was the whole point. That was the only way it would work, as it had worked with Harra. Somehow, this adult woman was interested in playing the same games he was.

Lying in his bed that night, Piri felt better than he had for months, since before Harra had become so distant. Now that he had a companion, he realized that maintaining a satisfying fantasy world by yourself is hard work. Eventually you need someone to tell the stories to, and to share in the making of them.

They spent the day out on the reef. He showed her his crab farm, and introduced her to Ocho the Octopus, who was his usual shy self. Piri suspected the damn thing only loved him for the treats he brought.

She entered into his games easily and with no trace of adult condescension. He wondered why, and got up the courage to ask her. He was afraid he'd ruin the whole thing, but he had to know. It just wasn't normal.

They were perched on a coral outcropping above the high tide level, catching the last rays of the sun.

"I'm not sure," she said. "I guess you think I'm silly, huh?"

"No, not exactly that. It's just that most adults seem to, well, have more 'important' things on their minds." He put all the contempt he could into the word.

"Maybe I feel the same way you do about it. I'm here to have fun. I sort of feel like I've been reborn into a new element. It's *terrific* down there, you know that. I just didn't feel like I wanted to go into that world alone. I was out there yesterday…"

"I thought I saw you."

"Maybe you did. Anyway, I needed a companion, and I heard about you. It seemed like the polite thing to, well, not to ask you to be my guide, but sort of fit myself into your world. As it were." She frowned, as if she felt she had said too much. "Let's not push it, all right?"

"Oh, sure. It's none of my business."

"I like you, Piri."

"And I like you. I haven't had a friend for…too long."

That night at the luau, Lee disappeared. Piri looked for her briefly, but was not really worried. What she did with her nights was her business. He wanted her during the days.

As he was leaving for his home, Harra came up behind him and took his hand. She walked with him for a moment, then could no longer hold it in.

"A word to the wise, old pal," she said. "You'd better stay away from her. She's not going to do you any good."

"What are you talking about? You don't even know her."

"Maybe I do."

"Well, do you or don't you?"

She didn't say anything, then sighed deeply.

"Piri, if you do the smart thing you'll get on that raft of yours and sail to Bikini. Haven't you had any…feelings about her? Any premonitions or anything?"

"I don't know what you're talking about," he said, thinking of sharp teeth and white death.

"I think you do. You have to, but you won't face it. That's all I'm saying. It's not my business to meddle in your affairs."

"I'll say it's not. So why did you come out here and put this stuff in my ear?" He stopped, and something tickled at his mind from his past life, some earlier bit of knowledge, carefully suppressed. He was used to it. He knew he was not really a child, and that he had a long life and many experiences stretching out behind him. But he didn't think about it. He hated it when part of his old self started to intrude on him.

"I think you're jealous of her," he said, and knew it was his old, cynical self talking. "She's an adult, Harra. She's no threat to you. And, hell,

I know what you've been hinting at these last months. I'm not ready for it, so leave me alone. I'm just a kid."

Her chin came up, and the moonlight flashed in her eyes.

"You idiot. Have you looked at yourself lately? You're not Peter Pan, you know. You're growing up. You're damn near a man."

"That's not true." There was panic in Piri's voice. "I'm only...well, I haven't exactly been counting, but I can't be more than nine, ten years—"

"Shit. You're as old as I am, and I've had breasts for two years. But I'm not out to cop you. I can cop with any of seven boys in the village younger than you are, but not you." She threw her hands up in exasperation and stepped back from him. Then, in a sudden fury, she hit him on the chest with the heel of her fist. He fell back, stunned at her violence.

"She *is* an adult," Harra whispered through her teeth. "That's what I came here to warn you against. *I'm* your friend, but you don't know it. Ah, what's the use? I'm fighting against that scared old man in your head, and he won't listen to me. Go ahead, go with her. But she's got some surprises for you."

"What? What surprises?" Piri was shaking, not wanting to listen to her. It was a relief when she spat at his feet, whirled, and ran down the beach.

"Find out for yourself," she yelled back over her shoulder. It sounded like she was crying.

That night, Piri dreamed of white teeth, inches behind him, snapping.

But morning brought Lee, and another fine breakfast in her bulging bag. After a lazy interlude drinking coconut milk, they went to the reef again. The pirates gave them a rough time of it, but they managed to come back alive in time for the nightly gathering.

Harra was there. She was dressed as he had never seen her, in the blue tunic and shorts of the reef maintenance crew. He knew she had taken a job with the disneyland and had been working days with her mother at Bikini, but had not seen her dressed up before. He had just begun to get used to the grass skirt. Not long ago, she had been always nude like him and the other children.

She looked older somehow, and bigger. Maybe it was just the uniform. She still looked like a girl next to Lee. Piri was confused by it, and his thoughts veered protectively away.

Harra did not avoid him, but she was remote in a more important way. It was like she had put on a mask, or possibly taken one off. She carried herself with a dignity that Piri thought was beyond her years.

Lee disappeared just before he was ready to leave. He walked home alone, half hoping Harra would show up so he could apologize for the way he'd talked to her the night before. But she didn't.

He felt the bow-shock of a pressure wave behind him, sensed by some mechanism he was unfamiliar with, like the lateral line of a fish, sensitive to slight changes in the water around him. He knew there was something behind him, closing the gap a little with every wild kick of his flippers.

It was dark. It was always dark when the thing chased him. It was not the wispy, insubstantial thing that darkness was when it settled on the night air, but the primal, eternal night of the depths. He tried to scream with his mouth full of water, but it was a dying gurgle before it passed his lips. The water around him was warm with his blood.

He turned to face it before it was upon him, and saw Harra's face corpse-pale and glowing sickly in the night. But no, it wasn't Harra, it was Lee, and her mouth was far down her body, rimmed with razors, a gaping crescent hole in her chest. He screamed again—

And sat up.

"What? Where are you?"

"I'm right here, it's going to be all right." She held his head as he brought his sobbing under control. She was whispering something but he couldn't understand it, and perhaps wasn't meant to. It was enough. He calmed down quickly, as he always did when he woke from nightmares. If they hung around to haunt him, he never would have stayed by himself for so long.

There was just the moonlit paleness of her breast before his eyes and the smell of skin and sea water. Her nipple was wet. Was it from his tears? No, his lips were tingling and the nipple was hard when it brushed against him. He realized what he had been doing in his sleep.

"You were calling for your mother," she whispered, as though she'd read his mind. "I've heard you shouldn't wake someone from a nightmare. It seemed to calm you down."

"Thanks," he said quietly. "Thanks for being here, I mean."

She took his cheek in her hand, turned his head slightly, and kissed him. It was not a motherly kiss, and he realized they were not playing the same game. She had changed the rules on him.

"Lee..."

"Hush. It's time you learned."

She eased him onto his back, and he was overpowered with *deja vu*. Her mouth worked downward on his body and it set off chains of associations from his past life. He was familiar with the sensation. It had happened to him often in his second childhood. Something would happen that had happened to him in much the same way before and he would remember a bit of it. He had been seduced by an older woman the first time he was young. She had taught him well, and he remembered it all but didn't want to remember. He was an experienced lover and a child at the same time.

"I'm not old enough," he protested, but she was holding in her hand the evidence that he was old enough, had been old enough for several years. *I'm fourteen years old*, he thought. How could he have kidded himself into thinking he was ten?

"You're a strong young man," she whispered in his ear. "And I'm going to be very disappointed if you keep saying that. You're not a child anymore, Piri. Face it."

"I...I guess I'm not."

"Do you know what to do?"

"I think so."

She reclined beside him, drew her legs up. Her body was huge and ghostly and full of limber strength. She would swallow him up, like a shark. The gill slits under her arms opened and shut quickly with her breathing, smelling of salt, iodine, and sweat.

He got on his hands and knees and moved over her.

He woke before she did. The sun was up: another warm, cloudless morning. There would be two thousand more before the first scheduled typhoon.

Piri was a giddy mixture of elation and sadness. It was sad, and he knew it already, that his days of frolicking on the reef were over. He would still go out there, but it would never be the same.

Fourteen years old! Where had the years gone? He was nearly an adult. He moved away from the thought until he found a more acceptable one. He was an adolescent, and a very fortunate one to have been initiated into the mysteries of sex by this strange woman.

He held her as she slept, spooned cozily back to front with his arms around her waist. She had already been playmate, mother, and lover to him. What else did she have in store?

But he didn't care. He was not worried about anything. He already scorned his yesterdays. He was not a boy, but a youth, and he remembered from his other youth what that meant and was excited by it. It was a time of sex, of internal exploration and the exploration of others. He would pursue these new frontiers with the same single-mindedness he had shown on the reef.

He moved against her, slowly, not disturbing her sleep. But she woke as he entered her and turned to give him a sleepy kiss.

They spent the morning involved in each other, until they were content to lie in the sun and soak up heat like glossy reptiles.

"I can hardly believe it," she said. "You've been here for…how long? With all these girls and women. And I know at least one of them was interested."

He didn't want to go into it. It was important to him that she not find out he was not really a child. He felt it would change things, and it was not fair. Not fair at all, because it *had* been the first time. In a way he could never have explained to her, last night had been not a rediscovery but an entirely new thing. He had been with many women and it wasn't as if he couldn't remember it. It was all there, and what's more, it showed up in his lovemaking. He had not been the bumbling teenager, had not needed to be told what to do.

But it was *new*. That old man inside had been a spectator and an invaluable coach, but his hardened viewpoint had not intruded to make last night just another bout. It had been a first time, and the first time is special.

When she persisted in her questions he silenced her in the only way he knew; with a kiss. He could see he had to rethink his relationship to her. She had not asked him questions as a playmate, or a mother. In the one role, she had been seemingly as self-centered as he, interested only in the needs of the moment and her personal needs above all. As a mother, she had offered only wordless comfort in a tight spot.

Now she was his lover. What did lovers do when they weren't making love?

They went for walks on the beach, and on the reef. They swam together, but it was different. They talked a lot.

She soon saw that he didn't want to talk about himself. Except for the odd question here and there that would momentarily confuse him, throw him back to stages of his life he didn't wish to remember, she left his past alone.

They stayed away from the village except to load up on supplies. It was mostly his unspoken wish that kept them away. He had made it clear to everyone in the village many years ago that he was not really a child. It had been necessary to convince them that he could take care of himself on his own, to keep them from being overprotective. They would not spill his secret knowingly, but neither would they lie for him.

So he grew increasingly nervous about his relationship with Lee, founded as it was on a lie. If not a lie, then at least a withholding of the facts. He saw that he must tell her soon, and dreaded it. Part of him was convinced that her attraction to him was based mostly on age difference.

Then she learned he had a raft, and wanted to go on a sailing trip to the edge of the world.

Piri did have a raft, though an old one. They dragged it from the bushes that had grown around it since his last trip and began putting it into shape. Piri was delighted. It was something to do, and it was hard work. They didn't have much time for talking.

It was a simple construction of logs lashed together with rope. Only an insane sailor would put the thing to sea in the Pacific Ocean, but it was safe enough for them. They knew what the weather would be, and the reports were absolutely reliable. And if it came apart, they could swim back.

All the ropes had rotted so badly that even gentle wave action would have quickly pulled it apart. They had to be replaced, a new mast erected, and a new sailcloth installed. Neither of them knew anything about sailing, but Piri knew that the winds blew toward the edge at night and away from it during the day. It was a simple matter of putting up the sail and letting the wind do the navigating.

He checked the schedule to be sure they got there at low tide. It was a moonless night, and he chuckled to himself when he thought of her reaction to the edge of the world. They would sneak up on it in the dark, and the impact would be all the more powerful at sunrise.

But he knew as soon as they were an hour out of Rarotonga that he had made a mistake. There was not much to do there in the night but talk.

"Piri, I've sensed that you don't want to talk about certain things."

"Who? Me?"

She laughed into the empty night. He could barely see her face. The stars were shining brightly, but there were only about a hundred of them installed so far, and all in one part of the sky.

"Yeah, you. You won't talk about yourself. It's like you grew here, sprang up from the ground like a palm tree. And you've got no mother in evidence. You're old enough to have divorced her, but you'd have a guardian somewhere. Someone would be looking after your moral upbringing. The only conclusion is that you don't need an education in moral principles. So you've got a co-pilot."

"Um." She had seen through him. Of course she would have. Why hadn't he realized it?

"So you're a clone. You've had your memories transplanted into a new body, grown from one of your own cells. How old are you? Do you mind my asking?"

"I guess not. Uh…what's the date?"

She told him.

"And the year?"

She laughed, but told him that, too.

"Damn. I missed my one-hundredth birthday. Well, so what? It's not important. Lee, does this change anything?"

"Of course not. Listen, I could tell the first time, that first night together. You had that puppy-dog eagerness, all right, but you knew how to handle yourself. Tell me: what's it like?"

"The second childhood, you mean?" He reclined on the gently rocking raft and looked at the little clot of stars. "It's pretty damn great. It's like living in a dream. What kid hasn't wanted to live alone on a tropic isle? I can, because there's an adult in me who'll keep me out of trouble. But for the last seven years I've been a kid. It's you that finally made me grow up a little, maybe sort of late, at that."

"I'm sorry. But it felt like the right time."

"It was. I was afraid of it at first. Listen, I *know* that I'm really a hundred years old, see? I know that all the memories are ready for me when I get to adulthood again. If I think about it, I can remember it all as plain as anything. But I haven't wanted to, and in a way, I still don't want to. The memories are suppressed when you opt for a second childhood instead of being transplanted into another full-grown body."

"I know."

"Do you? Oh, yeah. Intellectually. So did I, but I didn't understand what it meant. It's a nine- or ten-year holiday, not only from your work, but from yourself. When you get into your nineties, you might find that you need it."

She was quiet for a while, lying beside him without touching.

"What about the reintegration? Is that started?"

"I don't know. I've heard it's a little rough. I've been having dreams about something chasing me. That's probably my former self, right?"

"Could be. What did your older self do?"

He had to think for a moment, but there it was. He'd not thought of it for eight years.

"I was an economic strategist."

Before he knew it, he found himself launching into an explanation of offensive economic policy.

"Did you know that Pluto is in danger of being gutted by currency transfers from the Inner Planets? And you know why? The speed of light, that's why. Time lag. It's killing us. Since the time of the Invasion of Earth it's been humanity's idea—and a good one, I think—that we should stand together. Our whole cultural thrust in that time has been toward a total economic community. But it won't work at Pluto. Independence is in the cards."

She listened as he tried to explain things that only moments before he would have had trouble understanding himself. But it poured out of him like a breached dam, things like inflation multipliers, futures buying on the oxygen and hydrogen exchanges, phantom dollars and their manipulation by central banking interests, and the invisible drain.

"Invisible drain? What's that?"

"It's hard to explain, but it's tied up in the speed of light. It's an economic drain on Pluto that has nothing to do with real goods and services, or labor, or any of the other traditional forces. It has to do with the fact that any information we get from the Inner Planets is already at least nine hours old. In an economy with a stable currency—pegged to gold, for instance, like the classical economies on Earth—it wouldn't matter much, but it would still have an effect. Nine hours can make a difference in prices, in futures, in outlook on the markets. With a floating exchange medium, one where you need the hourly updates on your credit meter to know what your labor input will give you in terms of material output—your personal financial equation, in other words—and the inflation multiplier is something you simply *must* have if the equation is going to balance and you're not going to be wiped out, then time is really of the essence. We operate at a perpetual disadvantage on Pluto in relation to the Inner Planet money markets. For a long time it ran on the order of point three percent leakage due to outdated information. But the inflation multiplier has been accelerating over the years. Some of it's been absorbed by the fact that we've been moving closer to the I.P.; the time lag has been getting shorter as we move into summer. But it can't last. We'll reach the inner point of our orbit and the effects will really start to accelerate. Then it's war."

"War?" She seemed horrified, as well she might be.

"War, in the economic sense. It's a hostile act to renounce a trade agreement, even if it's bleeding you white. It hits every citizen of the Inner Planets in the pocketbook, and we can expect retaliation. We'd be introducing instability by pulling out of the Common Market."

"How bad will it be? Shooting?"

"Not likely. But devastating enough. A depression's no fun. And they'll be planning one for us."

"Isn't there any other course?"

"Someone suggested moving our entire government and all our corporate headquarters to the Inner Planets. It could happen, I guess. But who'd feel like it was ours? We'd be a colony, and that's a worse answer than independence, in the long run."

She was silent for a time, chewing it over. She nodded her head once; he could barely see the movement in the darkness.

"How long until the war?"

He shrugged. "I've been out of touch. I don't know how things have been going. But we can probably take it for another ten years or so. Then we'll have to get out. I'd stock up on real wealth if I were you. Canned goods, air, water, so forth. I don't think it'll get so bad that you'll need those things to stay alive by consuming them. But we may get to a semi-barter situation where they'll be the only valuable things. Your credit meter'll laugh at you when you punch a purchase order, no matter how much work you've put into it."

The raft bumped. They had arrived at the edge of the world.

They moored the raft to one of the rocks on the wall that rose from the open ocean. They were five kilometers out of Rarotonga. They waited for some light as the sun began to rise, then started up the rock face.

It was rough: blasted out with explosives on this face of the dam. It went up at a thirty-degree angle for fifty meters, then was suddenly level and smooth as glass. The top of the dam at the edge of the world had been smoothed by cutting lasers into a vast table top, three hundred kilometers long and four kilometers wide. They left wet footprints on it as they began the long walk to the edge.

They soon lost any meaningful perspective on the thing. They lost sight of the sea-edge, and couldn't see the dropoff until they began to near it. By then, it was full light. Timed just right, they would reach the edge when the sun came up and they'd really have something to see.

A hundred meters from the edge when she could see over it a little, Lee began to unconsciously hang back. Piri didn't prod her. It was not something he could force someone to see. He'd reached this point with others, and had to turn back. Already, the fear of falling was building up. But she came on, to stand beside him at the very lip of the canyon.

Pacifica was being built and filled in three sections. Two were complete, but the third was still being hollowed out and was not yet filled with water except in the deepest trenches. The water was kept out of this section by the dam they were standing on. When it was completed, when all the underwater trenches and mountain ranges and guyots and slopes had been built to specifications, the bottom would be covered with sludge and ooze and the whole wedge-shaped section flooded. The water came from liquid hydrogen and oxygen on the surface, combined with the limitless electricity of fusion powerplants.

"We're doing what the Dutch did on Old Earth, but in reverse," Piri pointed out, but he got no reaction from Lee. She was staring, spellbound, down the sheer face of the dam to the apparently bottomless trench below. It was shrouded in mist, but seemed to fall off forever.

"It's eight kilometers deep," Piri told her. "It's not going to be a regular trench when it's finished. It's there to be filled up with the remains of this dam after the place has been flooded." He looked at her face, and didn't bother with more statistics. He let her experience it in her own way.

The only comparable vista on a human-inhabited planet was the Great Rift Valley on Mars. Neither of them had seen it, but it suffered in comparison to this because not all of it could be seen at once. Here, one could see from one side to the other, and from sea level to a distance equivalent to the deepest oceanic trenches on Earth. It simply fell away beneath them and went straight down to nothing. There was a rainbow beneath their feet. Off to the left was a huge waterfall that arced away from the wall in a solid stream. Tons of overflow water went through the wall, to twist, fragment, vaporize and blow away long before it reached the bottom of the trench.

Straight ahead of them and about ten kilometers away was the mountain that would become the Okinawa biome when the pit was filled. Only the tiny, blackened tip of the mountain would show above the water.

Lee stayed and looked at it as long as she could. It became easier the longer one stood there, and yet something about it drove her away. The scale was too big, there was no room for humans in that shattered world. Long before noon, they turned and started the long walk back to the raft.

She was silent as they boarded, and set sail for the return trip. The winds were blowing fitfully, barely billowing the sail. It would be another hour before they blew very strongly. They were still in sight of the dam wall.

They sat on the raft, not looking at each other.

"Piri, thanks for bringing me here."

"You're welcome. You don't have to talk about it."

"All right. But there's something else I have to talk about. I...I don't know where to begin, really."

Piri stirred uneasily. The earlier discussion about economics had disturbed him. It was part of his past life, a part that he had not been ready to return to. He was full of confusion. Thoughts that had no place out here in the concrete world of wind and water were roiling through his brain. Someone was calling to him, someone he knew but didn't want to see right then.

"Yeah? What is it you want to talk about?"

"It's about—" she stopped, seemed to think it over. "Never mind. It's not time yet." She moved close and touched him. But he was not interested. He made it known in a few minutes, and she moved to the other side of the raft.

He lay back, essentially alone with his troubled thoughts. The wind gusted, then settled down. He saw a flying fish leap, almost passing over the raft. There was a piece of the sky falling through the air. It twisted and turned like a feather, a tiny speck of sky that was blue on one side and brown on the other. He could see the hole in the sky where it had been knocked loose.

It must be two or three kilometers away. No, wait, that wasn't right. The top of the sky was twenty kilometers up, and it looked like it was falling from the center. How far away were they from the center of Pacifica? A hundred kilometers?

A piece of the sky?

He got to his feet, nearly capsizing the raft.

"What's the matter?"

It was *big*. It looked large even from this far away. It was the dreamy tumbling motion that had deceived him.

"The sky is..." he choked on it, and almost laughed. But this was no time to feel silly about it. "The sky is falling, Lee." How long? He watched it, his mind full of numbers. Terminal velocity from that high up, assuming it was heavy enough to punch right through the atmosphere...over six hundred meters per second. Time to fall, seventy seconds. Thirty of those must already have gone by.

Lee was shading her eyes as she followed his gaze. She still thought it was a joke. The chunk of sky began to glow red as the atmosphere got thicker.

"Hey, it really is falling," she said. "Look at that."

"It's big. Maybe one or two kilometers across. It's going to make quite a splash, I'll bet."

They watched it descend. Soon it disappeared over the horizon, picking up speed. They waited, but the show seemed to be over. Why was he still uneasy?

"How many tons in a two-kilometer chunk of rock, I wonder?" Lee mused. She didn't look too happy, either. But they sat back down on the raft, still looking in the direction where the thing had sunk into the sea.

Then they were surrounded by flying fish, and the water looked crazy. The fish were panicked. As soon as they hit they leaped from the water again. Piri felt rather than saw something pass beneath them. And then, very gradually, a roar built up, a deep bass rumble that soon threatened to turn his bones to powder. It picked him up and shook him, and left him limp on his knees. He was stunned, unable to think clearly. His eyes were still fixed on the horizon, and he saw a white fan rising in the distance in silent majesty. It was the spray from the impact, and it was still going up.

"Look up there," Lee said, when she got her voice back. She seemed as confused as he. He looked where she pointed and saw a twisted line crawling across the blue sky. At first he thought it was the end of his life, because it appeared that the whole overhanging dome was fractured and about to fall in on them. But then he saw it was one of the tracks that the sun ran on, pulled free by the rock that had fallen, twisted into a snake of tortured metal.

"The dam!" he yelled. "The dam! We're too close to the dam!"

"What?"

"The bottom rises this close to the dam. The water here isn't that deep. There'll be a wave coming, Lee, a big wave. It'll pile up here."

"Piri, the shadows are moving."

"Huh?"

Surprise was piling on surprise too fast for him to cope with it. But she was right. The shadows were moving. But *why*?

Then he saw it. The sun was setting, but not by following the tracks that led to the concealed opening in the west. It was falling through the air, having been shaken loose by the rock.

Lee had figured it out, too.

"What is that thing?" she asked. "I mean, how big is it?"

"Not too big, I heard. Big enough, but not nearly the size of that chunk that fell. It's some kind of fusion generator. I don't know what'll happen when it hits the water."

They were paralyzed. They knew there was something they should do, but too many things were happening. There was not time to think it out.

"Dive!" Lee yelled. "Dive into the water!"

"What?"

"We have to dive and swim away from the dam, and down as far as we can go. The wave will pass over us, won't it?"

"I don't know."

"It's all we can do."

So they dived. Piri felt his gills come into action, then he was swimming down at an angle toward the dark-shrouded bottom. Lee was off to his left, swimming as hard as she could. And with no sunset, no warning, it got black as pitch. The sun had hit the water.

He had no idea how long he had been swimming when he suddenly felt himself pulled upward. Floating in the water, weightless, he was not well equipped to feel accelerations. But he did feel it, like a rapidly rising elevator. It was accompanied by pressure waves that threatened to burst his eardrums. He kicked and clawed his way downward, not even knowing if he was headed in the right direction. Then he was falling again.

He kept swimming, all alone in the dark. Another wave passed, lifted him, let him down again. A few minutes later, another one, seeming to come from the other direction. He was hopelessly confused. He suddenly felt he was swimming the wrong way. He stopped, not knowing what to do. Was he pointed in the right direction? He had no way to tell.

He stopped paddling and tried to orient himself. It was useless. He felt surges, and was sure he was being tumbled and buffeted.

Then his skin was tingling with the sensation of a million bubbles crawling over him. It gave him a handle on the situation. The bubbles would be going up, wouldn't they? And they were traveling over his body from belly to back. So down was that way.

But he didn't have time to make use of the information. He hit something hard with his hip, wrenched his back as his body tried to tumble over in the foam and water, then was sliding along a smooth surface. It felt like he was going very fast, and he knew where he was and where he was heading and there was nothing he could do about it. The tail of the wave had lifted him clear of the rocky slope of the dam and deposited him on the flat surface. It was now spending itself, sweeping him along to the edge of the world. He turned around, feeling the sliding surface beneath him with his hands, and tried to dig in. It was a nightmare; nothing he did had any effect. Then his head broke free into the air.

He was still sliding, but the huge hump of the wave had dissipated itself and was collapsing quietly into froth and puddles. It drained away with amazing speed. He was left there, alone, cheek pressed lovingly to the cold rock. The darkness was total.

He wasn't about to move. For all he knew, there was an eight-kilometer drop just behind his toes.

Maybe there would be another wave. If so, this one would crash down on him instead of lifting him like a cork in a tempest. It should kill him instantly. He refused to worry about that. All he cared about now was not slipping any further.

The stars had vanished. Power failure? Now they blinked on. He raised his head a little, in time to see a soft, diffused glow in the east. The moon was rising, and it was doing it at breakneck speed. He saw it rotate from a thin crescent configuration to bright fullness in under a minute. Someone was still in charge, and had decided to throw some light on the scene.

He stood, though his knees were weak. Tall fountains of spray far away to his right indicated where the sea was battering at the dam. He was about in the middle of the tabletop, far from either edge. The ocean was whipped up as if by thirty hurricanes, but he was safe from it at this distance unless there were another tsunami yet to come.

The moonlight turned the surface into a silver mirror, littered with flopping fish. He saw another figure get to her feet, and ran in that direction.

GOOD-BYE, ROBINSON CRUSOE

✦

The helicopter located them by infrared detector. They had no way of telling how long it had been. The moon was hanging motionless in the center of the sky.

They got into the cabin, shivering.

The helicopter pilot was happy to have found them, but grieved over other lives lost. She said the toll stood at three dead, fifteen missing and presumed dead. Most of these had been working on the reefs. All the land surface of Pacifica had been scoured, but the loss of life had been minimal. Most had had time to get to an elevator and go below or to a helicopter and rise above the devastation.

From what they had been able to find out, heat expansion of the crust had moved farther down into the interior of the planet than had been expected. It was summer on the surface, something it was easy to forget down here. The engineers had been sure that the inner surface of the sky had been stabilized years ago, but a new fault had been opened by the slight temperature rise. She pointed up to where ships were hovering like fireflies next to the sky, playing searchlights on the site of the damage. No one knew yet if Pacifica would have to be abandoned for another twenty years while it stabilized.

She set them down on Rarotonga. The place was a mess. The wave had climbed the bottom rise and crested at the reef, and a churning hell of foam and debris had swept over the island. Little was left standing except the concrete blocks that housed the elevators, scoured of their decorative camouflage.

Piri saw a familiar figure coming toward him through the wreckage that had been a picturesque village. She broke into a run, and nearly bowled him over, laughing and kissing him.

"We were sure you were dead," Harra said, drawing back from him as if to check for cuts and bruises.

"It was a fluke I guess," he said, still incredulous that he had survived. It had seemed bad enough out there in the open ocean; the extent of the disaster was much more evident on the island. He was badly shaken to see it.

"Lee suggested that we try to dive under the wave. That's what saved us. It just lifted us up, then the last one swept us over the top of the dam and drained away. It dropped us like leaves."

"Well, not quite so tenderly in my case," Lee pointed out. "It gave me quite a jolt. I think I might have sprained my wrist."

A medic was available. While her wrist was being bandaged, she kept looking at Piri. He didn't like the look.

"There's something I'd intended to talk to you about on the raft, or soon after we got home. There's no point in your staying here any longer anyway, and I don't know where you'd go."

"No!" Harra burst out. "Not yet. Don't tell him anything yet. It's not fair. Stay away from him." She was protecting Piri with her body, from no assault that was apparent to him.

"I just wanted to—"

"No, no. Don't listen to her, Piri. Come with me." She pleaded with the other woman. "Just give me a few hours alone with him, there's some things I never got around to telling him."

Lee looked undecided, and Piri felt mounting rage and frustration. He had known things were going on around him. It was mostly his own fault that he had ignored them, but now he had to know. He pulled his hand free from Harra and faced Lee.

"Tell me."

She looked down at her feet, then back to his eyes.

"I'm not what I seem, Piri. I've been leading you along, trying to make this easier for you. But you still fight me. I don't think there's any way it's going to be easy."

"No!" Harra shouted again.

"What are you?"

"I'm a psychiatrist. I specialize in retrieving people like you, people who are in a mental vacation mode, what you call 'second childhood.' You're aware of all this, on another level, but the child in you has fought it at every stage. The result has been nightmares—probably with me as the focus, whether you admitted it or not."

She grasped both his wrists, one of them awkwardly because of her injury.

"Now listen to me." She spoke in an intense whisper, trying to get it all out before the panic she saw in his face broke free and sent him running. "You came here for a vacation. You were going to stay ten years, growing up and taking it easy. That's all over. The situation that prevailed when you left is now out of date. Things have moved faster than you believed possible. You had expected a ten-year period after your return to get things in order for the coming battles. That time has evaporated. The Common Market of the Inner Planets has fired the first shot. They've instituted a new system of accounting and it's locked into their computers and running. It's aimed right at Pluto, and it's been working for a month now. We cannot continue as an economic partner to the C.M.I.P., because from now on every time we sell or buy or move money the inflationary multiplier is automatically juggled against us. It's all perfectly legal by all existing treaties, and it's necessary to their economy. But it ignores our time-lag disadvantage. We have to consider it as a hostile act, no matter what the intent. You have to come back and direct the war, Mister Finance Minister."

The words shattered what calm Piri had left. He wrenched free of her hands and turned wildly to look all around him. Then he sprinted down the beach. He tripped once over his splay feet, got up without ever slowing, and disappeared.

Harra and Lee stood silently and watched him go.

"You didn't have to be so rough with him," Harra said, but knew it wasn't so. She just hated to see him so confused.

"It's best done quickly when they resist. And he's all right. He'll have a fight with himself, but there's no real doubt of the outcome."

"So the Piri I know will be dead soon?"

Lee put her arm around the younger woman.

"Not at all. It's a reintegration, without a winner or a loser. You'll see." She looked at the tear-streaked face.

"Don't worry. You'll like the older Piri. It won't take him any time at all to realize that he loves you."

He had never been to the reef at night. It was a place of furtive fish, always one step ahead of him as they darted back into their places of concealment. He wondered how long it would be before they ventured out in the long night to come. The sun might not rise for years.

They might never come out. Not realizing the changes in their environment, night fish and day fish would never adjust. Feeding cycles would be disrupted, critical temperatures would go awry, the endless moon and lack of sun would frustrate the internal mechanisms, bred over billions of years, and fish would die. It had to happen.

The ecologists would have quite a job on their hands.

But there was one denizen of the outer reef that would survive for a long time. He would eat anything that moved and quite a few things that didn't, at any time of the day or night. He had no fear, he had no internal clocks dictating to him, no inner pressures to confuse him except the one overriding urge to attack. He would last as long as there was anything alive to eat.

But in what passed for a brain in the white-bottomed torpedo that was the Ghost, a splinter of doubt had lodged. He had no recollection of similar doubts, though there had been some. He was not equipped to remember, only to hunt. So this new thing that swam beside him, and drove his cold brain as near as it could come to the emotion of anger, was a mystery. He tried again and again to attack it, then something would seize him with an emotion he had not felt since he was half a meter long, and fear would drive him away.

Piri swam along beside the faint outline of the shark. There was just enough moonlight for him to see the fish, hovering at the ill-defined limit of his sonic signal. Occasionally, the shape would shudder from head to tail, turn toward him, and grow larger. At these times Piri could see nothing but a gaping jaw. Then it would turn quickly, transfix him with that bottomless pit of an eye, and sweep away.

Piri wished he could laugh at the poor, stupid brute. How could he have feared such a mindless eating machine?

Good-bye, pinbrain. He turned and stroked lazily toward the shore. He knew the shark would turn and follow him, nosing into the inter-dicted sphere of his transponder, but the thought did not impress him. He was without fear. How could he be afraid, when he had already been swallowed into the belly of his nightmare? The teeth had closed around him, he had awakened, and remembered. And that was the end of his fear.

Good-bye, tropical paradise. You were fun while you lasted. Now I'm a grownup, and must go off to war.

He didn't relish it. It was a wrench to leave his childhood, though the time had surely been right. Now the responsibilities had descended on him, and he must shoulder them. He thought of Harra.

GOOD-BYE, ROBINSON CRUSOE

"Piri," he told himself, "as a teenager, you were just too dumb to live."

Knowing it was the last time, he felt the coolness of the water flowing over his gills. They had served him well, but had no place in his work. There was no place for a fish, and no place for Robinson Crusoe.

Good-bye, gills.

He kicked harder for the shore and came to stand, dripping wet, on the beach. Harra and Lee were there, waiting for him.

LOLLIPOP AND
THE TAR BABY

With the following two stories—and this will serve as an introduction to both of them—we leave the comfortable, well-traveled spacelanes of the solar system as we think of it, and set our course outward bound for the wild places. Think of it as our cruise ship departing charted waters and entering the vast zones labeled only "Here be dragons."

First we come to the Kuiper Belt, a region that extends from the orbit of Neptune all the way out to twice the distance of Pluto from the sun. It is the home of the other dwarf planets that we know of (except Eris, which is more distant), and one thousand known smaller objects, over sixty miles in diameter. Astronomers believe there are around seventy thousand of these Kuiper Belt Objects (KBOs), and there could be many thousands or millions or billions more, too small for us to see. So there's a lot of work still to be done!

Beyond that is a region almost unimaginably huge, known as the Oort Cloud. This is where comets go to spend the winter, and it reaches out almost a light-year from the sun, or as much as three light-years, depending on whose estimate you believe.

Exactly what is out there is partly known (or believed with pretty good evidence), and partly a mystery. There are almost certainly more dwarf planets still to be discovered, and thousands of KBOs. There are certainly a large number of comets, and by "large," I mean the estimate is that there are billions of them larger than 10 miles across, and about a trillion smaller than that. Sounds crowded, but it's not. Compared to the Oort Cloud, the sparsely populated Asteroid Belt is as tightly packed as grains of sand on a beach.

At the furthest theoretical edges of the cloud, the sun is no longer the dominant gravitational force. We may be trading comets with Proxima Centauri, the nearest star.

So what else might be out there? For an SF writer, just about anything you want to imagine, I guess, as long as it's too small to see with our telescopes. And the things I imagined out there are very small indeed.

I first heard of the concept of quantum black holes in a column by Jerry Pournelle in *Galaxy* magazine. He was talking about the new ideas coming from a man named Stephen Hawking, who I had never heard of at the time. Hawking theorized that, during the Big Bang, the conditions existed to form black holes of all different sizes. They should still be out there, somewhere. (But it turned out, later, that the very smallest of them would eventually evaporate due to quantum fluctuation. Whatever that is.)

These weren't the galaxy-gobbling monsters like the one that seems to be in the middle of the Milky Way; some of them might be as small as an atomic nucleus. I didn't see how those could be useful, but what about holes somewhere in between? Floating out there in the Oort Cloud, or passing through the Kuiper Belt. If they had a magnetic charge you might find them—very carefully!—and tow them back into the solar system. There (even more carefully) you could put them in orbit and feed them asteroids. Once the asteroids passed the event horizon they would be of no further use to us, but on the way in…well, I'd read descriptions of the accretion discs of black holes, and they would release a *huge* amount of energy. And thus, a smallish black hole could become a prize worth much more than its weight in diamonds. And where there are riches to be mined, people will go.

But it would be incredibly lonely out there…

"Zzzzello. Zzz. Hello. Hello." Someone was speaking to Xanthia from the end of a ten-kilometer metal pipe, shouting to be heard across a roomful of gongs and cymbals being knocked over by angry giant bees. She had never heard such interference.

"Hello?" she repeated. "What are you doing on my wavelength?"

"Hello." The interference was still there, but the voice was slightly more distinct. "Wavelength. Searching, searching wavelength…get best reception with… Hello? Listening?"

"Yes, I'm listening. You're talking over... My radio isn't even..." She banged the radio panel with her palm in the ancient ritual humans employ when their creations are being balky. "My goddamn *radio* isn't even on. Did you know that?" It was a relief to feel anger boiling up inside her. Anything was preferable to feeling lost and silly.

"Not neccessary."

"What do you mean not—who are you?"

"Who. Having...*I'm*, pronoun, yes, I'm having difficulty. Bear with. Me? Yes, pronoun. Bear with me. I'm not who. What. *What* am I?"

"All right. *What* are you?"

"Spacetime phenomenon. I'm gravity and causality-sink. Black hole."

Xanthia did not need black holes explained to her. She had spent her entire eighteen years hunting them, along with her clone-sister, Zoetrope. But she was not used to having them talk to her.

"Assuming for the moment that you really are a black hole," she said, beginning to wonder if this might be some elaborate trick played on her by Zoe, "just taking that as a tentative hypothesis—how are you able to talk to me?"

There was a sound like an attitude thruster going off, a rumbling pop. It was repeated.

"I manipulate spacetime framework...no, please hold line...*the* line. I manipulate the spacetime framework with controlled gravity waves projected in narrow...a narrow cone. I direct at the speaker in your radio. You hear. Me."

"What was that again?" It sounded like a lot of crap to her.

"I elaborate. I will elaborate. I cut through space itself, through—hold the line, hold the line, reference." There was a sound like a tape reeling rapidly through playback heads. "This is the BBC," said a voice that was recognizably human, but blurred by static. The tape whirred again, "gust the third, in the year of our Lord nineteen fifty-seven. Today in—" Once again the tape hunted.

"Chelson-Morley experiment disproved the existence of the ether, by ingeniously arranging a rotating prism—" Then the metallic voice was back.

"Ether. I cut through space itself, through a—hold the line." This time the process was shorter. She heard a fragment of what sounded like a video adventure serial. "Through a spacewarp made through the ductile etheric continuum—"

"Hold on there. That's not what you said before."

"I was elaborating."

"Go on. Wait, what were you doing? With that tape business?"

The voice paused, and when the answer came the line cleared up quite a bit. But the voice still didn't sound human. Computer?

"I am not used to speech. No need for it. But I have learned your language by listening to your radio transmissions. I speak to you through use of indeterminate statistical concatenations. Gravity waves and probability, which is not the same thing in a causality singularity, enables a nonrational event to take place."

"Zoe, this is really you, isn't it?"

Xanthia was only eighteen Earth-years old, on her first long orbit into the space beyond Pluto, the huge cometary zone where space is truly flat. Her whole life had been devoted to learning how to find and capture black holes, but one didn't come across them very often. Xanthia had been born a year after the beginning of the voyage and had another year to go before the end of it. In her whole life she had seen and talked to only one other human being, and that was Zoe, who was one hundred and thirty-five years old and her identical twin.

Their home was the *Shirley Temple*, a fifteen-thousand-tonne fusion-drive ship registered out of Lowell, Pluto. Zoe owned *Shirley* free and clear; on her first trip, many years ago, she had found a scale-five hole and had become instantly rich. Most hole hunters were not so lucky.

Zoe was also unusual in that she seemed to thrive on solitude. Most hunters who made a strike settled down to live in comfort, buy a large company or put the money into safe investments and live off the interest. They were unwilling or unable to face another twenty years alone. Zoe had gone out again, and a third time after the second trip had proved fruitless. She had found a hole on her third trip, and was now almost through her fifth.

But for some reason she had never adequately explained to Xanthia, she had wanted a companion this time. And what better company than herself? With the medical facilities aboard *Shirley* she had grown a copy of herself and raised the little girl as her daughter.

Xanthia squirmed around in the control cabin of *The Good Ship Lollipop*, stuck her head through the hatch leading to the aft exercise room, and found nothing. What she had expected, she didn't know. Now she crouched in midair with a screwdriver, attacking the service panels that protected the radio assembly.

"What are you doing by yourself?" the voice asked.

"Why don't *you* tell *me*, Zoe?" she said, lifting the panel off and tossing it angrily to one side. She peered into the gloomy interior, wrinkling her nose at the smell of oil and paraffin. She shone her pencil beam into the space, flicking it from one component to the next, all as familiar to her as neighborhood corridors would be to a planet-born child. There was nothing out of place, nothing that shouldn't be there. Most of it was sealed into plastic blocks to prevent moisture or dust from getting to critical circuits. There was no tampering.

"I am failing to communicate. I am not your mother. I am a gravity and causality—"

"She's not my mother," Xanthia snapped.

"My records show that she would dispute you."

Xanthia didn't like the way the voice said that. But she was admitting to herself that there was no way Zoe could have set this up. That left her with the alternative: she really was talking to a black hole.

"She's not my mother," Xanthia repeated. "And if you've been listening in, you *know* why I'm out here in a lifeboat. So why do you ask?"

"I wish to help you. I have heard tension building between the two of you these last years. You are growing up."

Xanthia settled back in the control chair. Her head did not feel so good.

Hole hunting was a delicate economic balance, a tightrope walked between the needs of survival and the limitations of mass. The initial investment was tremendous and the return was undependable, so the potential hole hunter had to have a line to a source of speculative credit or be independently wealthy.

No consortium or corporation had been able to turn a profit at the business by going at it in a big way. The government of Pluto maintained a monopoly on the use of one-way robot probes, but they had found over the years that when a probe succeeded in finding a hole, a race usually developed to see who would reach it and claim it first. Ships sent after such holes had a way of disappearing in the resulting fights, far from law and order.

The demand for holes was so great that an economic niche remained which was filled by the solitary prospector, backed by people with tax writeoffs to gain. Prospectors had a ninety percent bankruptcy rate. But as with gold and oil in earlier days, the potential profits were huge, so there was never a lack of speculators.

Hole hunters would depart Pluto and accelerate to the limits of engine power, then coast for ten to fifteen years, keeping an eye on the mass detector. Sometimes they would be half a light-year from Sol before they had to decelerate and turn around. Less mass equaled more range, so the solitary hunter was the rule.

Teaming of ships had been tried, but teams that discovered a hole seldom came back together. One of them tended to have an accident. Hole hunters were a greedy lot, self-centered and self-sufficient.

Equipment had to be reliable. Replacement parts were costly in terms of mass, so the hole hunter had to make an agonizing choice with each item. Would it be better to leave it behind and chance a possibly fatal failure, or take it along, decreasing the range, and maybe miss the glory hole that is sure to be lurking just one more AU away? Hole hunters learned to be handy at repairing, jury-rigging, and bashing, because in twenty years even fail-safe triplicates can be on their last legs.

Zoe had sweated over her faulty mass detector before she admitted it was beyond her skills. Her primary detector had failed ten years into the voyage, and the second one had begun to act up six years later. She tried to put together one functioning detector with parts cannibalized from both. She nursed it along for a year with the equivalents of bobby pins and bubblegum. It was hopeless.

But *Shirley Temple* was a palace among prospecting ships. Having found two holes in her career, Zoe had her own money. She had stocked spare parts, beefed up the drive, even included that incredible luxury, a lifeboat.

The lifeboat was sheer extravagance, except for one thing. It had a mass detector as part of its astrogational equipment. She had bought it mainly for that reason, since it had only an eighteen-month range and would be useless except at the beginning and end of the trip, when they were close to Pluto. It made extensive use of plug-in components, sealed in plastic to prevent tampering or accidents caused by inexperienced passengers. The mass detector on board did not have the range or accuracy of the one on *Shirley*. It could be removed or replaced, but not recalibrated.

They had begun a series of three-month loops out from the mother ship. Xanthia had flown most of them earlier, when Zoe did not trust her to run *Shirley*. Later they had alternated.

"And that's what I'm doing out here by myself," Xanthia said. "I have to get out beyond ten million kilometers from *Shirley* so its mass doesn't affect the detector. My instrument is calibrated to ignore only the mass of this ship, not *Shirley*. I stay out here for three months, which is a reasonably safe time for the life systems on *Lollipop*, and time to get pretty lonely. Then back for refueling and supplying."

"The *Lollipop*?"

Xanthia blushed. "Well, I named this lifeboat that, after I started spending so much time on it. We have a tape of Shirley Temple in the library, and she sang this song, see—"

"Yes, I've heard it. I've been listening to radio for a very long time. So you no longer believe this is a trick by your mother?"

"She's *not*..." Then she realized she had referred to Zoe in the third person again.

"I don't know what to think," she said, miserably. "Why are you doing this?"

"I sense that you are still confused. You'd like some proof that I am what I say I am. Since you'll think of it in a minute, I might as well ask you this question. Why do you suppose I haven't yet registered on your mass detector?"

Xanthia jerked in her seat, then was brought up short by the straps. It was true, there was not the slightest wiggle on the dials of the detector.

"All right, why haven't you?" She felt a sinking sensation. She was sure the punchline came now, after she'd shot off her mouth about *Lollipop*—her secret from Zoe—and made such a point of the fact that

Zoe was not her mother. It was her own private rebellion, one that she had not had the nerve to face Zoe with. Now she's going to reveal herself and tell me how she did it, and I'll feel like a fool, she thought.

"It's simple," the voice said. "You weren't in range of me yet. But now you are. Take a look."

The needles were dancing, giving the reading of a scale-seven hole. A scale seven would mass about a tenth as much as the asteroid Ceres.

"Mommy, what *is* a black hole?"

The little girl was seven years old. One day she would call herself Xanthia, but she had not yet felt the need for a name and her mother had not seen fit to give her one. Zoe reasoned that you needed two of something before you needed names. There was only one other person on *Shirley*. There was no possible confusion. When the girl thought about it at all, she assumed her name must be Hey, or Darling.

She was a small child, as Zoe had been. She was recapitulating the growth Zoe had already been through a hundred years ago. Though she didn't know it, she was pretty: dark eyes with an oriental fold, dark skin, and kinky blonde hair. She was a genetic mix of Chinese and Negro, with dabs of other races thrown in for seasoning.

"I've tried to explain that before," Zoe said. "You don't have the math for it yet. I'll get you started on spacetime equations, then in about a year you'll be able to understand."

"But I want to know now." Black holes were a problem for the child. From her earliest memories the two of them had done nothing but hunt them, yet they never found one. She'd been doing a lot of reading—there was little else to do—and was wondering if they might inhabit the same category where she had tentatively placed Santa Claus and leprechauns.

"If I try again, will you go to sleep?"

"I promise."

So Zoe launched into her story about the Big Bang, the time in the long-ago when little black holes could be formed.

"As far as we can tell, all the little black holes like the ones we hunt were made in that time. Nowadays other holes can be formed by the collapse of very large stars. When the fires burn low and the pressures that are trying to blow the star apart begin to fade, gravity takes over and starts to pull the star in on itself." Zoe waved her hands in the air, forming cups to show bending space, flailing out to indicate pressures of fusion. These explanations were almost as difficult for her as stories of sex had been for earlier generations. The truth was that she was no relativist and didn't really grasp the slightly incredible premises behind black-hole theory. She suspected that no one could really visualize one, and if you can't do that, where are you? But she was practical enough not to worry about it.

"And what's gravity? I forgot." The child was rubbing her eyes to stay awake. She struggled to understand but already knew she would miss the point yet another time.

"Gravity is the thing that holds the universe together. The glue, or the rivets. It pulls everything toward everything else, and it takes energy to fight it and overcome it. It feels like when we boost the ship, remember I pointed that out to you?"

"Like when everything wants to move in the same direction?"

"That's right. So we have to be careful, because we don't think about it much. We have to worry about where things are because when we boost, everything will head for the stern. People on planets have to worry about that all the time. They have to put something strong between themselves and the center of the planet, or they'll go down."

"Down." The girl mused over that word, one that had been giving her trouble as long as she could remember, and thought she might finally have understood it. She had seen pictures of places where down was always the same direction, and they were strange to the eye. They were full of tables to put things on, chairs to sit in, and funny containers with no tops. Five of the six walls of the rooms on planets could hardly be used at all. One, the "floor," was called on to take all the use.

"So they use their legs to fight gravity with?" She was yawning now.

"Yes. You've seen pictures of the people with the funny legs. They're not so funny when you're in gravity. Those flat things on the ends are called feet. If they had peds like us, they wouldn't be able to walk so good. They always have to have one foot touching the floor, or they'd fall toward the surface of the planet."

Zoe tightened the strap that held the child to her bunk, and fastened the velcro patch on the blanket to the side of the sheet, tucking her in.

Kids needed a warm, snug place to sleep. Zoe preferred to float free in her own bedroom, tucked into a fetal position and drifting.

"G'night, Mommy."

"Good night. You get some sleep, and don't worry about black holes."

But the child dreamed of them, as she often did. They kept tugging at her, and she would wake breathing hard and convinced that she was going to fall into the wall in front her.

"You don't mean it? I'm rich!"

Xanthia looked away from the screen. It was no good pointing out that Zoe had always spoken of the trip as a partnership. She owned *Shirley* and *Lollipop*.

"Well, you too, of course. Don't think you won't be getting a real big share of the money. I'm going to set you up so well that you'll be able to buy a ship of your own, and raise little copies of yourself if you want to."

Xanthia was not sure that was her idea of heaven, but said nothing.

"Zoe, there's a problem, and I...well, I was—" But she was interrupted again by Zoe, who would not hear Xanthia's comment for another thirty seconds.

"The first data is coming over the telemetry channel right now, and I'm feeding it into the computer. Hold on a second while I turn the ship. I'm going to start decelerating in about one minute, based on these figures. You get the refined data to me as soon as you have it."

There was a brief silence.

"What problem?"

"It's talking to me, Zoe. The hole is talking to me."

This time the silence was longer than the minute it took the radio signal to make the round trip between ships. Xanthia furtively thumbed the contrast knob, turning her sister-mother down until the screen was blank. She could look at the camera and Zoe wouldn't know the difference.

Damn, damn, she thinks I've flipped. But I *had* to tell her.

"I'm not sure what you mean."

"Just what I *said*. I don't understand it, either. But it's been talking to me for the last hour, and it says the *damnedest* things."

There was another silence.

"All right. When you get there, don't do anything, repeat, *anything*, until I arrive. Do you understand?"

"Zoe, I'm not crazy. I'm *not*."

"Of course you're not, baby, there's an explanation for this and I'll find out what it is as soon as I get there. You just hang on. My first rough estimate puts me alongside you about three hours after you're stationary relative to the hole."

Shirley and *Lollipop*, traveling parallel courses, would both be veering from their straight-line trajectories to reach the hole. But Xanthia was closer to it; Zoe would have to move at a more oblique angle and would be using more fuel. Xanthia thought four hours was more like it.

"I'm signing off," Zoe said. "I'll call you back as soon as I'm in the groove."

Xanthia hit the off button on the radio and furiously unbuckled her seatbelt. Damn Zoe, damn her, damn her, *damn her*. Just sit tight, she says. I'll be there to explain the unexplainable. It'll be all right.

She knew she should start her deceleration, but there was something she must do first.

She twisted easily in the air, grabbing at braces with all four hands, and dived through the hatch to the only other living space in *Lollipop*: the exercise area. It was cluttered with equipment that she had neglected to fold into the walls, but she didn't mind; she liked close places. She squirmed through the maze like a fish gliding through coral, until she reached the wall she was looking for. It had been taped over with discarded manual pages, the only paper she could find on *Lollipop*. She started ripping at the paper, wiping tears from her cheeks with one ped as she worked. Beneath the paper was a mirror.

How to test for sanity? Xanthia had not considered the question; the thing to do had simply presented itself and she had done it. Now she confronted the mirror and searched for…what? Wild eyes? Froth on the lips?

What she saw was her mother.

Xanthia's life had been a process of growing slowly into the mold Zoe represented. She had known her pug nose would eventually turn down. She had known that baby fat would melt away. Her breasts had grown just into the small cones she knew from her mother's body and no farther.

She hated looking in mirrors.

Xanthia and Zoe were small women. Their most striking feature was the frizzy dandelion of yellow hair, lighter than their bodies. When the time had come for naming, the young clone had almost opted for Dandelion until she came upon the word *xanthic* in a dictionary. The radio call-letters for *Lollipop* happened to be X-A-N, and the word was too good to resist. She knew, too, that Orientals were thought of as having yellow skin, though she could not see why.

Why had she come here, of all places? She strained toward the mirror, fighting her repulsion, searching her face for signs of insanity. The narrow eyes were a little puffy, and as deep and expressionless as ever. She put her hands to the glass, startled in the silence to hear the multiple clicks as the long nails just missed touching the ones on the other side. She was always forgetting to trim them.

Sometimes, in mirrors, she knew she was not seeing herself. She could twitch her mouth, and the image would not move. She could smile, and the image would frown. It had been happening for two years, as her body put the finishing touches on its eighteen-year process of duplicating Zoe. She had not spoken of it, because it scared her.

"And this is where I come to see if I'm sane," she said aloud, noting that the lips in the mirror did not move. "Is she going to start talking to me now?" She waved her arms wildly, and so did Zoe in the mirror. At least it wasn't that bad yet; it was only the details that failed to match: the small movements, and especially the facial expressions. Zoe was inspecting her dispassionately and did not seem to like what she saw. That small curl at the edge of the mouth, the almost brutal narrowing of the eyes…

Xanthia clapped her hands over her face, then peeked out through the fingers. Zoe was peeking out, too. Xanthia began rounding up the drifting scraps of paper and walling her twin in again with new bits of tape.

The beast with two backs and legs at each end writhed, came apart, and resolved into Xanthia and Zoe, drifting, breathing hard. They caromed off the walls like monkeys, giving up their energy, gradually getting breath back under control. Golden, wet hair and sweaty skin brushed against each other again and again as they came to rest.

Now the twins floated in the middle of the darkened bedroom. Zoe was already asleep, tumbling slowly with that total looseness possible only in free fall. Her leg rubbed against Xanthia's belly and her relative motion stopped. The leg was moist. The room was close, thick with the smell of passion. The recirculators whined quietly as they labored to clear the air.

Pushing one finger gently against Zoe's ankle, Xanthia turned her until they were face to face. Frizzy blonde hair tickled her nose, and she felt warm breath on her mouth.

Why can't it always be like this?

"You're not my mother," she whispered. Zoe had no reaction to this heresy. "You're *not*."

Only in the last year had Zoe admitted the relationship was much closer. Xanthia was now fifteen.

And what was different? Something, there had to be something beyond the mere knowledge that they were not mother and child. There was a new quality in their relationship, growing as they came to the end of the voyage. Xanthia would look into those eyes where she had seen love and now see only blankness, coldness.

"Oriental inscrutability?" she asked herself, half-seriously. She knew she was hopelessly unsophisticated. She had spent her life in a society of two. The only other person she knew had her own face. But she had thought she knew Zoe. Now she felt less confident with every glance into Zoe's face and every kilometer passed on the way to Pluto.

Pluto.

Her thoughts turned gratefully away from immediate problems and toward that unimaginable place. She would be there in only four more years. The cultural adjustments she would have to make were staggering. Thinking about that, she felt a sensation in her chest that she guessed was her heart leaping in anticipation. That's what happened to characters in tapes when they got excited, anyway. Their hearts were forever leaping, thudding, aching, or skipping beats.

She pushed away from Zoe and drifted slowly to the viewport. Her old friends were all out there, the only friends she had ever known, the stars. She greeted them all one by one, reciting childhood mnemonic riddles and rhymes like bedtime prayers.

It was a funny thought that the view from her window would terrify many of those strangers she was going to meet on Pluto. She'd read that many tunnel-raised people could not stand open spaces. What it was that scared them, she could not understand. The things that scared her were crowds, gravity, males, and mirrors.

"Oh, damn. Damn! I'm going to be just *hopeless*. Poor little idiot girl from the sticks, visiting the big city." She brooded for a time on all the thousands of things she had never done, from swimming in the gigantic underground disneylands to seducing a boy.

"To *being* a boy." It had been the source of their first big argument. When Xanthia had reached adolescence, the time when children want to begin experimenting, she had learned from Zoe that *Shirley Temple* did not carry the medical equipment for sex changes. She was doomed to spend her critical formative years as a sexual deviate, a unisex.

"It'll stunt me forever," she had protested. She had been reading a lot of pop psychology at the time.

"Nonsense," Zoe had responded, hard-pressed to explain why she had not stocked a viro-genetic imprinter and the companion Y-alyzer. Which, as Xanthia pointed out, *any* self-respecting home surgery kit should have.

"The human race got along for millions of years without sex changing," Zoe had said. "Even after the Invasion. We were a highly technological race for hundreds of years before changing. Billions of people lived and died in the same sex."

"Yeah, and look what they were like."

Now, for another of what seemed like an endless series of nights, sleep was eluding her. There was the worry of Pluto, and the worry of Zoe and her strange behavior, and no way to explain anything in her small universe which had become unbearably complicated in the last years.

I wonder what it would be like with a man?

Three hours ago Xanthia had brought *Lollipop* to a careful rendezvous with the point in space her instruments indicated contained a black hole. She had long since understood that even if she ever found one she would never see it, but she could not restrain herself from squinting into the starfield for some evidence. It was silly; though the hole massed ten to the fifteenth tonnes (the original estimate had been off one order of magnitude) it was still only a fraction of a millimeter in diameter. She was staying a good safe hundred kilometers from it. Still, you ought to be able to sense something like that, you ought to be able to *feel* it.

It was no use. This hunk of space looked exactly like any other.

"There is a point I would like explained," the hole said. "What will be done with me after you have captured me?"

The question surprised her. She still had not got around to thinking of the voice as anything but some annoying aberration like her face in the mirror. How was she supposed to deal with it? Could she admit to herself that it existed, that it might even have feelings?

"I guess we'll just mark you, in the computer, that is. You're too big for us to haul back to Pluto. So we'll hang around you for a week or so, refining your trajectory until we know precisely where you're going to be, then we'll leave you. We'll make some maneuvers on the way in so no one could retrace our path and find out where you are, because they'll know we found a big one when we get back."

"How will they know that?"

"Because we'll be renting...well, *Zoe* will be chartering one of those big monster tugs, and she'll come out here and put a charge on you and tow you...say, how do you feel about this?"

"Are you concerned with the answer?"

The more Xanthia thought about it, the less she liked it. If she really was not hallucinating this experience, then she was contemplating the capture and imprisonment of a sentient being. An innocent sentient being who had been wandering around the edge of the system, suddenly to find him or herself...

"Do you have sex?"

"No."

"All right, I guess I've been kind of short with you. It's just because you *did* startle me, and I *didn't* expect it, and it was all a little alarming."

The hole said nothing.

"You're a strange sort of person, or whatever," she said.

Again there was silence.

"Why don't you tell me more about yourself? What's it like being a black hole, and all that?" She still couldn't fight down the ridiculous feeling those words gave her.

"I live much as you do, from day to day. I travel from star to star, taking about ten million years for the trip. Upon arrival, I plunge through the core of the star. I do this as often as is necessary, then I depart by a slingshot maneuver through the heart of a massive planet. The Tunguska Meteorite, which hit Siberia in 1908, was a black hole gaining momentum on its way to Jupiter, where it could get the added push needed for solar escape velocity."

One thing was bothering Xanthia. "What do you mean, 'as often as is necessary'?"

"Usually five or six thousand passes is sufficient."

"No, no. What I meant is *why* is it necessary? What do you get out of it?"

"Mass," the hole said. "I need to replenish my mass. The Relativity Laws state that nothing can escape from a black hole, but the Quantum Laws, specifically the Heisenberg Uncertainty Principle, state that below a certain radius the position of a particle cannot be determined. I lose mass constantly through tunneling. It is not all wasted, as I am able to control the direction and form of the escaping mass, and to use the energy that results to perform functions that your present-day physics says are impossible."

"Such as?" Xanthia didn't know why, but she was getting nervous.

"I can exchange inertia for gravity, and create energy in a variety of ways."

"So you can move yourself."

"Slowly."

"And you eat..."

"Anything."

Xanthia felt a sudden panic, but she didn't know what was wrong. She glanced down at her instruments and felt her hair prickle from her wrists and ankles to the nape of her neck.

The hole was ten kilometers closer than it had been.

"How could you *do* that to me?" Xanthia raged. "I trusted you, and that's how you repaid me, by trying to sneak up on me and...and—"

"It was not intentional. I speak to you by means of controlled gravity waves. To speak to you at all, it is necessary to generate an attractive force between us. You were never in any danger."

"I don't believe that," Xanthia said angrily. "I think you're double-talking me. I don't think gravity works like that, and I don't think you really tried very hard to tell me how you talk to me, back when we first started." It occurred to her now, also, that the hole was speaking much more fluently than in the beginning. Either it was a very fast learner, or that had been intentional.

The hole paused. "This is true," it said.

She pressed her advantage. "Then why did you do it?"

"It was a reflex, like blinking in a bright light, or drawing one's hand back from a fire. When I sense matter, I am attracted to it."

"The proper cliché would be 'like a moth to a flame.' But you're not a moth, and I'm not a flame. I don't believe you. I think you could have stopped yourself if you wanted to."

Again the hole hesitated. "You are correct."

"So you were trying to...?"

"I was trying to eat you."

"Just like *that*? Eat someone you've been having a conversation with?"

"Matter is matter," the hole said, and Xanthia thought she detected a defensive note in its voice.

"What do you think of what I said we're going to do with you? You were going to tell me, but we got off on that story about where you came from."

"As I understand it, you propose to return for me. I will be towed to near Pluto's orbit, sold, and eventually come to rest in the heart of an orbital power station, where your species will feed matter into my gravity well, extracting power cheaply from the gravitational collapse."

"Yeah, that's pretty much it."

"It sounds ideal. My life is struggle. Failing to find matter to consume would mean loss of mass until I am smaller than an atomic nucleus. The loss rate would increase exponentially, and my universe would disappear. I do not know what would happen beyond that point. I have never wished to find out."

How much could she trust this thing? Could it move very rapidly? She toyed with the idea of backing off still further. The two of them were now motionless relative to each other, but they were both moving slowly away from the location she had given Zoe.

It didn't make sense to think it could move in on her fast. If it could, why hadn't it? Then it could eat her and wait for Zoe to arrive—Zoe, who was helpless to detect the hole with her broken mass detector.

She should relay the new vectors to Zoe. She tried to calculate where her twin would arrive, but was distracted by the hole speaking.

"I would like to speak to you now of what I initially contacted you for. Listening to Pluto radio, I have become aware of certain facts that you should know, if, as I suspect, you are not already aware of them. Do you know of Clone Control Regulations?"

"No, what are they?" Again, she was afraid without knowing why.

The genetics statutes, according to the hole, were the soul of simplicity. For three hundred years, people had been living just about forever. It had become necessary to limit the population. Even if everyone had only one child—the Birthright—population would still grow. For a while, clones had been a loophole. No more. Now, only one person had the right to any one set of genes. If two possessed them, one was excess, and was summarily executed.

"Zoe has priority property rights to her genetic code," the hole concluded. "This is backed up by a long series of court decisions."

"So I'm—"

"Excess."

Zoe met her at the airlock as Xanthia completed the docking maneuver. She was smiling, and Xanthia felt the way she always did when Zoe smiled these days: like a puppy being scratched behind the ears. They kissed, then Zoe held her at arm's length.

"Let me look at you. Can it only be three months? You've *grown*, my baby."

Xanthia blushed. "I'm not a baby anymore, Mother." But she was happy. Very happy.

"No. I should say not." She touched one of Xanthia's breasts, then turned her around slowly. "I should say not. Putting on a little weight in the hips, aren't we?"

"And the bosom. One inch while I was gone. I'm almost there." And it was true. At sixteen, the young clone was almost a woman.

"Almost there," Zoe repeated, and glanced away from her twin. But she hugged her again, and they kissed, and began to laugh as the tension was released.

They made love, not once and then to bed, but many times, feasting on each other. One of them remarked—Xanthia could not remember who because it seemed so accurate that either of them might have said it—that the only good thing about these three-month separations was the homecoming.

"You did very well," Zoe said, floating in the darkness and sweet exhausted atmosphere of their bedroom many hours later. "You handled the lifeboat like it was part of your body. I watched the docking. I *wanted* to see you make a mistake, I think, so I'd know I still have something on you." Her teeth showed in the starlight, rows of lights below the sparkles of her eyes and the great dim blossom of her hair.

"Ah, it wasn't that hard," Xanthia said, delighted, knowing full well that it *was* that hard.

"Well, I'm going to let you handle it again the next swing. From now on, you can think of the lifeboat as *your* ship. You're the skipper."

It didn't seem like the time to tell her that she already thought of it that way. Nor that she had christened the ship.

Zoe laughed quietly. Xanthia looked at her.

"I remember the day I first boarded my own ship," she said. "It was a big day for me. My own ship."

"This is the way to live," Xanthia agreed. "Who needs all those people? Just the two of us. And they say hole hunters are crazy. I...wanted to..." The words stuck in her throat, but Xanthia knew this was the time to get them out, if there ever would be a time. "I don't want to stay too long at Pluto, Mother. I'd like to get right back out here with you." There, she'd said it.

Zoe said nothing for a long time.

"We can talk about that later."

"I love you, Mother," Xanthia said, a little too loudly.

"I love you, too, baby," Zoe mumbled. "Let's get some sleep, okay?"

She tried to sleep, but it wouldn't happen. What was *wrong*?

Leaving the darkened room behind her, she drifted through the ship, looking for something she had lost, or was losing, she wasn't sure which. What had happened, after all? Certainly nothing she could put her finger on. She loved her mother, but all she knew was that she was choking on tears.

In the water closet, wrapped in the shower bag with warm water misting around her, she glanced in the mirror.

"Why? Why would she do a thing like that?"

"Loneliness. And insanity. They appear to go together. This is her solution. You are not the first clone she has made."

She had thought herself beyond shock, but the clarity that simple declarative sentence brought to her mind was explosive. Zoe had always needed the companionship Xanthia provided. She needed a child for diversion in the long, dragging years of a voyage, she needed someone to talk to. *Why couldn't she have brought a dog?* She saw herself now as a shipboard pet, and felt sick. The local leash laws would necessitate the destruction of the animal before landing. Regrettable, but there it was. Zoe had spent the last year working up the courage to do it.

How many little Xanthias? They might even have chosen that very name; they would have been that much like her. Three, four? She wept for her forgotten sisters. Unless...

"How do I know you're telling me the truth about this? How could she have kept it from me? I've seen tapes of Pluto. I never saw any mention of this."

"She edited those before you were born. She has been careful. Consider her position: there can be only one of you, but the law does not say which it has to be. With her death, you become legal. If you had known that, what would life have been like in *Shirley Temple*?"

"I don't believe you. You've got something in mind, I'm sure of it."

"Ask her when she gets here. But be careful. Think it out, all the way through."

She had thought it out. She had ignored the last three calls from Zoe while she thought. All the options must be considered, all the possibilities planned for. It was an impossible task; she knew she was far too emotional to think clearly, and there wasn't time to get herself under control.

But she had done what she could. Now *The Good Ship Lollipop*, outwardly unchanged, was a ship of war.

Zoe came backing in, riding the fusion torch and heading for a point dead in space relative to Xanthia. The fusion drive was too dangerous for *Shirley* to complete the rendezvous; the rest of the maneuver would be up to *Lollipop*.

Xanthia watched through the telescope as the drive went off. She could see *Shirley* clearly on her screen, though the ship was fifty kilometers away.

Her screen lit up again, and there was Zoe. Xanthia turned her own camera on.

"There you are," Zoe said. "Why wouldn't you talk to me?"

"I didn't think the time was ripe."

"Would you like to tell me how come this nonsense about talking black holes? What's gotten into you?"

"Never mind about that. There never was a hole, anyway. I just needed to talk to you about something you forgot to erase from the tape library in the *Lol*—...in the lifeboat. You were pretty thorough with the tapes in *Shirley*, but you forgot to take the same care here. I guess you didn't think I'd ever be using it. Tell me, what are Clone Control Regulations?"

The face on the screen was immobile. Or was it a mirror, and was she smiling? Was it herself, or Zoe she watched? Frantically, Xanthia thumbed a switch to put her telescope image on the screen, wiping out the face. Would Zoe try to talk her way out of it? If she did, Xanthia was determined to do nothing at all. There was no way she could check out any lie Zoe might tell her, nothing she could confront Zoe with except a fantastic story from a talking black hole.

Please say something. Take responsibility out of my hands. She was willing to die, tricked by Zoe's fast talk, rather than accept the hole's word against Zoe's.

But Zoe was acting, not talking, and the response was exactly what the hole had predicted. The attitude control jets were firing, *Shirley Temple* was pitching and yawing slowly, the nozzles at the stern hunting for a speck in the telescope screen. When the engines were aimed, they would surely be fired, and Xanthia and the whole ship would be vaporized.

But she was ready. Her hands had been poised over the thrust controls. *Lollipop* had a respectable acceleration, and every gee of it slammed her into the couch as she scooted away from the danger spot.

Shirley's fusion engines fired, and began a deadly hunt. Xanthia could see the thin, incredibly hot stream playing around her as Zoe made finer adjustments in her orientation. She could only evade it for a short time, but that was all she needed.

Then the lights went out. She saw her screen flare up as the telescope circuit became overloaded with an immense burst of energy. And it was over. Her radar screen showed nothing at all.

"As I predicted," the hole said.

"Why don't you shut up?" Xanthia sat very still, and trembled.

"I shall, very soon. I did not expect to be thanked. But what you did, you did for yourself."

"And you, too, you…you *ghoul*! Damn you, damn you to hell." She was shouting through her tears. "Don't think you've fooled me, not completely, anyway. I know what you did, and I know how you did it."

"Do you?" The voice was unutterably cool and distant. She could see that now the hole was out of danger, it was rapidly losing interest in her.

"Yes, I do. Don't tell me it was a coincidence that when you changed direction it was just enough to be near Zoe when she got here. You had this planned from the start."

"From much further back than you know," the hole said. "I tried to get you both, but it was impossible. The best I could do was take advantage of the situation as it was."

"Shut up, shut up."

The hole's voice was changing from the hollow, neutral tones to something that might have issued from a tank of liquid helium. She would never have mistaken it for human.

"What I did, I did for my own benefit. But I saved your life. She was going to try to kill you. I maneuvered her into such a position that, when she tried to turn her fusion drive on you, she was heading into a black hole she was powerless to detect."

"You *used* me."

"You used me. You were going to imprison me in a power station."

"But you said you wouldn't *mind*! You said it would be the perfect place."

"Do you believe that eating is all there is to life? There is more to do in the wide universe than you can even suspect. I am slow. It is easy to catch a hole if your mass detector is functioning: Zoe did it three times. But I am beyond your reach now."

"What do you mean? What are you going to do? What am *I* going to do?" That question hurt so much that Xanthia almost didn't hear the hole's reply.

"I am on my way out. I converted *Shirley* into energy; I absorbed very little mass from her. I beamed the energy very tightly, and am now on my way out of your system. You will not see me again. You have two options. You can go back to Pluto and tell everyone what happened out here. It would be necessary for scientists to rewrite natural laws if they believe you. It has been done before, but usually with more persuasive evidence. There will be questions asked concerning the fact that no black hole has ever evaded capture, spoken, or changed velocity in the past. You can explain that when a hole has a chance to defend itself, the hole hunter does not survive to tell the story."

"I will. I *will* tell them what happened!" Xanthia was eaten by a horrible doubt. Was it possible there had been a solution to her problem that did not involve Zoe's death? Just how badly had the hole tricked her?

"There is a second possibility," the hole went on, relentlessly. "Just what *are* you doing out here in a lifeboat?"

"What am I...I told you, we had..." Xanthia stopped. She felt herself choking.

"It would be easy to see you as crazy. You discovered something in *Lollipop*'s library that led you to know you must kill Zoe. This knowledge was too much for you. In defense, you invented me to trick you into doing what you had to do. Look in the mirror and tell me if you think your story will be believed. Look closely, and be honest with yourself."

She heard the voice laugh for the first time, from down in the bottom of its hole, like a voice from a well. It was an extremely unpleasant sound.

Maybe Zoe had died a month ago, strangled or poisoned or slashed with a knife. Xanthia had been sitting in her lifeboat, catatonic, all that time, and had constructed this episode to justify the murder. It *had* been self-defense, which was certainly a good excuse, and a very convenient one.

But she knew. She was sure, as sure as she had ever been of anything, that the hole was out there, that everything had happened as she had seen it happen. She saw the flash again in her mind, the awful flash that had turned Zoe into radiation. But she also knew that the other explanation would haunt her for the rest of her life.

"I advise you to forget it. Go to Pluto, tell everyone that your ship blew up and you escaped and you are Zoe. Take her place in the world, and never, *never* speak of talking black holes."

The voice faded from her radio. It did not speak again.

After days of numb despair and more tears and recriminations than she cared to remember, Xanthia did as the hole had predicted. But life on Pluto did not agree with her. There were too many people, and none of them looked very much like her. She stayed long enough to withdraw Zoe's money from the bank and buy a ship, which she named *Shirley Temple*. It was massive, with power to blast to the stars if necessary. She had left something out there, and she meant to search for it until she found it again.

THE BLACK HOLE PASSES

Jordan looked up from the log of the day's transmissions and noted with annoyance that Treemonisha was lying with her legs half-buried in the computer console. He couldn't decide why that bothered him so much, but it did. He walked over to her and kicked her in the face to get her attention, his foot sailing right through her as if she wasn't there, which she wasn't. He waited, tapping his foot, for her to notice it.

Twenty seconds later she jumped, then looked sheepish.

"You blinked," Jordan crowed. "You blinked. You owe me another five dollars." Again he waited, not even conscious of waiting. After a year at the station he had reached the point where his mind simply edited out the twenty-second time lag. Given the frantic pace of life at the station, there was little chance he would miss anything.

"All right, so I blinked. I'm getting tired of that game. Besides, all you're doing is wiping out your old debts. You owe me...four hundred and fifty-five dollars now instead of four hundred sixty."

"You liked it well enough when you were *winning*," he pointed out. "How else could you have gotten into me for that kind of money, with my reflexes?"

(Wait) "I think the totals show who has the faster reflexes. But I told you a week ago that I don't appreciate being bothered when I'm reading." She waved her facprinted book, her thumb holding her place.

"Oh, listen to you. Pointing out to me what you don't like while you're all spread out through my computer. You *know* that drives me up the wall."

(Wait) She looked down at where her body vanished into the side of the computer, but instead of apologizing, she flared up.

"Well, so what? I never heard of such foolishness; walking around chalk marks on the floor all the time so I won't melt into your precious furniture. Who ever heard of such—" She realized she was repeating herself. She wasn't good at heated invective, but had been getting practice at improving it in the past weeks. She got up out of the computer and stood glowering at Jordan, or glowering at where he had been.

Jordan had quickly scanned around his floor and picked out an area marked off with black tape. He walked over to it and stepped over the lines and waited with his arms crossed, a pugnacious scowl on his face.

"How do you like that?" he spat out at her. "I've been very scrupulous about avoiding objects in your place. Chalk marks, indeed. If you used tape like I told you, you wouldn't be rubbing them off all the time with that fat ass of yours." But she had started laughing after her eyes followed to where he was now standing, and it soon got out of control. She doubled over, threatened to fall down she laughed so hard. He looked down and tried to remember what it was that the tape marked off at her place. Was that where she kept the toilet?

He jumped hastily out of the invisible toilet and was winding up a scathing remark, but she had stopped laughing. The remarks about the fat ass had reached her, and her reply had crawled back at the speed of light.

As he listened to her, he realized anything he could say would be superfluous; she was already as angry as she could be. So he walked over to the holo set and pressed a switch. The projection he had been talking to zipped back into the tank, to become a ten-centimeter angry figure, waving her arms at him.

He saw the tiny figure stride to her own set and slap another button. The tank went black. He noticed with satisfaction, just before she disappeared, that she had lost her place in the book.

Then, in one of the violent swings of mood that had been scaring him to death recently, he was desolately sorry for what he had done. His hands trembled as he pressed the call button, and he felt the sweat popping out on his forehead. But she wasn't receiving.

"Great. One neighbor in half a billion kilometers, and I pick a fight with her."

He got up and started his ritual hunt for a way of killing himself that wouldn't be so grossly bloody that it would make him sick. Once again he came to the conclusion that there wasn't anything like that in the station.

"Why couldn't they think of things like that?" he fumed. "No drugs, no poison gas, no nothing. Damn air system has so goddam many safeties on the damn thing I couldn't raise the CO_2 count in here if my life depended on it. Which it *does*. If I don't find a painless way to kill myself, it's going to drive me to suicide."

He broke off, not only because he had played back that last rhetorical ramble, but because he was never comfortable hearing himself talk to himself. It sounded too much like a person on the brink of insanity.

"Which I *am*!"

It felt a bit better to have admitted it out loud. It sounded like a very sane thing to say. He grasped the feeling, built steadily on it until it began to feel natural. After a few minutes of deep breathing he felt something approximating calm. Calmly, he pressed the call button again, to find that Treemonisha was still not at home. Calmly, he built up spit and fired it at the innocent holo tank, where it dripped down obscenely. He grinned. Later he could apologize, but right now it seemed to be the right course to stay angry.

He walked back to the desk and sat down before the computer digest of the three trillion bits that had come over the hotline in the last twenty-four hours. Here was where he earned his salary. There was an added incentive in the realization that Treemonisha had not yet started her scan of her own computer's opinions for the day. Maybe he could scoop her again.

Jordan Moon was the station agent for Star Line, Inc., one of the two major firms in the field of interstellar communication. If you can call listening in on a party line communication.

He lived and worked in a station that had been placed in a slow circular orbit thirteen billion kilometers from the sun. It was a lonely area; it had the sole virtue of being right in the center of the circle of greatest signal strength of the Ophiuchi Hotline.

About all that anyone had ever known for sure about the Ophiuchites was the fact that they had one hell of a big laser somewhere in their planetary system, 70 Ophiuchi. Aside from that, which they couldn't very well conceal, they were an extremely closemouthed race. They never volunteered anything about themselves directly, and human civilization was too parsimonious to ask. Why build a giant laser, the companies asked when it was suggested, when all that lovely information floods through space for free?

Jordan Moon had always thought that an extremely good question, but he turned it around: why did the *Ophiuchites* bother to build a giant laser? What did they get out of it? No one had the slightest idea, not even Jordan, who fancied himself an authority on everything.

He was not far wrong, and that was his value to the company.

No one had yet succeeded in making a copyright stand up in court when applied to information received over the Hotline. The prevailing opinion was that it was a natural resource, like vacuum, and free to all who could afford the expense of maintaining a station in the cometary zone. The expense was tremendous, but the potential rewards were astronomical. There were fifteen companies elbowing each other for a piece of the action, from the giants like Star Line and HotLine, Ltd., down to several free-lancers who paid holehunters to listen in when they were in the vicinity.

But the volume of transmissions was enough to make a board chairman weep and develop ulcers. And the aliens, with what the company thought was boorish inconsideration, insisted on larding the valuable stuff with quintillions of bits of gibberish that might be poetry or might be pornography or recipes or pictures or who-knew-what, which the computers had never been able to unscramble and which had given a few the galloping jitters. The essential problem was that ninety-nine percent of what the aliens thought worth sending over the Line was trash to humans. But that one percent...

...the Symbiotic Spacesuits, that had made it possible for a human civilization to inhabit the Rings of Saturn with no visible means of support, feeding, respirating, and watering each other in a closed-ecology daisy chain.

...the Partial Gravitational Rigor, which made it possible to detect and hunt and capture quantum black holes and make them sit up and do tricks for you, like powering a space drive.

…Macromolecule Manipulation, without which people would die after only two centuries of life.

…Null-field and all the things it had made possible.

Those were the large, visible things that had changed human life in drastic ways but had not made anyone huge fortunes simply because they were so big that they quickly diffused through the culture because of their universal application. The real money was in smaller, patentable items, like circuitry, mechanical devices, chemistry, and games.

It was Jordan's job to sift those few bits of gold from the oceans of gossip or whatever it was that poured down the Line every day. And to do it before Treemonisha and his other competitors. If possible, to find things that Treemonisha missed entirely. He was aided by a computer that tirelessly sorted and compared, dumping the more obvious chaff before printing out a large sheet of things it thought might be of interest.

Jordan scanned that sheet each day, marking out items and thinking about them. He had a lot to think about, and a lot to think with. He was an encyclopedic synthesist, a man with volumes of major and minor bits and pieces of human knowledge and the knack of putting it together and seeing how it might fit with the new stuff from the Line. When he saw something good, he warmed up his big laser and fired it off special delivery direct to Pluto. Everything else—including the things the computer had rejected as nonsense, because you never could tell what the monster brains on Luna might pick out of it on the second or third go-round—he recorded on a chip the size of a flyspeck and loaded it into a tiny transmitter and fired it off parcel post in a five-stage, high-gee message rocket. His aim didn't have to be nearly as good as the Ophiuchites'; a few months later, the payload would streak by Pluto and squeal out its contents in the two minutes it was in radio range of the big dish.

"I wish their aim had been a *little* better," he groused to himself as he went over the printout for the fourth time. He knew it was nonsense, but he felt like grousing.

The diameter of the laser beam by the time it reached Sol was half a billion kilometers. The center of the beam was twice the distance from Pluto to the sun, a distance amounting to about twenty seconds of arc from 70 Ophiuchi. But why aim it at the sun? No one listening there. Where would the logical place be to aim a message laser?

Jordan was of the opinion that the aim of the Ophiuchites was better than the company president gave them credit for. Out here, there was very little in the way of noise to garble the transmissions. If they had directed the beam through the part of the solar system where planets are most likely to be found—where they all *are* found—the density of expelled solar gases would have played hob with reception. Besides, Jordan felt that none of the information would have been much good to planet-bound beings, anyway. Once humanity had developed the means of reaching the cometary zone and found that messages were being sent out there rather than to the Earth, where everyone had always expected to find them, they were in a position to utilize the information.

"They knew what they were doing, all right," he muttered, but the thought died away as something halfway down the second page caught his eye. Jordan never knew for *sure* just what he was seeing in the digests. Perhaps a better way to make cyanide stew, or advice to lovelorn Ophiuchites. But he could spot when something might have relevance to his own species. He was good at his work. He looked at the symbols printed there, and decided they might be of some use to a branch of genetic engineering.

Ten minutes later, the computer had lined up the laser and he punched the information into it. The lights dimmed as the batteries were called upon to pour a large percentage of their energy into three spaced pulses, five seconds apart. Jordan yawned and scratched himself. Another day's work done; elapsed time, three hours. He was doing well—that only left twenty-one hours before he had anything else he needed to do.

Ah, leisure.

He approached the holo tank again and with considerable trepidation pressed the call button. He was afraid to think of what he might do if Treemonisha did not answer this time.

"You had no call to say what you said," she accused, as she appeared in the tank.

"You're absolutely right," he said, quickly. "It was uncalled for, and untrue. Tree, I'm going crazy, I'm not myself. It was a childish insult and you know it was without basis in fact."

She decided that was enough in the way of apology. She touched the projection button and joined him in the room. So beautiful, so alive, and so imaginary he wanted to cry again. Jordan and Treemonisha were the system's most frustrated lovers. They had never met in the flesh, but had spent a year together by holo projection.

Jordan knew every inch of Treemonisha's body, every pore, every hair. When they got unbearably horny, they would lie side by side on the floor and look at each other. They would strip for each other, taking hours with each garment. They developed the visual and aural sex fantasy to a pitch so fine that it was their own private language. They would sit inches apart and pass their hands close to each other, infinitely careful never to touch and spoil the illusion. They would talk to each other, telling what they would do when they finally got together in person, then they would sit back and masturbate themselves into insensibility.

"You know," Treemonisha said, "you were a lousy choice for this job. You look like shit, you know that? I worry about you, this isolation is... well, it's not good for you."

"Driving me crazy, right?" He watched her walk to one of the taped-off areas on his floor and sit; as she touched the chair in her room, the holo projector picked it up and it winked into existence in his world. She was wearing a red paper blouse but had left off the pants, as a reproach, he thought, and a reminder of how baseless his gibe had been. She raised her left index finger three times. That was the signal for a scenario, "Captain Future Meets the Black Widow," one of his favorites. They had evolved the hand signals when they grew impatient with asking each other, "Do you want to play 'Antony and Cleopatra'?"—one of *her* favorites.

He waved his hand, negating his opening lines. He was impatient with the games and fantasies. He was getting impatient with everything. Besides, she wasn't wearing her costume for the Black Widow.

"I think you're wrong," he said. "I think I was the perfect choice for this job. You know what I did after you shut off? I went looking for a way to kill myself."

For once, he noticed the pause. She sat there in her chair, mouth slightly open, eyes unfocused, looking as though she was about to drool all over her chin. Once they had both been fascinated with the process by which their minds suspended operations during the time lag that was such a part of their lives. He had teased her about how stupid she looked when she waited for his words to catch up with her. Then once he had caught himself during one of the lags and realized he was a slack-jawed imbecile, too. After that, they didn't talk about it.

She jerked and came to life again, like a humanoid robot that had just been activated.

"Jordan! Why did you do that?" She was half out of the chair in a reflex comforting gesture, then suppressed it before she committed the awful error of trying to touch him.

"The point is, I didn't. Try it sometime. I found nine dozen ways of killing myself. It isn't hard to do, I'm sure you can see that. But, you see, they have gauged me to a nicety. They know exactly what I'm capable of, and what I can never do. If I could kill myself painlessly, I would have done it three months ago, when I first started looking. But the most painless way I've doped out yet still involves explosive decompression. I don't have the guts for it."

"But surely you've thought of…ah, never mind."

"You mean you've thought of a way?" He didn't know what to think. He had been aware for a long time that she was a better synthesist than he; the production figures and several heated communications from the home office proved that. She could put nothing and nothing together and arrive at answers that astounded him. What's more, her solutions worked. She seldom sent anything over her laser that didn't bear fruit and often saw things he had overlooked.

"Maybe I have," she evaded, "but if I did, you don't think I'd tell you after what you just said. Jordan, I don't want you to kill yourself. That's not fair. Not until we can get together and you try to live up to all your boasting. After that, well, maybe you'll *have* to kill yourself."

He smiled at that, and was grateful she was taking the light approach. He *did* get carried away describing the delights she was going to experience as soon as they met in the flesh.

"Give me a hint," he coaxed. "It must involve the life system, right? It stands to reason, after you rule out the medical machines, which no one, *no* one could fool into giving out a dose of cyanide. Let's see, maybe I should take a closer look at that air intake. It stands to reason that I could get the CO_2 count in here way up if I could only—"

"No!" she exploded, then listened to the rest of his statement. "No hints. I don't know a way. The engineers who built these things were too smart, and they knew some of us would get depressed and try to kill ourselves. There's no wrenches you could throw into the works that they haven't already thought of and countered. You just have to wait it out."

"Six more months," he groaned. "What does that come to in seconds?"

"Twenty less than when you asked the question, and didn't that go fast?"

Looked at that way, he had to admit it did. He experienced no subjective time between the question and the answer. If only he could edit out days and weeks as easily as seconds.

"Listen, honey, I want to do anything I can to help you. Really, would it help if I tried harder to stay out of your furniture?"

He sighed, not really interested in that anymore. But it would be something to do.

"All right."

So they got together, and she carefully laid out strips of tape on her floor marking the locations of objects in his room. He coached her, since she could see nothing of his room except him. When it was done, she pointed out that she could not get into her bedroom without walking through his auxiliary coelostat. He said that was all right as long as she avoided everything else.

When they were through, he was as depressed as ever. Watching her crawl around on her hands and knees made him ache for her. She was so lovely, and he was so lonely. The way her hair fell in long, ashen streams over the gathered materials of her sleeves, the curl of her toes as she knelt to peel off a strip of tape, the elastic give and take of the tendons in her legs—all the myriad tiny details he knew so well and didn't know at all. The urge to reach out and touch her was overpowering.

"What would you like to do today?" she said when they were through with the taping.

"I don't know. Everything I *can't* do."

"Would you like me to tell you a story?"

"No."

"Would you tell *me* a story?" She crossed her legs nervously. She didn't know how to cope with him when he got in these unresponsive moods.

Treemonisha was not subject to the terrors of loneliness that were tearing Jordan apart. She got along quite well by herself, aside from the sometimes maddening sexual pressures. But masturbation satisfied her more than it did Jordan. She expected no problems while waiting out the six months until they were rotated back to Pluto. There was even a pleasurable aspect of the situation for her: the breathless feeling of anticipation waiting for the moment when they would finally be in each other's arms.

Jordan was no good at all at postponing his wants. Those wants, surprisingly to him, were not primarily sexual. He longed to be surrounded by people. To be elbow to elbow in a crowd, to smell the human smell of them around him, to be jostled, even shoved. Even to be punched in the face if necessary. But to be *touched* by another human being. It didn't have to be Treemonisha, though she was his first choice. He loved her, even when he yelled at her for being so maddeningly insubstantial.

"All right, I'll tell you a story." He fell silent, trying to think of one that had some aspect of originality. He couldn't, and so he fell back on "The Further Exploits of the Explorers of the Pink Planet." For that one, Treemonisha had to take off all her clothes and lie on her back on the floor. He sat very close to her and put the trio of adventurers through their paces.

Captain Rock Rogers, commander of the expedition, he who had fearlessly led the team over yawning wrinkles and around pores sunk deep into the treacherous surface of the pink planet. The conqueror of Leftbreast Mountain, the man who had first planted the flag of the United Planets on the dark top of that dangerously unstable prominence and was planning an assault on the fabled Rightbreast Mountain, home of the savage tribe of killer microbes. Why?

"Because it's there," Treemonisha supplied.

"Who's telling this story?"

Doctor Maryjane Peters, who single-handedly invented the epidermal polarizer that caused the giant, radioactive, mutated crab lice to sink into the epithelium on the trio's perilous excursion into the Pubic Jungle.

"I still think you make that up about the crab lice."

"I reports what I sees. Shut up, child."

And Trog, half-man, half-slime mold, who had used his barbarian skills to domesticate Jo-jo, the man-eating flea, but who was secretly a spy for the Arcturian Horde and was working to sabotage the expedition and the hopes of all humanity.

As we rejoin the adventurers, Maryjane tells Rock that she must again venture south, from their base at the first sparse seedlings of the twisted Pubic Jungle, or their fate is sealed.

"Why is that, my dear?" Rock says boyishly.

"Because, darling, down at the bottom of the Great Rift Valley lie the only deposits of rare musketite on the whole planet, and I must have some of it to repair the burnt-out denoxifier on the overdrive, or the ship will never…"

Meanwhile, back at reality, Treemonisha caused her Left Northern Promontory to move southwards and rub itself lightly through the Great Rift Valley, causing quite an uproar among the flora and fauna there.

"Earthquake!" Trog squeaks, and runs howling back toward safety in the great crater in the middle of the Plain of Belly.

"Strictly speaking, no," Maryjane points out, grabbing at a swaying tree to steady herself. "It might more properly be called Treemonisha-qua—"

"Treemonisha. Must you do that while I'm just getting into the story? It plays hell with the plot line."

She moved her hand back to her side and tried to smile. She was willing to patronize him, try to get him back to himself, but this was asking a lot. What were these stories for, she reasoned, but to get her horny and give her a chance to get some relief?

"All right, Jordan. I'll wait."

He stared silently down at her. A tear trembled on the tip of his nose, hung there, and fell down toward her abdomen. And of course it didn't get her wet. It was followed by another, and another, and still she wasn't wet, and he felt his shoulders begin to shake. He fell forward onto the soft, inviting surface of her body and bumped his head hard on the deck. He screwed his eyes shut tight so he couldn't see her and cried silently.

After a few helpless minutes, Treemonisha got up and left him to recover in privacy.

Treemonisha called several times over the next five days. Each time Jordan told her he wanted to be alone. That wasn't strictly true; he wanted company more than he could say, but he had to try isolation and see what it did to him. He thought of it as destructive testing—a good principle for engineering but questionable for mental equilibrium. But he had exhausted everything else.

He even called up The Humanoid, his only other neighbor within radio range. He and Treemonisha had named him that because he looked and acted so much like a poorly constructed robot. The Humanoid was the representative of Lasercom. No one knew his name, if he had one. When Jordan had asked passing holehunters about him, they said he had been out in that neighborhood for over twenty years, always refusing rotation.

It wasn't that The Humanoid was unfriendly; he just wasn't much of anything at all. When Jordan called him, he answered the call promptly, saying nothing. He never initiated anything. He would answer your questions with a yes or a no or an I-don't-know. If the answer required a sentence, he said nothing at all.

Jordan stared at him and threw away his plan of isolating himself for the remainder of his stay at the station.

"That's me in six months," he said, cutting the connection without saying good-bye, and calling Treemonisha.

"Will you have me back?" he asked.

"I wish I could reach out and grab you by the ears and shake some sense back into you. Look." She pointed to where she was standing. "I've avoided your tape lines for five days, though it means threading a maze when I want to get to something. I was afraid you'd call me and I'd pop out in the middle of your computer again and freak you."

He looked ashamed; he *was* ashamed. Why did it matter?

"Maybe it isn't so important after all."

She lay down on the floor.

"I've been dying to hear how the story came out," she said. "You want to finish it now?"

So he dug out Rock Rogers and Maryjane and sent them into the bushes and, to enliven things, threw in Jo-jo and his wild mate, Gi-gi.

For two weeks Jordan fought down his dementia. He applied himself to the computer summaries, forcing himself to work at them twice as long as was his custom. All it did was reconfirm to him that if he didn't see something in three hours, he wasn't going to see it at all.

Interestingly enough, the computer sheets were getting gradually shorter. His output dwindled as he had less and less to study. The home office didn't like it and suggested he do some work on the antennas to see if there was something cutting down on the quality of the reception. He tried it, but was unsurprised when it changed nothing.

Treemonisha had noticed it, too, and had run an analysis on her computer.

"Something is interfering with the signal," she told him after studying the results. "It's gotten bad enough that the built-in redundancy isn't sufficient. Too many things are coming over in fragmentary form, and the computer can't handle them."

She was referring to the fact that everything that came over the hotline was repeated from ten to thirty times. Little of it came through in its totality, but by adding the repeats and filling in the blanks the computer was able to construct a complete message ninety percent of the time. That average had dropped over the last month to fifty percent, and the curve was still going down.

"Dust cloud?" Jordan speculated.

"I don't think it could move in that fast. The curve would be much shallower, on the order of hundreds of years, before we would really notice a drop-off."

"Something else, then." He thought about it. "If it's not something big, like a dust cloud blocking the signal, then it's either a drop-off in power at the transmitter, or it could be something distorting the signal. Any ideas?"

"Yes, but it's very unlikely, so I'll think about it some more."

She exasperated him sometimes with her unwillingness to share things like that with him. But it was her right, and he didn't probe.

Three days later Treemonisha suddenly lost a dimension. She was sitting there in the middle of his room when her image flattened out like a sheet of paper, perpendicular to the floor. He saw her edge-on and had to get up and walk around the flat image to really see it.

"I'll call it 'Nude Sitting in a Chair,'" he said. "Tree, you're a cardboard cutout."

She looked up at him warily, hoping this wasn't the opening stanza in another bout with loneliness.

"You want to explain that?"

"Gladly. My receiver must be on the fritz. Your image is only two-dimensional now. Would you like to stand up?"

She grinned, and stood. She turned slowly, and the plane remained oriented the same way but different parts of her were now flattened. He decided he didn't like it, and got out his tools.

Two hours of checking circuitry told him nothing at all. There didn't seem to be anything wrong with the receiver, and when she checked her transmitter, the result was the same. Midway through the testing she reported that his image had flattened out, too.

"It looks like there really is something out there distorting signals," she said. "I think I'll sign off now. I want to check something." And with that she cut transmission.

He didn't care for the abruptness of that and was determined that she wouldn't beat him to the punch in finding out what it was. She could only be searching for the source of the distortion, which meant she had a good idea of what to look for.

"If she can figure it out, so can I." He sat down and thought furiously. A few minutes later he got up and called her again.

"A black hole," she said, when she arrived. "I found it, or at least a close approximation of where it must be."

"I was going to say that," he muttered. But he hadn't found it. He had only figured out what it must be. She had known that three days ago.

"It's pretty massive," she went on. "The gravity waves were what fouled up our reception, and now it's close enough to ruin our transmissions to each other. I thought at first I might be rich, but it looks far too big to handle."

That was why she hadn't said anything earlier. If she could locate it and get a track on it, she could charter a ship and come back to get it later. Black holes were fantastically valuable, if they were small enough to manipulate. They could also be fantastically dangerous.

"Just how big?" he asked.

"I don't know yet, except that it's too big to chase. I..."

Her image, already surreal enough from the flattening, fluttered wildly and dissolved. He was cut off.

He chewed his nails for the next hour, and when the call bell clanged, he almost injured himself getting to the set. She appeared in the room. She was three-dimensional again, wearing a spacesuit, and she didn't look too happy.

"What the hell happened? You didn't do that on purpose, did you? Because—"

"Shut up." She looked tired, as though she had been working.

"The stresses. I found myself falling toward the wall, and the whole station shipped around it like *zzzip!* And all of a sudden everything was creaking and groaning like a haunted house. Bells clanging, lights… Scared the *shit* out of me." He saw that she was shaking, and it was his turn to suffer the pain of not being able to get up and comfort her.

She got control again and went on.

"It was tidal strains, Jordan, like you read about that can wreck a holehunter if she's not careful. You don't dare get too close. It could have been a lot worse, but as it is, there was a slow blowout, and I only just got it under control. I'm going to stay in this suit for a while longer, because everything was bent out of shape. Not enough to see, but enough. Seams parted. Some glass shattered. Everything rigid was strained some. My laser is broken, and I guess every bit of precision equipment must be out of alignment. And my orbit was altered. I'm moving toward you slightly, but most of my motion is away from the sun."

"How fast?"

"Not enough to be in danger. I'll be in this general area when they get a ship out here to look for me. Oh, yes. You should get off a message as quick as you can telling Pluto what happened. I can't talk to them, obviously."

He did that, more to calm himself than because he thought it was that urgent. But he was wrong.

"I think it'll pass close to you, Jordan. You'd better get ready for it."

Jordan stood in front of the only port in the station, looking out at the slowly wheeling stars. He was wearing his suit, the first time he had had it on since he arrived. There had just been no need for it.

The Star Line listening post was in the shape of a giant dumbbell. One end of it was the fusion power plant, and the other was Jordan's quarters. A thousand meters away, motionless relative to the station, was the huge parabolic dish that did the actual listening.

"Why didn't they give these stations some means of movement?"

He was talking into his suit radio. Treemonisha's holo set had finally broken down and she could not patch it up. There were too many distorted circuits deep in its guts; too many resistances had been altered, too many microchips warped. He realized glumly that even if the passage of the hole left him unscathed he would not see her again until they were rescued.

"Too expensive," she said patiently. She knew he was talking just to keep calm and didn't begrudge providing a reassuring drone for him to listen to. "There's no need under normal circumstances to move the things once they're in place. So why waste mass on thrusters?"

"'Normal circumstances,'" he scoffed. "Well, they didn't think of everything, did they? Maybe there *was* a way I could have killed myself. You want to tell me what it was, before I die?"

"Jordan," she said gently, "think about it. Isn't it rather unlikely for a black hole to pass close enough to our positions to be a danger? People hunt them for years without finding them. Who expects them to come hunting *you*?"

"You didn't answer my question."

"After the passage, I promise. And don't worry. You know how unlikely it was for it to pass as close as it did to me. Have some faith in statistics. It's surely going to miss you by a wide margin."

But be didn't hear the last. The floor started vibrating slowly, in long, accelerating waves. He heard a sound, even through the suit, that reminded him of a rock crusher eating its way through a solid wall. Ghostly fingers plucked at him, trying to pull him backwards to the place where the hole must be, and the stars outside the port jerked in dance rhythms, slowing, stopping, turning the other way, sashaying up and down, then starting to whirl.

He was looking for something to grab onto when the port in front of him shattered into dust and he was expelled with a monstrous whoosh as everything in the station that wasn't bolted down tried to fit itself through that meter-wide hole. He jerked his hands up to protect his faceplate and hit the back of his head hard on the edge of the port as he went through.

✦

The stars were spinning at a rate fast enough to make him dizzy. Or were the stars spinning *because* he was dizzy? He cautiously opened his eyes again, and they were still spinning.

His head was throbbing, but he couldn't sync the throb rate with the pain. Therefore, he declaimed to himself, the stars *are* spinning. On to the next question. Where *am* I?

He had no answers and wished he could slip back into that comforting blackness. Blackness. Black.

He remembered and wished he hadn't.

"Treemonisha," he moaned. "Can you hear me?"

Evidently she couldn't. First order of business: stop the spin before my head unscrews. He carefully handled the unfamiliar controls of his suit jets, squirting streams of gas out experimentally until the stars slowed, slowed, and came to rest except for a residual drift that was barely noticeable.

"*Very* lonely out here," he observed. There was what must be the sun. It was bright enough to be, but he realized it was in the wrong place. It should be, now let's see, where? He located it, and it wasn't nearly as bright as the thing he had seen before.

"That's the hole," he said, with a touch of awe in his voice. Only one thing could have caused it to flare up like that.

The black hole that had wrecked his home was quite a large one, about as massive as a large asteroid. But with all that, it was much smaller than his station had been. Only a tiny fraction of a centimeter across, in fact. But at the "surface," the gravity was too strong to bear thinking about. The light he saw was caused by stray pieces of his station that had actually been swept up by the hole and were undergoing collapse into neutronium, and eventually would go even further. He wondered how much radiation he had been exposed to. Soon he realized it probably wouldn't matter.

There were a few large chunks of the station tumbling close to him, dimly visible in the starlight. He made out one of the three-meter rockets he used to send the day's output back to Pluto. For a wild second he thought he saw a way out of his predicament. Maybe he could work out a way of using the rocket to propel him over to Treemonisha. Then he remembered he had worked all that out on the computer during one of his lonelier moments. Those rockets were designed for accelerating a pea-sized transmitter up to a tremendous velocity, and there was no provision for slowing it down again, or varying the thrust, or turning it on and off. It was useless to him. Even if he could rig it some way so that it would move him instead of drilling straight through his back, the delta-vee he could get from it was enough to let him reach Treemonisha in about three weeks. And that was far, far too long.

He started over to it, anyway. He was tired of hanging out there in space a billion kilometers from anything. He wanted to get close to it, to have something to look at.

He clanged onto it and slowly stopped its rotation. Then he clung to it tightly, like an injured monkey to a tree limb.

A day later he was still clinging, but he had thought of a better metaphor.

"Like a castaway clinging to a log," he laughed to himself. No, he wasn't sure he liked that better. If he cast loose from the rocket, nothing at all would happen to him. He wouldn't drown in salty seas or even choke on hard vacuum. He was like the monkey: very scared and not about to let go of the security that his limb afforded him.

"…calling. Treemonisha calling Jordan, please answer quickly if you can hear me, because I have the radio set to…"

He was too astounded to respond at once, and the voice faded out. Then he yelled until he was hoarse, but there was no answer. He abandoned himself to despair for a time.

Then he pulled himself together and puzzled out with what wits he had left what it was she might be doing. She was scanning the path of strewn debris with a tight radio beam, hoping he was one of the chunks of metal her radar told her were there. He must be alert and yell out the next time he heard her.

Hours later, he was trying to convince himself it hadn't been a hallucination.

"…hear me, because—"

"Treemonisha!"

"—I have the radio set to scan the wreckage of your station, and if you take your time, I won't hear you. Treemonisha call…"

It faded again, and he jittered in silence.

"Jordan, can you hear me now?" The voice wavered and faded, but it was there. She must be aiming by hand.

"I hear you. I figured it out."

"Figured what out?"

"Your painless way of committing suicide. But you were wrong. It's true that if I had stepped outside the station wearing my suit, I would have died of CO_2 poisoning eventually, but you were wrong if you thought I could take this isolation. I would have jetted back to the station in just a few hours—" His voice broke as he forced himself to look again at the bottomless depths that surrounded him.

"You always take the hard way, don't you?" she said, in a voice so gentle and sympathetic that she might have been talking to a child. "Why would you have to step out?"

"Aaaaa..." he gurgled. One step ahead again. Why step outside, indeed? Because that's what you *do* in a spacesuit. You don't wear it inside the station, sealed off from the fail-safe systems inside unless you want to die when the oxygen in your tanks runs out.

"I'm not that dense, and you know it. You want to tell me why I didn't see that? No, wait, don't. Don't outfigure me in that, too. I'll tell you why. Because I didn't really want to kill myself. If I had been sincere, I would have thought of it."

"That's what I finally hoped was the case. But I still didn't want to take the chance of telling you. You might have felt pressured to go through with it if you knew there was a way."

Something was nagging at him. He furrowed his brow to squeeze it out in the open, and he had it.

"The time lag's shorter," he stated. "How far apart are we?"

"A little over two million kilometers, and still closing. The latest thing I can get out of my computer—which is working in fits and starts—is that you'll pass within about one point five million from me, and you'll be going five thousand per, relative."

She cleared her throat. "Uh, speaking of that, how much reserve do you have left?"

"Why bother yourself? I'll just fade away at the right time, and you won't have to worry because you know how long I have to live."

"I'd still like to know. I'd rather know."

"All right. The little indicator right here says my recyclers should keep right on chugging along for another five days. After that, no guarantees. Do you feel better now?"

"Yes, I do." She paused again. "Jordan, how badly do you need to talk to me right now? I can stay here as long as you need it, but there's a lot of work I have to do to keep this place running, and I can't afford the power drain to talk to you continuously for five days. The batteries are acting badly, and they really do need constant attention."

He tried not to feel hurt. Of course she was fighting her own fight to stay alive—she still had a chance. She wouldn't be Treemonisha if she folded up because the going got rough. The rescue ship would find her, he felt sure, working away to keep the machines going.

"I'm sure I can get along," he said, trying his best to keep the reproach out of his voice. He was ashamed at feeling that way, but he did. The bleak fact was that he had felt for a brief moment that dying wouldn't be so hard as long as he could talk to her. Now he didn't know.

"Well, hang on, then. I can call you twice a day if my figures are right and talk for an hour without draining too much power for what I have to do. Are you *sure* you'll be all right?"

"I'm sure," he lied.

And he was right. He wasn't all right.

The first twelve-hour wait was a mixture of gnawing loneliness and galloping agoraphobia.

"About half one and half the other," he commented during one of his lucid moments. They were rare enough, and he didn't begrudge himself the luxury of talking aloud when he was sane enough to understand what he was saying.

And then Treemonisha called, and he leaked tears through the entire conversation, but they didn't enter into his voice, and she never suspected. They were happy tears, and they wet the inside of his suit with his boundless love for her.

She signed off, and he swung over to hating her, telling the uninterested stars how awfully she treated him, how she was the most ungrateful sentient being from here to 70 Ophiuchi.

"She could spare the power to talk just a few minutes longer," he raged. "I'm *rotting* out here, and she has to go adjust the air flow into her bedroom or sweep up. It's so damn important, all that housekeeping, and she leaves me all alone."

Then he kicked himself for even thinking such things about her. Why should she put her life on the line, wasting power she needed to keep breathing, just to talk to him?

"I'm dead already, so she's wasting her time. I'll tell her the next time she calls that she needn't call back."

That thought comforted him. It sounded so altruistic, and he was uncomfortably aware that he was liable to be pretty demanding of her. If she did everything he wanted her to, she wouldn't have any time to do anything else.

"How are you doing, Rock Rogers?"

"Treemonisha! How nice of you to call. I've been thinking of you all day long, just waiting for the phone to ring."

"Is that sincere, or are you hating me again today?"

He sobered, realizing that it might be hard for her to tell anymore, what with his manic swings in mood.

"Sincere. I'll lay it on the line, because I can't stand not talking about it anymore. Have you thought of anything, *anything* I might do to save myself? I've tried to think, but it seems I can't think in a straight line anymore. I get a glimpse of something, and it fades away. So I'll ask you. You were always faster than me in seeing a way to do something. What can I do?"

She was quiet for a long time.

"Here is what you *must* do. You must come to terms with your situation and stay alive as long as you can. If you keep panicking like you've been doing, you're going to open your exhaust and spill all your air. Then all bets are off."

"If you were betting, would you bet that it matters at all how much longer I stay alive?"

"The first rule of survival is never give up. *Never.* If you do, you'll never take advantage of the quirks of fate that can save you. Do you hear me?"

"Treemonisha, I won't hedge around it any longer. Are you doing something to save me? Have you thought of something? Just what 'quirks' did you have in mind?"

"I have something that might work. I'm not going to tell you what it is, because I don't trust you to remain calm about it. And that's all you're getting from me."

"Haven't you considered that not knowing will upset me more than knowing and worrying about it?"

"Yes," she said, evenly. "But frankly, I don't want you looking over my shoulder and jostling my elbow while I try to get this together. I'm doing what I can here, and I just told you what *you* have to do out *there*. That's all I can do for you, and you won't change it by trying to intimidate me with one of your temper tantrums. Go ahead, sound off all you want, tell me I'm being unfair, that you have a right to know. You're not rational, Jordan, and *you* are the one who has to get yourself out of that. Are you ready to sign off? I have a lot of work to do."

He admitted meekly that he was ready.

Her next call was even briefer. He didn't want to remember it, but he had whined at her, and she had snapped at him, then apologized for it, then snapped at him again when he wheedled her for just a teeny tiny hint.

"Maybe I was wrong, not telling you," she admitted. "But I know this: if I give in and tell you now, the next phone call will be full of crap from you telling me why my scheme won't work. Buck up, son. Tell yourself a story, recite prime numbers. Figure out why entropy runs down. Ask yourself what The Humanoid does. But don't *do* what he does. That isn't your style. I'll see you later."

The next twelve hours marked the beginning of rising hope for Jordan, tinged with the first traces of confidence.

"I think I might be able to hold out," he told the stars. He took a new look at his surroundings.

"You aren't so far away," he told the cold, impersonal lights. It sounded good, and so he went on with it. "Why, how can I feel you're so far away when I can't get any perspective on you? You might as well be specks on my faceplate. You *are* specks." And they were.

With the discovery that he had some control of his environment, he was emboldened to experiment with it. By using his imagination, he could move the stars from his faceplate to the far-away distance, hundreds of meters away. That made the room he was in a respectable size, but not overwhelming. He tuned his imagination like a focusing knob, moving the stars and galaxies in and out, varying the size of space as he perceived it.

When she called again, he told her with some triumph that he no longer cared about the isolation he was floating in. And it was true. He had moved the stars back to their original positions, light-years away, and left them there. It no longer mattered.

She congratulated him tiredly. There was strain in her voice; she had been working hard at whatever mysterious labors had kept her from the phone. He no longer believed the story about maintenance occupying all her time. If that were true, when would she find time to work on rescuing him? The logic of that made him feel good all over.

He no longer clung to his bit of driftwood as an anchor against the loneliness. Rather, he had come to see it as a home base from which he could wander. He perched on it and looked out at the wide universe. He looked at the tiny, blinding spark that was the sun and wondered that all the bustling world of people he had needed so badly for so long could be contained in such a small space. He could put out his thumb and cover all the inner planets, and his palm took in most of the rest. Billions of people down there, packed solid, while he had this great black ocean to wallow around in.

Jordan's time was down to five hours. He was hungry, and the air in his helmet stank.

"The time," Treemonisha stated, "is fourteen o'clock, and all is well."

"Hmm? Oh, it's you. What is time?"

"Oh, brother. You're really getting into it, aren't you? Time is: the time for my twice-daily call to see how things are in your neck of space. How are you doing?"

"Wonderful. I'm at peace. When the oxygen runs out, I'll at least die a peaceful death. And I have you to thank for it."

"I always hoped I'd go kicking and screaming," she said. "And what's this about dying? I told you I had something going."

"Thank you, darling, but you don't need to carry on with that anymore. I'm glad you did, because for a time there if I hadn't thought you were working to save me, I never would have achieved the peace I now have. But I can see now that it was a device to keep me going, to steady me. And it worked, Tree, it worked. Now, before you sign off, would you take a few messages? The first one is to my mother. 'Dear mom...'"

"Hold on there. I refuse to hear anything so terribly personal unless there's a real need for it. Didn't I find a way for you to kill yourself after you had given it up? Don't I always pull more gold out of those transmissions than you do? *Haven't you noticed anything?*"

The time lag!

Panic was rising again in his voice as he hoarsely whispered, "Where are you?"

And instantly:

"A thousand kilometers off your starboard fo'c'sle, mate, and closing fast. Look out toward Gemini, and in about thirty seconds you'll see my exhaust as I try to bring this thing in without killing both of us."

"This thing? What *is* it?"

"Spaceship. Hold on."

He got himself turned in time to see the burn commence. He knew when it shut off exactly how long the burn had been; he had seen it enough times. It was three and five-eighths seconds, the exact burn time for the first stage of the message rockets he had launched every day for almost a year.

"Ooh! Quite a few gees packed into these things," she said.

"But how?"

"Hold on a few minutes longer." He did as he was asked. "Damn. Well, it can't be helped, but I'm going to go by you at about fifty kilometers per hour, and half a kilometer away. You'll have to jump for it, but I can throw you a line. You still have that rocket to push against?"

"Yes, and I have quite a bit of fuel in my backpack. I can get to you. That's pretty good shooting over that distance."

"Thanks. I didn't have time for anything fancy, but I—"

"Now you hush. I'm going to have to see this to believe it. Don't spoil it for me."

And slowly, closing on him at a stately fifty kilometers per, was…a thing…that she had offhandedly called a spaceship:

It was all roughly welded metal and ungainly struts and excess mass, but it flew. The heart of it was a series of racks for holding the message rocket first stages in clusters of ten. But dozens of fourth and fifth stages stuck out at odd angles, all connected by wire to Treemonisha's old familiar lounging chair. All the padding and upholstery had frozen and been carelessly picked off. And in the chair was Treemonisha.

"Better be ready in about fifty seconds."

"How did you do it? How long did it take you?"

"I just asked myself: 'What would Rock Rogers have done?' and started whipping this into shape."

"You don't fool me for an instant. You never cared for Rock. What would Maryjane Peters, superscientist, have done?"

He could hear the pleased note in her voice, though she tried not to show it.

"Well, maybe you're right. I worked on it for three days, and then I had to go whether it was ready or not, because it was going to take me two days to reach you. I worked on it all the way over here, and I expect to nurse it all the way back. But I intend to *get* back, Jordan, and I'll need all the help I can get from my crew."

"You'll have it."

"Get ready. Jump!"

He jumped, and she threw the line out, and he snagged it, and they slowly spun around each other, and his arms felt as though they would be wrenched off, but he held on.

She reeled him in, and he climbed into the awkward cage she had constructed. She bustled around, throwing away expended rocket casings, ridding the ship of all excess mass, hooking him into the big oxygen bottle she had fetched.

"Brace yourself. You're going to have bruises all over your backside when I start up."

The acceleration was brutal, especially since he wasn't cushioned for it. But it lasted only three and five-eighths seconds.

"Well, I've lived through three of these big burns now. One more to go, and we're home free." She busied herself with checking their course, satisfied herself, then sat back in the chair.

They sat awkwardly side by side for a long twenty seconds.

"It's…it's funny to be actually sitting here by you," he ventured.

"I feel the same way." Her voice was subdued, and she found it hard to glance over at him. Hesitantly, her hand reached out and took his. It shocked him to his core, and he almost didn't know what to do. But something took over for him when he finally appreciated, through all the conditioned reflexes, that it was *all right*, he could touch her. It seemed incredible to him that the spacesuits didn't count for anything; it was enough that they could touch. He convulsively swept her into his arms and crushed her to him. She pounded his back, laughing raggedly. He could barely feel it through the suit, but it was wonderful!

"It's like making love through an inflated tire," she gasped when she had calmed down enough to talk.

"And we're the only two people in the universe who can say that and still say it's great because, before, we were making love by postcard." They had another long hysterical laugh over that.

"How bad is it at your place?" he finally asked.

"Not bad at all. Everything we need is humming. I can give you a bath—"

"A bath!" It sounded like the delights of heaven. "I wish you could smell me. No, I'm glad you can't."

"I wish I could. I'm going to run the tub full of hot, hot water, and then I'm going to undress you and lower you into it, and I'm going to scrub all those things I've been staring at for a year and take my time with it, and then—"

"Hey, we don't need stories anymore, do we? Now we can do it."

"We need them for another two days. More than ever now, because I can't reach the place that's begging for attention. But you didn't let me finish. After I get in the tub with you and let you wash me, and before we head hand in hand for my bedroom, I'm going to get Rock Rogers and Maryjane Peters and the Black Widow and Mark Antony and Jo-jo and his wild mate and hold their heads under the water until they *drown*."

"No you don't. *I* claim the right to drown Rock Rogers."

THE UNPROCESSED WORD

I was one of the last SF writers to switch from a typewriter to a word processor. (Not the very last; I know for a fact that Harlan Ellison has never used a computer, and he never will.) It was not really a hatred of computers that kept me from joining the rush, it was a reluctance to stop using something that worked so well as my IBM Correcting Selectric. If it ain't broke, don't fix it.

But I'll admit that there was an element of digging in my heels when I listened to people rhapsodize about the damn things. They made writing so efficient, corrections so easy, global changes a snap instead of a nightmare. And in the very next breath they would, every one of them, tell a horror story of a hard drive crash, a file lost forever in the cybercabinet, the difficulty of installing new software, new drivers, new operating systems, whatever those were. No, thank you.

Eventually computers got simple enough that you could take them out of the box and start writing on them. And I do, and I like it. I write and receive a lot of emails. I have a website (varley.nct), and I use the Internet extensively for research. But to this day I don't have a Facebook page, nor any other of those awful social media. I don't tweet. If I have a single "app" on this computer it must have sneaked in while I wasn't looking. (Another thing that never bothered my IBM Selectric: viruses, malware, spybots, Nigerian get-rich scams, fundraising emails from Rick Santorum…the list of computer nightmares is long.) Basically, I use this computer as a fancy typewriter, a research tool, and a mailbox. That's it.

I wrote this little story/essay at the height of my resistance to the new age. It's silly, as it was meant to be, but I still like it.

John Varley
555 Mozart Place
Eugene, Oregon 97444

Susan Allison
Editor, Berkley Books
The Berkley Building
1 Madison Avenue
New York, New York 10010

Dear Susan,

You and I have talked before about word processors, and how I'm one of the last science fiction writers who doesn't use one. Now I feel it is time to take aggressive action against the blight of computers.

What I want you to do is run the following notice right before the title page of the new book, and in all books after this, and in any re-print editions of previous books written by me. Though this kind of self-promotion is personally repugnant to me, I feel it is time to speak out before it is Too Late. Also, it might help to sell books to people who feel the same way I do.

You may be wondering just what VarleyYarns is. Well, I've re-organized, partly for tax purposes, partly for other reasons. I've formed a corporation called VarleyYarns, Inc., to market and promote my books. It's a step that's been long overdue. From now on, you can make out all my royalty checks to VarleyYarns.

Best,
John

THE UNPROCESSED WORD

INTRODUCING VARLEYYARNS®

THE UNPROCESSED WORD

This symbol is your assurance that the following yarn was composed entirely without the assistance of a word processor.

Each VarleyYarn® is created using only natural ingredients: The purest paper, carbon typewriter ribbons, pencils, ballpoint pens, thought, and creativity. Manuscript corrections are done entirely by hand. Final drafts are lovingly re-typed, word by word, in the finest typefaces available—no dot-matrix printers allowed!

The manuscript of each VarleyYarn® is then carried by the United States Postal Service—First Class!—to the good offices of the Berkley/Putnam Publishing Group in Manhattan, New York City, New York. Not a word is ever phoned in via modem.

Not One Word!

Here the VarleyYarn® is given to skilled artisans, men and woman who learned their craft from their parents, and from their parents before them…many of them using the tools and even the same offices their grandparents used. Crack teams of proofreaders pore over the manuscript, penciling corrections into the wide margins left for that purpose. Messengers hand-carry the VarleyYarn® from floor to floor of the vast Berkley Building, delivering it to deft Editors, clever Art Directors, and lofty Vice-Presidents.

When all is in readiness, the VarleyYarn® is rushed to the typesetter, who once again re-types the manuscript—*word by word!*—on the typesetting machine. Then the bulky lead plates are trucked to New Jersey and given to the printer, who uses technologies essentially unchanged from the days of Gutenberg.

And the end result? The book you now hold in your hands, as fine a book as the economic climate will allow.

So look for the sign of the twin typewriter keys—your symbol of quality in

100% guaranteed non-processed fiction!

✦

John Varley
555 Mozart Place
Eugene, Oregon 97444

Dear John,

You asked to hear from me as soon as we had some concrete sales figures on the new book. As you know, we ran your "promotional" notice as you instructed, just after the title page. The book has been out for a month now, and I'm sorry to say there's no measurable impact. It's selling about as well as the previous collection.

We have received some rather strange mail, though, which I am forwarding to you under a separate cover.

John, I'm not completely sure the public *cares* whether fiction was written on a typewriter, a word processor, or with a quill pen and ink. I know this is an important issue with you and I was happy to help you try and get your message across, but maybe it's best for now if we just forget it. Unless I hear back from you soon, I'm going ahead with the twenty-eighth printing of WIZARD without the VarleyYarn seal of approval in front.

Yours,
Susan Allison

THE UNPROCESSED WORD

Susan Allison
Berkley

Dear Susan,

Of *course* they care. You can't tell me people can't tell the difference when it is so obvious to any literate person. They just haven't been given the choice in recent years…and more importantly, they haven't heard the message. I'm afraid putting it in just my books was a mistake, as that is simply preaching to the converted. What I want you to do now is use the advertising budget for the new book and, instead of running the standard promo, use the following material instead. I'd like to see it in all the trade publications and as many national magazines as we can afford. And, far from letting you remove the original message from the new printing of WIZARD, I want to keep it, and run this new one on stiff paper—like you used to use for cigarette ads—somewhere in the middle of the book. Full color won't be necessary; just print the underlined parts in red caps.

John

WHY VARLEYYARNS®?

Perhaps you asked yourself: "Why should I buy and read Berkley's VarleyYarns® when cheaper, more plentiful 'processed' fiction puts me to sleep just as quickly?"

Here are some things we at VarleyYarns® think you should know:

Processed fiction can contain harmful additives.

When fiction is produced on a Word Processor each keystroke is first converted to a series of "on" and "off" signals in the microprocessor unit. Some of these signals go to the video screen and are displayed. The rest are "tagged" by various electronic additives and stored in the "memory" for later retrieval. Inevitably, these tags cling to the words themselves, and no amount of further processing can wash them away. Even worse, while in the memory these words are subject to outside interference such as power surges, changes in the Earth's magnetic field, sun spots, lightning discharges, and the passage of Halley's Comet—due back in 1986...*and every 76 years thereafter!* VarleyYarns® are guaranteed to contain no sorting codes, assemblers, inelegant "languages" like FORTRAN or C.O.B.O.L., and to be free of the fuzzy edges caused by too much handling (more commonly known as "hacker's marks").

Floppy disks lack sincerity.

Think about it. When the "word processor" turns off his or her machine...*the words all go away!* The screen goes blank. The words no longer exist except as encoded messages on a piece of plastic known as a floppy disk. These words cannot be retrieved except by whirling the disk at great speed—a process that can itself damage the words. Words on a floppy disk are un-loved words, living a forlorn half-life in the memory until they are suddenly spewed forth at great and debilitating speed by a dot-matrix printer *that actually burns them into the page*!

VarleyYarn® words go directly from the writer's mind onto the printed page, with no harmful intermediate steps. At night, when the typewriter is turned off, they repose peacefully in cozy stacks of paper on the writer's desk, secure in the knowledge they are cherished as words.

Microprocessors are Un-American.

That's right, we said Un-American. At the heart of every word processor is something called a microchip. Due to cheap labor costs, these chips are made in places like Taiwan, Singapore, Hong Kong, and Japan. Now, we at VarleyYarns® have nothing against the Japanese (though Pearl Harbor *was* a pretty cowardly attack, don't you think?), but ask yourself this: Do you want to entrust your precious fiction to a machine *that doesn't even speak English?*

So ask your grocer, druggist, airport manager, and bookseller to stock up on Berkley's VarleyYarns® today. And next time someone offers to let you read processed fiction, you can say:

"No thanks! I'd rather read a VarleyYarn®!"

✦

John Varley
555 Mozart place
Eugene, Oregon 97444

Dear John,

As you must have seen by now, I did as you asked. But let me tell you, it was a struggle. I fought pretty hard for that ad budget, such as it was, and it was quite a trick to turn around and tell everyone you now want this other material to run in place of the ads we'd prepared.

A word to the wise, my friend. You're not the only author on the Berkley list. I called in a lot of favors on this one.

And I'm sorry to tell you it doesn't seem to have worked. All of them—*The Times, Rolling Stone, Publishers Weekly, Variety, USA Today, Locus*—report negative responses to the ad as run. Maybe this will convince you that people really aren't concerned—as I know you are—about the spread of word processors.

One more thing you might not have considered. All the other Berkley authors use word processors. More than a few of them have called or written about your ad. So far the tone has been more puzzled than anything else, but I'm afraid that if we went on with this it could only get worse. See, they're beginning to think you're saying something negative about *their* fiction.

For this reason, if for no other, I'm pulling your ad from all the printed media, and canceling the upcoming radio and television campaign. The forty-third printing of TITAN goes to the presses next week, and it will do so without either the VarleyYarns "symbol of quality" or the two-color slick paper insert.

Yours truly,
Susan

✦

Dear Susan,

You can't do this to me! You're simply not giving this a chance to work. Naturally there's going to be some initial resistance. It's a new idea to most people out there that word additives can be harmful to one's fiction. Remember how people fought the idea of ecology in the late '60s? Remember how the AEC used to tell us that radiation was good for you? This is just like that. The word has to get out now, before it's too late.

So here's what I want you to do. Forget all the book advertising. I want to go right on to direct mail. See if you can obtain the lists of everyone who ever voted for Eugene McCarthy, and send them all a copy of the enclosed exposé. It's time their eyes were really opened.

I have gone to a great deal of trouble obtaining these testimonials. I expect you to do your part. And, oh, sure, I know the lawyers on your end are going to give you a hard time about some of this, but you'll notice I've concealed the names of the people involved.

Here's to an unprocessed future…

John

The Shame of MacWrite
Brought To You By

VarleyYarns®

Home Of The Unprocessed Word

Almost without our realizing it, a generation has grown up in America that has never read an unprocessed word, never heard an unprocessed line of dialogue. This is tragic enough…but have you ever considered the effect of the Word Processor upon today's writers? Many of them have never seen a typewriter. Their familiarity with pen and ink extends only to the writing of checks to pay for a new addition to their computer systems.

And now, slowly, insidiously, hidden from public view, the results of their new toys are beginning to be felt.

John Varley

We at VarleyYarns® feel it is time for someone to speak out, to rip away the veil of secrecy that has, until now, prevented these writers from coming forward to speak of their shame, their anguish, their heartbreak. You probably don't know any writers personally. Most people don't. Here are some facts you should know:

Fact #1: Writers can't handle money, and are suckers for shiny new toys.

Writers are a simple folk, by and large. Awkward in social situations, easily deceived, childishly eager to please, the typical writer never had the advantages of a normal childhood. He was the dreamy one, the friendless one, object of scorn and ridicule to his classmates. Living in his own fantasy world, writing his "fiction," he is ill-equipped for the pitfalls of money or technology.

Fact #2: Writers come in two types—compulsives, and procrastinators.

The Type A writer will labor endlessly without food, water, or sleep. His output of fiction is prodigious. Many claim they would write fiction even if they were not being paid for it—a sure danger signal.

Type B writers live to sharpen pencils, straighten their desks, create elaborate filing systems, and answer the telephone and the doorbell. A productive day for the Type B writer consists of half a paragraph—which may end up in the wastepaper basket at the end of the day. This writer will work only under deadline pressure. Any excuse to leave the typewriter is welcomed.

Conclusion: The Word Processor is precisely the <u>wrong</u> tool to put into a writer's hands!!

If you don't believe it, listen to these unsolicited testimonials from some of the most pitiful cases of computaholism:

<u>"SK," Jerusalem's Lot, Maine</u>

I was one of the first writers to get a word processor. My God, if only I had known...if only...I was always pro-lific. I write every day but Guy Fawkes Day, Bastille Day, and the anniversary of the St. Valentine's Day Massacre. When I got my computer my output increased dramatically. My family didn't see me for days at a time...then weeks at a time! I was sending in novels at the rate of three a month...and in addition, was writ-ing and selling dozens of short stories every day. Thinking of pseudonyms became a major task in itself, a task I faced with a deepening sense of horror. Have you ever heard of John Jakes? That's really me! And what about Arthur Hailey, I'll bet you've heard of him. That's me, too! And Colleen McCullough, and William Goldman, and Richard Bachman...John D. MacDonald really died in 1976...but nobody knows it, because I took over his name! Soon I was writing movie scripts. (Have you heard of Steven Spielberg? That's me, too.) In 1980 I began writing the entire line of Harlequin Romances. I was making money faster than General Dynamics...but my kids didn't know me. As I sat at my Word Processor, a strange change would come over me. I would become these other people. Friends would mistake me for Truman Capote, or J. D. Salinger. But I could have lived with that...if not for the children. I can hear them now, crying in the kitchen. "Mommy, mommy," they weep. "Who is daddy today?" If only I could save another writer from this nightmare...if only...if only...

John Varley

I used to write with a pencil and paper—I never even used a typewriter for my first drafts…until the day someone convinced me to buy a Macintosh Computer, known in the industry as a Fat Mac. I loved it! In only three or four months I taught myself to type and wrote seventy or eighty letters. I purchased a MacPaint program, and soon was turning out wonderful dot-matrix artwork to amuse my friends. Then I brought a MacAlien program and had hours of fun every day eluding the space monsters that tried to eat me alive. (The MacWrite program still had a few glitches, but I knew I'd work them out…one of these days…when I got around to it…mañana…what's the rush?) In the meantime, I was having too much fun…

Well, you've probably guessed I'm a Type B writer. It was always easy enough to find an excuse not to write…and the Mac made it even easier! Now winter is coming on, I've missed a dozen deadlines, my family is starving, and bill collectors are pounding on the door.

Thank God for the people at VarleyYarns®!

When they heard of my plight they rushed over with a typewriter, reams of paper, and a package of pencils.

I know it will be a long hard path back to sanity…

…but with the help of VarleyYarns®, I think I can lick it!

"DT" Oakland, California

Born Again!

That's what I told my friends when I finally "made the switch" to a word processor. The ease, the speed, the versatility... I began buying new programs as quickly as they came out. I even got to "road-test" a few of them, developed by friends in the industry, before they were available to the general public. I really liked the MacPlot at first. When you "Booted it up," MacPlot would suggest alternate story lines...while at the same time conducting a global search of all stories written by anyone, anywhere, at any time, to see if an idea was "old hat." Soon all my friends had copied it and were using it, too. Then came MacClimax!, which analyzed your prose for the "high points," and added words and phrases here and there to "punch it up." You've all heard how a word processor can aid you if you decide to change a character's name in the course of a story. With MacCharacter, I was able to change a whimp into a hero, a Presbyterian into an alien suffering from existential despair, or a fourteenth century warlord into a Mexican grape-picker...all with only a few keys...all without lapses in story logic! Before long I had them all: MacConflict, MacDialogue, MacMystery, MacWestern, Adverb-Away. VisiTheme, MacDeal-With-The-Devil...

Then I noticed a strange thing.

I'm a Type A writer, like Mr "SK/Bachman/Goldman/ETC." I'm not happy unless I'm writing most of the day. And now, writing was so easy I could simply write a first line, punch a few keys, and sit back and watch the story write itself. It was so easy, I was miserable. Now, in today's mail, comes MacFirstline, but I don't think I'll run it. I think I'll kill myself instead.

<u>Now where's the MacHara-Kiri suicide-note-writing program...?</u>

Sad, isn't it? And there isn't even enough time to tell you of the incalculable amounts of money squandered by writers on expensive systems that were obsolete within a few weeks' time, or to print the countless other testimonials that have been pouring into VarleyYarns® since this crusade of salvation began.

We're trying to help. Won't you? Only with your support can we stamp out this dread killer, this hidden disease called Computaholism. Write your Congressperson today. Form a committee. Give generously. Be sure to vote.

And don't forget...to buy and read Berkley's VarleyYarns®.

✦

Dear John,

All right, enough is enough. I don't think you realize it, but I put my career on the line over your *last* insane request. If you think I'm going to publish and mail that diatribe, you've got another think coming.

I went so far as to show it to our lawyers. You said you disguised the names, but how many writers do you think there are in Halifax, Nova Scotia? Or in *Maine*, for that matter. And do you have any idea how much money that guy has? Enough to keep you in court for the next twenty years.

Maybe I'll regret this later, but there are a few things I've been dying to get off my chest, so here goes. First...was that some kind of crack, back in your first ad? Something like "as fine a book as the economic climate will allow"? Let me tell you, we editors work *hard* and we do the best job we can. So we don't usually have much of an advertising budget. So DEMON *was* printed on newsprint. So *sue* me, okay?

As for your horror stories about excessively prolific authors... boy, don't I *wish*! I could say a thing or two about missed deadlines, that's for sure. And did you read what Norman Spinrad and Algis Budrys had to say about your last two epics? So much for the inherent superiority of the typewriter.

TITAN parts four, five, and six are due at the end of the month, don't forget. You may not find the editors here at Berkley quite so forgiving the next time you ask for a deadline extension.

Yours,
Susan

SUSAN ALLISON
BERKLEY PUBLISHING
NEW YORK

DEAR SUSAN,

HOLD EVERYTHING! NO NEED TO GET UPSET. HELL, YOU DIDN'T THINK I WAS SERIOUS, DID YOU? THE THING IS, SEE, I WAS TALKING TO HARLAN ELLISON THE OTHER DAY, AND WHILE HE AGREED WITH MY STAND AGAINST THE WORD PROCESSOR, HE FELT THE WHOLE VARLEYYARNS BUSINESS SMACKED OF TOO MUCH SELF PROMOTION.

BUT BEYOND THAT, AS YOU MIGHT HAVE GUESSED FROM THE HOLES ALONG THE SIDE OF THE PAPER, I'VE BOUGHT A WORD PROCESSOR. (SORRY ABOUT THIS TYPEFACE: MY LETTER-QUALITY PRINTER IS "DOWN" AGAIN. I'M USING AN OLD "WORDSPITTER" PRINTER I BORROWED FROM THE E STATE OF "DT" IN OAKLAND.)

I'M WRITING THIS ON AN EXXON OFFICE SYSTEMS "ANNIE" COMPUTER. AS YOU MAY HAVE HEARD, EXXON GOT OUT OF THE COMPUTER BUSINESS AFTER A FEW YEARS OF POOR SALES, SO I GOT THIS MACHINE AT A BARGAIN-BASEMENT PRICE! FOR ONLY

John Varley

$5000 I GOT A MAINFRAME MORE POWERFUL THAN THE ONE NASA USED TO SEND MEN TO THE MOO N IN 1969, A DISK DRIVE, A "SANDY" PRINTER, A "PUNJAB'S CRYSTAL" MONITOR SC REEN, AND A LITTLE DEVICE SIMILAR TO THE APPLE MOUSE, WHICH EXXON CALLS AN "ASP." I'VE BEEN TOLD THIS IS WHAT IS KNOWN AS AN ORPHAN COMPUTER, BUT IT SHOULDN'T MATTER, AS IT WILL RUN SOME OF THE APPLE SOFTWARE, AND THE SALESMAN--A MR. PANGLOSS--ASSURES ME EXXON WILL CONTINUE TO SERVICE IT AND PRODU CE MORE PROGRAMS.

SO FAR HE'S BEEN AS GOOD AS HIS WORD. THE LASER-DRIVEN HYPERSPEED WHIRL-WRITE "SANDY" PRINTER HAS BROKEN DOWN EIGHT TIMES SO FAR, AND THE SERVICE MANAGER, MR. GOLDBERG, IS ALWAYS HERE WITHIN A WEEK OR TWO. (HE'S HERE RIGHT NOW-- HEY, RUBE!--SO PRETTY SOON I CAN PUT THE PRINTER "ON-LINE" AGAIN. HE SAYS IT'S JUST RUN OUT OF PHOTONS AGAIN.)

I'VE BEEN HAVING A BALL. I'VE USED THE MACWARBUCKS PROGRAM TO BALANCE MY CH ECKBOOK AND PLAN MY FINANCIAL FUTURE. MY OUTPUT OF FICTION HAS REALLY INCREASED. YOU'LL RECEIVE SHORTLY, UNDER SEPARATE COVER, TWO TRILOGIES AND FIVE OTHER NOVELS. JUST THIS MORNING I TRIED PHONING ANOTHER NOVEL TO YOUR OFFICE VIA MODEM, BUT EITHER MY MACHINE OR YOUR COMPUTER ROOM OR POOR OLD MA BELL SEEM TO HAVE LOST IT. OH, WELL, NO BIG DEAL, THERE'S PLENTY MORE WHERE THAT ONE CAME FROM!

TO FACILITATE YOUR ACCOUNTING DEPARTMENT'S WRITING OF MY CHECKS, IN THE FUTURE I SHALL SIGN MYSELF WITH THE UNIVERSAL WRITERS CODE (UWC) SYMBOL YOU SEE BELOW, RECENTLY APPROVED BY THE WRITERS GUILD. SO IT'S GOODBYE, JOHN VARLEY, HELLO 2100061161...BUT YOU CAN CALL ME 210, IF WE'RE STILL FRIENDS.

THE MANHATTAN
PHONE BOOK
(ABRIDGED)

There's not much I can say about this final story. There are things in the world so awful that you can't even think about them for very long. The global atrocities the United States and the Soviet Union contemplated are enough to make you vomit. And if you think it's over, that we're reasonably safe now, you really ought to take a look around you.

The Doomsday Clock maintained by the directors of the *Bulletin of the Atomic Scientists* stands now at five minutes to midnight. The best it has ever been in my lifetime was 11:43, with the collapse of the Soviet Union. I have no argument with any of those figures. Nukes no longer exist in the insane, genocidal numbers we saw at the height of the Cold War, but there are still plenty of them out there, some of them not adequately guarded. More countries have nukes now than did when I wrote this, some of them in countries that are volatile, to say the least, and more countries are working hard to get them. The only country to reject their use by destroying a nuclear weapon stockpile is South Africa. Total disarmament is only a distant dream.

It is my fervent hope that the events described in this story happen to none of you, nor to anyone. Good luck to you all.

This is the best story and the worst story anybody ever wrote.

There's lots of ways to judge the merit of a story, right? One of them is, are there a lot of people in it, and are they real. Well, this story has more people in it than any story in the history of the world. The Bible? Forget it. Ten thousand people, tops. (I didn't count, but I suspect it's less than that, even with all the begats.)

And real? Each and every character is a certified living human being. You can fault me on depth of characterization, no question about it. If I'd had the time and space, I could have told you a lot more about each of these people…but a writer has dramatic constraints to consider. If only I had more room. Wow! What stories you'd hear!

Admittedly, the plot is skimpy. You can't have everything. The strength of this story is its people. I'm in it. So are you.

It goes like this:

Jerry L. Aab moved to New York six years ago from his home in Valdosta, Georgia. He still speaks with a southern accent, but he's gradually losing it. He's married to a woman named Elaine, and things haven't been going too well for the Aab family. Their second child died, and Elaine is pregnant again. She thinks Jerry is seeing another woman. He isn't, but she's talking divorce.

Roger Aab isn't related to Jerry. He's a native New Yorker. He lives in a third-floor walk-up at 1 Maiden Lane. It's his first place; Roger is just nineteen, a recent high school graduate, thinking about attending City College. Right now, while he makes up his mind, he works in a deli and tries to date Linda Cooper, who lives two blocks away. He hasn't really decided what to do with his life yet, but is confident a decision will come.

Kurt Aach is on parole. He served two years in Attica, up-state, for armed robbery. It wasn't his first stretch. He had vague ideas of going straight when he got out. If he could join the merchant marine he figures he just might make it, but the lousy jobs he's been offered so far aren't worth the trouble. He just bought a .38 Smith and Wesson from a guy on the docks. He cleans and oils it a lot.

Robert Aach is Kurt's older brother. He never visited Kurt in prison because he hates the worthless bum. When he thinks of his brother, he hopes the state will bring back the electric chair real soon. He has a wife and three kids. They like to go to Florida when he gets a vacation.

Adrienne Aaen has worked at the Woolworths on East 14th Street since she was twenty-one. She's pushing sixty now, and will be retired soon, involuntarily. She never married. She has a sour disposition, mostly because of her feet, which have hurt for forty years. She has a cat and a parakeet. The cat is too lazy to chase the bird. Adrienne has managed to save a little money. Every night she thanks God for all her blessings, and the City of New York for rent control.

Molly Aagard is thirty, and works for the New York Transit Police. She rides the subway every day. She's charged with stopping the serious crimes that infest the underground city, and she works very hard at it. She *hates* the wall-to-wall grafitti that blooms in every car like a malign fungus.

Irving Aagard is no relation. He's fifty-five, and owns an Oldsmobile dealership in New Jersey. People ask him why he lives in Manhattan, and he is always puzzled by that question. Would they rather he lived in Jersey, for chrissake? To Irving, Manhattan is the only place to live. He has enough money to send his three kids—Gerald, Morton, and Barbara—to good schools. He frets about crime, but no more than anyone else.

Shiela Aagre is a seventeen-year-old streetwalker from St. Paul. Her life isn't so great, but it's better than Minnesota. She uses heroin, but knows she can stop whenever she wants to.

Theodore Aaker and his wife, Beatrice, live in a fine apartment a block away from the Dakota, where John Lennon was killed. They went out that night and stood in the candlelight vigil, remembering Woodstock, remembering the summer of love in the Haight-Ashbury. Theodore sometimes wonders how and why he got into stocks and bonds. Beatrice is pregnant with their first child. She is deciding how much time she should take off from her law practice. It's a hard question.

(162,000 characters omitted)

Clemanzo Cruz lives on East 120th Street. He's unemployed, and has been since he arrived from Puerto Rico. He hangs out in a bar at the corner of Lexington and 122nd. He didn't used to drink much back in San Juan, but now that's about all he does. It's been fifteen years. You might say he is discouraged. His wife, Ilona, goes to work at five P.M. at the Empire State Building, where she scrubs floors and toilets. She's been mugged a dozen times on the way home on the number 6 Lexington local.

Zelad Cruz shares an apartment with two other secretaries. Even with roommates it's hard to make ends meet with New York rents the way they are. She always has a date Saturday night—she's quite a beauty—and she swings very hard, but Sunday morning always finds her at early mass at St. Patrick's. There's this guy who she thinks may ask her to get married. She's decided she'll say yes. She's tired of sharing an apartment. She hopes he won't beat her up.

Richard Cruzado drives a cab. He's a good-natured guy. He's been known to take fares into darkest Brooklyn. His wife's name is Sabina. She's always after him to buy a house in Queens. He thinks one of these days he will. They have six children, and life is tough for them in Manhattan. Those houses out in Queens have back yards, pools, you name it.

(1,250,000 characters omitted)

Ralph Zzyzzmjac changed his name two years ago. His real name is Ralph Zyzzmjac. A friend persuaded him to add a Z to be the last guy in the phone book. He's a bachelor, a librarian working for the City of New York. For a good time he goes to the movies, alone. He's sixty-one.

Edward Zzzzyniewski is crazy. He's been in and out of Bellevue. He spends most of his time thinking about that bastard Zzyzzmjac, who two years ago knocked him out of last place, his only claim to fame. He broods about him—a man he's never met—fantasizing that Zzyzzmjac is out to get him. Last year he added two Z's to his name. Now he's thinking about stealing a march on that bastard Zzyzzmjac. He's sure Zzyzzmjac is adding two more Z's this year, so he's going to add *seven*. Ed Zzzzzzzzzzzzyniewski. That'd be nice, he decides.

Then one day seventeen thermonuclear bombs exploded in the air over Manhattan, The Bronx, and Staten Island, too. They had a yield of between five and twenty megatons each. This was more than enough to kill everyone in this story. Most of them died instantly. A few lingered for minutes or hours, but they *all* died, just like that. I died. So did you.

I was lucky. In less time than it takes for one neuron to nudge another I was turned into radioactive atoms, and so was the building I was in, and the ground beneath me to a depth of three hundred meters. In a millisecond it was all as sterile as Edward Teller's soul.

You had a tougher time of it. You were in a store, standing near a window. The huge pressure wave turned the glass into ten thousand slivers of pain, one thousand of which tore the flesh from your body. One sliver went into your left eye. You were hurled to the back of the store, breaking a lot of bones and suffering internal injuries, but you still lived. There was a big piece of plate glass driven through your body. The bloody point emerged from your back. You touched it carefully, trying to pull it out, but it hurt too much.

On the piece of glass was a rectangular decal and the message "Mastercard Gladly Accepted."

The store caught fire around you, and you started to cook slowly. You had time to think "Is this what I pay my taxes for?" and then you died.

This story is brought to you courtesy of The Phone Company. Copies of the story can be found near every telephone in Manhattan, and thousands of stories just like it have been compiled for every community in the United States. They make interesting reading. I urge you to read a few pages every night. Don't forget that many wives are listed only under their husband's name. And there are the children to consider: very few have their own phone. Many people—such as single women—pay extra for an unlisted number. And there are the very poor, the transients, the street people, and folks who were unable to pay the last bill. Don't forget any of them as you read the story. Read as much or as little as you can stand, and ask yourself if this is what you want to pay your taxes for. Maybe you'll stop.

Aw, c'mon, I hear you protest. *Some*body will survive.

Perhaps. Possibly. Probably.

But that's not the point. We all love after-the-bomb stories. If we didn't, why would there be so many of them? There's something attractive about all those people being gone, about wandering in a depopulated world, scrounging cans of Campbell's pork and beans, defending one's family from marauders. Sure, it's horrible, sure we weep for all those dead people. But some secret part of us thinks it would be good to survive, to start all over.

Secretly, we know we'll survive. All those *other* folks will die. That's what after-the-bomb stories are all about.

All those after-the-bomb stories were lies. Lies, lies, lies.

This is the only true after-the-bomb story you will ever read.

Everybody dies. Your father and mother are decapitated and crushed by a falling building. Rats eat their severed heads. Your husband is disemboweled. Your wife is blinded, flashburned, and gropes along a street of cinders until fear-crazed dogs eat her alive. Your brother and sister are incinerated in their homes, their bodies turned into fine powdery ash by firestorms. Your children...ah, I'm sorry, I hate to tell you this, but your children live a *long* time. Three eternal days. They spend those days puking their guts out, watching the flesh fall from their bodies, smelling the gangrene in their lacerated feet, and asking you why it happened. But you aren't there to tell them. I already told you how you died.

It's what you pay your taxes for.